A Friend is

SOMEBODY

ISBN: 148196562X
ISBN 13: 9781481965620

Library of Congress Control Number: 2013900909
CreateSpace Independent Publishing Platform
North Charleston, SC

A Friend is
SOMEBODY

R J FURTH

**A friend is somebody you know very well
and like anyway.**

DEDICATION: This novel is dedicated to all third culture kids, those born into one culture and raised in a different one. Although you may feel like you don't have a homeland, the entire world is your home. We will all be better off when more people develop a global perspective.

PROLOGUE—TODAY

Tom was sitting on his favorite cane rocker in the screened-in porch, listening to the cricket symphony as he had done most evenings in Charleston since his retirement, when the phone rang. Over the years he'd gotten used to other people answering phones: secretaries or maids or wives. He no longer had any of those around. Reluctantly, he stood and walked into the kitchen, muttering at the caller to hold his horses.

"Hello," he said when he finally picked up the wireless phone and pushed the correct button. He was neither that old nor technophobic; it was a new phone and he hadn't mastered its intricacies yet.

"Tom?"

The woman's voice carried a hint of a question and a bit of hope. It was faintly familiar, a ghost of a memory from long, long ago.

"Yes, this is Tom. Who's calling?"

"Suzie."

"Suzie? Suzie Chomsky?"

He hadn't talked with Suzie for years, at least a decade, he figured. Hadn't even thought about her, yet her name and face jumped immediately to mind. And her body, though it was the body from her youth.

"Yup. It's me."

"Well I'll be damned."

"Most likely," she said, followed by a husky bark of a laugh.

"This is a surprise."

"A pleasant one?"

"Of course. You know you've always had a place in my heart."

"You haven't called since that senile actor was president."

"It hasn't been that long. Besides, you haven't called either."

"Who knew where the hell you were? Paris, Tokyo, I lost track years ago. Anyway, that's the past. No point in looking backward."

He smiled. "You haven't changed. Still a Buddhist?"

"Sort of. Still a world-famous diplomat?"

"No, I left the foreign service years ago. I taught at Columbia for a while; now I'm working on an autobiography. Sounds egotistical, but my kids say—insist—the world should know about my career." He laughed. "As if anybody cares about a failed diplomat."

"You're being too hard on yourself. You had quite a few adventures."

"I suppose that's true, though I think the kids are just trying to keep me busy. They worry that my brain will turn to mush if I don't use it. So how'd you locate me here in South Carolina?"

"I found your son Keith on the Internet. I googled him. Pretty impressive kid. Really sweet on the phone."

"Yeah. He turned out pretty well, in spite of everything."

There was a brief moment of silence, then Suzie got to the reason for her call.

"Ira passed away recently."

"Oh." He had no idea what Suzie expected him to say, but "oh" didn't seem sufficient. "He was pretty young. For dying, I mean. What was he? Sixty-eight? Sixty-nine?"

"Something like that, though he was never really young, not even when we first met him. Know what I mean?"

"Most definitely."

Another silence ensued, only longer this time.

"Anyway, I thought you'd want to know, and I figured you probably hadn't heard. It's not like Ira was going to get an obit in the *Times* or the *Post*."

"You're right about that, and no, I hadn't heard. Thanks."

"Well, nice talking with you."

"Where are you calling from? I mean, where do you live these days?"

"I'm on a small farm outside of Burlington, Vermont. My partner and I raise goats and make artisan goat cheese. We live in this old farmhouse in a pretty little valley. Business was slow at first, but we've developed a loyal following of high-end restaurants and specialty markets in New England and New York. We're finally starting to make a decent living."

"It sounds wonderful."

"It is. Maybe you'll come up and visit us some day."

"I'd like that. Give me your phone number."

She began to recite her number.

"Got it. Thanks again for the call."

"Keith said you hadn't talked with Ira for years."

"At least twenty years."

"Sorry."

"Sorry? About what?"

"You two were very close for a long time."

"Things change. Nothing lasts forever."

"Now you're the one who's sounding Buddhist."

He smiled again. "I got that from you."

"You must have gotten a lot from Ira as well. I mean, friends for over forty years."

"Closer to thirty."

"Gosh, Tom, you're kinda anal about dates."

"My diplomatic training. Dates play an important role. It's necessary to be precise."

"Except when the government wants to keep the people in the dark and dodge responsibility, then they're purposely vague."

"Same Suzie."

"Same Tom." She hesitated a moment. "Friendships are different. They're not about precision and dates. They transcend time. You and I haven't talked forever, yet here we are chatting like we'd smoked a joint yesterday."

"That's you, Suzie. You never let time or age change you. I've always respected that."

"What about you?"

"I've changed a lot, in some ways for the better, in some ways maybe not."

"Is that what happened between you and Ira? You changed and he didn't?"

3

"Tell you what. Why don't I give you a call sometime and come visit the farm? We could smoke a J and talk about life—past, present, and future—unless that violates your Buddhist beliefs."

"Like I said, I'm sort of a Buddhist. You still smoke? I would have thought that was a no-no in the diplomatic corps."

"It is, but I'm retired and the thought of smoking a doobie with you and your partner on the farm is quite appealing."

"Cool. So I'll hear from you sometime soon?"

"Definitely."

"Great. Tom, are you OK with Ira's passing? Do you have anybody to be with?"

"I'm fine. It's been a long time since I thought of Ira. I'll drink a cheap beer to his memory and reminisce about the good times we shared."

"OK, but if you don't call I'm going to come down south and whip your ass with a magnolia branch."

"Sounds kinky."

"You used to like it kinky."

"Thanks for calling, Suzie. It's great to hear your voice. I'll see you soon."

"I really hope so."

Tom went back to the cane rocker and began to slowly rock. Although the crickets were still filling the humid summer evening with their songs, he was no longer listening. His mind had wandered back nearly fifty years, to when he was a teenager, a green hick from Indiana who'd wound up in New York City. He'd been homesick and felt like he'd landed on a strange and frightening planet, the Planet of the Incredibly Tall Concrete and Steel Monsters. He was soon to learn that he'd actually taken the first step on what would be a lifelong odyssey of personal discovery. And Ira Blue, born Ira Jacob Kornblue, would be a mileage marker and reference point for most of that journey.

CHAPTER 1—1958

"What the hell is this?"

"Uh, your tip," the young man said, though his voice came out sort of squeaky with a hint of a question.

"This ain't no tip. It ain't enough to feed the fuckin' pigeons."

Tom grabbed his two suitcases and stumbled out of the taxi.

"Hey, get back here," the taxi driver yelled.

A few heads turned to see what the yelling was about, but this being New York City they only glanced for a second, then got on with their lives. Tom lugged the suitcases into the Columbia University student center, checked in as a new student, and was given the keys and verbal directions to his dorm.

"Um, where is the dorm?" Tom asked, his voice shaky with uncertainty.

"I just told you."

"I know, but, well, I just got here and I don't know the street names and..."

"Hey, Suzie," the middle-aged woman behind the counter shouted. "Come 'ere."

A young woman detached herself from a group of four students who were chatting around a table that was piled high with student welcome folders and overflowing ashtrays and half-finished mugs of coffee. She was medium height and full-figured, though it was difficult to determine her shape due to her baggy clothes. Her blue-jean skirt appeared to be a couple of sizes too big, as was the light-blue man's shirt she wore untucked.

Her hair was shoulder length and frizzier than any hair he'd ever seen, and she didn't wear any makeup. She strolled over to the counter.

"Yeah, waddya want?"

"Would ya show this man to JJ?"

"Sure, come on." She indicated with a nod of the head that Tom should follow.

"Thanks."

"Don't mention it. So where ya from?"

"Fort Wayne, Indiana. Well, not right in Fort Wayne, sort of nearby. My family has a dairy farm with three hundred cows, and the town's real small, you wouldn't have heard of it..."

She turned and gave Tom an amused look. "Sweetheart, I couldn't find Indiana on a map if my life depended on it, much less Fort whatever, so I sure as hell don't need to know where you park your cows. No offense meant."

"That's all right. No offense taken."

Suzie walked a few steps before stopping and turning around again. "This your first time
in New York?"

"First time out of Indiana, except for one trip to Chicago to visit the museums and a forensics tournament in Ohio last year."

"Wow. A real hayseed."

Tom blushed a brilliant red and began to sweat. His hands got slippery, and he put down the two suitcases and rubbed his palms against his gray slacks.

"Sorry. Look, sweetheart," Suzie began, placing her hand on his forearm, "you're in the big city now, and there's something you gotta learn from the start. We New Yorkers got big mouths and we love to use 'em. We are not shy and we don't pull our punches."

"So I've discovered."

"The important thing is not to take it personally. It's not about you; it's about us. We love being loud and brash, and we think that the only place in America that matters at all is right here: New York City. We love to brag about our sports teams and our museums and our food, and we don't give a shit about anything west of the Hudson. Mind if I give you some advice?"

"No, not at all. In fact, I'd appreciate it."

"Play down the farm-boy cowshit stuff. Tell 'em you're from south of Chicago or something like that. And while you're at it, let that flat-top buzz cut grow out. You look like some damn soldier or farmer."

"I am a farmer."

"No. You *were* a farmer. Now you're a student at Columbia University. The Big Time. You must be smart or they wouldn'a let you in. Do what ya want, but I doubt that you came here to study agriculture and irrigation and stuff like that."

Tom smiled for the first time since leaving Indiana. "You're right about that."

"You got a major in mind?"

"I've been considering political science or English literature, though I'm open minded."

Suzie studied Tom's face for the first time, then boldly checked out his body. He was slim and tall, an inch over six feet. His erect posture made her think of a sandy-haired Abe Lincoln. The hint of a smile on his lips gave her the impression that he was playing the farm boy. "Just goes to show that first impressions are not always correct. Here I took you for a hayseed, when all along you're a different kind of seed, though what you'll be when you're properly watered and nurtured, who's to say. You got a lot of potential, kid."

"Thanks, I guess."

"Pick up your bags and let me show you JJ hall. That's John Jay, named after the first judge of the Supreme Court."

"The first chief justice."

"What?"

"John Jay was first chief justice of the Supreme Court."

"See. I knew you weren't stupid."

"Thanks.

Suzie checked him into his dorm and saw him settled into his room.

"I gotta go back to the student union. I'm a volunteer to help new students settle in and find their way around."

"Which you've done admirably."

"'Admirably,' huh. I bet you did really well on your SATs. Hey, listen, there's this small club not far from here, a coffee house where there's music and poetry readings and lots of interesting people. If you want, I could pick you up around eight o'clock. I mean, if you got nothing better to do."

7

"Nothing better to do? I've got nothing to do at all, except unpack, and I'll be done long before eight. Sure, I'd like to go."

"Am I being too forward? This isn't a date or anything. I don't know if girls in Indiana invite guys to go out."

"No, they don't usually, except for the Sadie Hawkins dance, but like you say, this isn't a date, and besides, you're not from Indiana. You're a New Yorker. You've got a big mouth and you're not shy."

She gave him a full, slightly seductive smile. "Oh, you're gonna do real well here in New York. Real well."

Tom ate at the dorm's cafeteria though he didn't taste a thing, his mind being elsewhere. Suzie had been right, he hadn't come to Columbia to study agriculture. Although he'd been a good farmer's son—did his chores without complaint, joined the 4H club, kept his hair short—he'd always felt estranged from his community. Even his parents knew that he was different. Tom had always been curious, even as a small child, continually asking questions yet feeling dissatisfied with the answers. "But why does an engine need gasoline?" "But why are we in a war in Korea?" "But why did the calf just die?" He even drove the minister crazy with his endless theological questions.

"Sometimes I wonder about you, Tom," his father would occasionally say.

"I think it was that full moon he was born under," his mother would usually interject with a wink.

"Don't start with that again. Tom's brain is already full of too much mush; you needn't be givin' him any peculiar ideas."

"Aw, Tom knows that I'm only kidding. Don't you, Tom?"

In fact, Tom was always too serious to realize when he was being kidded, and even though he nodded to acknowledge his mother's little joke, he wondered what she'd meant about being born under a full moon. He'd gone to the public library the next day and asked the librarian, and she'd started to talk about something called astrology. Then she'd abruptly stopped.

"That's not a subject that is appropriate for eight-year-olds. I've got a new Hardy Boys mystery that you'll really like a lot."

Some of his teachers thought of him as a brilliant, though challenging, student. Tom unnerved them; he made them doubt their own intelligence because they could never satisfactorily answer his questions. Miss Learnard, his freshman world history teacher, rather than be intimidated by Tom, had been enamored of him. For four years she urged him to take the most challenging social studies courses, to write on the most obscure topics, to read lesser-known authors. Miss Learnard was a spinster, the type of teacher who gave all of her energy, all of her love, to her students, and Tom was her favorite. It was Miss Learnard who urged Tom to spread his wings and fly, which he ultimately did in a northeasterly direction, to Columbia University.

He was standing outside JJ's entrance when Suzie turned the corner and spied him.

"Eager to go out, eh?" she called out as she approached.

"I didn't come all the way to New York to sit in my dorm."

"That's the spirit. Come on."

Tom turned and walked beside her.

"This being your first night in the big city, I assume you haven't been to a coffee house."

"Coffee house? I've had a few mugs at Edna's Diner."

Suzie gave Tom a sideways glance.

"Are you pulling my leg?"

"I wish."

He was stunned by his own boldness. Although Tom had slowly developed a wry sense of humor and could be playful with peers, he had never practiced his budding wit on strangers, thinking it rude.

"Well, well, well. You are full of surprises."

"Sorry. I didn't mean to be fresh. It just sort of popped out. I hope I didn't offend you."

"Offend me? Hell, no, I'm flattered that you'd want to pull my leg."

"I was only kidding."

"Oh. So you don't want to pull my leg?" She sounded slightly hurt.

"No, really, I'd love to pull your leg, or any part of your anatomy. Uh, I mean...Heck. I'm not getting off to a very good start."

"*Au contraire.* You're doing great. Keep it up. New Yorkers like people who can give as good as they get, though at the Blue Moon you might want to sit back and observe for a while before you try to pick up a girl."

"I wasn't trying..."

Suzie froze him with a look. "Don't ruin the moment. Women like to think they're attractive. They want guys to flirt. And even if you aren't flirting, it doesn't hurt to let 'em think you are. Understand?"

"Yup."

"Now, back to the Blue Moon. It's a coffee house, meaning it serves coffee rather than booze, but a coffee house is more than that. It's a place to hang out, play music, and read poetry. The best coffee houses, the ones with the coolest people, are in the Village. That's Greenwich Village. You've heard of it?"

"I'm from Indiana, not Tibet. We get *Time* magazine and I listen to Chicago radio stations. Besides, the Village has been a literary center for over a century."

"I suppose that was an AP US History question."

"Not last year, though I was ready if it had been."

"I bet you would have been. You seem ready for just about anything." She gazed at him a second before continuing. "The Blue Moon isn't happening, not like places in the Village, but it has the best scene in upper Manhattan. Here we are."

Had he been on his own, Tom would have walked by the Blue Moon without giving it a glance. The entrance was poorly lit, and you had to peer carefully to see the sign. It was not an inviting exterior, and the interior was no better. Dimly lit, the smallish room was enveloped in a dense cloud of cigarette smoke. Even when Tom's eyes had adjusted to the darkness, there was little to see. A dozen people lounged around on wooden chairs or on one of the two old, sagging sofas. Music was playing softly in the background, driven by a sweet, low saxophone. Suzie grabbed his sleeve and pulled him toward a table at which a man sat by himself.

"Hey, Ira."

"Hey, babe. Where'd you find the square?"

"Take it easy on him. It's his first night in New York."

"Are you jivin' me?"

"Would I do that? Ira, this is Tom. Tom, Ira."

Tom reached out his hand. Ira hesitated, then gave a weak shake.

It was too dark to see clearly, yet Tom had the impression of seeing an older man. Ira was slouched in his chair, his head slightly tipped forward. His hair had a reddish tint to it, though that might have been a trick of the light. When they had been sitting for a minute and their eyes adjusted to the light, Tom realized that Ira was only a few years older. His thin hair, through which the light shone and glared off of his skull, added to the impression of age. He had a longish, thin face and sported a scraggly, untrimmed beard.

"You must be a new student at Columbia."

"Wow. You're a real genius," Suzie said.

"That's why you like to hang with me, for the stimulating conversation and intellectual challenge."

"No. I like to hang with you 'cuz you're so fuckin' weird."

Ira smiled. "I am what I am. So why're you hanging with Mr. Brown-Shoed Square?"

"Tom, grab a seat and ignore Ira. He loves being a jerkoff. I used to think he worked on it. Now I realize it's his natural condition."

"I just tell it like I see it. Like Ginsberg or Burroughs. You shouldn't censor yourself, worry about how people are going to react. That leads to a tight asshole and constipation. You gotta let it flow. Can you dig it, Tom?"

"Sure. My momma always says: You can get blocked up if you hold things in."

Ira smiled. "Your momma's a smart woman."

"You like the music?" Suzie asked, changing the subject. "It's called jazz."

"Not just any jazz. That's Charley 'Bird' Parker," Tom replied.

"My, oh, my," said Ira. "Seems like I was off base calling you a brown-shoed square."

"I'm pretty square compared to most."

"How do you know Charley Parker?" Suzie asked.

"We have radios where I live, and electricity."

"Zap!" said Ira. "So you've heard Bird fly."

"Often. He's one of my favorites, along with Miles Davis and John Coltrane."

"Except Bird spent too much time flying in the gutter with a needle in his arm," said Suzie. "You have heard about heroin, haven't you?"

"I've read about it."

"It's good you know how to read," said Ira. "So where are you from?"

"Uh, south of Chicago."

"Sure you are. Way south."

"Close enough to get radio reception. I've been listening to jazz for a few years now."

The music stopped, and a dim spotlight illuminated a corner of the room where a short, thick man with longish gray hair and a beard stood. He blinked a few times under the diffused glare of the light.

"Good evening, and welcome to poetry night at the Blue Moon. For those who are new to poetry night, here's how it goes. I start with some free verse, something to get the creative juices flowing—my own very brief moment in the spotlight—then the spot is yours. The main rule is that there are no rules. "

The emcee started to string words together, playing with the sounds of each word and altering the rhythm of each phrase. Tom had read the usual poetry in high school: Wordsworth and Longfellow, English and American masters. He'd participated in discussions on the nature of poetry in his honors lit classes. None of that prepared him for what he was hearing. There were no rhyme schemes, no structure of any kind, yet something about the poetry reached out to him. Tom found himself hanging on each word, searching for meaning with the same intensity that he'd used in French 4. Suddenly, he was stunned to realize that he was understanding the message of the poem: everybody on earth—beggars and soldiers, actors and farmers—everybody was connected. We are all brothers and sisters, basking in the light of eternal love.

"Gosh," Tom gasped when the emcee had concluded. He raised his hands to clap, then noticed that people were nodding their approval or tapping their tables or calling out praise like, "Cool, man" and "Dig it."

"You liked it?" Suzie asked with a note of skepticism.

"Oh, yes. There was something fresh and unrestrained about it, something I've never heard before."

"Looks like our cat from south of Chicago has an ear for Beat poetry," said Ira.

"Beat poetry?"

"Yeah, man. We've been called the Beat Generation, 'cuz we dance to a different beat than other cats. Speakin' of beats, I think I'll lay down a few of my own."

Ira got up and strolled to the performers' corner. He stood under the spotlight for a moment, his head down, his shoulders slumped forward, and then he looked up and words started to flow from his mouth. At first the words were disjointed, random, with long pauses that left the audience leaning forward just a little, as if waiting to catch the next wisp of an idea. Then Ira seemed to grow focused. His voice took on a note of urgency and purpose. The words flowed faster, and the pauses grew shorter before disappearing entirely. His shoulders straightened and his hands became animated, as if they were required to pull the words from Ira's mouth and shape them into coherent thoughts. Tom had struggled to focus at the start of Ira's poem, then with a start, Tom realized that the poem was about him.

"New kid in an old town. Old ideas carrying clods of dirt. Raised on a farm, planted in the concrete and steel jungle, watered with sweat and blood and beer and piss and cum. Hayseeds sprouting into mighty oaks of thought and desire in the soil fertilized with the bodies of immigrants from Middle America. The Big City has everything…and nothing. It has a heart that beats and blood that course through its sewage-clotted veins and still, more than ever, it craves fresh blood, new energy, babes from the woods who offer their virgin bodies to be sacrificed to the gods of *progress*. Those who giveth also receiveth and those who give openly and freely are those who receive the biggest slice of the pie in the sky. Open your minds, open your hearts, and the Big City will open its legs wide to receive your driving jackhammer of youthful purpose. Spill your hayseeds in the old town's still-fertile womb and give birth to a new world. Your future awaits. Strip yourself bare. Learn all. *Be all*."

Ira returned to the table followed by a smattering of praise and tapping on tabletops. He sat and lit a cigarette, drew in a deep lungful, then slowly let it out.

"So waddya think?" he asked Tom.

"Very impressive. To create that right after you met me. Wow, I don't know if it's something I could do."

"It wasn't about you."

"Oh."

"It was inspired by what you are."

"What am I?"

"I just told you, in the poem. It was all in the words."

"Ira, don't be an asshole," Suzie said.

"Suzie, sweetie, the kid came to New York for an education. Not all learning is in a textbook or explained by a professor. Those things that we learn best are those that we have to struggle to understand. Besides, I don't think Tom needs a one-sentence summary to grasp its meaning. Right, Tom?"

"Most people live quiet lives, unaware of anything beyond their farm or factory, be it in Europe or Indiana."

Ira nodded.

"And those who seek knowledge also carry knowledge, and the meeting of old and new, city and country, Beat and straight, leads to something new. Something better?"

"The Marxist dialectic," said Suzie. "The clash of opposites leads to something new. Better?" She shrugged. "It is what it is. The kid gets it, Ira."

"Maybe. Let's see. The spotlight's waiting."

Tom looked at the performer's corner. "What? Me get up? I don't think so."

"You're not going to be graded," Ira said. "It won't hurt your GPA."

"I've never done it before."

"Never spoken in front of a group of people?" Suzie asked.

"Sure, I've given speeches and debated in front of hundreds, but it was all prepared."

"I bet you've got some things to say about your first day in New York City. Go on, you don't have to say much. A couple of sentences."

Tom glanced at the spotlit corner.

"That," said Suzie, pointing at the corner, "is why you came to New York."

He looked at her, raised his eyebrows, and nodded once. "Right."

Tom stood. Suzie grabbed his hand and pulled him toward her.

"For luck."

She reached up and kissed him, a warm, wet kiss with a hint of tongue, then she let him go. Tom looked into Suzie's eyes for a second before turning and walking to the spotlight.

He took a deep breath and looked around the room. A dozen people were patiently waiting. He closed his eyes, allowed an image to form, opened his eyes, and began. "Gray, hard, rough, loud, busy overwhelming. Lost, unsure, overwhelmed. The urge to flee, return to bosom of loved ones, to be a boy forever, to be safe. Then light, warmth, the human touch. Strength from others that reveals strength within. Fear not the unknown. Seek it, embrace it, revel in it. Life continues and is reborn and begins anew."

Tom's hands were shaking, and his palms and underarms were sweaty, yet he felt inebriated, as if he'd just chugged a six-pack. He returned to the table, aware of snippets of praise and even some mild applause, which was coming from his own table.

"Bravo," said Suzie who rose to give him a hug. He hugged her back, then they kissed again, a deeper, longer kiss that hinted of things to come.

"Not bad," Ira said.

Tom and Suzie sat down. Suzie kept her eyes on Tom, while he turned to Ira.

"Thanks."

"Not bad?" Suzie said. "The kid's a natural."

"Yeah, maybe. Maybe."

"It wasn't anything like yours or the emcee's," said Tom, his heart racing. "I just said what came to mind. It wasn't poetry. You wove words into something more than words. You created a rhythm and purpose and feeling. You created poetry."

"Yeah, I did, didn't I. Still, yours was a good first effort, kid. You got a bright future in poetry."

"I don't think my future lies in poetry."

"You got other plans?" Suzie asked.

"Not plans, really, more of a feeling. I see grander things for myself."

"Grander things? Nothing as frivolous as poetry, eh?" Ira challenged. "You going to run for president? A good, God-fearing, Protestant from the heartland. Clean-shaven, hair trimmed neat, clothes spotless. Tom is your man. If he can't do it, nobody can."

"I didn't mean to sound like I was criticizing poetry. I respect it."

"You goddamned better, 'cuz without words and the power of words we are nothing. Nothing. Poets are like priests, and poems are the modern gospel. It ain't scientists or politicians who are going to save the world. It's artists."

"Hail to Rabbi Ira, the new savior," snickered Suzie.

"Why not me?" Ira asked.

"Excuse me. While you save this sinner's soul, I'm going to use the facilities."

When she'd left the table Ira turned to Tom.

"She's got the hots for you."

"Hey, look, if she's your girlfriend..."

Ira laughed. "She's everybody's girlfriend."

"Oh." Tom looked disappointed.

"She's not a slut, if that's what you're thinking. She's a free spirit. Suzie's got to feel something before she sleeps with someone, and I can see she feels something for you."

"Have you and Suzie, um, well..."

"Have we made it? On many levels. That's not important. Go with the flow. It's your first night in the big city. Feel the love. Ever make it with a Jewish chick?"

"No, but..."

"What are you boys talking about?" asked Suzie as she approached the table.

"Beauty and love and you," said Ira.

"Well, this beauty has an early morning tomorrow, helping the last group of freshman to settle in. Want to be a gentleman and walk me home?" she asked Tom.

"I'd love to. Nice meeting you, Ira. Are you a student at Columbia?"

Suzie laughed. "Ira has been, and will be, a student at Columbia for as long as he can."

"My old man believes in education. It's a Jewish thing. You got any Jews where you come from?"

"No, but I've read about them."

"Funny guy," said Ira. "Education is the most important things for Jews. My old man will support me as long as I remain in school, so I plan on remaining in school for as long as I can."

"I guess I'll see you on campus sometime."

"You'll have a better chance of seeing Ira at the Blue Moon," said Suzie. "He only takes one or two courses a semester."

"And I only attend one or two classes per course. My education is taking place in a multitude of places."

"Interesting. Well, see you around."

Suzie lived a few blocks from the Blue Moon.

"Wanna come up and see my place?" she asked.

"Sure."

The apartment was on the top floor of a four-story walkup. The tiny living room was dominated by a sagging, faded sofa and a small round kitchen table dotted with dirty cups and overflowing ashtrays.

"The place is kind of a pit. My roommate is a waitress and doesn't get home 'til late and can't bother to do housework. Then again, I can't be bothered with it either. Want to see my room?"

"Sure."

Suzie's unmade bed was buried under dirty clothes and books, as was the floor. As Tom entered, Suzie turned, wrapped her arms around him, grabbed his ass with both hands, and pulled him to her. Their lips met, tongues probing. Suzie shuffled backward until she hit the bed, then they both tumbled onto it.

"Shit," Suzie muttered. She rolled to her side and pulled a massive book from the bed. "Too much crap. We need room to move."

She stood up, grabbed the blanket, and tugged, as if trying to pull a tablecloth out from under a fully set table. Tom went rolling off the bed and landed with a thud. Books and dirty clothes went flying.

"That's better."

She stood on the bed and motioned for him to join her. Suzie pulled Tom's shirt over his head, then dropped to her knees and began to un-buckle his belt.

"Wow!" Tom sighed.

"Do girls do this to you in Indiana?"

"Definitely not."

"Am I being too forward?"

"Not in the least."

She pulled down his zipper, then yanked his pants down to his ankles. He started to lose his balance and grabbed her shoulders. Suzie took his cock into her mouth and began to suck until it became fully erect.

"Now it's your turn." She took a step back and waited expectantly.

Tom stood and pulled Suzie's sweater over her head. It took him a mo-ment to unclasp the plain white bra, which released large yet firm breasts.

"Too big, eh?"

"Hell, no. They're fantastic."

Tom dropped to his knees and suckled her breasts while fumbling blindly with her belt and zipper. Finally, he pulled her pants down. Suzie fell to her back and allowed Tom to remove her pants and panties. She lifted her knees and spread her legs.

"Do you go down on girls on the farm?

"I tried once, but the girl was too embarrassed."

"You won't have that problem with me. If you don't mind me being pushy, I like to be done a certain way."

"I'm in New York to be educated."

"The professor is ready. Pussy Licking 101."

An hour later they lay on the sweat-soaked bed. Tom stared at the ceiling, a smile on his face.

"You look happy," Suzie said.

"Who wouldn't be? Here I am in New York City. I've read poetry at a coffee shop and had wild sex with a hot woman."

"I'm not too fat."

"You're voluptuous, like the women in a Renoir painting. You know, where the men are fully dressed at a picnic and there are nude women lying about. You have a classic body."

"You don't find me too pushy? Too strong? My mom tells me I scare away men."

"You didn't scare me away. Actually, when we met Ira, I was disappointed because I thought maybe you two were going together."

"Me and Ira? Together?" She snorted a laugh.

"What's so funny? He's not bad looking, I guess. He seems interesting."

"You just met him and you already think he's interesting?"

"I've never met a poet."

"Well, you still haven't. Ira's a part-time student, part-time poet."

"Did you two, well...."

"I like sex, as you can tell, but I only do it with people I find interesting. Or if they're so hot looking I can't say no. Yeah, Ira's an interesting guy, so we slept together, once. Believe me, it was no big deal, and it won't happen again. We're just friends."

"Will it happen again with me? Or are we just friends?"

"It's too soon to know if we'll be friends. I do know we'll have sex again. Right now, in fact."

The rest of the night was spent having wild, abandoned sex, with a few hours of sleep interspersed. Tom did things he had never dreamed of, mainly because he had no idea people did those kinds of things. By the time the sky began to lighten, he'd lost count of how many positions they'd tried, how many new ways he'd learned to please a woman.

"I'd better get ready to go to school," Suzie said, "though I don't know if I'll be able to walk."

"Sorry," Tom said, though he obviously didn't mean it.

"I'm going to shower and get dressed. You should go back to your dorm."

"So I'm being dismissed."

"For now. I'll see you around campus or at the Blue Moon. Hey, it was fun."

"Yeah. It's a night I'll never forget."

And he never did.

CHAPTER 2—1958/1959

Tom's first few months at Columbia were a blur of classes and late-night study sessions. He had always spent his days doing chores on the farm or playing sports at school, followed by hearty meals of farm-fresh food. Now his life consisted of bad cafeteria food, no exercise, and no sunshine. He got up early, studied, spent all day in classrooms and the library, then read until he fell asleep. Life in Indiana, the evening at the Blue Moon, the wild night with Suzie, all faded into distant, hazy memories.

One day he was carrying a tray of institutional food in one hand, a huge stack of books in the other, searching for an empty chair in the cafeteria, when somebody called to him.

"Hey, South of Chicago."

Tom looked over and saw Ira sitting alone at a table, a cigarette in his hand.

"Mind if I join you?" Tom asked.

"I was kind of holding these seats for Ike and Nixon, in case they're in the neighborhood and want to stop by for a snack and a bull session."

Tom hesitated.

"Sit down," said Ira. "You don't want your food to grow cold. I hate it when everything congeals on the plate."

Tom set down his tray and attacked his lunch. After wolfing down a few bites, he looked up so see Ira nodding his head.

"What?"

"I see the transformation has begun," Ira replied.

"What transformation?"

"High school BMOC into faded, jaded Columbia student."

"I was never a big man on campus."

"You mean you weren't captain of the football team? Weren't balling a cheerleader?"

"I didn't play football. Didn't have sex with any cheerleaders. I was kind of a loner."

"Oh, that's right. You're not a brown-shoed square, and you listen to jazz. I don't suppose that goes over big in the prairies. I'm still right about your transformation, though."

"How so?"

"It's pretty standard, actually. Whether you're from Long Island or way, way south of Chicago, you show up bright-eyed and eager to excel. Columbia is your ticket to wealth and fame, or at least some important job with the government or some huge industrial organization. Then reality hits. You bust your gut to get the work done, spend all of your time in the library. First you lose that tan you got milking cows or cutting hay or whatever it is you farmers do. Your skin becomes pasty and translucent, like the belly of a dead fish. Then your hair starts to get longer and you don't comb it as often. You say it's because you don't have the time or money to get it cut, but in reality you want to look less like a high school geek. Your clothes start to look like they're permanently wrinkled and carry a faint odor of dirty dorm rooms."

"I look that bad?"

"I didn't say you look bad. Hell, you'll probably get laid more now that you've lost that 'new kid on the street' look."

"I guess I still have a long way to go. I haven't been laid since school began."

"Not since your first night in New York, anyway."

Tom didn't reply, choosing to attack his food instead.

"Suzie's a lot of fun."

Tom kept eating.

"I see. You don't screw and tell."

Tom shrugged. "It's personal."

"Suzie doesn't mind. In fact, she loves it when people talk about her. It's her insecurity, 'cuz she sees herself as fat. The way she tells it, she was the fattest kid in school. Everybody always made fun of her. You know how kids are. So she lost some weight and discovered sex."

Tom squirmed.

"It's all right. She'd tell you the same thing. She was the big slut of her high school. Then she came to Columbia. I met her the first week. I was taking American Lit for the second time, having flunked it freshman year due to nonattendance. Suzie was lucky she met me, otherwise she might have sucked her way through the entire campus. I clued her in, told her that her problem was one of self-image. Reminded her how difficult it was to get into Columbia, told her how special she was. I still got a great blowjob."

"Jerk."

"It was only that one time. Since then it's been a platonic friendship. I've helped her to gain confidence, feel good about herself. As you saw, she's a really strong person now."

"So now you're just friends?"

"You ever have any girl friends? I mean girls who are friends?"

"Not really."

"Suzie prides herself on being open minded. She has male friends and female friends, city friends and farmer friends, even some colored friends. She likes me 'cuz I'm different than her other friends."

"Yeah? What makes you different?"

"That's something you're going to have to find out for yourself."

"If I had the time."

"You've got all the time in the world."

"Sure, if I stop going to class and stop doing my homework."

"Look, South of Chicago..."

"Call me Tom."

"OK, Tom. You could have gone to college anywhere if all you're going to do is go to class and sit in a library. You could be back in the Midwest, picking corn. You're not, though. Remember why you came here?"

"Because it was far from Indiana and it's where I can listen to live jazz."

"So have you listened to any?"

"No, because..."

Ira held up his hand. "Stop. This Friday night I'm taking you to a jazz club. It's a little place in the Village, no big names, which is why we can afford it. I'll even bring Suzie along, if you'd like. We won't talk school, and maybe you'll figure out why Suzie would want to hang out with a loser like me."

"I never called you a loser."

"You didn't have to. Nobody's impressed with a guy who's on the ten-year plan."

"I never gave it much thought, other than wondering why somebody would work to get into Columbia, then not work once you got here."

"Hang around and you'll discover why, though be careful. You might catch what I have."

"I doubt it."

Ira, Suzie, and Tom met outside the subway and took the #1 line to the Village. The club was dark and smoky, as was the jazz. They found a table in the corner, a quiet spot for talking while the trio played in the background. Ira jumped right into the topic he'd opened at the cafeteria.

"Our kid Tom wants to know why you hang out with a loser like me."

Suzie looked at Tom when she answered. "No matter how down I am, no matter how fat I feel or how badly I did on a test, I can look at Ira and know that I'm not the biggest loser in New York."

Ira grinned. "It's nice to be needed, if not loved."

"Poor Ira thinks that his family doesn't love him."

"I'm not what they wanted. Dear Dad was hoping I'd look less Jewish, which would be a good trick since both my parents are Semitic to the core: frizzy hair, hooked noses, the works. I was born Kornblue, but dear Dad is in advertising and fears that anything that smacks of Jewishness will endanger his career. Thus, the change to Blue, which I like 'cuz it sounds like the blues, which gave birth to jazz. I dug my name enough to get into the blues and jazz, which I listened to all the time, when I wasn't reading Ginsberg or Burroughs or Kerouac. I should have dropped out of high school and got a job busing tables at Fugazzi's, where Ginsberg worked for a while, but I'm a pussy, so I went to Columbia."

"You just want to keep sucking at the big teat," said Suzie.

"Why shouldn't I live off of dear Dad? The wealthy have a public duty to support artists. So I take a class or two each semester, Dad pays the bills and can tell his friends that his son attends Columbia, and we're all happy. Does that answer your Q?"

"Sure. We're all outcasts, looking for a place where we belong, looking for people we can relate to. You're the Jewish kid with a father who rejected his religion, leaving you with nothing to identify with or belong to. You feel some guilt for taking your father's money, yet justify it by claiming artists' rights. You like to come off as some Beat poet so squares like me will be in awe, though you've never actually published anything or hung out with your Beat heroes."

"I see you've taken Intro to Psychology," said Ira. "Great. My turn to explain why Suzie likes to hang with me. Suzie is pretty and sexy and very smart, but she doesn't think so. Kids always made fun of her 'cuz she was fat and her mother encouraged her to diet and exercise, which made Suzie feel fatter and unwanted, so she became a slut in order to feel wanted. Then she met me, who didn't care about sex and liked her for her mind, and I encourage her to be strong. She's not sure if Beat is where she's at, but it's about rebellion, and so is she. For now. See? Two losers who found comfort in each other."

"My turn," said Suzie. "Why would a genius like Tom want to hang out with two losers like Ira and me? Tom was the odd kid in Indiana. He was smarter than everybody else and didn't really care that much about farming or football, preferring to listen to jazz and read articles in *Time* magazine about the Beat Generation. He had a few friends back home, though all they had in common was that they didn't belong. Being accepted to Columbia was the best thing that ever happened to him, and he was lucky when he met me and I opened the door to a new world, though he's still not sure he wants to step too far into it. He digs the idea of hot sex and cool jazz, and he's heard about pot, which intrigue him, but he doesn't want to end up like Ira. He's ambitious, though he has no idea where his destiny is leading him. He likes hanging with us because we're exotic. For now."

"Does that answer your Q?" Ira asked again.

"More than I expected. Psychoanalysis on the cheap."

"So wanna go outside and smoke a joint? Get high?" Ira asked. "It's good for your head."

"I don't think so. Don't let me stop you. Go ahead if you want to."

"How enlightened. Tell you what, kid. I've got a homework assignment for you."

"I've got plenty of homework."

"Not like this. Besides, it's for Christmas vacation. You going to the farm?"

"No. Can't afford the train, and I need to make some money. I thought I'd get a job at Macy's."

"Good. That'll give you some free time. You've read *about* the Beat poets and all, but have you actually read any?"

"No."

"Start with some of Corso's poems, then Ginsberg's *Howl*, then top it off with Kerouac's *On the Road.*"

"Why should I spend my vacation reading Beat literature?"

"'Cuz that's why you came to New York. To expand your mind. Go to more jazz clubs, more poetry readings. After Christmas you'll be ready for the next thing: smoking pot."

"Why would a smart guy like me listen to a ten-year man like you?"

"You want to expand your mind, and you know you can only go so far in a classroom and by reading textbooks."

"Under one condition. After Christmas I don't want to be the 'kid.' Suzie's about my age, and you aren't much older, even if you think you are."

"It's a deal, kid."

Tom worked at Macy's during the holidays, stocking shelves and doing other menial jobs. Though it wasn't stimulating work, it gave him the free time to explore New York's many neighborhoods. He enjoyed listening to the sounds of the city and lapped up its ethnicity, trying different foods and inhaling unusual smells. The first time he entered Harlem he was quickly overwhelmed by its blackness and fled back to the relative whiteness of the Columbia campus. Eventually he grew comfortable and found he could walk around almost any neighborhood without feeling self-conscious or fearful of assault. He ventured into the numerous museums and discovered a fondness for modern art at the MOMA. His hair grew longer and shaggier, and he took to wearing dark shirts instead of the white ones he'd arrived with. His nice slacks remained on their hangers, replaced by jeans, which he'd always associated with farmers. He now wore them as a sign of his solidarity with workers and cool students. The night before the start of the second semester Tom met Ira at Suzie's apartment.

"You're looking good," Suzie said when she opened the door, "like you've lived in New York all your life."

"Am I that pale?"

"It's not about skin tone, man," chimed in Ira from couch. "It's about attitude, and I can see you've developed some."

Tom noted Ira's use of 'man' instead of 'kid,' and it made him feel like he belonged. He hugged Suzie and they exchanged wet kisses.

"How's the poetry?" Tom asked Ira.

"Very cool. Ginsberg told me he liked what I had to say."

"Allen Ginsberg?"

"No. Mort Ginsberg, from Carnegie Deli. Of course Allen Ginsberg."

"Wow. Big Time."

"Yeah, it was very cool. It was at a poetry reading in the Village. I asked him if I could send him some poems, you know, to get his opinion. I got the feeling he didn't want to give me his address, so he told me to send a few to local rags in order to get published. I think I need the credibility before I'm accepted."

"That'd be great. To be published and hang out with Ginsberg and Kerouac."

"So you read *Howl* and *On the Road*?"

"Yeah."

"So waddya think?"

"I don't think I'm ready to quit school and hitch to Denver, but they've given me a lot to consider."

"That's a start. We can talk later about next summer. Maybe hitch out west, check out the Beat scene in San Francisco. Do our own road trip."

While Tom and Ira were talking, Suzie had gone to her room and emerged holding a hand-rolled cigarette.

"This'll give you even more to consider. You ready to try some pot?"

"I don't suppose a little will do any permanent danger. You both still seem somewhat normal."

"Thanks, I guess," said Suzie.

She lit the joint, took a few deep drags, then passed it to Ira. He kept it for a while before passing it to Tom.

"Inhale a little at a time," cautioned Suzie, "otherwise you'll cough it up."

Tom did as instructed, then took a few more small drags when the joint came around the second time. He didn't feel anything at first and soon became lost in a deep discussion about Beat poetry and poets, then about the use of language, then about the alphabet and how twenty-six letters didn't seem sufficient, and how language in general seemed inadequate to express feelings. Suzie mentioned that she was starving, and Ira mentioned that she looked like she was in need of a meal, and Suzie told him to fuck off and everybody started laughing uncontrollably. Finally, the laughter faded away and left them short of breath.

"So how do you like being stoned?" Ira asked.

"Gosh. I almost forgot," Tom answered, which led to another fit of the giggles.

"Let's go explore the city," Ira suggested, "chase down some music."

"Let's find some food," added Suzie. "That's the problem about being stoned. I get hungry and don't care how much I eat."

"That's fine with me," said Tom. "I like your full fleshiness."

"Oh, my. A horny stoner," said Suzie.

"Let's get something to eat," said a blushing Tom.

They gobbled down coffee and burgers at a local dinner, buttoned up their coats, and went looking for adventure. Rather than head to the Village for jazz and poetry, Ira suggested heading north into Harlem in search of blues. Tom's forays into Harlem had relieved his anxiety about Negroes, and the idea of hearing real blues in a Harlem club appealed to him. Ira suggested a club that was known for its music, as well as its rough characters, which only added to its appeal. The three took the subway north to 140th Street, then headed to the club. A knot of tough-looking men loitered near the entryway, smoking hand-rolled cigarettes that reeked of pot.

"Lookee what we got here. Whitey is slumming tonight." Though the speaker wasn't particularly tall, he had wide shoulders and a massive chest and muscles that strained to break free from his black T-shirt. "You folks are about a hundred blocks too far north."

Ira stepped up with a bit of a swagger. "We're here for some music."

"What? You didn't stop by for chitlins and biscuits?"

Suzie grabbed Tom's arm and started moving backward.

"Oh, oh, it would appear that the young lady is ready to head home," said the shortest of the men. "She ain't even heard any music yet."

"Careful," cautioned Muscles. "You don't want to hurt George's feelings." He nodded to the man who stood next to him, a huge man nearly six feet six and close to two hundred fifty pounds, who wore a ragged leather jacket.

"We're here for music, man, not trouble," said Ira, who'd lost his swagger.

"Music? What you white people know about music besides Eye-talian drunks and twanging hillbillies?"

Just then a man stepped out of the club. "Break time's over. You niggers better start playing if you want to get paid."

Tom, Suzie, and Ira stood with their mouths gaping.

"You folk keep them mouths open," said Muscles, "and you never know what people are gonna put in 'em, 'specially that sweet gal with them full, moist lips."

Suzie snapped her mouth shut and the band doubled over in laughter.

"Come on in," smiled Muscles. "I guess we owe you a beer for scaring you like that, though you white people are too damn easy to scare. Isn't much sport in it."

It was the middle of the night when Tom, Suzie, and Ira stumbled out of the nameless club. They'd smoked a joint with the band during the next break and had bought the band and themselves beer until they ran out of money. Though it was a long walk back to Columbia, they were high on the music and the adventure they'd just had.

"Hell of a lot more fun than studying," said Ira.

"You're right about that," agreed Tom. "We should do it again sometime."

"Sometime? Let's do it again tomorrow night."

"It is tomorrow, and I'll have homework tonight."

"Damn, man. You still don't get it."

"Get what?" asked Tom. "Get that I should stop studying and start getting stoned all the time and staying out all night listening to music?"

"Why not? Books are full of the past. They don't tell you shit about the here and now or the future. What we did tonight was real. Same as when

Sal Paradise hitched cross-country. That was real. Listen to Beat poetry. Read Beat books. That's where you'll get a real education."

Tom looked at Suzie. "What do you think?"

"I think Ira is right and wrong. Books only teach about the past. I can't relate to what I hear in the classroom. On the other hand, hitchhiking and spending all night in smoky bars doesn't seem to lead anywhere worthwhile."

"So where is it you want to be led?" Ira asked.

"Right now I only want to be led to my bed."

"It's that time of semester," Ira smirked at Tom. "You got any energy left?"

Tom glanced shyly at Suzie.

Suzie smiled. "So tell us, Indiana Slim. Got any energy left?"

"I started last semester exhausted, and I still landed pretty good grades. I think I can do the same this semester."

"Good grades?" muttered Ira. "Good grief. You're the only one who can grade yourself."

Something changed for Tom during the second semester. Or changed *within* Tom. He slept with Suzie more often, and they started to fuck in the morning rather than go to class. He went to more jazz clubs in the Village and more blues clubs in Harlem, and his classwork became sloppy. He started smoking cigarettes and bought his first bag of pot. Tom would spend long evenings discussing the meaning of life with Ira, rather than prepare for the next day's class.

The day approached when he would need to declare his major in order to be able to register for the right classes for sophomore year. He had originally considered political science, which would lead to a job with the government, or English literature, which would lead to a teaching job or even a position at the University of Indiana or Columbia itself. Now he began to contemplate philosophy, which wouldn't lead to much besides writing or a professorship. Suzie was taking Intro to Religions, and they would spend hours in bed naked considering the role of religion in society and comparing Eastern and Western religions. Suzie had become intrigued with Buddhism and had even demonstrated in opposition to

China's invasion of Tibet a few times in front of the United Nations building. Ira had joined her solely for the experience: he didn't care about Tibet, didn't believe that demonstrations achieved anything. Tom had also accompanied Suzie, partly because he was curious about the power of demonstrations.

Things changed dramatically for Tom when he received his quarter grades: two Bs, two Cs, and one D. He'd had fun for two months, loved the sex and the devil-may-care attitude, but those grades were like a splash of ice-cold water. He felt like he'd woken from a long—though pleasant—dream. The morning he learned about his grades he marched over to the registrar's office and declared a major in political science with a minor in French, one of the main languages of international diplomacy. It was time to get back to being a serious student. He stopped sleeping with Suzie, stopped going to clubs with Ira, stopped smoking pot, and only drank a beer or two on the weekends.

Tom had raised his grades back to acceptable levels, and final exams were a week away, when, while on his way to the library to study, he turned a corner and bumped into Ira.

"Well, if it isn't the ex-beatnik."

"I was never a beatnik. Those musicians in Harlem were right: I was just slumming."

"I don't buy that, man. I've looked into your heart and it's the heart of a poet."

"You were stoned at the time."

"Pot doesn't lie. It only reveals what is already within."

"Look, I'm late for a study session. Tell you what. Let's go hear some jazz the night of my last final. I'll call Suzie. It'll be like old times."

"I don't want old times. I want new times. A new world. A world where we're not expected to conform to society's expectations. Come up to my place and we'll smoke a joint and plot a new course for America."

"I have to run. See you later."

"You can run, but you can't hide. I'm in your brain."

"If so, I hope you know something about Europe between the wars."

"We're still at war, though now it's with our own government and advertisers who are trying to control our minds."

"Goodbye, Ira."

CHAPTER 3—1961

Tom gradually became a BMOC at Columbia. He excelled in all subjects, and his professors recommended him to be the student representative on various committees. He was elected student body vice president for his junior year and led the campus campaign for Kennedy's successful 1960 presidential run. There was even a picture in the *New York Times* of Tom shaking hands with Kennedy. Tom could be found at nearly every football and basketball game leading cheers and urging the team on. Although his hair had grown longer, he kept it neatly combed and in place with Brylcreem. He bumped into Suzie from time to time and—unknown to all except Ira—they still enjoyed wild alcohol- and pot-fueled sex at the beginning of every semester. This biannual bacchanalia was perhaps less surprising than Tom's frequent evenings with Ira. A young man having sex is to be expected; a mainstream, fairly straight-laced, and ambitious student meeting often with a shiftless beatnik was incongruous. Yet for Tom, his friendship with Ira was of vital importance, though he couldn't say why. It was a point that Ira often touched on during their time together.

"Hail to the VP," Ira called out as Tom entered a Village jazz club one night soon after spring break. "The election for next year must be soon. Time to plan your presidential campaign. Better be careful. Kennedy beat the standing VP, so a precedent might have been set. Then again, you're a lot smarter and better looking than Nixon. Here's to the next president of the student body of Columbia University. Hail to the chief!" He raised his beer and belched loudly as Tom sat down.

"Show a little respect," said Tom.

"That's as little as I can muster."

Tom wearily shook his head.

"Why do you keep coming back for another beating?" Ira said.

"Good question, though 'beating' is an exaggeration. You merely ruffle my feathers."

"Well, my fine-feathered turkey, I'll tell you why. You're ashamed of what you've become, and being with me helps you to convince yourself that you're not a totally lost cause."

"Is that a fact? What have I become that is so shameful as to drive me to waste countless hours drinking cheap beer with an eternal student? Maybe it's my 3.8 GPA. Or perhaps it's the respect I get from my professors, who often ask for my opinion on student issues. No, I've got it—it's my election as vice president of the student body, which you loudly mock. You're right, Ira. I've got a shitload to be ashamed of."

"You failed to mention the shallow bluebloods you've been balling."

"Jealous?"

Ira shot Tom a look that said, "Are you serious?" As far as Tom could tell, Ira was asexual. He might have slept with Suzie years before, yet Tom had never seen Ira with a woman during the three years they'd known each other.

"All right, so you're not jealous," Tom conceded. "Why should I be ashamed of balling some of the hottest women on campus?"

"Because they're only hot on the outside, and that's only because they trowel on the makeup."

"You're wrong there. I guarantee they were sizzling on the inside, too."

"I'm talking about their soul, not their pussies, as you are very well aware. You seem to seek out the shallowest, richest, snobbiest women on campus."

"Guilty as charged, though I'm not ashamed of it. In fact, I enjoy the irony. None of these women would have given me a second look when I stepped off the train from Indiana. The poor hayseed is balling the cream of the elite crop."

"That's why you came to Columbia? So fawning professors could kiss your ass and rich bitches could suck your dick?"

"That and for New York pizzas."

"You can joke, but you know exactly what I'm saying. That's why you hang out with me. So you can be reminded why you're really here."

"If that's the case, then please tell me. Why am I here?"

"Because Indiana was too small for your big dreams. You wanted Ivy League and New York City. You wanted to do something important. To be somebody special."

"Believe me, I am special to the women I ball."

Ira slammed his empty glass on the table.

"You're so full of shit that it's pouring out of your mouth in buckets. There's more to life than sex and grades and meetings to discuss who Columbia should invite to give the commencement speech, and you know it. Somewhere deep inside your well-dressed, squeaky-clean exterior lurks something of substance. You occasionally let it out during poetry readings, which, by the way, you have a talent for. Though it's on the rare occasions when you smoke some weed that the real you emerges."

"It's not the real me if I'm stoned."

"How many times must I tell you? The pot only reveals what exists inside you. It cuts through the ego and the bullshit and the defense mechanisms you use to mask the truth."

"Lord save me from another Freudian rant."

"Lord save you from yourself, if there was a 'Lord.' I worry about you, Tom. Who's going to be around to tell you the truth when you graduate in a year?"

"You'll always be around. It's your calling in life."

"Naw. I'll be in San Francisco. I'm going to move there this summer."

"A year ago you said you were moving to the Village. It never happened, and you'll never move to San Francisco. You're a talker, not a doer."

"And you're a doer, not a thinker. Not a deep thinker, anyway. That's another reason you keep following me around like a lost puppy. I'm the only one who really makes you look inside yourself, who shames you into more profound thoughts. As long as we remain friends, you're not a completely lost cause."

"In that case, I owe you a lot. How about I buy you a fifty cent beer?"

They had the same conversation—with minor variations—every month or two. Tom scoffed at Ira's overblown image of his own importance, though he knew that there was a kernel of truth in what Ira said. There *was* something missing from his life. The praise he received rang hollow in his ear. The pretty daughters of wealthy East Coast barons meant nothing to him. They discussed holiday plans and movies and clothes; nothing of substance. The annoying fact was that Ira was right. Tom had developed a grudging respect for the apparently hopeless Ira. Whereas Tom still had no idea what he wanted to do with his life with one year remaining at Columbia, Ira was supremely confident about his own future. He would stay at Columbia as long as he could, then pursue a literary career that would bring him the recognition he craved. Not fame, because fame was a mass thing and Ira scorned the uneducated masses. Not fortune, because money was only the measure of how greedy and selfish a person was. Ira was going to be the next Allen Ginsberg, the next Jack Kerouac. He was going to write important poems that would endure and change lives long after he was dead. In fact, he'd already had a few poems printed in a third-rate poetry magazine. The poems were full of righteous indignation, and although few people actually read the rag, Ira saw it as the beginning.

Suzie joined the two friends from time to time, but she'd found another focus: Buddhism. What had started with the Intro to Religions class and demonstrations against China's invasion of Tibet was now a quest for Buddhist knowledge. Suzie had explored Tibetan and Theravada Buddhism before eventually latching on to Zen Buddhism. She had become a regular at a Zen temple not far from Columbia and often spent weekends in meditation sessions or at a meditation retreat in upstate New York. She was a lit major and had planned on getting a teaching certificate and finding a job at a school in the inner city. Now she struggled with a moral dilemma: help poor, underprivileged kids or seek inner peace. After Tom and Ira had finished debating their lives and futures, the conversation would usually turn to Suzie.

"What's new with our Long Island Buddhist?" Tom would ask.

"She's hoping to find enlightenment right after Passover."

"I don't suppose you bother to mask your cynicism when you see her."

"Would you believe me if I started to fawn over you and tell you what a brilliant, perceptive student leader you are? Of course not. Same with Suzie. Then again, after Kerouac published *The Dharma Bums* last year, I decided to give Suzie less grief for dabbling in voodoo."

"So if it's OK with Kerouac, it's OK with you. I'm glad you show respect for somebody."

"I won't make a habit of it."

The three friends had agreed to meet a few nights before Suzie's graduation to celebrate the event. Tom had been dating a blueblood from Darien, Connecticut—Barbara Bennett—who he invited to the dinner. He had warned her that she would not like his friends, but she insisted on joining them. They met at a small Italian restaurant that featured red-and-white checkered table clothes, Chianti bottles as candleholders, and Sinatra in the background. Tom and Barbara were already sipping Chianti when Ira and Suzie arrived.

"I hope that you don't mind that we started without you," Tom said, as he raised his wine glass.

"That's all right," replied Ira. "We smoked a joint to enhance our appetites."

Barbara grew tense and Tom cringed. He'd told Ira that Barbara was a conservative Republican who thought that all pot smokers were communist junkies. Tom had also mentioned Barbara's dislike for jazz, the "music of Negro drug addicts" according to her, which explained Ira's next comment.

"Not to worry. I brought another one for afterward. I thought we'd run up to Harlem and find some smoky jazz club."

"Shut up, Ira," said Suzie. She held her hand out to Barbara. "Hi. I'm Suzie. Don't mind Ira. He's preparing for his final exam in How to Be a Major Asshole."

Suzie was trying to break the ice and put Barbara at ease, but she'd picked the wrong method. Barbara did not use profanities and disdained those who did. Barbara gave Suzie a weak handshake, and quickly put her hands in her lap lest Ira try to shake.

"So, Barbara," began Ira, "do your people like Italian food? I mean, I was under the impression that they didn't like ethnic things, you know, jazz and colored people and such."

Tom shot Ira a withering look.

"Let's start all over again," suggested Suzie. She raised her glass. "Here's to old Columbia U. Although we may be from different backgrounds and are following different paths, Columbia brought us together."

They clinked glasses and drained them. Ira refilled each and signaled for the waiter to bring another bottle.

"A better bottle," Ira said to the waiter. He turned to Tom. "I assume you and Barbara are paying for dinner."

Tom shook his head, exasperated.

"Here's to New York City," Ira toasted, "where everybody is welcome: rich and poor, black and white, the powerful and the powerless."

Tom heaved a sigh of relief, having expected the worst. He should have known better. As Barbara brought her glass to her lips, Ira continued.

"Even if the rich and powerful spend their days pissing on the poor."

Barbara put her glass down before her lips touched it.

"Here's to friends," Tom jumped in. "I'm going to miss you, Suzie. You'd better stay in touch, even if you move to the Far East."

Barbara grew tense again and hesitated a moment before raising her glass.

"Your turn, Barbie," said Ira.

Ira's reference to the new doll that had captivated little girls across the country did not go unnoticed. Barbara glared at Ira.

"I prefer Barbara."

"Well everybody else prefers Barbie," Ira said, "though I don't get it. Who the hell is really shaped like that? Those perfect long, slim legs and perfect long, blond hair, and perfect tits that don't require a bra. No woman could possibly look like that in real life. Of course, except for the perfect tits, you could be a dead ringer for the other Barbie."

Barbara had always been self-conscious about her breasts, which barely filled a B cup. Ira's remarks were more than she could tolerate. She raised her glass toward Ira.

"Here's to the little people who do the lousy jobs that make it possible for important people to make this world a better place." She drained her glass before anybody else had even raised theirs. "Oh, by the way," she sneered at Ira, "what is it you're going to do after your father finally cuts you off? Tom tells me you're a Beat poet. Exactly how much does that pay?"

"Here's to the little people," Tom said, raising his glass before Ira had a chance to reply.

Suzie joined Tom in draining her glass, then she slammed it down and let out a bellow of a laugh. "What the hell. I didn't want a tea party anyway.

You two," she nodded toward Ira and Barbara, "can attack each other with knives if you like. This is a celebration, and I'm going to get drunk. You with me, Tom?"

Tom glanced at Barbara, then shrugged. "What the hell. Barbara, have another drink. Have a bunch. No more toasting, though."

"Fucking right," Suzie agreed. "No more fucking toasting. Just drinking and bullshitting. Oops, pardon my French."

Tom decided to change the subject. "Suzie, I was shocked when Ira told me that you've decided not to be a teacher after all."

"Really?" Barbara said. "Tom had told me that you were committed to helping inner-city children. Such a noble thing to do, until you start a family, anyway."

Ira opened his mouth to say something, but yelped in pain instead. "Ouch. Who kicked me?"

"Suzie must have beat me to it," Tom said.

"My leg cramped," said Suzie with a wink at Tom. "Actually, I haven't given up on teaching. I'm putting it on hold while I explore other things. There's a Buddhist monastery near San Francisco, and I thought I might do some meditation before committing to something like teaching."

"A Buddhist monastery?" Barbara had a perplexed look on her face, as if Suzie had said she was planning to walk on the moon.

"Hasn't Tom told you that I've studied Buddhism since freshman year?"

Tom hadn't. He knew that Barbara hadn't been thrilled to be dining with two Jews, and he'd thought it best to not mention Buddhism, hoping the subject wouldn't come up.

"I wonder what else Tom neglected to mention," said Ira, a hint of a smile on his lips.

It was Tom's turn to glare at Ira. Once again, Suzie tried to save the evening.

"Teaching inner-city kids is important. I just think people need to find themselves before they can help others."

The perplexed look remained on Barbara's face.

"Look, Barbara, you seem confident in who you are..."

"WASP," Ira coughed.

"...and where you're going. Right?"

"Sure. When I graduate with my BA in French, I'll teach at a boarding school until I get married." She smiled at Tom, then looked coolly at Ira. "And yes, I'm a white Anglo-Saxon Protestant."

"Great," Suzie quickly said. "That's really neat. In my case, though, it's not so easy. My dad is Jewish, but my mom is half Jewish, half atheist. I'm part Russian, part Polish, part Bohemian, part who-knows what. I was bat mitzvahed, but I haven't been to synagogue since. There are also some other, um, issues that I've been struggling with." She thought it prudent not to mention the few lesbian flings she'd had in the past year. She hadn't even discussed those with Ira or Tom. "Anyway, I'm hoping to find some answers in California."

"Well, that's, uh, nice," Barbara said.

"I think it's wonderful," said Tom. "Now I'll have somebody to visit in California." Out of the corner of his eye he saw Barbara grow tense. "I mean, I've been to the East Coast, now I can visit the West Coast."

"You finally going to follow Kerouac's *On the Road*," Ira smiled."

"I think Tom has more important things in mind," said Barbara.

"What's more important than finding out who you are?" challenged Ira.

"Career. Family."

"Making money and babies," sneered Ira. "I imagine you're a natural for both."

Barbara stood and knocked her chair over backward.

"That's it. I don't have to stand for this. Let's go, Tom."

"Go? We haven't ordered dinner yet."

"I've lost my appetite. Are you coming or not?"

Tom looked from Suzie to Ira and back at Suzie again.

"Forget it," Barbara snapped. "I'll take a taxi."

"No, I'll take you back to your apartment."

"That's not necessary. Stay here and get drunk with your friends." She spat the last word.

Tom walked Barbara out the door.

"I warned you."

"Yes, you did. I just didn't believe that anybody could be so detestable."

"Ira is unique."

"Unique?"

Barbara was so furious that she was unable to get another word out until she had gotten into the cab. Tom was about to shut the door when she held it open and looked up at him standing on the curb.

"I think you'd better look long and hard at tonight. If you really want to have a bright future, you're going to have to consider who your true friends are. My family can open doors for you. What do those two offer you? Good night."

She grabbed the door handle and slammed it shut.

When Tom approached the table Ira and Suzie stopped talking. He sat down and took a gulp of wine. "That didn't go too well."

Ira and Suzie burst out laughing.

"You two can laugh. I'm the one who's going to have to deal with Barbara tomorrow."

"Have to?" asked Ira. "You don't 'have to' do anything with that flat-chested bitch."

"She has her good points," Tom said weakly. "You never gave her a chance."

"I don't care how good she is in bed. I bet you have a lot more fun once a semester with our steamy Suzie."

"Fuck off, Ira." Suzie looked at Tom." In spite of three years under Ira's tutelage, you're still a gentleman and a good friend. You chose Ira and me over Barbie tonight."

"I didn't choose anybody. I warned Barbara against coming, but she insisted. This is our night." Tom raised his glass. "To friends for life."

"Friends for life," Suzie echoed.

"However long that may be," said Ira.

"Seriously, Tom, why do you go out with her?" asked Suzie. "It's certainly not for the intellectual stimulation. What is it?"

Tom considered the question while sipping his wine.

"Do you remember why I came to Columbia?"

"Sure. You knew you didn't belong behind a plow, knew bigger and better things beckoned, and you sensed that those things might be found in the big city."

"That's about right, and I did find bigger and better things."

"You found Beat poetry and writing, and jazz and Harlem, and a taste for kosher meat," added Suzie with a grin.

"So why settle for the WASP bitch?" asked Ira.

"I haven't settled for anything. I'm still trying different things. Look, Ira, my future is not being a Beat poet or hitting the road or meditating in a Buddhist monastery, though I have enormous admiration for those who do. I'll be honest. I'm intrigued by the rich and powerful, two things I've never been."

"I suppose that explains your peculiar involvement in school politics," said Ira.

"There's nothing peculiar about it at all. You're cynical about all politics. You didn't do a single thing to help Kennedy win."

"Aha. Now I get it. You see yourself as the next John Kennedy. Except you lack his money and connections."

"Harry Truman lacked Kennedy's money and connections. He was a haberdasher from Missouri."

"My, my, my. Our young hayseed has visions of becoming a mighty oak. What do you think, Suzie? Would you vote for Tom for president?"

"Sure, why not."

"Thanks for the enthusiastic endorsement," said Tom. "First things first. I'm considering running for student body president in September."

"Now I get it," said Ira. "You think Barbara would make a better impression on the voters than a Long Island Jew."

"I have friends from many different backgrounds."

"Acquaintances," Ira corrected.

Tom shrugged. "I'm not going out with her because she'll enhance my electability. I first asked her out because I heard some guys mention they were intimidated by her beauty and wealth. I took it as a challenge. Later, after spending a weekend at her family's summer home in the Hamptons, I realized how much I enjoyed the good things in life."

"Oh, god," gasped Suzie. "Don't tell me you're going to marry her for her money."

"I'm not marrying her at all. I'm balling her."

"And you call me cynical," said Ira.

"Look, nobody's talking marriage. We're just having fun together. Do you really think the Bennetts want a farmer in the family? I know damn well that Barbara and I have no future. It's part of the adventure. Something different."

"Like going to Harlem to hear hot blues," said Ira, "except you have colored servants mixing martinis instead of colored musicians rolling joints."

"Exactly."

"Speaking of joints, I was serious about having a joint. There's this folk singer named Bob Dylan who's playing at Gerde's. What do you say we order some dinner, step outside for a joint afterward, then go hear some music?"

"Sounds perfect. What does the graduate have to say?"

"Sure. One thing, though. Tom, I understand that balling Barbara is part of your big adventure. You're tasting different flavors as it were. But if you end up marrying that skinny bitch and running for senator, I'm coming back from California to kick your corn-fed ass."

Tom and Ira had dinner with Suzie and her family the night of graduation. Afterward, the three friends went to the Village to listen to jazz together for what they knew might be the last time. When the club closed, Ira went home, and Tom climbed into bed with Suzie.

"That was the perfect end to four years at Columbia," said Suzie as they lay back in the afterglow.

"I hope you'll come back to return the favor next year when I graduate."

"Were you doing me a favor?"

Tom rolled over, caressed Suzie's breast, then gave her a deep, slow kiss. "Just a phrase. It was all pleasure, as was knowing you the past three years."

Suzie smiled. "Yeah. It was really nice."

"I don't want to lose touch with you after you move to California. You mean a lot to me."

"As much as Ira does?" Suzie teased.

"Differently. Ira has been important to my head. He makes me think, stops me from following the easy path."

"Is that good?"

"For me it is. I could have cruised, taken a few fluff classes, sweet-talked professors."

"You *have* sweet-talked professors."

"Yeah, but I feel some guilt about it. Ira's made me look at things from a different angle. He's pushed me to challenge myself, to use my head for more than getting good grades."

"So what have I done for you? Besides getting your rocks off."

"You've been important to my heart. You've helped me to feel. I had friends back home, yet none close. None with whom I shared my heart. You're the first person I think I truly love. Not in the marriage sense," he quickly added.

"Don't get nervous. I know you're not proposing. It's possible to love a friend."

"I knew you'd understand. That's part of why I love you. You understand me and still accept me for who I am. I never want to lose you as a friend."

"You never will. We're connected."

They made love one more time before going to sleep.

CHAPTER 4—1961/1962

Tom won the election for student body president. His main opponent was a brash, aggressive New Yorker who alienated all but the most fervent New Yorkers. For the mellower in-staters and nearly every student from out of state Tom was the easy choice. He never appeared overly ambitious—even when he was. He was earnest, yet friendly; had a vision, yet never seemed to push it; was as humble and relaxed with professors as with cafeteria staff. In short, Tom was a natural diplomat, a quality that did not go unnoticed. His academic advisor, a political science professor who had been in Franklin Roosevelt's New Deal administration, urged Tom to take either the civil service or the foreign service exam. He'd even assured Tom that he could pull strings to assure that Tom landed a plum position. Having led Kennedy's campaign at Columbia, Tom also had connections with the new administration.

In spite of the disastrous pregraduation dinner with Ira and Suzie, Tom and Barbara continued to be an item. Barbara's father—Henry Bennett, a Wall Street investment banker—invited Tom to lunch with him once a month at his private Manhattan club. Henry Bennett was a lifelong Republican who fervently believed that the New Deal was an insidious communist plot. He usually spent the first half of lunch railing against the Kennedy clan and the Jewish conspiracy ("that damn Jewsevelt nearly ruined America"), then eventually got around to Tom's future. Tom always sensed that Henry Bennett looked down on him—a farmer's son from Indiana—but at the same time Bennett was willing to overlook Tom's shabby background. Henry Bennett would do anything for his daughter, including accepting a son-in-law of inferior breeding. More importantly, Henry saw enormous potential in Tom, someone who could use his humble upbringing to rise in Washington, much as Abe Lincoln had used the log cabin and rail splitting. Henry believed that Tom could be a valuable political tool, a wholesome public face to provide cover for possible corporate shenanigans. Besides, he was neither a Jew nor a Catholic, so he was acceptable.

Not surprisingly, the higher Tom's star rose, the more shit he received from Ira. But whereas others might have taken exception to Ira's constant criticism and insults, Tom provoked it. He reported in great detail his lunches with Henry Bennett: the opulence of the club, the whiteness of the starched uniforms of the Negro waiters, the exorbitant cost of a simple hamburger. Ira would mutter ("Ground sirloin? Ground bullshit!"), and he would grow particularly irate when Tom detailed Bennett's plans for his future. Tom took particular glee in discussing his life with Barbara: thousand dollar shopping sprees, her descriptions of the opulent mansion she would one day own and stock with custom-made furniture, the children she would have and the private boarding schools they would attend. Tom enjoyed seeing how furious he could make Ira.

Three things combined to bring the game to an abrupt end one month before Tom graduated: Barbara, a job offer, and preparation for the commencement speech he would deliver as student body president.

Although Barbara appeared to be a spoiled princess, she had been, at times, a hell of a lot of fun. She was far hotter and adventurous in bed than one might have expected and she was graced with a sharp, incisive sense of humor. Tom had grown so fond of Barbara that he no longer felt obliged to rationalize to Ira his desire to be with her. He wasn't that bothered by her politics, was impressed by her family's wealth, and was proud to be seen with her in public.

One month before graduation Tom and Barbara were dining at a fancy French restaurant—Tom was comfortable with Barbara picking up the check—when Barbara brought up a topic that had hovered in the air, though never discussed.

"Tom, dear, I think we should talk about our engagement."

"Our engagement?"

"I know that it's the man who traditionally brings up the topic, but you've been so busy with your duties as president and preparing for exams and everything, and, well, I know we feel the same way about each other. We're obviously compatible in bed," she smiled and raised her eyebrows, "and with my father's help you'll be able to choose your career. It just seems like the time to take the next logical step."

"Engagement? To be married?"

Barbara threw her head back and laughed. "You're too much. Of course, we needn't rush the marriage. I'm content with a long engagement, six months to a year. That will give you time to start work and get settled in. You'll be too busy to get into trouble and I'll have time to design our new house."

"Barbara, honey, you know I'm fond of you..."

"Fond?"

"I'm crazy about you. It's just, well, I haven't even graduated yet and..."

"I'm not asking you to get down on your knees and declare your everlasting love. I'm not some silly schoolgirl. What I am asking for is a commitment, a commitment to your future, to our future together."

Tom took a couple of deep breaths and contemplated his dark red St. Emilion.

"Barbara, I haven't given much thought to anything beyond graduation."

"You've talked about taking the civil service or foreign service exam."

"Yes, though only in general terms, as possibilities. I worked pretty hard in high school to get into Columbia, and I've worked hard for four years to get top grades. The only future I've decided on is taking a year to travel around America. I want to get to know my country, get to know the people. Maybe buy a cheap car and do odd jobs, be a short-order cook for a few months or pick grapes in California."

"Pick grapes near the Buddhist monastery where that Suzie is meditating?"

"She left the monastery months ago."

"So you're still in touch with her?"

"Of course, she's a friend."

"You fucked her, didn't you?"

It was the first time Tom had heard Barbara swear. His mouth fell open.

"Yes, I know how to swear; I'm just too much of a lady to do it. Maybe you'd like me better if I lowered myself to the level of that Jewish slut."

"I won't tolerate you calling her a slut. And whether or not I've had sex with Suzie is not your business."

"Oh, it isn't?"

"I told you, Suzie is a friend, one of the best friends I've ever had. She is not a slut, and her religion is irrelevant to me. And before you start attacking Ira as a Jewish commie, I warn you that I take my friendships very seriously."

"As I've seen, even when they threaten your future."

"How does my friendship with Ira threaten my future?"

"Don't think that I don't know what your 'friend' has been telling you. It's obvious that he hates me and everything I represent. He resents my family's wealth and success, and he fears losing your friendship when you decide to ditch him for a better life. So he fills your head with beatnik nonsense about 'hitting the road' and 'finding yourself.' As for that Buddhist or Jew or whatever the hell she is, that bitch is no different. Go ahead, ruin your life if you want, but I warn you. If you go to California and fuck her you can say goodbye to me and your future, because I won't be waiting when you get back."

The last bit was delivered with such venom and volume that the entire restaurant came to a silent stop. Tom looked around at the other dinners and the staff, then calmly folded his napkin and placed it on the table.

"I'm glad we've had this talk. It'll certainly give me something to think about as I consider my future."

The fury suddenly drained from Barbara's face. "Oh, Tom. I'm sorry. I lost my temper. I've enjoyed our year together, and I don't want it to end. We belong together. I just go nuts when I think that your so-called friends are trying to tear us apart."

Tom sat silently for a moment, then said, "Give me a little time. You kind of took me by surprise, and I've got a lot to consider. I've got the commencement speech to write, and, well, you know, everything."

"I understand. Take your time. Graduation isn't for nearly a month. We could announce our engagement during graduation weekend, when both of our families are here."

"Right, good idea. Should we order dessert now?"

Two days later he was called out of class by his advisor's secretary. There were two gentlemen who wanted to have a word with him. The tall one was thin, with short, sandy-colored hair. The short one was stocky and sported a brown buzz cut. Both wore black suits, highly polished black shoes, white shirts, and black ties. The secretary led them to an empty classroom and closed the door when she left.

"Mr. Kington, I'm Officer Smith," began the tall, thin one, "and this is Officer Jones. We work for the Central Intelligence Agency. I assume a bright young man like you has heard of the CIA."

Tom almost laughed out loud. Some people might have been unaware of the CIA's existence prior to April, 1961, but not after the failed Bay of Pigs invasion on April 15 of that year. The clumsy CIA attempt to overthrow Fidel Castro and "liberate" Cuba from communist rule had shaken Kennedy's presidency, though he had quickly regained the public's trust by introducing the space program and the Peace Corps.

"Yes, I am well aware of the CIA's existence."

"Good, though I'm doubt that you are aware of the full extent of our work. Mr. Kington, the CIA is always on the lookout for special people, and you've been identified as one."

"Really?"

"There's no need to be modest with us. The person who brought you to our attention—sorry, we cannot reveal his name—thinks you have a lot to offer your government. Frankly, after some preliminary investigating, we concur. You're bright, hard working, a natural leader, Christian, and a good American. From the courses you've taken to papers you've written to your near fluency in French, it is apparent that you have an interest in the greater world. It is our hope that you'll consider joining us to make that a better world, one guided by American principles of democracy and liberty."

"I'm flattered."

"You should be. We're very selective. We're looking for America's best and brightest, and you've been identified as one of them."

"We do have a few questions," began Officer Jones, "before we proceed."

"If you're interested, that is," said Officer Smith.

"I've given serious consideration to working for the government. Actually, I've already looked into taking the civil service or foreign service exam." Tom said.

"That won't be necessary if you join the CIA."

"Great. However, I don't think I'm ready to commit to anything at this time."

"Of course not," smiled Officer Smith. "You haven't even graduated yet. Heck, we yanked you out of class and dropped this in your lap; I imagine your head is spinning a bit. Besides, this is all preliminary stuff, checking each other out. You might decide the CIA isn't right for you. We might discover some things that would cause us to rescind our invitation. It's kinda like the first date. We're not ready to jump into bed together yet."

Officer Smith grinned. Officer Jones did not

"In that case," Tom said, "proceed with your questions."

Officer Jones took a small notebook from the inner pocket of his black suit, flipped it open, checked some notes, then looked at Tom.

"You are friends with one Ira Blue." It wasn't a question. "Are you aware that Mr. Blue was born Kornblue?"

"Yes, he told me that."

"Are you aware that Mr. Blue is a communist?"

Tom couldn't stop a laugh from slipping out.

"You find that funny?" Officer Jones challenged.

"If you knew Ira, you'd find it funny too. He may have attended a meeting or read a magazine about communism, but he isn't a communist. He's a cynic."

"That's your professional opinion?" asked Jones.

"Professional opinion?"

"You seem so sure of yourself. Is that based on your knowledge of communism and communists? On research you've conducted? People you've interviewed?"

"No, but..."

"Leave the analysis to us, Mr. Kington. That's what we do, and we do it well."

Tom nearly mentioned the analysis that led to the Bay of Pigs.

Officer Smith joined in. "The depth of Mr. Blue's commitment to communism is not important at this time. What matters is that your loyalty to your country be beyond question. We know you're not a communist;

others may come to different conclusions due to the people you associate with."

Officer Jones continued his line of questioning. "You've also spent time with one Suzie Chomsky. Close, personal time, I might add."

Tom bristled. "I don't see how my personal life is your business."

"If you decide to join the CIA, everything about you will be our business."

"Are you familiar with the term 'honey trap'?" Officer Smith asked.

"No."

"A honey trap is when the enemy uses a woman to lure our officers into committing treason. Some people will do anything for love."

"Or sex," Officer Jones added pointedly.

Tom's face grew red, and he was on the point of standing up and ending the meeting.

"Tom. Do you mind if I call you Tom?" Officer Smith asked.

Tom nodded his approval.

"Tom, fighting America's enemies is serious business. I won't apologize if our questions upset you. That's our job. If you want to call it quits, we can just pretend that we never met. Forget the entire thing."

"I wouldn't think the CIA forgets anything."

Officer Smith grinned. "See, Officer Jones? I told you he was sharp." He turned to Tom. "Should we continue?"

"Sure."

"Are you aware that Miss Chomsky has also attended communist meetings?" asked Officer Jones.

"I wasn't aware, though I'm not surprised. Miss Chomsky is a searcher."

"Excuse me?" asked Officer Jones.

"A searcher. Suzie is searching for the meaning of life."

"Is that why she's demonstrated in front of the UN building in support of Tibet?"

"I thought she was a communist." Tom taunted. "Communist China invaded Tibet. Why would she support the communists *and* their enemies?"

Officer Smith grinned some more. Officer Jones glared.

"Suzie Chomsky is an inquisitive person who explores the world in trying to understand all sides of an issue. I'm sure she's read communist and socialist literature. She's also read Greek and Roman lit; gone to Catholic churches, Jewish synagogues, Hindu and Buddhist temples, and

Sikh *gudwaras*. She was a student at Columbia University. We're encouraged to expand our minds, even if that means attending communist meetings or demonstrating in front of the UN"

"You're a loyal friend, Tom," said Officer Smith. "What if you had to choose between your friends and your country?"

"I thought being an American meant not having to choose. We believe in freedom, the freedom to have friends with different beliefs."

"Freedom is not free, Mr. Kington," Mr. Jones declared. "Half a million Americans died during the last war to ensure that you would be free to attend school. The world is now divided between free and communist. Though you may think it's pleasant to 'explore' both sides, there are still men out there fighting to make sure that your children will be able to do the same thing in twenty years. Sooner or later, you're going to have to choose sides. That may mean leaving friends behind."

Officer Smith glanced at his watch. "Officer Jones and I have another meeting, so we're going to have to wrap this up. Any other questions, Officer Jones?"

Officer Jones shook his head.

"Take some time to think over what we've discussed," said Officer Smith. "I must insist that our meeting be kept confidential. I know we've asked some disturbing questions, but these are disturbing times. I think you'd fit in well with us, though you've got to be sure. One hundred percent sure. We'll be in touch after graduation."

They shook hands and parted.

Tom didn't tell Ira about the meeting, nor had he mentioned his recent dinner with Barbara and her engagement proposal. Tom knew what Ira's response would be to both meetings, and he wasn't interested in listening to one of Ira's rants. He did, however, seek out Ira for ideas for his commencement speech. Ira insisted on meeting at a folk club where Bob Dylan was playing. Tom had reluctantly agreed. They had barely sat down when Tom got to business.

"This is not the best place for discussing my speech, especially with you stoned."

"On the contrary, it's the right place, though it would be better if you were stoned too."

"How do you figure?"

"Because I know you better than you know yourself, and I know you're planning on sucking up to the rich and powerful. You want to leave a good impression, show 'em what a fine young man you are. Shit, you've been doing that for four years."

"Assuming you're correct, how will getting stoned and listening to some folkie alter that?"

"'Cuz you're a deeper thinker when you're stoned, and you might make a statement that actually matters."

"Really. What kind of statement do you have in mind?"

"You've listened to Beat poets and Dylan, and you've heard Woody Guthrie songs, and I know you've heard what they say."

Tom nodded.

"But I'd be willing to bet everything I'm worth..."

Tom snorted at the absurdity of the statement. Ira owned absolutely nothing of value.

"...that 99 percent of the commencement audience haven't listened to a single Beat poet or protest song. They're clueless. This is your opportunity to clue them in."

"To what?"

"To the truth. Students are led to believe that they can make a difference in the world, but they can't as long as the military-industrial complex controls things. Ike told 'em that a few years back, and all the Republican bastards in the audience will have to acknowledge that. Tell 'em that the first thing they need to do is change their own government, elect people who really know the score. Or even better, tell 'em that we need an entirely new system of government, one where the will of the people is more important than the profit margin of giant corporations."

"That'll go over well with the fathers who work for General Electric and Standard Oil."

"You're not speaking to the fathers. It's not your job to increase donations to dear old Columbia. You were elected by the student body. Your speech should be aimed at the heart of each student. Every single one of them should take a year to get to know the real people. People who won't be getting cars for graduation, 'cuz they couldn't afford to attend college.

People who worry about feeding their families. Each graduate should spend a year picking grapes in California or caring for starving kids in India. Don't baby these kids. Tell 'em straight, 'cuz I know that you get it. In spite of Barbie and sucking up to professors and dreaming of wealth and power, you get it. You've studied history, you know that the powers-to-be are ruining it. There are little wars popping up all over the world, wars that our government sponsors, and we the people ignore them. People are starving while the rich drive around in big cars and waste tons of food."

"Although you may really be a communist, your single defining characteristic is insanity."

"First of all, I'm not a communist. As you well know, I don't subscribe to any single philosophy. I don't know why anybody with half a brain would think that."

Tom smiled at the thought of Officer Jones.

"Secondly, stop thinking about how 'important people' will react. The only truly important people at graduation are the graduates. You owe them honesty. For once in your life, use your heart, not your head."

Tom felt a shiver run up his spine. Ira had finally said something that hit home. Tom hadn't made it to Columbia by simply using his head. Sure, he'd gotten top grades in high school, but his head also told him that he should attend agriculture school, help his father to manage the family farm, marry a local girl, and raise a family in Indiana. His heart cried out for something different. That is what brought him to Columbia. Ira had also been correct about Tom's four years at Columbia. Although he'd dabbled with following his heart (Beat poetry readings, sex with Suzie, smoking pot, and listening to jazz), he'd mostly followed his head: taking only serious classes with practical goals, running for student government, dating Barbara. People were expecting a conservative speech, something that would please all and offend none. Ira was correct; Tom had an opportunity to do something memorable.

Tom's reverie was interrupted by the club's emcee.

"Welcome to Gerde's Folk City. We're thrilled to welcome back an old friend—well, a young friend, but one who's played here before—somebody who will sing right to your very soul. Listen to this cat, 'cuz he's got a message everybody should hear. He's gonna play some songs he's been working on for an album he's doing for Columbia Records, which has no connection to our own beloved university of the same name."

There were snickers from the audience.

"Please give a warm welcome to Bob Dylan."

The young folk singer rambled to the stage, sat down, adjusted his harmonica rack so it sat comfortably around his neck, then leaned into the mic.

"This is a love song, I suppose, though it's about pain, which is sort of the same thing."

He played a song called "Don't Think Twice, It's All Right." After the applause, he gazed around the room and then spoke.

"Some will tell you that the answer to every question can be found in a book. I don't agree. Sometimes it ain't that easy. Sometimes you gotta search. You gotta look and listen. Sometimes the answer is blowin' in the wind.

As Tom listened to "Blowin in the Wind" his commencement speech started to take shape.

Tom's family was not coming to graduation. May was a hectic time on the farm, and his father couldn't afford to miss a week going to New York. The truth was, Tom had grown apart from his family during his four years at Columbia. His parents loved him, yet they had never understood him. They accepted that he was different, accepted his move to New York, and eventually accepted the fact that he would never return to Indiana. He'd come home after freshman year and had helped around the farm, but the summer after sophomore year he'd taken a job helping to run a summer camp in Central Park for inner-city kids. Junior year he'd hit the jackpot, thanks to Barbara's father. Tom had been hired to work at a resort in the Hamptons on Long Island. He began parking cars and washing dishes, then moved up to waiter by midsummer. Henry Bennett had introduced him to members of the New York elite, providing connections that Tom hoped would come in handy in the future. The result was that Tom hadn't seen his family in two years. He promised to send them pictures of him wearing his graduation gown and mortarboard.

A few nights before graduation Tom was still working on his speech. He had gone over it dozens of times and was now getting hung up on individual words, a sure sign that he should put it away for a while and clear his head with a walk. He stood up, stretched, and glanced once more at the first line: "Students and faculty, relatives and friends, we are here today to celebrate..." The word "friends" jumped out at Tom. He would know hundreds of students and dozens of faculty at graduation. He knew most of Barbara's relatives who would attend. Friends were something else. Suzie was in California. Ira was far too cynical to consider attending. He spent a lot of time with Barbara, yet had never considered her a friend. It suddenly struck Tom that after four years at Columbia he only had two friends. Although he'd had a few friends in high school, he had lost touch with all of them when he'd moved to New York. "Lost touch with them." Tom shook his head. The phrase made it sound like they'd been misplaced. The truth was that he'd consciously decided to leave them behind when he left Indiana. He also realized that he'd been gathering election support rather than making true friends during the past four years. Tom sat down again, placed a clean sheet of paper into his Remington typewriter, and began to type.

Graduation was sunny and warm, a perfect May day in Manhattan. Tom sat on the stage flanked by the university's president and the reverend who would be giving the benediction. He scanned the edges of the audience until he finally located Ira. Ira had laughed when Tom asked him to attend graduation, not thinking it necessary to put his rejection into words.

"I want you to be there," Tom had insisted.

"Why would you want a cynical bastard like me to attend? I'll make rude comments and jokes until they kick me out."

"If you don't come, I won't have a single friend or relative there."

Ira's eyebrows arched. "I didn't know you felt that way."

"I'm serious. It would mean a lot to me."

"Then I'm there, though I refuse to be straight."

"Smoke yourself stupid. It won't take much."

"Very funny."

Tom nodded at Ira, who pretended to be smoking a joint. Tom smiled and shook his head. The morning dragged on until it was finally Tom's turn to speak. He stood up, walked to the podium, cleared his throat, then began.

"As president of the Columbia student body, I'd like to welcome you all. You've already heard some inspiring speeches, and it'll take a good part of the remaining morning to distribute the diplomas, so I'll keep this short. As is the case with my fellow graduates, I spent my four years in high school working so that I would be accepted to a fine university. During my four years at Columbia I've worked hard to position myself for an important and, hopefully, lucrative job."

There were some chuckles from the audience and appreciative hoots from among the graduates. Tom did not smile or acknowledge the responses.

"Yet, while I was preparing this speech I reflected on the history of Columbia University and it came to me: Columbia was not created so that its graduates would become wealthy or powerful. Rather than to enrich ourselves, we have received an education in order to enrich others: our community, our nation, the world. By now I suppose you're bracing yourself for 'The Future is Yours' speech, whereby I urge you to make a mark in the world, invent a cure for the incurable, bring peace to a troubled world. I had even included that wonderful line from President Kennedy's inaugural speech: 'Ask not what your country can do for you; ask what you can do for your country.' Rather, I beseech you to follow your dreams. Not your parents' dreams. Not Columbia University's dreams. Not even John Kennedy's dreams. Follow your own.

"Why am I counseling you, in the words of William Shakespeare, 'To thine own self be true?' Because, ultimately, you must face yourself in the mirror each morning. You must determine whether your life has meaning. Whether or not you've done something worthwhile. Some of us have been flattered to be offered lucrative jobs upon graduation. Others have been urged to help our federal government to combat communism and other evils that threaten our great nation. I know students who are going into teaching because it's a nice, clean profession and they don't know what else to do while they wait for a marriage proposal."

There were mutterings from the audience, a growing sense of unease.

"I praise all of you who know what you want to do. Teaching is a noble profession. Earning money provides for the comfort of our families and provides necessary tax revenue for our government. Working for that government is vital to our national health. To the graduates who will be scientists, doctors, professors, diplomats, whatever, I applaud you."

Tom turned and clapped toward the sitting graduates. There was a hesitation, then the audience joined in, a few at first, then all of them.

"Many of you, however, are like me. You don't know what you want to do. You can't do nothing; that would seem wasteful after four years at an expensive university."

More muttering from the audience.

"Many of you are feeling intense pressure from family, professors, friends, and recruiters. You want to make the right decision, because you believe you only get one chance in life and this is it. Well, I'm here to tell you that's a load of crap."

This time, the muttering was replaced by loud shouts for Tom to get off the stage, though most of the shouts were from the audience. Tom looked to the graduates and noticed that more than a few were leaning forward, the better to hear what he had to say. He nodded toward the sitting class of '62 before turning back toward the microphone.

"I apologize if I've offended anybody. That was not my intention. The thing is, I've been working on a speech that I hoped would impress our honored guests, maybe land me a few more job offers. Then, just a few nights ago, it struck me: I was elected by the student body and my speech should be directed at them, for them. Not for me. Not for my career or my ego. I realized I should offer something meaningful to you," Tom indicated his fellow graduates, "not to your parents or prospective employers. So here's my advice to you. 'To thine own self be true.' Follow your own dream. Find out who *you* are. Find out who *you* want to be. Consider what legacy *you* would like leave behind. You are about to be faced with an important decision—what you should do after graduation—yet it need not be the final choice for your life. We are young. The future *is* ours. Don't rush into doing something you might regret later. And if you do make a choice, you can always change your mind. That goes for what you're going to do, where you're going to live, even who you're going to marry."

There were a few gasps from the audience.

"I've been confronted by all of these choices and I've made my decision: I'm putting off choosing. Yesterday I sent in my application to the Peace Corps. Although I have enormous respect for President Kennedy, I'm not doing it in order do something for my country. I'm joining the Peace Corps so that I can do something for myself: I want to know who I am.

"Many of you are wondering what you're going to do after you graduate. Where are you going to find the answers to your pressing questions about career and family? In the words of a young poet from Minnesota, 'The answer my friend is blowing in the wind.' Go for a long walk. Take a drive in the countryside with the windows rolled down. Listen for the answer. It may be blowing in the wind. It may be in your own heart."

The reception to the speech was, not surprisingly, mixed. Tom looked at Ira, who was hunched over in laughter. When Ira caught Tom's eye, he shook his head and continued to laugh. Some people booed, others cheered wildly, though most of the cheers were from the class of '62. After all the diplomas had been handed out and the ceremony ended, Tom made his way into the audience. A few parents glared at him. Many students clapped him on the back and shook his hand. He was chatting with a fellow political science student when a shock of blond entered his peripheral vision. Tom excused himself from the poli sci student and turned to greet Barbara.

"You bastard," she snarled. Her fists were clenched, and Tom braced himself for a blow. "How could you? I've never been so humiliated in my life. The least you could have done was warn me. I might have been able to convince my father that you were merely performing for your peers, attempting to be cool, but no. You had to make a statement."

Barbara's voice grew louder and more strident. Heads began to turn in their direction.

"I'm sorry. It was something I had to do."

"What? Humiliate me? Tell thousands of people that you've been using me for the past year? Slap my father in the face so that your Jewish friend Ira would like you?"

"It may come as a shock to you; not everything is about Barbara Bennett."

The slap resounded like a shot.

"I hope you rot in hell," Barbara turned and stormed off through the crowd.

"Does that mean you're not going to be dining tonight with the Bennett's?" came Ira's voice from behind Tom.

"Apparently not."

"Then dinner's on me."

Tom turned to face Ira. "That's a first."

"It won't be at a private club."

"Unless Fratelli's Pizzeria has gone private. Have they gotten a liquor license?"

"No."

"So we'll be celebrating with pepperoni and coke."

"I'll pop for sausage and 7Up if you prefer. Besides, I'm not celebrating. You are. I still have about thirty semester hours left."

"How many years is that?"

"Depends on how long my father's patience lasts."

They met at Fratelli's for dinner, then went to a jazz club in the Village for drinks and some music. As the trio wove tunes in the background, Tom sipped his wine.

"You haven't said anything all night about my speech."

"What do you want me to say?"

"It's not that I want you to say anything. I kind of thought you'd have something to say."

"You mean like telling you how brave you were and how proud I am of you."

"Yeah, something like that, though the way you put it makes me sound like some insecure kid craving approval."

"Well?"

"I see your point."

"You've spent four years having people praise you: your professors and peers and Democrats and Barbara and her family. Even Suzie sang your praises as a lover. Now you want me to do the same."

Tom shrugged. "It would be nice."

"We've known each other four years and you expect me to be nice?" Ira shook his head. "Maybe the Peace Corps wasn't such a bad idea after all. You've got some learning to do."

"Not a bad idea?"

"It's better than working for Barbara's family."

"You've been ranting about living an authentic life. Hitting the road. Experiencing things. Well, I'm doing that. I'll be living in some village with real people, instead of sitting in a bar in *The Village*, talking about living the real life."

Ira ignored the dig. "Kerouac was one of the people. He talked with them and drank with them and fucked them. You're going to be a colonial master. A white man who condescends to help the poor, ignorant savages."

"You don't know shit about what the Peace Corps does. Have you talked to anyone from the Peace Corps? Have you even read any of their literature? What have you done in life besides bitch and moan? You're just a backseat driver, giving directions because you don't have the guts to grab the wheel and drive. You're the person who tells somebody to turn left; then you criticize them for driving the wrong way down a one-way street."

"Clever image, though it's not my fault if the driver listens to me. I don't tell people what to do. I merely suggest paths. It's up to the individual to make choices."

"Right. I make choices, then have to listen to you tell me why I've made the wrong one."

"You're an adult. You should take responsibility for your actions."

"I do. Once I enter the Peace Corps I'll be supporting myself. I'll no longer rely on my father to support me. When I get out in two years, I'll pursue a career that'll make a difference."

"Goody for you."

"Jerk. I've had enough."

Tom stood to leave.

"What did Thomas Paine do for a living?" Ira asked.

"What?"

"You do know Thomas Paine?"

"The author of *Common Sense*, a pamphlet that came out in 1776 and urged American colonists to declare independence from England. It had a huge impact."

"Very good, professor. So, what did Paine do for a living?"

"I don't remember."

"What about Engels and Marx?"

"If I remember correctly, they lived off of the income Engels received from his father."

Ira smirked.

"Are you comparing yourself to Paine and Marx?"

"Not yet. The point I'm making is that it's not your career path that's important. It's what you achieve. Tell me, Tom, were you planning on entering the Peace Corps a month ago?"

Tom sat down. "No."

"Did you have other career choices?"

"Yes."

"Barbara's father was going to introduce you to some 'important' people, meaning rich and powerful. You were going to land some fat job as a fresh, young face for some old, incredibly corrupt corporation. Maybe be a lobbyist who could ease nasty legislation through Congress. You could use your Kennedy connections."

"That was a possibility. There were other options."

"Really. You've never mentioned any."

"I was under orders not to mention one."

The perpetually slouching Ira sat up. "That's intriguing. Now that you've spilled the beans, don't hold me in suspense. Who was it?"

Tom drained his glass. "The CIA."

"You're bullshitting."

"Am I?"

"No, you're not. I should have guessed it. You're perfect for those assholes."

"Perfect except for one thing: They had questions about two of my friends."

"Really? Fantastic. What were they worried about? Wait a sec. Aha! That's where you got the idea that I was a commie. What did they nail Suzie for?"

"Communism. Demonstrating in front of the UN"

Ira slapped the table and began to laugh so loudly the other customers shot him annoyed looks. "That's wonderful. So what'd you say? No, let me guess. You told 'em to fuck off." This produced another round of laughter from Ira. "Just kidding. You told 'em you were flattered and that you had to think about it. Now you'll call to thank 'em and tell 'em you may contact them after the Peace Corps if they're still interested. Am I right?"

"I'm not going to burn any bridges."

"Of course not, not even bridges built and run by spies and liars."

"It's not as simple as you make it sound. The CIA has blundered, sure. They've also provided valuable information on our enemies."

"Yeah? Who told you that? The officer who contacted you?"

"Where do you get your info on the CIA? What makes you so damn sure they're evil?"

"It's the nature of the beast. Didn't they question the patriotism of Suzie and me?"

"In so many words."

"Do you question our patriotism?"

"Of course not."

"Let me ask another question. Did our talk at Gerde's last month affect your decision?"

Tom hesitated, then nodded his head. "Yeah, it did."

A self-satisfied smile came over Ira's face. "I may not be a Paine or Marx, yet, but I'm already making a difference in the world."

"Oh, you're a pain all right."

"I hope so, and I've started to make my mark on the world."

"By reading Beat poetry and advising college students on career choices?"

"Paine didn't start by writing *Common Sense*, and Marx didn't start by writing The *Communist Manifesto*."

"So I'm only the beginning of a long and illustrious career for you. I can tell people that I owe the presidency of the United States to Ira Blue, communist agitator and Pulitzer Prize–winning poet."

Ira raised his glass. "Here's to the future president of the United States and his chief advisor."

Tom clinked glasses. "Heaven help the nation."

CHAPTER 5—1964/1965

When the plane's door opened it was as if somebody had slapped Tom with a blanket that had just been yanked from a bucket of hot water. He'd been warned about Vietnam's heat and humidity, yet it still came as a shock, though not an unpleasant one. His two years in the Peace Corps in the Ivory Coast—Côte d'Ivoire as the French-speaking natives called it—had been his baptism in tropical climates. Rather than be overwhelmed as some Peace Corps volunteers had been, Tom had loved living in shorts and sandals, loved sleeping under a mosquito net with just a sheet, loved not having to bundle up with layers of wool as he had during winters in Indiana and New York. Perhaps it was his experience near the equator in a French-speaking country that led the State Department to send him to Vietnam for his first assignment. Vietnam was also near the equator, had also been a French colony.

Tom walked down the stairs onto the tarmac at Tan Son Nhut airbase. He allowed his eyes to adjust to the tropical glare for a moment before glancing around. Although a US military base, Tan Son Nhut had rapidly become one of the busiest airports in Asia. Military vehicles were zipping back and forth, and it seemed as if half a dozen transport planes were disgorging hundreds of GIs at the same time. Tom had been reading about it since the 1964 Gulf of Tonkin incident and Lyndon Johnson's subsequent Gulf of Tonkin Resolution, which called for more troops to protect American interests in the region. He'd received more details about the increase from the State Department during his training, and still he hadn't been prepared for the immensity of what he saw during his first moments at Tan Son Nhut.

"It's pretty impressive, isn't it, sir," said the Army lieutenant who had met him at the bottom of the stairs.

"It is that."

"I'm told that a couple of days ago the first official combat troops landed."

"Official?"

The lieutenant looked uncomfortable.

"Don't sweat it, lieutenant. I'm just gathering information. Trying to figure this all out."

"Good luck, sir."

Tom again scanned the hive of activity. "I suppose we're starting to have an impact on the nation."

"Sir?"

"Oh, nothing. I was just thinking."

"I suppose that's your job. My job is to do what I'm told, and I'm under orders to get you to the embassy as soon as possible."

"In that case, let's go."

Tom reached for his bag, but the lieutenant grabbed it first and tossed it in the back of the jeep. Tom climbed into the passenger seat, put his head back, and his eyelids soon started to grow heavy. He slipped into a light sleep before they'd left Tan Son Nhut. His last thought before losing consciousness was: this is a long, long way from New York.

Tom's two years in the Peace Corps had been uneventful, though vital to his personal growth. Rather than be in some primitive village—the image most people have of Peace Corps volunteers—Tom spent his entire time in Abidjan, the economic and cultural capital of the Ivory Coast. Due to his political science background, the Peace Corps placed Tom in the National University of Côte d'Ivoire, where he taught classes in French and English. Although French was the national language, Ivoirian leaders knew that fluency in English was essential in the modern world. Enrollment in Tom's French-language poli sci classes remained moderate, but his English-language classes soon became among the most popular in the university.

As well, students raved to their parents about Tom's passionate teaching and insights into international diplomacy, and Tom became a regular at parties thrown by some of Abidjan's top families. By the end of his second year, Tom was often invited to small, informal gatherings hosted by important members of government who craved a different view than the one pressed upon them by the US and French ambassadors. Tom was always careful to offer a variety of perspectives without actually endorsing any, thus avoiding being identified with any specific political agenda. It would be one of the last times that Tom would be able to have political discussions that were purely theoretical.

Tom completed his Peace Corps commitment, then traveled for three months in North Africa and Europe. As well, Tom considered his next career move, though he had no serious doubts about what that would be. The Wednesday before Thanksgiving, 1964, Tom flew from London to New York and went directly to Ira's apartment in the Village.

Ira had graduated from Columbia after his father had finally lost patience and had given him just enough money to last one year. He talked himself into a position at *The Village Voice*, and though it was only as proofreader and general gofer he was pleased to have landed at one of the hippest papers in the nation. As a graduation present, Ira convinced his father to put down a deposit on a two-bedroom apartment in the Village. The *Voice* didn't pay much and Ira occasionally took in roommates to help cover the bills. Fortunately, the second room was vacant when Tom arrived.

"Welcome to my humble abode," Ira said as he opened the door.

They exchanged Black Power handshakes and awkwardly hugged, then Tom followed Ira into the apartment. Not surprisingly, the place was a pit, strewn with old newspapers, books, empty booze bottles, overflowing ashtrays, and unmatched shoes. Tom looked around the room while still holding his suitcase.

"Yeah, I know it's a mess." Ira shrugged. "I was gonna throw all this shit into the second bedroom and shut the door, but it's full of shit that my last roommate left behind. At least I cleared off the bed for you. The mattress isn't too bad, if you cover it with something to hide the stains. Hey, it's gotta be better than where you lived in Africa, wherever the hell that was."

"Actually, my place in Abidjan was very clean. I had a girl come in every week to dust and mop the floors."

"That's not going to happen here. Tell you what. If you clean up this place, you can stay in the second bedroom for free. For a while. If you're planning on staying longer, we can talk about rent."

"I won't be here that long, though I'll accept the first part of your offer."

"Big plans already. You've saved Africa, now the world."

"I didn't save anybody, just educated some people."

"So what's next?"

"I explained that in my letters. You did read my letters, didn't you?"

"I sorta glanced at them; I've been kinda busy."

"Apparently not with cleaning."

"Why don't I put on some coffee and clear off a couple of chairs, and you can tell me in person about your next step toward the presidency."

It took nearly an hour for Tom to settle into the second bedroom and clean up a corner of the living room. When the coffee was ready they poured themselves mugs and sat down.

"So, seriously," Tom began, "did you read my letters?"

"Sure. They're here somewhere." He waved his hand around to indicate that the letters were buried under the crap piled around the apartment. "You said something about working for the government." He said "government" as if it was something odious.

"The State Department, if I pass the foreign service exam."

"Oh, you'll pass the exam. You always seem to get what you want, though I don't see how foreign service will lead to the White House."

Tom ignored the jab. "One thing I learned in Côte d'Ivoire is that I'm good at what I do."

"So what is it you do?"

"I understand how governments work and how they can work better. I can also help others to understand and to see other viewpoints. In Cape D'Ivoire I saw how people could get along even though they've been enemies for centuries. I know that nations can overcome differences, and I can help that process.

"Maybe I underestimated you. The White House is too small for your ambitions."

"Ira, it's not about personal ambitions. I'm talking about using a skill I seem to have been born with. You remember when I ran for student government president at Columbia?"

"Sure. You appealed to all types, from abrasive New Yorkers to country bumpkins, like yourself."

"The same thing was true in Côte d'Ivoire. Regardless of tribe or religion, people trusted me, sought my counsel."

"Sounds like they stroked your ego."

"I suppose my ego played a role, but they trusted me because I had nothing to gain."

"Except reputation, which will inevitably lead to something bigger, more important."

"As your poetry led to your position at *The Village Voice*."

Ira frowned. "It sure as hell wasn't my poetry that got me hired. It was my persistence. I bugged them until they hired me. Plus, I was willing to work for slave wages."

"Then Thanksgiving dinner is on me tomorrow night."

"All right. At least I'll have one good meal this week. So what are you going to do while you wait to take the foreign service exam and then wait for the results? Gonna get a job? Maybe Barbie's daddy can help you land a job in the Hamptons again."

"That won't be necessary. I've enough money from the Peace Corps to last me five or six months. I'm going to buy an old car and drive to California. This is it, Ira, the road trip you've been talking about since I met you."

"I can't go. I've got my job."

"The one that pays slave wages."

"It covers my mortgage, barely."

"Then sell this dump and hit the road. Here's your chance to write something special. I'll pay for gas. All you've got to do is read the map. We can crash with Suzie in San Fran and you can check out the hip scene there."

Ira shrugged. "I don't think so. If I hang in long enough I'll get to write something serious for the *Voice*. I've had some minor pieces published, a few short pieces on poetry readings and a couple of reviews of folk concerts. I think I'm about to make a breakthrough"

"Somehow I suspect that Kerouac and Burroughs would do things differently."

"I'm not Kerouac or Burroughs. I respect what they've done, but I'm following a different path."

Tom spent a week with Ira. During that time he completed his application for the foreign service exam, bought a '58 Chevy that didn't have too many miles, and planned his trip west—which would include a stop in Indiana to visit family. Tom left New York with a sense that Ira might finally be exhibiting some ambition. Ira seemed energized by the few articles that he had published, and he finally appeared ready to stop talking and start achieving. Tom was happy for Ira, and he hit the road in the first week of December with a sense that all was right in the world.

Tom pulled up in front of the old three-story house in San Francisco's Haight-Ashbury just before sunset and shut off the engine. The week-long drive from New York had been everything he'd hoped for and more. He had dreaded the visit to Indiana, fearing that he'd outgrown his roots. Instead, his parents and brother and sister had made him feel welcome. They'd asked hundreds of questions about his life, and he'd responded by catching up on the doings of friends and relatives. Even though he'd never felt that he fully belonged, he now realized that home was where he'd picked up his values of hard work, loyalty, and honesty. The rest of the drive west had been memorable for breathtaking views, hitchhikers who wove colorful stories, and hours of silent contemplation behind the wheel.

Tom slowly climbed out of the car, stretched his arms toward the sky, arched his back, then reached down to touch his toes.

"Nice butt," came a familiar voice from behind Tom.

He turned and saw Suzie sitting on the steps of the three-story house.

"If I'd known I had an audience I would have combed my hair and flexed my muscles."

"You look good with ruffled hair, and you never had enough muscles to flex."

Tom walked up to the stairs and gave Suzie a full-body hug and a long, passionate kiss.

"You're getting pretty close to public indecency," said a woman from the porch.

"Jealous?" asked a male.

"Absolutely."

"Yeah, but of which one?"

Suzie slowly pulled away. "Let me introduce you to my housemates."

Two long-haired men were sitting on an old, ratty couch. One had black hair, and the other was blondish-red. A short, muscular woman with brown hair in a butch cut sat in a wooden rocking chair. One of the men took a drag on a fat joint and passed it to the other man, who took a deep drag and passed it to the woman. Suzie made the introductions.

"Tom, this is Miguel." She indicated the black-haired man. "And Carl. You shouldn't have much trouble telling them apart."

Tom smiled and nodded a welcome to each.

"And this is Tony, short for Antoinette."

"You can see that Tony fits better," the woman said with a smirk.

"Everybody, this is my soul brother Tom."

Tony took a hit on the joint and offered it to Tom. He began to reach for it, then shook his head.

"Thanks, I've got to pass."

There was an awkward silence, then Suzie reached for the joint and took a drag.

"You in one of your straight periods?" Suzie asked." I mean, your hair is kinda long and you're in San Francisco, so I naturally thought..." She turned to her housemates. "Whenever Tom got really serious about something at Columbia, like raising his grades, he'd go cold turkey." She turned back toward Tom. "So have you permanently given up weed or are you into something serious?"

"The latter. I just took the foreign service exam and I'm waiting for the results."

"Wow, man," said Carl. "You joining the Foreign Legion? I loved that movie with Cary Grant and Douglas Fairbanks. What was it called?"

"*Gunga Din*," said Tom, "and no, I'm not joining the Foreign Legion. That's French. I'm hoping to work for the US State Department."

"Wow. For which state?" Carl asked.

"Don't mind Carl," said Suzie. "He likes to wake and bake, so he's been stoned for ten hours already. Carl, the State Department is the section of the US government that deals with foreign affairs, everything that occurs outside of the United States. Tom's going to be a diplomat, and the government doesn't like its diplomats to be wasted."

"That's too bad," said Miguel. "It'd be a better world if people were smoking together instead of shooting each other."

Suzie smiled at Tom. "Welcome to the Haight. Can I get you something to drink? A beer or wine? Some herbal ice tea?"

"Tea sounds great."

They sat on the porch and talked as the sun set, ate a macrobiotic vegetarian dinner cooked by Miguel, then talked late into the night. After Suzie left Columbia, she had moved to an ashram in northern California, where she spent six months meditating. When she felt that she had no more to gain from the aesthetic life, she moved to a nearby commune. She continued to meditate daily and read every book on Buddhism she could get her hands on. Suzie also revealed to Tom that she'd had a very active sex life on the commune, where sex was viewed as natural and healthy. She had multiple partners, of both sexes, often at the same time. Eventually, she grew tired of life down on the farm and, badly in need of an urban fix, moved to San Francisco with Miguel. The obvious destination was the Haight-Ashbury district.

The Haight, as it was called, was a depressed area of San Francisco where houses were big, rundown, and cheap. By 1965 many had become mini–urban communes with up to a dozen people living in four-bedroom houses. Suzie and Miguel were given the address of a house whose residents had connections to their commune, and they soon settled in, though each had their own room. Tony already lived in the house, and she and Suzie hit it off from the start and spent many nights together. As was common at the time, their relationship was not exclusive. Suzie got a job at a high school in the Mission District, the Hispanic section of San Francisco, and taught English lit and philosophy. She was still heavily into Buddhism and occasionally went to an ashram for weekend meditation retreats.

As midnight approached Carl excused himself and went to bed, followed soon by Miguel. Finally, Suzie stood up.

"I don't know about you, but I've got to get up early for work."

"Yeah, I'm beat. Where do I sleep?"

"It better be next to me or I'll be very upset," said Suzie.

"Aren't you the lucky one," Tony said to Tom.

Tom looked from Suzie to Tony and back to Suzie.

Suzie laughed. "It's cool, Tom. Tony and I don't sleep together every night, as I explained."

"Oh, OK. I just wasn't sure of the etiquette. This, uh, lifestyle is all new to me."

"Looks like I'll be showing you the ropes, like your first day at Columbia."

It was Tom's turn to smile. "This trip just gets better and better."

"I know you're going to have a good time here. It'll be good for your head. I have to go to work tomorrow, but Tony has a day off. Maybe she'll show you around."

"I don't want to be a bother."

"No bother at all," said Tony. "From what Suzie has told me, I think we'll have a real good time together. That is, if you're as open minded as you were at Columbia."

Suzie took Tom's hand and pulled him to his feet. "Me first."

Tom and Suzie made love, then fell asleep in each other's arms. He faintly sensed her getting out of bed in the morning and getting ready for work, but was too tired from his cross-country trip to open his eyes. Sometime later he began to have an erotic dream. A hand was stroking his cock, bringing it to life. It slowly dawned on him that he was not dreaming. When he opened his eyes he looked upon Tony's smiling face.

"Good morning. Time to wake up. Or stand up, as the case may be."

Tom silently reached out and fondled her naked breast, which was small yet firm with a prominent nipple. Tony sat up and kissed the top of Tom's erection.

"Suzie was right. You have a very nice cock."

"I didn't know cocks were your thing."

"Sex is my thing. That's why Suzie and I get along so well. As you know, our friend Suzie is a passionate woman. Men, on the other hand, are usually assholes. They want to jump on, stick it in, shoot their load, then go to sleep. Suzie tells me you're not like that at all."

"Damn right. I'm a diplomat. I want everybody to be pleased."

Tony turned out to be a funny, energetic tour guide, and the two spent the day walking around San Francisco. That week was one of the best of Tom's life. Besides the pleasure of sex with Suzie and Tony—frequently and often together—Tom became intimately familiar with the hip San Francisco scene. They listened to live music most nights, drank liberally, and even though Tom did not smoke a joint, he was often high from the massive cloud of smoke that usually permeated the air. Tom's last evening before heading back east was spent solely with Suzie. They had a quiet Italian dinner, then strolled to Buena Vista park where they sat on a bench and looked upon the lights of San Francisco and the bay.

"Thanks for an amazing week," said Tom.

"I had a great time too, as did Tony, though I was worried that you'd turn her straight."

"With a sensuous woman like you around? Not likely."

Suzie kissed Tom's cheek. "You've always made me feel good about myself, in spite of my insecurities."

"Has your study of Buddhism also helped?"

"Immensely. I feel more at peace, better understand the impermanence of everything."

"How does that help you to feel at peace?"

"Because I realize that little things have no meaning. I may be overweight, yet in the grand scheme of things it has no importance. Not when people are suffering. Not when people are enslaved or when they're murdered by their own government. Or by our government."

Tom flinched slightly.

"Sorry, Tom. I didn't mean to get political with you."

"You can get anything you want with me." He put his arm around her waist and gave a gentle squeeze. "Afraid that I'm going to become a bad guy?"

"Not at all. You've got a good heart. It's just, well, you try so hard to please everybody. At Columbia you had a good word for everyone and always avoided harsh criticism. That's why you were elected student body president. I can appreciate it for something like a campus election. Working for the government is different."

"Why? Do you see our government as inherently evil?"

"No, but the government has done some evil things, like using military solutions when there were nonviolent ones."

"That's a matter of opinion. Maybe force is necessary to stop things like communism."

"You know damn well that there's nothing wrong with the communist philosophy."

"True, but it's being used by crazies to appeal to the poor. It worked for Lenin in Russia. It worked for Mao in China. It may work for Ho Chi Minh in Vietnam."

"If it's good for the people, what difference does it make what it's called?"

"It makes a huge difference to the US government."

"That's what worries me. The US government is opposed to communism. You go to work for the US government, you have to be opposed to communism. The US government supports corrupt governments. You go to work for the US government, you support corrupt governments."

"I don't think it's that simple. Besides, we're getting ahead of things. I haven't even passed the foreign service exam yet."

"Have you seen the photo of the monk who self-immolated last year in Vietnam?"

"Yeah. Pretty grim."

"He was protesting a government that we support. A Catholic government in a Buddhist country. How can we justify that shit?"

Tom shrugged again.

"Is there a chance you'll be sent to Vietnam?"

"I suppose so, if I pass the exam. Since the Gulf of Tonkin Resolution we've been building up our forces there. More soldiers probably means more diplomats."

"Plus you're fluent in French. Since Vietnam was a French colony for so long, I figure you have a good chance of being sent there."

Tom smiled. "You've been giving this some thought."

"I think of you a lot. You're my friend and my lover and my brother."

Tom leaned over and gave Suzie a very unbrotherly kiss.

Suzie took his hand and looked into his eyes. "Tom, wherever you go, do good."

"That's my goal. I want you to be proud of me."

"I always am. Here I've been seeking self-fulfillment in California while you've been in Africa helping others. You're a good man. I know you'll do good things. I just worry that you'll get sucked into the whole military-industrial complex thing and you'll do bad things even though you don't mean to."

"You've got my word. I will do good things. You'll see."

Tom had been hanging around New York for two weeks before the letter from the State Department arrived congratulating him on passing the foreign service exam. At the beginning of March he was to report to Washington, DC, where he would receive his assignment and enter into an intensive month-long course to prepare him. Ira had immediately gotten on Tom's case.

"Vietnam. They're going to send you to Vietnam to help the murderers do their job."

"I assume you're referring to the US military."

"Who the fuck else would I be referring to? Who else is bombing innocent civilians?"

"The Vietcong. The North Vietnamese."

"Freedom fighters trying to end centuries of colonialism."

Tom wearily shook his head. "You're so predictable."

"Constant. That's what I am. I work constantly for the little people."

"You're a gofer at *The Village Voice*."

"I've reviewed some poetry and a few concerts and I've been discussing some longer pieces with the editors. They're considering an epic poem about the military-industrial complex's role in America's new imperialism."

"Whatever. I don't want to get into it. Besides, I have no idea where I'll be sent."

"Vietnam."

"That's what Suzie said."

"Great minds think alike. Do me a favor. Do yourself a favor. You've got plenty of time before you report. Read some books about US foreign policy. Educate yourself."

"My degree in poli sci included quite a few courses on US foreign policy. I've read Kennan, Lodge, dozens."

"Old books by old authors."

"I suppose you have some recommendations."

"Start with Greene's *The Quiet American.*"

"He's British, isn't he?"

"Yup. The book is a brilliant look at how Americans blunder in foreign policy. Takes place in Vietnam, yet it could apply to anywhere. Greene is brilliant."

"OK. I've been meaning to read some of his books."

"Next, *The Ugly American.*"

"I'm familiar with it. Pretty controversial. It's supposed to be very critical of US foreign policy. It also takes place in Vietnam. "

"Coincidental. Whether you agree with its views or not, Lederer and Burdick's book will give you lots to think about. Lastly, David Halberstam recently won the Pulitzer Prize for reporting on the war in Vietnam. Drag your ass down to the public library and read his articles. Even if you're sent to Timbuktu, you'll be the wiser for it."

"Sounds good, Professor. Any other suggestions?"

"Yes. Stop working for the government."

"I want to do big things. Nothing's bigger than the US government. So what about you?"

"When the *Voice* finally recognizes that they're underutilizing a major talent, they'll give me my own column. Then I'll shake the foundations of this country."

"Why limit yourself to the country? Why not shake the world?"

"I'm serious. America has gone from the supposed heroes of World War II to the villains of Southeast Asia."

"I don't see it that way. Except for a few blunders, we've consistently tried to maintain world peace, promote democracy, and stop ruthless dictators from doing serious damage."

"We allied ourselves with that Russian butcher Stalin."

"In order to stop a greater evil: Hitler."

"We're pouring in thousands of troops into Vietnam to support an unpopular Catholic president in a Buddhist country."

"Suzie said pretty much the same thing."

"And?"

"I don't have enough information to know what's actually happening."

"So you don't buy your government's explanation."

"I'm keeping an open mind."

"There's hope for you yet."

"I wish I could say the same thing about you."

As predicted by Suzie and Ira, Tom was assigned to the US embassy in Saigon as a political attaché. The training in Washington went smoothly, though there were highs and lows. His French was deemed excellent—by State Department standards—so he spent four hours every morning for two weeks on intensive Vietnamese language training. As well, Tom's afternoons were spent preparing for his role as a political officer, though that didn't go as smoothly as his language training. The political instructors seemed bent on indoctrinating Tom in the administration's foreign policy, rather than instructing him in the art of international diplomacy. When Tom persisted on asking questions, he was called in for a private meeting and told that he didn't know enough to ask questions, and that his insistence on asking questions might have adverse affects on his career. Not wanting to be washed out before he'd even had a chance, Tom bowed to the will of his superiors and stopped asking questions. Still, he couldn't help but think about *The Quiet American* and *The Ugly American* and the writings of David Halberstam. All had a common theme: the American government too often acted as if it already knew everything and had nothing to learn from anybody. With a jolt, Tom was snapped out of his reverie. Looking about, he realized that the jeep had stopped in a walled compound.

"The US embassy, sir," said the lieutenant. "Welcome to American soil."

CHAPTER 6—1965

"What about the Buddhist factions?" Tom asked.
The other political officers looked down awkwardly at their notes.

Tom's first forty-eight hours in Vietnam had been a disorienting blur. After a whirlwind tour of the embassy, he'd been shown his quarters. The State Department leased a three-story apartment block near the US embassy where it housed all of its personnel, except for the top-level diplomats who had more sumptuous dwellings. Tom shared an apartment with Stefan Boudreau, from Baton Rouge, Louisiana. The first night Stefan took Tom out to introduce him to Saigon. The city was throbbing with activity: bicycles and whining motorcycles jammed the streets; throngs of Vietnamese men in slacks and collared shirts, and Vietnamese women in traditional outfits, strolled the streets next to American soldiers in uniform; stalls lined the sidewalks, stacked with cheap consumer goods and steaming woks of food. Tom was bumped by a whining motorcycle as they crossed Hai Ba Trung and was out of breath by the time they reached the far sidewalk.

"Damn, that was a thousand times worse than the busiest Manhattan street during rush hour."

"I'll take your word for it," said Stefan, "though I'd rather be hit by one of these dinky little Honda 90s than a Buick."

"Good point."

"How's a cold beer sound to you?"

"Heavenly."

Stefan led them to a stall in front of an old colonial house set back from the street. They sat on red plastic chairs around a shaky aluminum table. Stefan ordered in halting Vietnamese. Immediately, two ice-cold beers were delivered by a teenaged Vietnamese boy, along with two chilled glasses. The boy returned in a moment with a small plate of peanuts and another that contained sliced green chilies floating in soy sauce.

"A little something to enhance your thirst," Stefan said, indicating the peanuts and chilies. "The Vietnamese are very clever—whatever you hear to the contrary—and outstanding businessmen. Things may look hectic and a bit helter skelter; don't let looks fool you."

Stefan Boudreau was a short, chubby man, about the same age as Tom. He pulled a handkerchief from his back pocket and wiped some of the sweat that streamed down his face. His checked cotton shirt was soaked, and his khaki pants clung to his damp, fleshy legs.

"I would have thought that a native of Louisiana wouldn't have a problem with humidity," said Tom.

"I suspect that the State Department thought the same thing, and, like them, you'd have thought wrong. I haven't stopped sweating since the plane door opened. I bet I lose twenty pounds a day in water weight."

"Either you arrived a lot larger or you've found a means to replace the loss."

Stefan's eyes opened wide in surprise, and then he let out a bark of a laugh. "Like Old Abe said, honesty is the best policy, and you sure call it like you see it. Indeed, what you see is Stefan Boudreau at his normal fighting weight, though said weight will go unmentioned. I've always been on the abundant side, thanks to generous portions of Louisiana gumbo and jambalaya. The food they serve here in Vietnam is quite delicious, but doesn't pack in the same calories. Therefore, I'm forced to drink the local brew, 333—that's *ba ba ba* in the native lingo. French brewed. Does the trick when it's ice cold. As I know they told you back in DC, it's essential that you replace your precious bodily fluids."

Tom raised his glass. "Here's to replacing precious bodily fluids."

They clinked glasses, drained them, then refilled them. Stefan raised his hand and called for another bottle in Vietnamese.

"You're pretty good with the language," said Tom, being more polite than honest.

"Damn right. I can order beer, rice, and noodles fluently. Beyond that I'm hopeless."

"How's your French?"

"Better than my Vietnamese, by a little, anyway."

"So how is it that somebody who suffers in the heat and humidity, and doesn't speak Vietnamese or French fluently, ends up in Saigon?"

"This your first overseas posting?"

"Yup."

"Welcome to the US Department of State. You seem a nice enough person and you've been honest regarding my girth; least I can do is be straight with you. This setup is a holy mess."

"You been posted somewhere else before?"

"No, so I have nothing to compare it to. I graduated from Tulane in December, having taken an extra semester to make up for classes I failed during a freshman year that remains an alcohol-fueled haze. I aced the foreign service exam—a testimony to good genes rather than hard work—and was assigned to Vietnam. In my brief month here I've been stunned by what's going on. I don't see how it can be worse anywhere else."

"What seems to be the problem? Wait a minute. I think we need another cold one." Tom ordered another bottle in rapid Vietnamese.

The corner of Stefan's lips curled up in a smirk. "Something tells me you already know the score here."

"I'm good with languages."

"Apparently. What else do you know?"

"I've read a few things here and there, all secondhand knowledge. A few books, a few articles."

"Don't let on to Hard Case that you already have some ideas about what's goin' on."

"Hard Case?"

"Howard Case, senior political attaché. He's your boss, and he will never let you forget it. If he wants your opinion on something, he'll give it to you first."

"Oh."

"Maybe I'd better back up first and fill you in. We've got a meeting tomorrow at 0900, as the military say. You'll do well to get off on the right foot with Hard Case, otherwise this will be a very, very long assignment."

"All right. Shoot."

"You may want to choose your words more carefully." Stefan nodded toward a group of armed soldiers who were walking by."

"Good advice."

"So here's the deal. As you well know, the political situation in Vietnam is a mess. After Diem's assassination—whether Kennedy authorized it or not is irrelevant—there was a power vacuum. There have been a series of leaders, none effective. The current prime minister, Dr. Quat, is just that: current, not future. The Buddhists loathed the previous officeholder, General Khanh, and they don't much like Dr. Quat."

"That's a problem in a Buddhist county."

"Not as big a problem as the rumblings from a cadre of ARVN officers. That's Army of the Republic of Vietnam. There's an ongoing power struggle between the air force and army. Each wants its own man at the top. As you are obviously aware, the Vietnamese don't have a history of democracy, though you can't fault 'em. I mean, the country has had emperors and been colonized by the Chinese and French and, if you believe our critics, Americans. There was supposed to be a national election back in the mid '50s, between Uncle Ho and Diem, but it never happened. Uncle Ho would have creamed Diem, so Diem came up with some pretext to cancel it. Pity. Vietnam would have definitely gone commie, but it woulda saved a hell of a lot of lives."

"So you don't buy into the domino theory? Russia fell, China fell; if Vietnam falls there goes the rest of Asia?"

"Maybe, maybe not. We gonna hold up dominos all across Asia? On our own? Besides, Russia and China don't seem to get along so well. I wouldn't be surprised if they ended up at each other's throats. The thing of it is, this isn't so much about stopping communism as it is about American politics. Truman got nailed for 'losing China.' Ike didn't want the same tag applied to Vietnam. Neither did Kennedy. Being soft on communism is about as popular as being caught with a boy in bed. Political death. Now we got that damn Texan. You can bet your spurs he won't back down, or listen to reason. That's why the State Department sent Hard Case last year. Case is a fellow Texan, graduate of SMU. The story is that Johnson called him to the White House and ordered him to get the political situation in order here in Vietnam. Said he would accept no excuses."

"What are we supposed to do? It's their country."

"You'll want to avoid saying that. We claim to be opposed to all forms of colonialism, but Hard Case is of the opinion that we may need to take over this place in order to stop the godless commies from doing so first. It may seem hypocritical, taking over before some else can, but we justify it 'cuz we're the good guys saving the poor heathens from the bad guys."

"You're a cynical bastard."

"Hopefully you're not. Hard Case don't like cynicism."

"So far I've learned what not to say at tomorrow's meeting. What *can* I say?"

"Good morning, sir. After that, you'd be well advised to shut up."

"I guess I better use my voice while I'm still allowed." Tom turned to the waiter and ordered another cold beer.

There were five men at the meeting the next morning: Tom and Stefan, the low-level political officers; two mid-level officers; and Howard Case, the senior political officer. Case was a tall, lean Texan with a weather-beaten face. He spoke with the expected drawl, though at a far faster clip than LBJ. He had landed on the Normandy beaches on D-Day, fought at the Battle of the Bulge, then left the military as soon as the war ended to complete his political science degree at Southern Methodist University. Although he had been in the State Depart for nearly twenty years, Case still carried himself with a distinct military bearing. He acknowledged Tom's presence with a curt nod, then got down to business at precisely 0900.

"If anybody has yet to meet our newest officer, Tom Kington, you may do so after this meeting. We have too much to accomplish to waste time on social graces. Mr. Kington, I'll tell you what I've told your fellow political officers: Although our job here is thankless, it is not unimportant. Vietnam is *the* hotspot at the moment. The most visible and well-covered aspects of diplomacy are carried out by the president, the secretary of defense, the secretary of state, and the ambassador, in that order. That means we are here to gather information and advise the ambassador and, if requested, the president, the secretary of defense and the secretary of state. We are not here to formulate or implement policy. We are not spokesmen; you are forbidden to voice your opinion or even to summarize your understanding of US foreign policy. Your job is to gather information and pass that information to me. I will then decide what is valuable enough to be passed up the chain. Are there any questions?"

Nobody spoke, so Case continued.

"Ambassador Taylor has asked me to update him weekly on the political situation. Mr. Lubner, any news from your military sources?"

"More of the same," said Brent Lubner, a middle-aged, mid-level officer from Cleveland. "Most still believe it's only a matter of time before Dr. Quat is history. He has no support in any section of the populace, and they know we won't stand in the way."

"How is it they *know* we won't stand in their way?"

"It's pretty obvious that we're not exactly rushing to shore him up."

"That is opinion. I want facts. Mr. Goldstein, do have any concrete information?"

"Same as Brent, just impressions," said Aaron Goldstein, an older, mid-level officer from Chicago. "Neither the newspapers nor radio nor the business community are jumping to support Quat. They see him as just the latest puppet and expect the military to step in soon."

"Mr. Boudreau?"

"Same with student leaders and the Catholics. Quat has no political support. If we back him, we back a three-legged horse in the Derby."

"That's your opinion, Mr. Boudreaux. I repeat, I want facts."

"What about the Buddhist factions?" Tom asked.

Case shot Tom a look that chilled him. "What about the Buddhists, Mr. Kington?"

"Do they support Dr. Quat?"

"I would have thought your training in Washington had addressed that question."

"My training barely touched on Buddhism."

"Exactly my point. The Buddhists are communist sympathizers. They do not believe in democracy, never have. Ever since that monk set himself on fire they've done nothing but try to subvert the political process. We keep an eye on them. We do not consult them."

"This is a Buddhist country. How can any government be viable without the support of the majority of the people?"

"I do not need a lecture on Vietnamese society, Mr. Kington," Case snapped. "The Buddhists are godless people. Their only thought is about attaining enlightenment, even if it means under a red flag. They have no concept of political responsibility."

"The monk who self-immolated was making a political statement."

"Is that a fact?"

"It's what I've come to understand."

"From your long career as a diplomat or from your many years in Vietnam or both?"

Since Tom couldn't very well say his understanding came from a few months of reading, he remained silent.

"I'll tell you what, Mr. Kington. Your assignment here in Vietnam will be to establish contacts with the Buddhist community and determine its role in the political process. How does that suit you?"

"Fine."

After another half hour of business, Case adjourned the meeting and stalked out of the room without a goodbye.

"I guess you forgot my advice about shutting up," quipped Stefan Boudreau.

"Our new colleague is a brave soul. Welcome aboard. I'm Aaron Goldstein.

"Or a foolish one. Brent Lubner." He nodded from across the table.

"I take it that you all believe I've gotten off on the wrong foot with Mr. Case."

"You're fortunate that he didn't bite off your foot," said Stefan. "You must have caught him in a good mood."

"Maybe," said Lubner, "though the damage's been done."

"What damage?" Tom asked. "We're supposed to gather political information. This is a Buddhist country. We should be collecting political information about the Buddhists."

"Why?" Lubner asked. "This war is not about Vietnam. It's about stopping communism, and the Buddhists don't give a hoot about communism."

"That's why Brent here is a favorite of Hard Case," said Stefan, "and why Brent's next posting will be plum..."

"Paris, London, Tokyo," Goldstein interjected.

"...whereas your next posting will be dung," concluded Stefan.

"Mongolia, Sudan, Iceland," said Goldstein.

"This is my first day on the job. I'll worry about my next posting in three years."

"It's your career," Goldstein shrugged.

"I don't get it," Tom said. "How are we supposed to win a war in a country where we ignore the will of the vast majority of the people?"

"Bombs," said Lubner. "Have you heard about Rolling Thunder?"

"Sure. We're going to bomb the hell out of the North until they stop supporting the Vietcong. It won't work."

"Oh, really?" asked Lubner. "Why not?"

"The Chinese Nationalists bombed Mao and the communists for years. Killed tens of thousands. It didn't work."

"The Chinese couldn't drop a turd in the toilet bowl if they were squatting on it," said Lubner. "We'll bomb these fuckers back to the Stone Age. The VC will wither without support."

"If we have so much faith in bombing raids, why are we bringing in a hundred thousand new troops?" Tom asked.

"The new kid has a good point," Goldstein conceded.

"Rolling Thunder's going to take time," said Lubner. "Right now we've got to deal with the VC, who are being supported by your Buddhist commies."

"They're not my Buddhists," said Tom.

"They are now," Stefan said. "You asked for 'em, and Hard Case complied."

"You should have listened to your roomie and shut up," said Lubner. "Unless we get a new head of section or things change pretty radically, you've been banished to the wilderness."

Tom's first three months in Vietnam were among the busiest of his life, though his colleagues at the embassy were either unaware or didn't care. Hard Case never called on him during meetings, never asked for written reports, and acted as if Tom didn't exist. David Halberstam had been correct in his reporting. The American government seemed to only want information that confirmed its predetermined view: the democratic, christian United States could defeat the communist heathens from North Vietnam through faith and firepower. Tom planned to gather information that proved otherwise. He would build an irrefutable case showing the flaws of the US strategy. When the time came, as it inevitably would, he would be ready to provide the critical information that would save the American mission.

He knew he was viewed by some as young and ignorant, possibly even arrogant. Tom viewed himself as a man of reason. He never believed something simply because he was told so. Rather than collect information that would confirm what LBJ and the Department of Defense already believed, Tom was determined to learn the truth about what was happening in Vietnam, regardless of what that truth was.

Tom knew that he had one thing in his favor: his gift for languages. Although he'd never be fluent in Vietnamese, he had learned enough to open a few doors. So few Americans bothered to learn any Vietnamese besides what was needed to buy food, booze, and women, that Tom's efforts were met with surprise and welcome. At those times when his limited Vietnamese ran out and the people he was meeting didn't speak English, his excellent French took over. He quickly picked up the French spoken by Vietnamese, which was accented and idiomatic. This further endeared him to the Vietnamese he met, though he soon realized that many Vietnamese refused to talk with Americans because most were arrogant know-it-alls.

Tom's first successful contact was with the owner of a noodle stall that he frequented. Tom practiced his Vietnamese and French with the man and eventually gained his trust. The stall owner introduced Tom to a young monk who knew other monks who were close to Tri Quang, the unofficial leader of the Vietnamese Buddhist community. It was a tenuous link, but Tom intended to fly to Hué in order to establish direct contact with Tri Quang. The day he was scheduled to fly to Hué—the old capital of Vietnam and a center of Buddhism—a cadre of young Catholic military officers ousted Dr. Quat and took over the government. After a week's delay, Tom finally succeeded in flying to Hué.

The taxi driver dropped Tom off at the Dieu De Buddhist temple near the Perfume River. His Saigon noodle connection had told him that the Dieu De temple was where Tri Quang made his headquarters. Tom spent the next forty-eight hours unsuccessfully trying to make contact with anyone willing to discuss politics. He spent hours over green tea and noodles discussing agriculture, the nature of religion in Vietnam (which blended Buddhism, Taoism, Confucianism, animism, and ancestor worship), colonial history, food, and just about everything else imaginable. Every time

Tom broached the subject of Vietnamese politics or the US military presence or communism, he was met with an uncomfortable silence. When Tom returned to Saigon he went to his favorite noodle stall and gently mentioned his frustrating and fruitless weekend in Hué.

"It is not easy to know who to trust," the noodle stall man said.

"I mentioned your name."

"Who am I? I cook noodles. I know many Americans. Too many."

"But I just want to talk. I want to understand and learn."

"I believe you. We have talked for many months and I know you are hungry for more than noodles. Others may not believe you. There is much to fear."

"What?"

The noodle man hesitated, then plunged in. "Maybe you are not with the embassy. Maybe you are with the CIA. Some may fear that you will identify leaders of the Buddhist movement and the leaders will be arrested. Or worse. Maybe you are with the embassy and really want to learn and understand, but what if the Vietcong are watching you? They might think that any Vietnamese who talks with you supports the government of the South, and that would be very dangerous. As long as your government supports Catholic governments, governments that come to power by military force, led by generals, your talk of democracy will not be believed."

"What should I do then?"

"Be patient. We Vietnamese have waited two thousand years to be free of foreign rule."

"I don't have two thousand years."

The next two months were times of change, none good from Tom's viewpoint. The coup that overthrew Dr. Quat led to the appointment of Air Vice Marshall Nguyen Cao Ky as prime minister and General Nguyen Van Thieu as head of state. Both were Catholic. Tom strongly believed that the United States remained on the wrong track and decided he had to renew his effort to win the trust of the Buddhist leadership. With that in mind, he returned to Hué half a dozen times between June and August.

Tom was packing his weekend bag one Friday when Stefan walked into his bedroom.

"More sightseeing, huh?"

"Yup."

"Hué again?"

"Uh huh. There's a lot to see for such a small city."

"Hard Case called me into his office this morning to ask what you've been up to."

"Why didn't he just ask me?"

"'Cuz he didn't like you. Me being from the South, he can relate, to some extent. You being an uppity New Yorker..."

"I'm from Indiana."

"Whatever. It's all up north to us.

"I thought Case wanted me to vanish. Isn't that why he agreed to let me gather information on the Buddhists? He sees it as a dead end, of no value to us."

"That's still true. How many times has he called on you during our Monday morning meetings to make a report?"

"Zero."

"How many times has he called you into his office to pick your brain?"

"Zero. So why's he asking you what I'm doing?"

"Like I said, he trusts me, and he's wondering what you're up to."

"So what'd you tell him?"

"I said you were trying to gather information, but having no luck making contacts."

"That must have pleased him."

"Not really. He doesn't trust you. Wants to know where you go on the weekends."

"Did you tell him?"

"You bet. I figured since he already knew you spent most of your weekends away from Saigon, it wouldn't be that difficult to access plane and train records. Hope you don't mind."

Tom had been taking the train, which was cheaper than flying. As well, the Friday night train arrived early Saturday morning, saving him the cost of a hotel, and the Sunday night train to Saigon arrived in plenty of time for Tom to make the regular 0900 Monday morning meeting.

"No, I don't mind. I wouldn't want you to get into trouble trying to cover for me. Besides, I'm not doing anything wrong. I'm supposed to gather info on the Buddhists. Right?"

"Right. Only, be careful."

"Careful of what?"

"Look, Tom, can I give you some advice? As a friend?"

"Are you my friend, Stefan?"

"Damn straight. I'm the best friend you got in Nam, the only one, as far as I know. That's the point. Hard Case is aware that you spend most of your time with Vietnamese, particularly at that noodle stall you frequent. The old bastard never trusts anybody he thinks is going native."

Tom wondered how Case knew where he spent his time; he assumed his roommate was the source.

"If you want Case off your case, you ought to spend more time with your fellow Americans. Hang out at the Continental, drink a few cold beers, tell some dirty jokes. He just wants to know that you're still part of the team."

"Even though I'm not treated as part of the team."

"You're new here. He doesn't expect much input from you yet. Things take time. Play the game and by next year you may be one of his most trusted officers."

"In the meantime we'll continue to back unpopular governments and lose the support of the people."

"Tom, you gotta have more faith in your government."

"Based on what?"

"So they haven't exactly done much to earn your faith. Then consider your career."

"Is that your advice as a friend? Put my career before my responsibility as a political officer in the State Department?"

Stefan shrugged. "I'm just being a realist. Nobody listens to us junior staffers. We're one notch above secretaries and cleaners. Look at Lubner. He's only been here a little more than a year and he already has Case's ear. Hell, by next year he might have Case's job, then he'll have the ambassador's ear. This ain't no different than any other job. You got to be patient, rise through the ranks, wait for your time."

"Thanks for the advice. You're the second person this week to counsel patience."

"Who was the other?"

"The guy who runs the noodle stall."

Stefan chuckled. "Then I'm in good company. Seems like you got two friends in Saigon."

Two friends indeed, but which one, if either, was the real friend?

Although Tom couldn't completely turn off his inner voice—the one that sounded suspiciously like a blend of Ira Blue and Suzie Chomsky—he decided to play the political game, for now. He reduced his trips to Hué, had a few beers at the Continental and got to know some journalists. During meetings he was careful to seem to hang on Case's words. He would nod as if to agree with Case's assessments, even when he found them to be asinine. The payoff came at the end of the second meeting of Tom's experiment.

"Tom, would you wait a minute after the meeting?" Case had asked as everybody rose.

When everybody else had left, Case nodded toward Tom's chair.

"Sit down a minute."

Tom did as instructed.

"How's the research on the Buddhists going?"

"Not particularly well." Although true, Tom was sure to put an additional dose of frustration into his voice.

"I thought you might find that to be the case. Like I told you, the Buddhists are not friends of democracy and have nothing to gain by cooperating with you. Just the opposite. It could put them in very real danger."

"Does that mean I'm in danger?" Again, Tom allowed his voice to shake just a tiny bit. He was, in fact, not in the least bit worried about his safety, yet knew that it might appeal to Case's paternalism.

"Naw, I can't see that anybody would be worried by some junior staffer asking a few questions. They're more likely to sell you more noodles and tell lies."

This was an implicit statement that Case knew with whom Tom had been talking.

"I still think there's potential value in establishing contacts. What do you think?"

"Can't hurt."

"All right. I don't know if you're aware that I've been traveling during the weekends."

"I've heard you've been up to Hué a few times."

"I've been hoping to meet with Tri Quang, the Buddhist leader."

"*One* of the Buddhist leaders, the closest to the Vietcong. He'll never see you, and if he does it'll only be to tell you lies."

"Thanks for the warning. I was told the same thing by Boudreau." It was a lie that would please Stefan. "It occurred to me that Tri Quang might have enemies among the Buddhists, enemies who might be willing to support our political choices in exchange for help in bringing Tri Quang down a notch or two." This too was a lie. Tom had only heard praise for Tri Quang.

"That's a dangerous game. Be very careful. Let one of them bring up the subject, never you. Never let them know who you back. And if you get any inkling that there are divisions among the Buddhists or any other local factions, you let me know first thing. Got it?"

"Yes, sir." Tom thought the "sir" might be a bit much, but Case's chest puffed out an extra inch in response.

"Tom, I'll be honest. I was not impressed with your attitude at first. A bit snotty Ivy League for my taste. I had more than enough dealing with the Kennedys and their people. Now you have your feet back on the ground, I think we'll be able to work together. I haven't told the others, but Washington is starting to put a little more thought into the political situation here. About time. This country has had more prime ministers than noodle stalls. That's gotta stop."

Tom waited until he had left the building before allowing himself a smile. Case believed that Tom had been put in his place and would be now playing by Case's rules. With Case off his back, Tom was free to pursue his own agenda.

CHAPTER 7—1965/1966

Tom sat at the noodle stall that had become his main hangout in Hué. His relationship with the stall's owner had gone through a few stages. The man had been superficially friendly at first, as he would be with any tourist. He would nod a welcome, give the faintest of smiles when Tom attempted humor, and respond with monosyllabic answers when Tom posed questions. As Tom's questions had grown more penetrating—moving from the weather and food to the war and politics—the man had become less and less responsive, until finally he would barely acknowledge Tom's presence. For several weeks, whenever Tom would appear at the stall, the owner would simply drop Tom's bowl of noodles onto the counter, each time causing Tom to jump back to avoid getting splashed. But the last time Tom had stopped by, the owner had begrudgingly nodded a welcome, as if to acknowledge that he was stuck with Tom and would no longer be rude. They'd spoken some French and a little Vietnamese, and eventually Tom sensed that he was developing a relationship with the owner, which is why he went straight to the noodle stall upon his first trip to Hué since his talk with Hard Case. There was one other reason why he was eager to return to the noodle stall: the owner's sister, who worked their occasionally, was a stunning beauty.

Tom had been celibate since arriving in Vietnam, a condition that didn't bother him. Except for a few brief affairs with other Peace Corps volunteers, he'd been celibate in Côte d'Ivoire as well. Tom had a healthy libido—as was evident in his times with Suzie and her roommate Tony—yet he was comfortable with long periods of abstinence. When colleagues visited brothels or picked up bar girls, Tom went back to his room to read or listen to Armed Forces Radio. Still, Tom was a healthy male, and the noodle stall owner's sister appeared to be a healthy, and lovely, female. At first, Tom assumed the woman was the owner's wife. One day, when she wasn't there, Tom asked where the owner's wife was.

"At home with our children," the man had answered in French.

"How many children do you have?"

"Three."

"Well, your wife is very lovely for a mother with three children."

The man had given Tom a quizzical look. "When did you see my wife?"

"The last time I was here. She cleared my bowl and washed it."

"Oh. That was my sister."

"Really. Is she married?"

The man had ignored the question. Tom realized he might have crossed a line and refrained from asking it again. The next time the woman worked the noodle stall Tom had tried to start a conversation; the woman's responses were briefer than her brother's and, if possible, conveyed even less welcome. Her obvious rejections only piqued Tom's interest. When he arrived at the stall this time, he was disappointed to find only the man working.

"Good morning," Tom said in his best Vietnamese.

"Good morning," replied the owner.

"I have missed your noodles. They are the best in Vietnam. Firm noodles, broth not too salty, tender chicken." Tom had practiced this little speech for days.

The man stopped chopping green onions and glanced at Tom. "You are too kind."

"No. It is a delicious meal."

"You have been practicing Vietnamese."

"Yes, though I do not know many words. I have much to learn."

"We all have much to learn. You can speak French if you wish."

"Thank you," Tom said in Vietnamese. Then he switched to French. "You are very busy. I do not want to bother you by practicing my Vietnamese."

"That is all right. It is rare to find a foreigner who tries to learn our language. It is not easy."

"No, it is very difficult for us *farang*. However, one must work and be patient if one wants to succeed."

The man nodded, then went back to his chopping. When Tom finished his noodles he put his money on the table and stood to leave.

"My name is Tom Kington."

"Tran Van Minh."

"Thank you, Tran."

Tom returned again the next day prior to going to the train station. He was again disappointed not to see Tran's sister, but he spent an hour talking with Tran, partly in Vietnamese, partly in French. Tran surprised Tom by wishing him a good voyage back to Saigon. Tom returned the next weekend. When the train arrived in Hué Tom took a pedal cab directly to the noodle stall. This time he was thrilled to see Tran's sister clearing bowls from the three small aluminum tables.

"Good morning," he said to the siblings in Vietnamese.

Both returned the greeting, though the sister's response was muted and guarded.

"It is truly a beautiful day," Tom said.

"Your accent is even better than last week," Tran said in rapid Vietnamese.

"Excuse me?"

Tran repeated his compliment in French.

"Thank you," Tom said in Vietnamese. "I still have much to learn."

Tom tried to strike up a conversation with Tran's sister, yet got nowhere. When he introduced himself she gave a quick nod in recognition, but did not offer her own name. Tom returned that evening and the next day. Though the sister was there both times, she continued to give Tom the cold shoulder, and he spent his time conversing with Tran.

When the Christmas holidays arrived, most of Tom's colleagues traveled out of Vietnam. Those that could afford it flew back to the States. A few took the opportunity to travel to Australia or Thailand, any place that allowed them to escape the growing anxiety of life in Vietnam. The military presence had escalated rapidly, and with it had come an increase in bar girls, drug peddlers, petty crime, and the occasional Vietcong bombing. Saigon was becoming crowded with military personnel and vehicles, as well as diplomats and journalist who packed the hotels, bars, and restaurants. Refugees from the war in the countryside also streamed into Saigon, creating even more crowding as sidewalks became jammed with beggars, the wounded, scarred and amputated, and those who had nowhere else to go.

Not surprisingly, many of the recent arrivals were assumed to be Vietcong using the mass migration as a cover to infiltrate the city. The result was that nearly every place frequented by Americans and Europeans bristled with armed guards. It was little wonder that most foreigners fled Vietnam every chance they got. Tom was different. He saw his two-week vacation as a golden opportunity to see South Vietnam—to explore the tropical country and to improve his Vietnamese. He headed south to Dalat, then took local buses to the Mekong Delta. After a week, he took the train north to Hué, where he planned on eating noodles until he either got sick of them or made a breakthrough with Tran's sister.

"Your Vietnamese is very good," Tran said after Tom finished his bowl of noodles.

"Thank you. I have spent the past week speaking it in the Mekong Delta. It is a lovely part of Vietnam."

"Yet you return to Hué."

"There is much to learn in Hué."

Tran put down his chopping knife and looked at Tom. "What is it that you are really doing here? You can get good noodles in Saigon."

Tom switched to French. "I told you many months ago when we met. I want to learn about Buddhism."

"You can learn everything about Buddhism in Saigon, too."

"That's true. However, Tri Quang lives in Hué."

It was a risky thing to say, yet Tom had been trying to make contact for six months and his time in the country was limited.

"I think you are not so interested in Buddhism."

"I am. I have Buddhist friends in America. I am also interested in the politics of Vietnam. That is why I am here."

"You Americans say you are here to stop communism."

"That is the goal of my government."

"It is not your goal?"

Tom was on treacherous ground. As an employee of the Department of State, his job was to implement US foreign policy. To do otherwise would be to jeopardize his career. Yet a voice kept whispering in his ear: "Wherever you go, do good."

"My goal is to make the world a safer place. That is good for Vietnam. It is also good for America."

As they were talking Tran's sister arrived by bicycle. As always, she was wearing the traditional *ao dai*: silk trousers with a long silk top that came to mid-thigh. She leaned the bicycle against the back of the stall and came around to the front.

"Sorry I am late," she said to her brother in Vietnamese.

"Tran cooked me a wonderful breakfast," said Tom, also in Vietnamese.

She seemed surprised by Tom's use of the language.

"Yes," began Tran, "our friend has been studying."

"I do not speak well. I need much practice."

Tran began to speak in rapid Vietnamese that Tom couldn't follow. Tran's sister responded with what appeared to be a reprimand, and the two got into a heated argument. When they stopped, the woman began to clear Tom's bowl and clean the tabletop.

"It is a lovely day," said Tom in Vietnamese.

"It is the same every day in Vietnam," she replied curtly in French. "We do not discuss the weather, like foreigners do. They either complain about the heat and humidity, or they tell me how nice it is, when they want to be my *friend*."

The meaning was clear. The woman believed that the Americans she met were either whiners or trying to get into her pants.

"I am not here to be your *friend*."

"My brother has told me why you are here."

"You do not believe me?"

She stopped wiping the table and looked at Tom. "You want to learn Vietnamese. I believe that. What I know is that you are an American, you work for the American government, and your job is to help America, not Vietnam."

"I can do both." He hesitated. "No, the truth is I can try to do both. It is not easy because most Americans only want to help themselves. Is that not true of all people? All people want to help their families, their tribes, their nations."

The woman looked into Tom's eyes, hesitated, then cleared his bowl and utensils.

"My name is Tom. Tom Kington."

She bent over and put the bowl and utensils into a bucket of soapy water, then straightened up and turned to face Tom.

"My name is Anh Co Minh."

"It is pleasure to meet you. Anh. I need a teacher to help me with my Vietnamese. Are you available?"

"You live in Saigon."

"True, but I come to Hué often. Do you work during the weekends?"

"Yes. I work with my brother."

"Sometimes," Tran said, "though as you can see, it does not require two people." He motioned with his hand to indicate the stalls two gas-powered woks, three small aluminum tables, and six chairs.

"Anh, what do you do during the week?"

"I work at the Buddhist Community Association."

"Really? What do you do there?"

"Many things. I am a secretary, interpreter, fund-raiser. I do what-ever needs to be done. We help the needy, organize festivals, repair old temples, and build new ones."

"Are you involved in any political activities?"

"I am interested in religion and my community. Not politics."

"Everything is politics. It was politics when Quang Duc set himself on fire three years ago."

"He was protesting the government's abuse of Buddhists. It was a re-ligious statement."

"With political goals."

Two other customers arrived. Anh took their orders and relayed them to Tran.

"I would like to continue this discussion some time when you are free," Tom said to Anh.

"I do not want to talk about your politics."

"Fine. I still need a tutor, and I'm willing to pay. How about a lesson this evening? At dinner?"

Anh shot him an accusing look, as if to say she'd expected this all along.

"I'm serious about learning Vietnamese. A meal, a walk, some talk. That is all."

Anh looked at Tran. He was busy cooking and gave a nearly imperceptible shrug.

"OK. Be here at seven o'clock."

"I can pick you up at your place."

"Be here at seven o'clock."

Tom went to Hué three or four times a month. Although his State Department salary was far from princely, it was sufficient for the overnight train, an inexpensive guesthouse near the Dieu De temple, and food. He and Anh would usually have a simple meal, sip tea, and walk around Hué. They found shady spots in temples or parks and sat for hours talking about many topics, though never politics. Just as it had taken patience to earn Tran's trust, Tom knew he would have to exercise patience before being able to broach the subject that brought him to Hué. Besides, he had completely fallen for Anh and didn't want to risk his relationship by dragging in his work. Not yet anyway. He convinced himself that it would be better to wait, earn Anh's trust, and gather valuable, reliable knowledge rather than rush ahead and be fed meaningless—and possibly false—information.

The political situation in Vietnam began to deteriorate in the spring. President Johnson had met Prime Minister Ky in Honolulu in February, and Johnson had responded by lavishly praising Ky. Ky possessed qualities that pleased Johnson: he was Christian and anticommunist. Ky seemed to view Johnson's praise as a go-ahead for establishing order in Vietnam, which did not include holding democratic elections. Instead, Ky tried to extend his control over regional military commanders, while at the same time ordering a crackdown on dissent. Vietnamese factions responded forcibly. Strikes and violence broke out in the central provinces. The Vietcong used this as an opportunity to strike. Rather than focus on the Vietcong, troops hostile to Ky rebelled and temporarily took over Danang and Hué. Tri Quang spoke out strongly against Ky, calling for his removal. This led Howard Case to become even more anti-Buddhist. The attaché ranted against the perceived ties between the Buddhists and the Communists, and he aimed one of these attacks directly at Tom.

"While you're still trying to make nice with those goddamned Buddhists, they're trying to cut Ky off at the knees. This would be a time to pull together to show the commies that the nation is united."

Tom knew that he should keep his mouth shut, but Case's profanity toward the Buddhists struck a nerve.

"The nation would have a better chance of being united if Ky tried to reach out to factions rather than squash them. The Vietnamese are a proud people. They will respect a monk or emperor and make sacrifices for the good of the nation. They don't react well to bullies with Napoleon complexes like Ky."

"I don't need a lecture on Vietnam's history and culture," Case snapped. "I need suggestions on how we can stabilize the political situation."

"Hold elections like we've said we were going to do," said Tom.

"That's Ky's call, and he don't seem inclined to hold an election."

"No wonder the people support the Vietcong and Tri Quang."

Tom knew it was a mistake the moment the words slipped out of his mouth. The official American line was that the people supported the government of South Vietnam, yet feared showing that support because they would either become a target of the Vietcong or be the subject of pressure from militant Buddhists.

"That's a myth," Case said while glaring at Tom. "Our sources continue to insist that the people want American-style democracy and American protection from the commies. Isn't that correct, Lubner?"

"Yes, sir, it is. It hasn't changed since Diem came to power in '54. The people fear that Uncle Ho and the Communists, with the support of Tri Quang and the Buddhists, will rig any election. Until we get both factions under control, it is not advisable to hold an election."

"There you have it from somebody who's been in country a hell of a lot longer than you," Case said. "You have anything else to add?" he challenged Tom.

Tom had a lot more to add, yet wisely choose not to. "No, sir."

"Good. By the way, with the situation looking so grim, this is not a good time for one of your excursions to Hué. You'll have to get word to your lady friend that she'll have to find other companionship for a while."

Tom's face turned scarlet. He had purposely told Stefan about Anh knowing the information would get to Hard Case. It was safer that Case thought Tom was having an affair rather than still trying to establish contact with Tri Quang. Still, it took an exceptional effort for Tom not to respond to this personal jab.

As the team filed out of the room, Case asked Tom to stay back a minute.

"You still part of this team?"

"Of course. I just think it's important to look at all angles. To play devil's advocate."

"That's fine, as long as you don't take the devil's side. And I'm serious. Until we've brought in enough troops and dropped enough bombs to bring law and order to this place, I want you close to home. They got a shitload of Buddhists here in Saigon. Confine your research to this vicinity."

"Yes, sir."

Tom had no intention of keeping his word.

It was too risky to take the train; Hard Case seemed to know when Tom was traveling. Feeling like the hero of the enormously popular James Bond series, Tom set his plan into action, and his roommate was a key to the plan. Regardless of whether Boudreau was feeding information to Case to advance his own career or merely to cover his own ass, Tom was pretty sure that much of Case's info about him came from Stefan. He planned on using the Louisianan.

"Hey, roomie, what about hitting the beach this weekend?"

Boudreau hated the beach. With his pale complexion and proclivity to sweat, the beach was the last place Stefan would ever want to be.

"The only water I plan on being near is the water I mix into my whiskey."

"All right. I'll bring you a bucket of sand, and you can play with it in the tub."

"You seem to be taking Case's travel ban pretty well."

"Hell, I'm not getting anywhere with Tri Quang in Hué."

"Yeah, but I thought you were getting somewhere with Ann."

Tom didn't bother to correct Boudreau's pronunciation.

"I told you, she's not a bar girl. I'm not going to get anywhere with Anh unless I marry her, and that's not in the cards."

"So why not hang out with me at the Continental? You haven't been there in months. I'm ready to make a breakthrough with this honey there, and she's got a couple of cute friends."

Boudreau tried to get Tom to join him nearly every week. Though Tom had complied when he was trying to get Case off his back, he hated the Continental. Hated all the places where Americans hung out. And as the steady stream of new GIs and refugees from the countryside flooded Saigon, he hated the city even more.

"I think I'll pass. Thanks for the offer. I'm going to take a bus to the beach, find a cheap room, and practice my Vietnamese."

"Doesn't sound like much fun."

"It's fun enough for me."

"So where you goin'?"

"Haven't decided yet. Any suggestions?"

"Yeah. Make sure the beach is far from Hué."

Tom's friend at the Saigon noodle stall had been asking around about anybody driving to Hué. Thursday night he informed Tom that a truck loaded with construction material would leave Saigon late Friday afternoon bound for Hué. Tom reached Hué by sunrise Saturday and arrived at Tran's noodle stall as the broth came to a boil. The two men chatted over breakfast, then Tom pulled a chair into the shade and waited for Anh to arrive. When she hadn't arrived by late morning, Tran sent a boy to find her. An hour later the boy returned and spoke in an excited tone that Tom was unable to understand.

"What's up?" he asked Tran.

"There is trouble in Danang. Ky's troops have attacked and hundreds are dead."

"That's bad," said Tom.

"Yes, very bad. The boy says that the soldiers attacked a Buddhist temple. Monks were killed, as well as soldiers and civilians. Anh is at the Buddhist Community Association headquarters. She will be there all day. The boy will take you there, but you must not go inside. The people are very angry, and they blame the Americans for supporting Ky. You stay outside, the boy will bring Anh to you."

The BCA's headquarters weren't far, yet in that short distance Tom noted something new in the air, a sense of dread and urgency. Rather than stroll toward work or social events, people rushed about as if on important missions, or eager to find a safe haven. The scene outside the BCA headquarters was even more frenetic. The boy indicated a partially hidden doorway where Tom could wait without attracting attention. Ten minutes later, he saw Anh exit the headquarters, look around to evaluate the scene, then walk toward him. He nearly rushed out to greet her, but wisely waited. Anh walked by and glanced briefly in Tom's direction while shaking her head, then kept walking. A minute later the boy who had escorted Tom walked up to him.

"Follow me," the boy said.

Tom followed for a few blocks until the boy stopped in front of a tea shop. The boy nodded toward the shop, then left. Tom entered and waited a moment until his eyes adjusted to the dim light. He spied Anh at a small table in the back, walked over, and sat down next to her.

"This is not a good time for you to be in Hué," said Anh

"It is always a good time to be with you."

"Stop! People are dying in Danang."

"Ky couldn't allow the rebellious troops to poison the rest of the army," Tom said.

"So you support the attack."

"Of course not. You know me better than that. I'm saying it was inevitable."

"Especially with you Americans giving Ky weapons and telling him to crush the rebels."

"Yes, my government supported Ky's move against the rebels, but you forget that it was US Marines a few weeks ago who stood between Ky and the rebels, and stopped bloodshed. My government hoped that a show of force would lead the rebels to back down."

"You keep saying, 'your government.' What is it that you truly believe? Everything your government tells you?"

"Of course not. I am not a puppet. I advise based on what I see and learn. This is what I believe: No government can survive for long without the support of the majority of the people. No amount of bombing or repression can win that support. In fact, it is just the opposite. My government, however, blames the Vietcong and Communist agitators and radical Buddhists, who they believe work closely with the Communists. My superior believes that all Vietnamese Buddhists are communist."

Anh looked shocked by this last bit. "That is stupid."

"Yes, it is. That's why I'm trying to prove them wrong. America can't defeat the Vietcong and North Vietnam without the support of the people of South Vietnam, and they will never win the support of the people while they view all Buddhists as enemies. That is why I need to learn more, meet some of the Buddhist leadership, maybe even meet Tri Quang. That is why I keep coming back to Hué. That and to see you."

Anh glanced down at her cup of tea. Tom thought she blushed slightly, though it was difficult to know for sure in the dim light of the tea shop.

"Wait here," said Anh. "I will go to BCA headquarters and talk with some people. They are very busy planning our response to the outrage in Danang. I will see what I can do."

She stood to go.

"Thank you, Anh."

Anh nodded, then walked out the door. She returned half an hour later with a Vietnamese man in his early thirties who wore dark slacks and a white button-down shirt. Like most Vietnamese he was relatively short and very thin.

"This is Nguyen," Anh said by way of introduction.

Nguyen is one of the most common names in Vietnam, similar to Jones or Smith in the States. Tom assumed it was an alias. The two men shook hands and sat down.

"We can talk in English, if you prefer," said Nguyen in nearly perfect English.

"I don't want to exclude Anh."

"I understand English, though not speak good," said Anh.

"My French is pretty good," Tom said, "but I want to be a hundred percent sure that I understand what you tell me. If it's OK with you, let's speak English."

"Fine," said Nguyen.

"Who are you?" Tom asked. "I mean, what is your position within the BCA?"

Nguyen smiled. "I understand. I might simply be an accountant." He motioned toward his neat European clothes. "In fact, I am an accountant. I have a master's degree from UCLA in business and finance. My father was a wealthy trader blessed with great vision. He knew ten years ago that the time of the French was passing and the time of the Americans was rapidly approaching. He sent me to California for the degree, but also to learn English and establish business connections."

"You said your father 'was' a wealthy trader. Has he passed away?"

"Financially, yes, though he still lives. He angered Diem with his Buddhist connections, and Diem made it very difficult for my father's business. Even after Diem was assassinated, those in power continued to hurt my family's business. We only trade domestically now. We've been squeezed out of the international market."

"So you have a grudge against your government."

"Yes, though I do not view it as my government. I suppose that in your eyes the information I give you has no value. My views are too biased. My anger too profound. You would be correct about my bias and my anger, yet that does not reduce my value to you. I will be honest with you. Anh tells me you are a good person, the type who can tell bias from fact."

"What can an accountant tell me about the Buddhist movement?"

"I have been the BCA's accountant since my return from California seven years ago. It is my father's way to gain merit. I work for the family business most of the time, and I spend about one day a week at BCA head-quarters. As such, I have earned the trust of the BCA leadership."

"Including Tri Quang?"

"Yes, including Tri Quang. We have shared many meals together, many discussions about Buddhism and Vietnam and politics."

"Since you have lived in America, you will understand if my questions are blunt. I do not have a lot of time, and I have many questions."

"I miss American bluntness. Here in Vietnam we often spend hours trying to be polite and not make somebody lose face. It is a Chinese thing. As you know, Vietnam was a Chinese tributary for a thousand years."

Tom appreciated that Nguyen credited him with knowledge of Vietnam. He nodded to confirm what Nguyen had said.

"Good," Nguyen responded, "then let's have a man-to-man talk, as you say in America."

"My government believes that Tri Quang is the leader of Vietnam's Buddhists. Is that true?"

"There is no official leader. There are many respected monks. Some stick to religion. Others get involved in politics. Tri Quang is one of those.

He is powerful because he is respected, not because he was elected or put in place like Ky."

"Are the leaders of the Buddhist community communist?"

"No, though many of the Communists are Buddhist."

"Is there a connection between the Buddhists and the Communists?"

"Yes, though it is not what the Americans think it is."

"What is it that we Americans think it is?"

"You think that we are working together to defeat America and assure victory for the Communists. Is that not the case?"

"That is what the government believes, and many Americans believe their government. However, that is rapidly changing. The American people are beginning to question what they have been told. So what is the truth?"

"The truth? We Buddhists and the Communists have some shared goals. Both want an end to colonialism. Had your government encouraged the French to leave peacefully in 1945, or even in 1954, there might not be war today."

"Might not?"

"Though we have some shared goals, there are some things on which the Buddhists and Communists do not agree. The Buddhists seek peace in which to practice our religion, and a government that respects us and our needs. The Communists wish to establish a communist state, though not the same as the one Mao has established in China. Mao, like Marx, opposes religion. Ho Chi Minh respects the beliefs of his ancestors. For Uncle Ho, communism is merely a means for uniting the nation and expelling the imperialists. He is first and foremost a Vietnamese nationalist. Still, there is always the possibility that, once you Americans have been expelled, the two factions may have a falling-out."

The discussion continued for nearly an hour until a man rushed in and spoke rapidly to Nguyen in Vietnamese.

"Sorry to cut this discussion short. I must go."

"Thank you for your time. I hope we can meet again and continue."

"That would be my pleasure. In the meantime, I urge you to exercise extreme caution while you remain in Hué."

"May I ask why?"

"It is time for action. We have prepared a large demonstration to protest the deaths in Danang. Though it is meant to be peaceful, one never knows how others will react, particularly Ky's forces. After all, the demonstrations in Danang were peaceful, but that did not stop Ky from starting a bloodbath." Nguyen switched to French. "Anh, you must take our friend to a safe place." He turned to Tom. "It would appear that you are not in agreement with your government. I know your career would be in danger if you appeared to sympathize with us Vietnamese nationalists, so I only ask one thing. If you are given an opportunity, try to explain that most of us are not communists, though we have been driven to collaborate with them at times. Backing Ky is a grave error that American will come to regret."

"I agree, and I have already told that to my superiors. They will not listen."

"Not now. Perhaps they will soon."

They rose and shook hands. Nguyen turned to Anh.

"You must go now. Wait until I have left. It would not be a good idea for me to be seen with somebody from the US embassy."

By the time Anh and Tom walked out of the tea shop, the streets were already buzzing with tension. People were standing around holding signs, preparing for a march. The messages on the signs were clear: "End Foreign Domination of Our Country!" "LBJ Bomb Your Own Country!" Anh led the way as they weaved their way through the crowd. Although quite a few people glared at Tom, he never felt in danger. He saw a few other Western faces, including some who he took to be journalists. He was watching one man snap a few shots when the man lowered his camera and looked directly at Tom. Something about the man was vaguely familiar, but before Tom could place the face his hand was grabbed by Anh and he was pulled down a side lane.

"We must find a safe place for you," said Anh.

"Safe from whom? Vietcong?"

"The Vietcong are not the only people who are against foreigners. Besides, you once told me that your superior doesn't want you in Hué."

Suddenly, Tom's gut tightened and he broke into a cold sweat. Something about the man with the camera tugged at Tom's memory. Who was he? Had he taken Tom's picture with Anh? She was right; he needed to find a safe place, somewhere far from the demonstration.

"Do you know where my guesthouse is?" he asked.

"Yes. We can get there by back streets. Come."

They wove through narrow back lanes until they came out half a block from his guesthouse. Few people were out, as most were either joining the anti-American demonstration or keeping off the streets. Tom led the way into the narrow building. The old woman who normally sat at the counter wasn't there. Anh and Tom stood awkwardly for a second.

"Come upstairs with me," he said simply.

Anh hesitated a moment, then nodded her assent. He took her hand and led her to his room. It was Spartan, containing a single bed, an old wooden chair, and a decrepit armoire. Tom locked the door and took Anh in his arms. They kissed passionately, then rapidly helped each other undress. Anh was tall for a Vietnamese, nearly five foot four. Her body was shapely, with sensuously curved hips and small, firm breasts. They fell onto the bed, entwined, and were soon deep in passionate lovemaking. Later, when their breathing had returned to normal, they lay on the sweat-soaked sheet.

"This was a mistake," Anh said. "It must not happen again."

Tom leaned on his side and kissed her. "I want it to happen again and again."

Anh stiffened. "I am not that type of woman."

"And I am not that type of man. This wasn't only about sex. I have much respect for you. You are beautiful and smart and brave and you love your country."

"Yes, I love Vietnam. That is why I should not be with you."

"You know that I want only good for Vietnam. That is why you are in bed with me. Plus, you like me."

Anh looked into Tom's eyes. A hint of a smile turned up the corners of her mouth and eyes. "You are right. I do like you. You are handsome and kind and you do care about Vietnam. I have wanted to be with you for many weeks."

"Many weeks? Not many months?"

She playfully pushed him away. "I did not trust you many months ago."

"So why do you trust me now?"

"Because you are too honest and kind to be an American agent."

Tom's gut constricted anew.

"Did I say something wrong?" Anh asked

"No. Not at all. I was just worrying about the demonstrators."

In truth, Anh's mention of 'an American agent' sent Tom's mind back to the Western photographer on the street. He realized that he had seen the man before, and now he remembered who the man was. The recollection did not please Tom.

Anh sighed. "I would like to remain here all day, but I must join the demonstrators. If people learn that I am sleeping with the enemy, it would not be good for either of us."

"Have I put you in danger?"

"My fellow Buddhists would never hurt me. However, my heart is with my people."

"All of it?"

"Not all. The part that is with you does not want you to be in trouble with your own people."

Again Tom flashed on the photographer.

"You are correct, of course. My trip here and meeting with Nguyen must remain secret."

Anh returned that evening and spent the night with Tom. She reported that the demonstration had been enormous, yet peaceful, which pleased them both. They made love the next morning and spent the day walking Hué, though sticking to side streets and quiet parks on the outskirts of town. Tom caught a ride back to Saigon with a truck driver and was able to catch a few hours of sleep before waking up for the 0900 meeting. As he and Stefan Boudreau walked to the embassy, his roommate grilled him on the weekend. Tom remained coy, told him he'd had a wild weekend, but refused to indulge Stefan with details. Tom was pretty sure that Boudreau bought the story because Tom had always been tight-lipped about his private life, a fact that Boudreau wrote off as a product of Tom's conservative Midwestern upbringing.

"You're one secretive dude," Boudreau muttered. "Ever consider a career with the CIA?"

"Not recently."

"You missed your calling, my friend."

"*Au contraire.* I think I'm doing the right thing, in the right place, at the right time."

CHAPTER 8—1966

"**D**amn it," Hard Case raged. "How are we supposed to do our job when these little pricks don't take our advice? We told 'em to go easy on their own people, that they needed to concentrate on the VC in the south and bomb the hell out of 'em up north. But do they listen? Hell, no."

The entire embassy bristled with tension. The marine guards at the front gate had been doubled and the entire staff had been put on a high state of alert. Case had started the meeting by summarizing the events of the past weekend. Prime Minister Ky had ordered that the rebellious troops be dislodged from Danang, and loyal troops had done so in a particularly brutal fashion. Hundreds of soldiers and civilians had been killed, including many who had sought shelter in Buddhist temples. It was this sacrilege, in particular, that led to demonstrations throughout South Vietnam. Although the one Tom had witnessed in Hué had been peaceful, it had also raised the greatest concern because of Tri Quang's assumed role as its leader. There were also rumors of a new round of self-immolation by Buddhist monks.

"Now it looks to all the world that Ky is fighting a civil war," Case continued. "How the hell are we going to sell the war to the American people when goddamned monks are setting themselves on fire and South Vietnamese soldiers are killing each other?"

Tom started to open his mouth, but a look from Case shut it.

"I sure as shit don't want to hear a fuckin' word about how we need to include the poor, underrepresented Buddhists in the political process."

Tom crossed his arms and stared blankly at some papers on the table.

"Sir," began Brent Lubner, "my contacts within the military are as concerned as we are. Though they agree that Ky is doing a good deal of damage, they still support the need for the prime minister to appear strong and resolute. The rebellion in Danang had to be swiftly crushed. Otherwise it might have spread through the ranks. I might add that we earned Brownie points in not being directly involved ourselves."

"I'd even go further," said Aaron Goldstein. "Business leaders are well aware that we tried to stop the bloodshed and that Ky ordered the assault against our wishes."

"Same with student leaders I talked with," added Stefan. "Let Ky be the heavy. We're still seen as a force of good that is focusing on the Communist insurgency."

"But we're supporting Ky," Case said, slamming the table for emphasis.

"For now," Tom muttered.

"Not that shit again," said Case.

"I'm not saying we should recommend another coup," Tom said. "I just don't think that Ky is the one who's going to take us to the finish line. We may recover from this business in Danang, but we can't afford much more of his heavy-handed tactics, not against his own people. Sooner or later, we're going to have to find somebody to take Ky's place, and it's going to have to look like it was his idea, not ours."

Everybody waited for an outburst from Hard Case. When none came, Lubner spoke up. "Tom has a point, though good luck pitching it to Lodge and Johnson."

"You're goddamned right about that," said Case. "How the hell can we convince 'em

back home that we've brought stability and security to Vietnam when the government changes more often than Joe Namath changes girlfriends? Look, I've got a meeting with the ambassador in an hour. I'll tell him our thoughts." He nodded toward Tom, a rare acknowledgement that Tom had made a valid point. "I want you all to bust your asses this week. Keep up with how your people are reacting to the demonstrations. Plan on meeting each morning at 0900 sharp to report to me. If Johnson asks for a report, I want to be ready. That's all for today."

When Tom returned to his desk there was a manila envelope sitting on it. There was no writing on the outside of the envelope, no indication of where it came from or what it contained. He sat down, opened it, and pulled out its contents: four photos. One was of Anh emerging from the BCA headquarters, the organization's sign clear behind her. Another photo was of Nguyen in the exact same location. A third was of Nguyen emerging from the tea shop where he'd met Tom and Anh. The final photo was of Tom and Anh emerging from the tea shop. The backs of all four photos were blank. He opened the envelope and found a small piece of paper folded in half. Tom pulled it out and opened it: Duffy's Pub, 776 Le Thanh Ton, 2100 tonight.

Tom walked into Duffy's at 2115. Being late was his way of saying he wasn't worried by the photos. The place was packed with Westerners— Tom heard various American accents as well as Australian, New Zealand, and South African—though no soldiers. It was a tough crowd, construction workers and private security types, long-time expats who drank freely and intimately knew many of Saigon's bar girls. Tom scanned the room until he saw the photographer sitting by himself at a table in the back. An empty chair awaited Tom. He walked over to the table and sat down.

"Been a while, Officer Smith. Or do you go by another name here in Vietnam?"

When Tom had realized—while lying in bed with Anh—that the photographer was Officer Smith of the CIA, the man who had attempted to recruit him at Columbia, he had a moment of panic. Soon, though, he calmed down. Yes, he had disobeyed orders by going to Hué, yet he hadn't committed a crime. Maybe he faced a reprimand. At worst he'd be thrown out of the foreign service. At this point, frustrated as he was with US policy in Vietnam and having to deal with ignorant bigots like Hard Case, he wasn't that concerned about his future. Regardless, Tom was not worried about Officer Smith. If Smith had wanted to bust him, he would have already. Rather than be worried, Tom was intrigued. Besides, unlike the hostile Officer Jones, he'd liked Officer Smith.

"Calling me Officer Smith seems a bit formal for this setting. Call me Sam."

"Is that your real name?"

"Does it matter?"

"Not in the least. So where's Officer Jones? Or is it John Jones? Or Jim or Joe?"

Smith waved to the waiter and indicated that two beers were required.

"We weren't married. He was just my partner for a while. I'm here on my own."

Two cold beers were plunked down on the table.

"Cheers," said Tom.

"To your health," Smith toasted.

They clinked glasses and took long sips.

"Ahhh. Lovely," said Smith. "This place is a dive, but the beer's always ice cold."

"Perfect place for a private meeting. Easy to be lost in a sea of white faces. Too loud for anybody to overhear or record. Too dim for photos."

Smith grinned at Tom. "Damn. It's just what I told Jones. You'd make an excellent officer. Bright, observant, ambitious. You know, it's not too late to join."

"I'm happy where I am right now."

"Really? Happy to have to sneak up to Hué? Happy to have a stupid boss who just doesn't get it? Happy to be treated like an idiot when you may be the only person in the entire fuckin' embassy who truly understands the politics of this country?"

Tom sipped some beer. "Tell me, Sam, why the hell am I here tonight?"

"I think we might be of use to each other."

"And to Vietnam?"

"Look, Tom, you're a real nice young guy, but let's face it, neither of us is in Vietnam for life. For you it's three years and out, for me it's only as long as I have a mission. Our country sent us here to do a job. When our time is up, mission accomplished or not, we'll be sent somewhere else. If you get too hung up on Vietnam, you're of little use to your own country. Now, if you are here to help your Uncle Sam, then you and I are on the same side."

"All right, let's say we're both here for the same reason: to help our nation stem the flow of communism and make the world safe for democracy. Then why try to intimidate me with those photos?"

Smith smiled sheepishly. "Yeah, that was a bit heavy-handed. It worked, though. I couldn't very well leave a calling card: S. Smith, CIA. I gotta maintain my cover. I could tell that you and that lovely lady were friends, and I figured you'd rush over to protect her. It worked, too, didn't it?"

"Plus, assuming that the lady and I are friends, and I cherish my job, I've got the possibility of extortion hanging over my head. I cooperate or else you tell my boss about my illicit trips to Hué; maybe show somebody that my friend is meeting with an American officer, which might put her in jeopardy with her own people."

"You've got a pretty active imagination."

"You work for an organization that has a reputation for underhanded tactics."

"Don't believe everything you hear."

"I believe what I see, and I've seen a blatant attempt at extortion."

"My apologies. Burn the photos if you want."

Tom stared at Smith.

"OK," said Smith, "I'll send you the negatives to show good faith."

"You can send the negatives to LBJ for all I care. You've got nothing on me."

"I've already apologized. I was just seeing what you're made of."

"Did I pass?"

"With flying fuckin' colors. You're loyal, committed to doing good, honest. Perhaps not the right qualities for my job, but I respect you and still believe we can help each other."

"Really? How is it we can help each other? No, wait, let me guess. You believe I'm making progress with establishing connections with the Buddhist community."

"Something the State Department has been too stupid and too big-oted to do to this point."

"I assume from your interest that it is also something the CIA has been unwilling or unable to do."

"You got that right."

Smith hadn't revealed whether the CIA had been unwilling or unable. Tom let it slide.

"So you're hoping that I'm willing to share my sources and information with you."

"Like I said, we're on the same side."

"Though maybe with different goals. I'm of the belief that we've made a grave error in ignoring the will of the majority, the Buddhists. We'll never succeed in stopping communism if we try to foist unpopular governments on the people."

"A noble view," said Smith.

"Yet what if you believe that the Buddhists are in cahoots with the Communists. You might attempt to penetrate the leadership and either corrupt it or eliminate it. That would go against everything I believe."

"What if I told you I meant no harm to the Buddhists?"

"Oh, and you'd give me your word?" Tom' s question dripped with skepticism.

"I see where that might be a problem. Given our reputation, there aren't a hell of a lot of people who will take our word on anything. It's a problem with being a spook. We don't inspire a lot of trust."

"That's half the problem. You claim that you can be of help to me, yet I don't see how. I'm focusing on the Buddhists. You don't seem to have any connections with them. Therefore, you don't have anything to offer me."

Smith smirked. "That's the first thing you've said that brings into question your intelligence. Or maybe it's just a sign of you being naïve. In order to gain the trust of the Buddhists, you're gonna have to do more than come across as a young buck who cares. 'I like you Buddhists. Now trust me and tell me what your plans are for Vietnam.' How far do think that's going to get you?"

Smith had a point. Anh had learned to trust Tom—after six months— and Nguyen seemed willing to discuss things in a general way. With one year gone and only two remaining, nothing of value had been achieved.

"How would it be," Smith continued, "if you could warn the Buddhists about a pending crackdown, or maybe give 'em some inside info about Ky's government that concerns 'em? You might very well earn their trust a bit quicker, gain access to the top leaders before you're shipped to Timbuktu or the Gobi desert. How would that suit you?"

"This isn't something they discussed with us in our State Department training sessions."

"No, I don't suppose so. Look, I'm not asking for a commitment, not requesting that you sign up as a junior CIA officer. All I'm saying is we should stay in contact. I learn something that may help you, I pass it on. You do the same in kind. I'm not talking classified information or national security secrets. I like you. I'm not aiming for you to end up in maximum security. This'd be hush-hush, not illegal."

Tom sipped his beer and looked around the bar.

"How would we contact each other?"

Smith smiled. "Kind of intrigued by this stuff, aren't you. Been reading James Bond. Seeing those sexy Bond girls."

"As long as nobody's going to be harmed..."

"We're engaged in a fuckin' war, Tommy boy. Of course people are going to be harmed. However, my goal is to win the fuckin' war, not to see how many bodies we can pile up."

"OK, I'll see where this leads, but I'm not promising anything."

"Terrific. So here's how it works. If you have anything that you think might interest me, tell the bartender here that you need to get in touch with Sam Smith."

"That bartender?" Tom nodded toward the tough-looking Vietnamese behind the bar.

"Any bartender. Word'll get to me. And don't worry none about me contacting you."

"That wasn't a concern. You managed to get a blank manila envelope onto my desk in the embassy. Obviously, you've got your ways."

"Indeed I do."

Tom drained his beer. "This one's on you, I assume."

"Hell, yes, as long as they accept checks from the CIA." Smith guffawed.

"One other thing. I'd rather not have you following me around with a camera."

"You only saw me 'cuz I wanted you to. I figured it would get your attention. If I really wanted to keep track of you, you'd never know. Anyway, it's not me you should worry about. If I can follow you and take pics, so can any number of people. I'd advise you to be a bit more cautious in the future."

"Good advice."

"That's free. Next time I'll expect something in return."

"The next beer's on me."

"That's a start."

The Buddhist situation deteriorated rapidly. Self-immolation by Buddhists monks increased, as did the rage of many Buddhists against

Ky's government. The daily political officers' meetings with Hard Case became more tense. Tom's gentle, yet persistent, suggestions that the United States start to incorporate more Buddhists into the dialogue were met with either glares from Case or commands to shut up. The progress that Tom thought he'd been making with Case proved illusory. By the end of the week Tom had stopped opening his mouth at the morning meetings. His frustration led to thoughts about requesting a transfer; he had even written a rough draft requesting one. Then one morning a blank envelope was waiting on his desk when he arrived at the embassy. The envelope contained a single sheet of paper with a single line: Arrest of Tri Quang imminent.

In spite of the urge to rush to Hué, Tom knew that was impossible. He remained at his desk until lunch, then hurried to the noodle stall. He ordered a bowl of noodles and waited until the other customers had left.

"I must get a message to Tri Quang," he told the stall owner.

"Perhaps I can find a phone number for the Dieu De temple."

"I cannot call myself. You understand?"

"Yes, I understand."

"If you can't reach the temple, perhaps you can reach my friend Tran or his sister Anh."

"I think I can do that."

"You must not use my name."

"That is OK. They will know it is you."

The assault on the Dieu De temple came two days later. Government forces had taken the temple, arrested Tri Quang and hundreds of followers, and had thrown them all in jail for undetermined lengths of time. According to Case, the string of self-immolations had been the last straw. Tri Quang had been present when an elderly Buddhist nun had doused herself with gasoline and lit herself on fire. He had then issued a statement blaming LBJ for the nun's horribly painful death, a death that Tri Quang claimed represented the horrible deaths of thousands of Vietnamese under Ky's repressive puppet government. A furious LBJ had ordered an end to Tri Quang's opposition movement, regardless of the cost.

Tom had left the meeting shaken. He didn't know if his message had gotten through to Tri Quang, wondered if the monk had purposely ignored it in order to become a martyr, and had no idea if Anh and Nguyen had been arrested. He couldn't go to Hué, and had no way of gaining any meaningful information. He briefly thought of contacting Smith, then wisely dropped the idea. Tom didn't want to give Smith any more leverage than necessary, and it would be foolish to call in a favor over a personal matter, especially since it would mean owing a favor in return.

With no true friends or allies in Vietnam, Tom wrote long letters to Suzie and Ira expressing his frustration and fury with his own government. Tom began to slide into a funk, even started hanging out with Stefan Boudreau, who consoled him with beer and sympathy.

"Tough luck, falling in love with a local girl. Never a good idea when you're working for State. Don't let it get you down. There's plenty of foxy women right here in Saigon."

Tom often had the urge to tell Boudreau to shut the fuck up, but he only opened his mouth to pour some more beer down it.

"Take it easy, boy. You haven't had a chance to build up a tolerance like I have."

Late in the evenings Tom would spout off, though he always maintained just enough control to say only what he knew Boudreau would want to hear.

"You were right all along, roomie. I was an idiot to fall for some babe in Hué when I could be having a great time right here in Saigon with you."

"Not *with* me," Stefan chuckled. "I hope not anyway. I was thinking more of one of these dark-haired beauties with firm tits."

Tom guffawed. "Of course that's what I meant. You're not my type."

At this point Boudreau would call over a bar girl and get her to sit on Tom's lap and whisper lewd suggestions in his ear. Though Tom would grin and act turned on, he never took one home. The next morning Tom would claim that he was too drunk to remember what he'd said or done, and Boudreau would assure him that he'd acted in a perfectly noble— meaning not manly—fashion. It was a good front, yet it wouldn't have lasted long except for three things: two letters and a message from Hué. The message was delivered via Tom's noodle man. Two weeks after the crackdown in Hué Tom was eating a bowl of noodles when the stall owner lowered his voice and leaned over the counter.

"Your friend in Hué has sent you a message."

The chopsticks slide from Tom's hands.

"Here is a clean pair," the noodle man said. "Your friend is fine. She was not arrested, though many were. She says it is not safe to visit at this time, it is still dangerous and she thinks she is being watched. She also sends her thanks for warning about the arrest of Tri Quang. He got the information, but still did what he had to do. She cautions patience."

"It seems the Vietnamese grow as much patience as they do rice."

"We have been invaded and occupied for two millennia. Over time one learns patience."

"I wish I had so much time."

Knowing that Anh and Tran were safe was a huge relief. Letters from Suzie and Ira were also enormous in elevating Tom's mood.

Dear Stud,

Life is good here in San Francisco. Tony has moved out, which was a relief. She became increasingly possessive and stopped the "bi" thing in order to concentrate on yours truly. I enjoyed the attention, but began to suffocate. I need my freedom. As well, I am currently more interested in spiritual pursuits (though not to the total exclusion of physical ones, with the right person).

Your news from VN is distressing. We hear a little in the States, though only a hint of what you wrote about. Our gov makes it sound like they're helping a popular president maintain order against the VC and Communist factions. They downplay the Buddhist thing for fear of giving ammo to the rapidly growing antiwar movement. By the way, I'm convinced it's not only in California, regardless of what the government says. Ira tells me that the antiwar movement is growing on the East Coast and only needs one incident to push the country against the war. I don't know if I believe him (you know Ira, ever the cynic who tries to make his opinion sound like fact), but I hope he's right. Your letter confirms what I've felt in my heart: no good can come from this war.

I can't adequately express in words how proud I am of you. I hope your friends are safe. Anh sounds special, though I would expect no less of the people you choose as friends. When you return I want details. Learn any new methods of pleasing a woman? More importantly, I'd like to know what you've learned about Buddhism and the spiritualism of the East. Maybe I'll visit next year, or we can meet in Tokyo or someplace where I can study Buddhism closer to its roots. It would be groovy.

Take good care of yourself. Don't forget to duck. Love always, Suzie

Ira's letter was pure Ira.

Tom,

You sign up to work for the bastards, then complain that they're a pack of bastards. I warned you! The government hires people for two reasons and two reasons only: to do the dirty work or to cover up the dirty work. The military-industrial complex is making a killing (literally and monetarily) while rubes like you are displayed to show that we're trying to understand the situation and aid the poor, helpless little brown people of Southeast Asia. What a crock of shit! The US government says it's studying and evaluating the situation, yet won't listen when honest putzes like you try to give them the real picture. Here's a piece of advice: Quit! You'll only grow more frustrated as we bungle our way deeper into the quagmire. What a fuckin' mess. Come home and join me in working against the war. Your firsthand knowledge would be invaluable to the growing antiwar movement. I could do an extended piece about you in the *Voice*, with an interview. It would be the right thing to do. As well, it would help my career, which is going nowhere fast.

Ira

Typical Ira. Telling Tom what to do with his life while still doing next to nothing with his own. Still, the arrival of the two letters, following closely on the news that Anh was fine, helped ease Tom out of his funk.

The next few months were a period of relative calm. The Buddhist movement had been seriously crippled by the mass arrests in Danang and Hué, and the Buddhist issue was rarely mentioned during the Monday-morning meetings. Though Tom still went out with Stefan Boudreau, he limited himself to a couple of beers. Boudreau stopped urging Tom to pick up one of the many bar girls who vied for his affection, reluctantly accepting that his roommate was still suffering from a broken heart. Tom spent most of his time studying Vietnamese, visiting Buddhist temples and establishing connections with the moderate Saigon Buddhist community. He was determined to rise in the State Department and fix what was obviously broken. He refused to become like Boudreau or Aaron Goldstein and Brent Lubner, who were content to do their research, write their reports, and accept whatever it was their superiors decided to do, or not to do. Tom swore that he'd make things better or get booted out trying.

Occasionally he stopped by Duffy's Pub, hoping to see Sam Smith. He had just finished his beer one evening when Smith walked in. The officer subtly scanned the room, strolled to the bar, ordered a beer, then sat down at Tom's table.

"What's a guy like you doing at a bar like this?" Smith quipped.

"Looking to thank you."

"Even though the information didn't save Tri Quang or the Buddhists from getting their asses kicked?"

"You knew it wouldn't help."

"Sure. Tri Quang can't afford to run and hide every time he hears there's gonna be a crackdown. That'd blow his credibility. Hell, these are people who would rather incinerate themselves than bow down to the military and a Catholic government. Think the threat of prison is gonna scare 'em? No fuckin' way. They gain more by being martyrs."

"Yet you warned me anyway."

"Sure. By sending a warning I earn Brownie points, gain some trust."

"I appreciate your honesty. So now I owe you a little, and the Hué Buddhists maybe owe me a little."

"Let's not talk debt among friends. I was glad to help, even if it didn't lead to immediate results. Hopefully your friend will appreciate the effort."

"Friends don't require presents."

"Maybe not, but they're nice to give anyway, as well as to receive."

"Thanks, friend," Tom said, ironically.

In September, four months after the May crackdown, Tom took the Friday evening train to Hué. Tran smiled when Tom strolled up to the stall.

"Mr. Tom, very nice to see you again."

"You too. I hope you and your family are well."

"Yes, all well. The troubles in May did not touch us."

"How is Anh?"

"You will see. She will be here any minute."

Tom surreptitiously looked around, half expecting to see Sam Smith. Instead, he saw Anh in the distance, biking toward the noodle stall. When she saw Tom she kept a straight face, though he could see in her eyes that she was happy to see him.

"Good morning," she said formally after leaning her bike behind the stall.

"Good morning," he replied, though he wanted to take her in his arms. "It's a lovely day, is it not?"

Anh allowed a smile to briefly grace her face. "Yes, it is a lovely day, though it will perhaps rain this afternoon."

Tom laughed. It was the rainy season; it rained every afternoon. They continued the small talk until Tom finished his noodles. As Anh cleared his bowl she leaned slightly toward him.

"Meet me at the An Cuu market at noon, in the vegetable section."

The An Cuu market was south of the Perfume River, on the southern edge of Hué. It was rarely visited by Westerners, so there was little chance of any Americans spotting the lovers. Tom walked the river until nearly noon, then made his way to the market. He was there a few minutes when a voice murmured in his ear.

"Hello, handsome."

Tom turned and smiled at Anh, though he refrained from embracing her.

"Come," Anh said. "I have a place for us."

He followed her through the maze of narrow streets until they stood in front of a small guesthouse.

"This is used by Vietnamese who don't have relatives in Hué when they come to visit temples. I know the owner, and she has agreed to rent us a room for the weekend."

"How kind."

They walked in and were greeted by a little old woman wearing the ubiquitous black silk *ao dai* worn by widows. Anh exchanged a few words with the woman, took the key that was offered, and led Tom to a room on

119

the third floor. It was sparsely decorated, containing a single bed, a small desk, and a bare bulb hanging from the ceiling. Wordlessly, Anh and Tom undressed, then fell onto the bed and made love. Afterward, they lay in each other's arms.

"I was frightened that you'd been hurt or arrested during the crackdown," Tom said.

"It was a terrible time, but I had a safe place to hide. After one week everything returned to normal."

"Normal? With Tri Quang in prison and hundreds dead?"

"You must understand. That is normal in Vietnam. The military attacks Buddhists or jails them in an attempt to intimidate us, we protest, they attack us some more, then life returns to normal. The same thing will continue as long as puppet governments remain in power."

"It must end some day."

"It will. The Buddha teaches that all things change, nothing is permanent."

"I will do my best to try to change the way my government operates in Vietnam, though nobody of importance listens to me."

"That too will change. I believe in you."

"Do any of the others in the Buddhist leadership believe in me?"

"Some. Nguyen does. He's the one I delivered your message to. Others think it was just a clumsy attempt by the Americans to gain our trust, to get a foot in the door, as you say. You cannot expect to be welcomed. Ever. You will always be a *farang*, a foreign invader."

"Then why do you welcome me?" Tom asked, stroking her breast.

"Because the Buddha taught love and acceptance. Also, I sense a Buddhist nature in you."

They spent the afternoon in bed, then walked the city at night, being careful to stay away from areas that Westerners frequented. Sunday was spent in parks and planning the near future. Anh knew of a small coastal city halfway between Hué and Saigon where they would be able to meet in private. She also provided Tom with the phone numbers of two friends who were willing to aid the lovers. They established a secret code—including pseudonyms—that would allow them to plan weekend rendezvous whenever Tom could safely get away. Tom boarded the train Sunday night in a state of euphoria, deeply in love with Anh. He was more determined than ever to push for changes in US political policy in Vietnam.

The rest of 1966 played out as it had begun. Ky remained in power and remained unpopular with most Vietnamese, though he still had the support of Lyndon Johnson. Government crackdowns were less frequent, in large part because most opposition leaders had been jailed or intimidated into silence. There was good news for Tom, however. Howard "Hard" Case's days in Vietnam were limited as his tour neared its end, as did those of Brent Lubner and Aaron Goldstein. Ever the optimist, Tom hoped for new colleagues who were more open minded, more willing to see the entire picture rather than the one LBJ wanted to be shown. Another piece of good news was that Suzie was coming to Thailand to spend a month in a Buddhist monastery. She had booked the trip to allow for a long weekend in Bangkok, and Tom had been granted leave to join her there. He flew to Bangkok the day after Thanksgiving.

Tom checked into the hotel and was informed that Suzie was waiting for him at the pool. He tipped the bellboy and asked him to put his suitcase in his room, then strolled to the pool. Suzie was lying on her stomach on a chaise lounge, wearing a bikini with the top unhooked.

"Hey, baby, looking for a good time?"

She raised her head and looked at Tom. "I thought that was a line for local hookers."

"I don't want to be sexist. Everybody should have the pleasure of being desired."

"Except the hookers only desire money. Besides, who in their right mind would try to pick up somebody who looked like a beached white whale."

"With all these skinny Thai girls, you stand out as one of the only real women here."

"That's why I love you, Tom."

Suzie tried to sit up while holding her bikini top in place.

"Let me help." Tom hooked the strap, then sat down and gave Suzie a long hug.

"Umm. That feels wonderful. Well worth the brutal trip it took to get here."

"Except you came for meditation, not to visit an old friend."

"I came to do both. I don't go to the monastery 'til Monday; that gives us plenty of time."

"Maybe I should go change into my swimming suit."

"Naw. I've had enough sun for one day. Let's get a drink. Come on."

They went up to Suzie's room. As soon as the door was shut Suzie put her arms around Tom, grabbed his butt, and gave him a long, wet kiss. His response was less warm than usual.

"Shit," Suzie said. "Am I sensing some hesitation?"

"No, not really," Tom said, though his words lacked conviction.

"Yes, really. You've got Anh on your mind, don't you?"

She pronounced it correctly, like 'on' instead of Ann, as Boudreau called her. Tom had written about his relationship with Anh. He hid nothing from Suzie, mainly because he never felt it necessary. Now he wondered if it might damage their relationship.

"Yeah. Anh is often on my mind."

"I wish I could meet her."

"Uh, I don't think she's as liberal as we are."

Suzie playfully pushed Tom away.

"Asshole. You think I'm looking for a threesome with your Vietnamese girlfriend?"

"It wouldn't be out of character."

"True, but I'd be happy to just have you between my legs."

Tom cringed.

"Will you lighten up," Suzie said. "I'm just kidding. We're friends. If we ball, that's wonderful. If we don't, that's fine too. I'm in Thailand to see a friend and continue to seek enlightenment. Everything else is just gravy."

Tom took Suzie by the waist and pulled her to him.

"Sorry I doubted you."

"Maybe you doubted yourself. Didn't think you'd have the willpower to keep your hands off me."

"I've always found you irresistible."

"Let's see if I still have the power of attraction. So what's the plan for the evening?"

"I thought we'd go to Wat Po, the Reclining Buddha. It's supposed to be spectacular."

"Cool. I've read that the soles of its feet are six feet high and covered entirely of mother-of-pearl. I'll rinse off."

"Great. I'll go to my room and unpack."

"Naw, keep me company. We only have the weekend together and I don't want to waste a single minute. That is, if it won't upset you to watch me shower and get dressed."

"I'm sure I can watch you without losing total control."

"In that case, come and sit in the bathroom while I shower."

Tom followed Suzie into the bathroom and sat on the toilet.

"Undo my top, if that's not asking too much."

He unhooked her top, then reached down and slid off her bottom.

"Thanks. How do I look?"

"Pretty damn good. I'd guess you lost ten or fifteen pounds."

"Twenty. It's my macrobiotic diet plus plenty of exercise; yoga and walking mostly."

Suzie turned on the shower and stepped in.

"Oh, this is lovely. Sure you don't want to rinse off after your flight?"

"Well..."

"Come on in and wash my back. I promise not to get frisky."

Tom hesitated. He loved Anh, yet they had never said as much, and neither had pledged fidelity. Besides, he and Suzie were old friends, and he was capable of being with her without having sex. Wordlessly he stripped and stepped into the shower.

"You're looking mighty thin, Tom. What have you been eating?"

"Mostly noodles, though plenty of fresh fruit and vegetables, lean chicken and fresh fish."

"Sounds healthy. Soap up my back."

He lathered up his hands and did as requested. Touching the familiar flesh caused Tom's heart to beat faster.

"That feels great," Suzie said. "Let me return the favor."

She turned to face him, lathered up her hands and reached around to soap his back. He put more soap on his hands and began to wash her front.

"You've still got magnificent breasts, in spite of your weight loss."

123

"And you've still got a magnificent dick," she said, grabbing his engorging penis.

They began to passionately kiss, then Suzie turned, put her hands against the wall, and spread her legs.

"How about one good fuck for old time's sake?"

Tom grabbed a breast with one hand and used the other to guide his erection into her. Afterward, they dried each other off and got dressed.

"You're a naughty boy, Tom."

"And you still turn me on. Now, let's seek some spiritual enlightenment."

They spent the weekend walking the streets of Bangkok, visiting temples, sunning by the pool, having sex, and talking. Their friendship, already a deep pool of memory and feelings, grew deeper still. Although casual observers may have assumed they were married or a longtime couple, theirs was a relationship that would last forever, yet never go beyond friendship. Not surprisingly, many of their discussions focused on Tom's role in Vietnam.

"I don't envy you," Suzie said during one of their last mornings together. They were sitting in the shade of one of Bangkok's many Buddhist temples. "Telling the State Department that they're fucking up Vietnam and stand no chance of defeating the 'enemy' with a repressive government could mean losing your job."

"That's only *if* anybody would listen to me."

"So why not take Ira's advice? Quit and try another career."

"I think the days of following Ira's advice are behind me."

"I hear what you're saying. Ira has always been good at giving advice, even when it has no rational basis. Besides, you and Ira are polar opposites."

"Sometimes I think that, other times I don't. We both believe the world can be a better place."

"But beyond that you've nothing in common. He blusters and complains, yet does nothing. You're a doer, a lifelong learner, whereas Ira thinks he already knows it all."

"Is that a fact? So tell me, what have I learned after twenty months in Vietnam?"

"Patience."

Tom smiled. "That seems to be The Word."

"Your lover Anh, Tri Quang, Nguyen, even Sam Smith, they've all bided their time 'cuz they had to. You've learned from them, and you'll use it to your benefit."

"I wish I had your confidence."

"It's from studying Buddhism. Siddhartha spent years trying to attain enlightenment. It wasn't until he tried everything—fasting for months, silent meditation, self-deprivation—that he decided to sit under the Boddhi tree and patiently wait for enlightenment. Forty days of sitting and meditating. Now that's patience. He wasn't eating noodles or sitting by a pool or slapping thighs with some dark-eyed beauty. So I have faith that you can spend three years in Vietnam trying to do good, even if you fall short of your goal."

"Which seems inevitable."

Now it was Suzie's turn to smile. "Notice how you said that falling short of your goal 'seems inevitable'? Ira would have said failure *was* inevitable. That's the difference between you and Ira. He doesn't even try 'cuz he knows he's going to fail, which he will every time. You keep trying, 'cuz even though failure seems likely, it's not inevitable.

Tom put his arm around Suzie's shoulder and squeezed.

"Thanks for being here with me. It couldn't have come at a better time."

"Even if you've been unfaithful to your lover?"

"Anh is beautiful and smart and strong; I may never find anybody like her again. However, I think we both know that there's no future for us. Vietnam is her home, always will be. For me it's a three-year assignment. I suppose that's why I let you seduce me."

"I didn't have to try very hard before you became very hard."

"True, and you never had to. You better take advantage of my weakness while you have the chance. One month in a monastery sounds like a whole lot of celibacy to me."

"I've gone longer without getting laid. Besides, who knows what really happens between Buddhist monks and nuns and guests."

"You're a deep-down-to-your-very-soul sinner, Suzie."

"It was one of Siddhartha's early steps toward enlightenment."

"Very early, I'd guess."

"At the start of the odyssey. So what? I'm still young."

CHAPTER 9—1967/1968

"So tell me, Tom, what's your assessment of the political situation here in Vietnam?"

Wayne Glass had replaced Howard Case as head of the political unit in Saigon at the start of the year. A man of no outstanding physical attributes—average height, average weight, sandy-brown hair with a receding hairline, late middle aged—Glass still managed to dominate a room. Perhaps it was his air of confidence, the way he looked you in the eye, his insistence on honesty and openness. He'd made a point of meeting privately with every member of his staff. Since nobody knew his political views or his opinion on the US effort in Vietnam, they tended to offer safe, neutral summaries restricted to their area of expertise. Stefan Boudreau had met with Glass the previous afternoon and told Tom he'd left Glass pretty much in the dark.

"Hell, I'm not going to risk my career by coming out on the wrong side. I mean, if I tell him we've screwed things up beyond repair, and he's an LBJ man, I'm in the shitcan. Same thing if I tell him we're winning and he's of the opinion that we need a totally new approach. Better to just give him a few platitudes, a few stats, and sit it out."

"What about our jobs? We've been asked to provide information."

"My job is to keep my job, and hope to Christ that I'm not sent to anymore war zones."

"Why'd you join the foreign service?"

"See the world. Land a cush job on the federal payroll. What about you?"

"I wanted to make a difference in the world."

Stefan chuckled. "Hell of a start."

Tom, however, didn't get the sense that Wayne Glass was out to discover his staffers' loyalties—or to cut young diplomats down to size. Something about the way Glass asked questions—as if he really wanted to know Tom's views—led Tom to open up with his new boss. Besides, he didn't join the State Department in order to "land a cush job on the government payroll." He could have worked for Barbara Bennett's father if his ultimate goal was to grow fat and rich.

"This place is a mess, sir."

"No need to call me "sir," Tom. I missed World War II and Korea because of flat feet, I'm not from the South, and we're both civilians. Call me Wayne."

"All right, Wayne. So where are you from?"

"Bedford, Oregon. Beautiful country."

"Why'd you leave it?"

"There's work to be done, and I figured to do some of it. I loved studying history and government at the University of Oregon, grew up with Japanese-American kids, and developed an interest in the wider world. What about you, Tom?"

Tom felt a thrill. Here was a like-minded person, somebody who seemed to share Tom's worldviews. Tom summarized his background, including a diplomatic review of his frustrating time in Vietnam.

"I met with Howard Case for a few days," said Glass, "seemed like a good man, though a bit set in his ways."

"You're a natural diplomat, Wayne."

"Never pays to trash a man simply because you don't agree with his views or methods. Sometimes you've got to work with people that you don't agree with. That's the nature of what we do. I began my career under Truman, then eight years under Ike, followed by Kennedy and now Johnson. Think I shared the same philosophy with them all?" He shook his head and smiled wryly. "No, you've just got to keep plugging away and staying true to your inner self."

"To thine own self be true."

"A literary man, eh? Can't go wrong with a little Shakespeare. Good to know I've got another literate man to converse with. So I'll ask again, Mr. Ivy League Liberal, what's your assessment of the political situation here? And I'm hoping for more than 'this place is a mess.' I've only been here a few days, and even I know that."

"Have you read Halberstam's *Making of a Quagmire*?"

"One of the first things I did when I landed this assignment. I have a great deal of respect for Halberstam. Been following his writing from the start."

"Then you already have a pretty good idea of what's happening here. Nobody wants to be the bearer of bad news, so everybody claims this war is winnable and says we're on the right track. All we need to do is keep bombing the North, keep pouring troops into the South, and keep supporting Ky because he's our man."

"So Rolling Thunder keeps rolling..."

"Which alienates the whole country and pushes the innocent victims toward the Communists."

"We approach having half a million men in country..."

"With questionable results, since the Vietcong just go underground and the ARVN boys are happy to sit back and let us fight their war."

"While Ky rules with an iron hand knowing that he's Johnson's man."

"Even though most of the people hate him and are rooting for Uncle Ho who they see as a national hero for fighting the Japanese, French, and now us."

"Pretty grim analysis," concluded Glass.

"If things weren't so grim, we wouldn't be sending half a million soldiers to fight in a jungle in Southeast Asia."

"Good point."

"So why doesn't LBJ see it?"

"Like every president, he can't help considering what the history books will say, not to mention his opponents. Johnson didn't start the war, but he inherited it and he'll be damned if he's going to lose it. You hit it on the head with the Halberstam stuff. LBJ keeps being told he can win, so he's going to do everything in his power to make it happen."

"Everything except listen to alternative ideas."

"That's what I'm here for. Somebody in the State Department apparently feels it's time to consider some different ideas. I'm known for keeping an open mind, for exploring options."

"Have you unearthed any viable options since arriving?"

"Not a single one. That's a problem at times with career diplomats. They start to think more about their careers than diplomatic possibilities. I sense you're different. "

"Maybe I'm more ambitious."

"Or maybe you really care. So talk to me."

"As you know, my area of expertise is the Buddhist community."

"Which Case allowed you to select because he figured it was a dead-end assignment."

"You're pretty well informed for somebody who recently arrived."

"I've had some unusual help. I was barely unpacked before I was contacted by the CIA."

Tom raised his eyebrows.

"An Officer Smith holds you in high regard. Seems to believe you're one of the only Americans in Vietnam who is committed to learning the entire story. Says you've taken your assignment to heart."

Tom squirmed in his chair.

"I'm not probing into your personal life. Smith says your fondness for Buddhist philosophy stretches back to your days at Columbia. He also says you don't let your personal life get in the way of your professional duty. That's good enough for me."

"Thanks."

"Just keep it that way, and be aware that others may not be as open minded as I am. Personal involvement may jeopardize your effectiveness, could be used to cast aspersion on your recommendations."

"I'll keep that in mind."

"So, what do you think needs to be done? Can anything begin to fix this mess?"

"Hold an honest, open election."

"Allow Buddhists and Communists to run?"

"Not the Communists. They've sworn to overthrow the government, so they've eliminated themselves. Buddhists? Got to have them."

"Antiwar candidates?"

"Anybody who doesn't have a criminal record and anybody who doesn't advocate the violent overthrow of the government."

"Washington won't go for it."

"We can't win this war, any war for that matter, without the support of the people."

They sat silently for a moment, each lost in their own thoughts.

"Thanks for your frankness," Glass finally said. "It's refreshing."

"May I ask a question?"

"Of course."

"My colleagues are under the impression that frankness can kill a career in the State Department. Is it possible to be frank and still advance?"

"As in any organization, one can speak one's mind if one is diplomatic, and if one finds somebody who is willing to listen."

"That's two 'ifs.'"

"I'm telling you like it is."

"I appreciate that."

"It remains to be seen whether the State Department will appreciate me telling them what it's really like here in Vietnam."

The State Department did not like Wayne Glass's recommendation for elections, but they accepted it. The next five months were taken up in meetings and negotiations with Prime Minister Ky and his advisors. Tom was glad that he had nothing to do with these meetings; such high-level discussions were usually carried out by Ambassador Lodge or Secretary of State Rusk and his people. Thanks to the departure of Case and the arrival of Glass—as well as the kind words from Sam Smith—Tom was now in the heart of matters in the political division. Neither Brent Lubner nor Aaron Goldstein resented Tom's elevated status, nor did Lubner's eventual replacement, who respected Tom's honesty and commitment. Stefan Boudreau appeared to have mixed feelings.

"You've managed to climb pretty high in under two years."

"I'm still doing what I was doing before: evaluating the Buddhists' role in Vietnamese politics."

"Yeah, but under Case that was like covering the role of albinos in American politics. Nowheresville. Now you're spending more time in Glass's office than the rest of us combined."

"I was damn close to being drummed out of the foreign service."

"You're right about that. If Hard Case had known about all your trips to Hué he'd have tossed you on the first plane out."

Tom was tempted to mention that Case only knew about some of his trips because Boudreau had been tipping him off. Then again, Boudreau himself only knew about some of the trips. It had been a lesson in trust and feigned friendship, one that Tom would never forget. Now that Tom was in good standing with his superiors, he could operate openly in Hué, though only professionally. His relationship with Anh, known only by the Buddhist community in Hué, still had the potential to cause problems if it became widely known in the American community. Sex with locals was accepted, as long as it wasn't flaunted. Intense emotional relationships might lead to questions about impartiality and misplaced loyalties.

Tom began to travel to Hué every other week, and he no longer needed to sit in the cabs of trucks leaving after dark. He flew on regular flights with Uncle Sam picking up the tab, and he rented a small apartment where Anh now lived. He paid the manager of a nearby hotel to take messages and accept mail so that the State Department would believe he was staying there. He also had enough money to pick up the tab when he met Nguyen at restaurants. Although Tom had hoped to meet some of the leaders of the Buddhist Community Association, that never happened. Nguyen remained his regular contact with the BCA, which was fine with Tom since he'd developed a close relationship with Nguyen and trusted him. Any tension that existed during their discussions had nothing to do with personalities or trust; the problem was, as it had been since the beginning, America's intentions.

"You claim that your nation is based on democracy, the will of the people," Nguyen said one evening over roast duck, steamed vegetables, rice, and beer, "yet you tell me that your government will not allow communists or pacifists to run for office."

"Nor anybody who is anti-American or favors negotiating with the North." Tom didn't agree with his government on these points, yet he could not openly disagree."

"That does not sound very democratic."

"There are restrictions on most freedoms in America. Free speech does not allow you to threaten lives or call for violent revolution. You are not free to murder somebody."

"Yes, yes, I understand that, but this is not the same thing. Pacifists do not advocate violence against anybody."

"My government will not allow anybody to run who advocates a policy that will lead to losing the war."

"So this is not about democracy. LBJ wants a well-crafted play that will give the appearance of democracy while assuring that their man wins the election."

Tom gnawed on a duck leg while he considered how to respond. He put the bone down and sipped some beer before answering.

"I'm looking for a more positive way of putting it."

"You're having trouble, though."

"Yes. Look, as you know, LBJ is from Texas."

"He is a cowboy, or at least sees himself as one. He is like John Wayne: big and tough and never backs down."

Tom grinned at the image. "You got that right. Since you understand the man, you'll understand that he absolutely will not allow South Vietnam to fall to the Communists."

"It is a political necessity as well as a personal one."

"Exactly."

"That means more American soldiers, more American bombs, more repression of my people."

"Maybe, maybe not. That's why I think this election is worth a chance. If it comes off smoothly, and if it's recognized by the international community, it may change things. The Vietnamese people might support their government rather than oppose it. That would lead to fewer crackdowns, perhaps more harmony. That would send a message to the North, which could lead to negotiations and a peaceful end to the war."

"That is a nice fairy tale, but I don't think you believe in fairy tales."

"No, I don't. I do believe that this is the best chance of establishing a stable government and reducing conflict within the South."

Nguyen silently nodded his head for a while, deep in thought.

"I will talk to my people and tell them what you have said."

"Good. I know this isn't perfect, far from it, yet I don't see a better option at this time."

"That is because President Johnson still believes he can win the war and ride off into the sunset with the girl."

Tom laughed. "You've seen too many Westerns."

"They are very instructive about the American way. I also like the action."

"If only all the action in the world could be restricted to movies."

The election turned out to be a worse fiasco than Tom could have imagined. Wayne Glass's valiant effort to produce a more democratic show was thwarted by Washington's fears. He even used Tom as point man on a few occasions.

"Play up the simple Midwesterner thing," Glass had counseled prior to Tom's big meeting with Ambassador Lodge and the Undersecretary of State for Southeast Asia. Glass thought that this meeting, held in late May, was the last chance to state their case. Once the decisions were made (when to hold the election, who could run with Washington's support, who would be barred) there would be no chance of changing them. "If you come off as some know-it-all punk, especially one who went to school in New York City, then the Texans will slam the door in our faces. On the other hand, if you're viewed as a bright young hayseed whose greatest wish is to see democracy spread across the globe—American-style democracy, be sure and trumpet that—then they might listen."

"A hayseed? One who's studied Buddhism and speaks Vietnamese?"

"All right, maybe that's laying it on a bit thick, but you see my point."

"You want me to be humble, yet confident in my knowledge and passionate in my belief in democracy and the American way."

"Damn, you're good. What am I worried about?"

"If we're thinking along the same lines, you're worried that the decision has already been made in Washington and this is only window dressing. If they really cared about our views we'd be meeting with LBJ and Rusk instead of the ambassador and an undersecretary."

"Yeah, that's what I'm worried about."

The meeting had been pleasant. The team from Washington appeared to be truly interested in Tom's views. The undersecretary was particularly impressed with Tom's knowledge of Vietnamese history, culture, and language. He and Ambassador Lodge asked Tom dozens of questions regarding the Buddhist community's opinion of the election. Tom urged the administration not to overlook the majority Buddhist population and to avoid the mistreatment of the Buddhists that had led to the failure of previous South Vietnamese governments. He was especially clear about the need for a unifying candidate, not simply another Catholic military leader who would immediately inspire fear and loathing from the masses. When the discussion ended everybody shook hands, and Tom received congratulations and thanks from Lodge for his valued contributions. Tom and Wayne Glass left the meeting feeling good and believing they stood a chance of affecting US policy.

As the summer progressed Tom gradually realized that his recommendations had been tossed in the shitcan. President Johnson had met with Ky and requested a special birthday present: a free and democratic election some time after Johnson's August birthday. As well, Johnson implied that his continued support for Ky would be in jeopardy if the election did not come off smoothly, since it was something the American public demanded. Ky's unpopularity led to a successful challenge from Head of State General Thieu. The result was that Thieu would run for president and Ky would become head of a powerful group that would guide national policy from behind the scenes. The initial appearance was of a new start for the government, though it was obvious to all that Thieu was just another power-hungry general who favored security and force over democracy. Antiwar candidates were barred from running, as was anybody who favored negotiations with the Vietcong or North Vietnam. The September election proved to be a global public-relations failure. Thieu won with a mere 35 percent of the votes. A dozen other candidates split the other 65 percent. Without a single candidate who was openly in favor of ending the war, the world knew that Thieu was yet another American puppet whose sole goal was defeating communism, regardless of the cost to his nation.

Tom only had six months remaining in Vietnam. In truth, he would have been eager to leave the country immediately if not for one thing: Anh. Though he had seen little of her in the months running up to the election, he planned on spending as much of his remaining time with her as possible. The weekend after the election Tom flew to Hué. As usual, Anh and he walked the streets of the city and spent hours in shady parks talking and holding hands. Sunday afternoon, a few hours before Tom's flight back to Saigon, they sat looking over the Perfume River.

"I'm going to miss you," Tom said, gazing into Anh's eyes.

"Not for long. You will have a new girlfriend very soon, I think. Or maybe you will marry your Buddhist friend from California."

The previous year, driven by guilt upon his return from the weekend in Bangkok with Suzie, Tom had confessed to sleeping with Suzie.

"Do you love her?" Anh had asked.

"Yes, though as a sister."

Anh's eyebrows shot up in surprise. "Do Americans usually have sex with their sisters?"

"All right, maybe not like a sister, more like a very close friend."

Anh's eyebrows arched again.

Tom shook his head. "I'm not explaining myself very well."

"What do you feel about this woman?"

"She's the best friend I ever had. She's smart and a good listener and a deep thinker. She forces me to be honest with myself, to be true to my ideals. I trust her and believe in her."

"And you like to have sex with her."

"Indeed I do."

"But you don't want to marry her?"

"No, and she doesn't want to marry me. We know we weren't destined to be married."

"So, what do you feel about me?"

Tom turned toward Anh and took her hand in his.

"You are smart and beautiful, and I have enormous respect for your commitment to your community and nation. I am the luckiest man alive to be with you, even if it's only for a few days every other week."

Anh smiled and squeezed Tom's hand, then let looked wistfully at the Perfume River.

"I noticed that you asked if I wanted to marry Suzie, yet didn't ask me the same question about you."

Anh turned from the river and gazed into Tom's eyes. "Sometimes, when I awake in the middle of the night and you are lying next to me, I wonder what it would be like to be married to you. Then I realize that will never happen. Like you and your friend Suzie, you and I are not destined to be married. You too know this to be true."

"Yes, I do, though I wish it were otherwise."

"Maybe at a different time, at a time without war, at a time when it would not matter that I am Vietnamese and you are American."

"I'll always carry a part of you in my heart."

Still, something kept stirring in the back of Tom's mind. Or was it deep in his heart?

The precipitous decline of the American mission in Vietnam began to accelerate in late 1967. Increased bombings by the United States, including the use of napalm and herbicides such as Agent Orange, alienated innocent civilians, as did the Americanization of Vietnam: gambling, prostitution, drugs. The faster the fall, the harder Westmoreland and LBJ tried to sell the war to the American people, yet the rising body count of young American GIs began to inexorably turn the public against the war. The rumbling of the nascent antiwar movement that had blossomed on US campuses started to filter through to the wider community. As the final few months of Tom's posting in Vietnam wound down, he felt the welling of a profound sadness. His three years of work, of studying the language and culture, of falling in love with the country and Anh, were drawing to a close. If this was what life in the State Department was all about, he had better rethink his future, because he wasn't sure he could tolerate a career of frustration, of failure, of saying goodbye every three years to something to which he had given so much of himself.

Tom's three-year assignment was scheduled to draw to a close at the end of February. Stefan Boudreau told him that new assignments were usually received two to three months before reporting date, enough time to prepare for the move, begin studying a new language if necessary, and wrap up the current assignment. After a hearty Thanksgiving dinner hosted by Wayne Glass and his wife, the five men of the diplomatic corps were sipping cognac when Tom broached a subject that was on his mind.

"Is it possible to get an extension on a posting?"

"You mean you want to stay *longer* in this tropical war zone?" asked Dick Dunn, the young man who had replaced Brent Lubner three months previously.

"Sounds like three years in Oslo spoiled you for humid climates," chuckled Boudreau.

"It's not just the humidity and bugs," replied Dunn, "it's everybody carrying guns that I'm having trouble with. Maybe you get used to it. The guns and the humidity."

"Our colleague Tom never seemed bothered by the climate," said Boudreau. "Hell, he seems to love it, though I suspect it's not the love of the climate that prompted his question."

"In response to your question, Tom," said Wayne Glass, "yes, extensions have been granted, and considering the work you've done here in Nam, I don't suppose you'd have too much trouble having it granted."

Something in Glass's voice sounded less than enthusiastic.

"Am I hearing a 'but'?" Tom asked.

"More of a 'however.' I think this is a discussion we should have in private, and not after having polished off half a dozen bottles of wine."

"This might be instructive for all members of State, especially junior members like Dick," said Boudreau. He clearly didn't want to be left out of what promised to be a juicy topic.

"My private life—assuming that's what you're referring to—hasn't been private since I joined the State Department," said Tom. "Wayne, if it's about my relationship with Anh, I have nothing to hide."

"Do you plan on making the State Department a career?"

"That was the plan."

"Do you intend on making Anh your wife?"

"That certainly wasn't my original intent. I mean, I've never given marriage much thought, and I had planned on concentrating on my work for a while before getting married and starting a family. Now, with time running out..."

"So now you're wondering what would be the effect on your career should you marry Anh," concluded Glass.

"Yes, though purely hypothetical."

"Let me ask you a question first. How do you think Anh would do in Oslo? Any Vietnamese restaurants in Norway, Dick?"

"None."

"Does it ever get hot in Norway?" Glass asked.

Dunn barked a laugh. "If you consider eighty degrees hot, and it only hits that a couple of days in July. Rest of the year you're lucky to see sixty degrees, and that's not even talking about the snow or endless nights during the winter."

Glass looked at Tom and raised his eyebrows in a question.

"I guess I hadn't considered that aspect," Tom said.

"People don't usually think of climate when they're in love. You asked about how marriage would affect your career; nobody asks how career will affect marriage."

"So how would asking for an extension affect my career?"

"If it's to further our mission, it could help your career, especially if we manage to finally have some success here. On the other hand, if it's about Anh, it may not be beneficial. What if you get posted to northern Europe or someplace equally inhospitable for a Vietnamese? That might be tough on Anh, and believe me, an unhappy wife makes for a difficult assignment." Glass looked at the doorway to see if his wife was in hearing distance. "I can't go into detail, but early in my career I was posted to the Congo. Put a severe strain on our marriage, and, I hate to admit it, I didn't do my best work. If my wife wasn't so well liked by the ambassador, it might have put a serious crimp in my career. That's another point to consider. I'm sure Anh is a lovely woman, but let's be honest, having a Vietnamese wife will not advance your career. And how comfortable will Anh be in Washington among the other government wives? So, bottom line? If you ask for an extension, and if you marry Anh during that year, your personal and professional life may suffer."

"Wayne's right about prejudice and our government," concurred Aaron Goldstein. Goldstein was on his second extension, something unusual in the foreign service. Since his work was not that vital or successful, everyone assumed his requests for extensions were for personal reasons. Although it was never discussed, Goldstein had been spotted a few times in the company of effeminate Vietnamese men, very young men. "Any variation from the norm of having a white wife and you can forget dreaming about being an ambassador or head of a branch. I've been turned down for every plum position I've ever applied for."

"If you want a friend's advice," said Stefan Boudreau, "have a great time with Anh while you're here, then accept your next posting. You've got a bright future in the State Department."

The truth was that Tom wasn't completely sure how he felt about Anh, wasn't sure how much of his feelings were infatuation and how much true love. Anh had as much as said that marriage wasn't in their future, that Vietnam was her home, and that she knew Tom's future was elsewhere. Would he jeopardize his career—and spend another year in this frustrating, seemingly hopeless assignment—while pursuing a relationship that most likely had no future?

"Thank you all for your honesty and candor. You've all given me a lot to consider."

Tom picked up his cognac, stared at the amber liquid, then drained his glass.

Tom and Anh spent Christmas on a beach near Hoi An. They slept late, drank a lot of coffee, read, and avoided any talk of the future. Tom had not received the orders for his next assignment, which meant there still might be time to request an extension. He was continuing to struggle over what to do. Finally, as they sipped beer and looked out over the South China Sea during their last night in Hoi An, it was Anh who broached the subject.

"Have you learned where you are to be assigned next?"

"Not yet. Actually, I've been thinking about that quite a lot lately, and..."

Anh reached over and gently placed her index finger on Tom's lips, silencing him.

"I have loved our time together. You will always be in my heart, but I am Vietnamese, and you are American. This is my home. When the war is finally over, I will be here. You will not."

"I've met many Frenchmen who remain in Vietnam, and I understand there are many Englishmen who live in Malaysia and Singapore. I imagine many Americans will stay here."

"Yes, though not you. You are doing important things here. Do you really believe you will be able to do important things if you stay here and stop working for your government?"

"You could come with me. Then I could do important things in other countries and you would still be with me."

"What would I do? In Vietnam I too am important. I am part of the effort to free my country from foreigners. People like you. What would I do in Paris or New York?"

"You would be beautiful."

"Is that why you love me? Only for my beauty?"

"Your beauty and your spirit and your mind."

"My beauty will fade some day, and my spirit lives here, in my country. As to my mind, I hope it is worth more than just to be a good wife. When Vietnam is free, really free, I will be needed."

"God, how I'll miss you."

"We are together now, and that is all that matters. The Buddha teaches that to live in the future is of as little value as living in the past. Let us enjoy each other today. Here. Now."

Tom leaned over and kissed Anh passionately.

"I wish we could stay in this moment forever," Tom said.

The next morning they took a taxi to the train station. Anh's train for Hué left an hour before Tom's headed south toward Saigon. They sat silently together on a wooden bench, holding hands, until Anh's train pulled into the station. Tom carried Anh's small suitcase to the train, and they stood at the foot of the steps, looking into each other's eyes. When the train sounded its whistle to announce its imminent departure, they kissed briefly and Tom handed Anh her suitcase.

"I'll see you soon," he said.

"Yes, very soon."

He watched her climb the steps, then walked down the platform until he saw her take her seat next to the window. They smiled at each other until the train started to move. Tom waved and continued to smile until Anh was out of sight. Even when the train disappeared from view he continued to stand on the platform, staring north toward where the train was heading. A sense of deep loss started to permeate his being. *Yes, all things are transient*, he acknowledged, *but does change have to be so painful?*

The winds of change were blustering across the United States and Vietnam at the dawn of 1968, though most people had yet to realize the depth of that change. In the States the antiwar movement was starting to emerge, especially in the form of Eugene McCarthy, the antiwar Democrat who had declared in late 1967 that he would challenge LBJ for the Democratic presidential nomination in 1968. Even more disturbing to the Texan was the early indication that Bobby Kennedy was also considering challenging Johnson for the nomination, based on Kennedy's own growing opposition to how the war was being managed. The emerging split in the Democratic Party foreshadowed the division that would soon split the nation: anticommunist and prowar versus emerging globalists and propeace.

America had started on the rough road from the 1967 San Francisco Summer of Love to the 1969 mayhem and murder of a fan at the Rolling Stone concert at Altamont. Some historians trace this precipitous decline to an event on January 31, 1968, that would forever alter the Vietnam War and the course of American history. That event occurred in South Vietnam.

Tom had taken to drinking at Duffy's Pub, though he knew it had less to do with thirst than with the hope of encountering Sam Smith. Tom was fully aware of the irony that he—an Ivy-educated diplomat who believed in the democratic process—would crave the friendship of a man who used covert operations to subvert legally elected governments and who himself might even be an assassin. Still, he preferred Smith's professional duplicity to the lazy, self-serving cynicism of Stefan Boudreau and his ilk. For some unfathomable reason, Tom trusted Smith more than any of his own State Department colleagues, save for Wayne Glass.

It was a mid-January evening, and there was a feeling of tension in the air at Duffy's, an unidentifiable sense that something wasn't quite right. The tough men who packed the tables leaned forward and talked in hushed tones, frequently glancing over their shoulders as if expecting something or somebody unsavory. Tom was sitting at his usual corner table, holding his beer with both hands, watching the men and catching some of their anxiety.

"Sorta spooky, eh?"

Tom looked up to see Sam Smith standing next to him.

"Is that supposed to be funny? Coming from a spook?" Tom said it low enough not to be overheard, though Smith didn't seem concerned.

"Nothing funny about it, and you're lucky I'm a friend and not Charley with a knife."

"I would have thought I was safe here in Saigon, especially with friends like you watching my back."

"Do we ever really know who our true friends are? As to being safe in Saigon, well, let me grab a cold one and we can discuss that topic. Ready for a fresh one? The way you're clutching that glass, the beer must be blood warm."

"Nice image. Yeah, I'd love a cold one."

When Smith returned with the beers they resumed their conversation.

"So you feel it too," Tom said.

"It's my job, and I'm damned good at it."

"Yet the war seems to be stalemated. No major victories or defeats for either side, our troop level is fairly stable, Thieu's government appears to be gaining a toehold, and all indications are that we'll be here a long time, supporting unpopular governments."

"You suppose that Uncle Ho and his cadres are content with a stalemate? Think they'll settle for us being here a couple of decades more?"

"No, that doesn't seem likely. So what do you guess is next?"

"I don't guess. I form hypotheses based on extensive research."

"What a bucket of bullshit."

Smith smiled. "Just trying to put it in terms an Ivy Leaguer would understand. So what do I think? I think the shit's gonna hit the fan sometime soon. Though the 'when' and 'where' and 'how' continue to elude me."

"So how did your 'extensive research' lead to that conclusion?"

"There's been some unusual activity lately, the kinda stuff Charley wouldn't normally do."

"For example."

"Khe Sanh."

Khe Sanh was a marine base near the border with North Vietnam. After a series of attacks on bases in the northern provinces of South Vietnam, the Vietcong seemed to be focusing their forces on Khe Sanh. Engaging in a set battle was contrary to the Vietcong's usual guerrilla tactics. At the same time, there was a significant movement of North Vietnamese forces toward the same area. In response, the United States had been moving troops to counter the buildup.

"Westmoreland says it's proof that the Communists are desperate," Tom said. "The good general claims it's a huge tactical blunder since they lack the firepower to stand up to us in a toe-to-toe fight."

"The 'good general' couldn't find his fuckin' nose with a mirror. Besides, he's got to say positive things, assure the rubes back home that we're kickin' ass. You've been here nearly three years. In your educated opinion, what quality would you say is the Vietnamese people's most effective weapon in dealing with foreign invaders?"

"Patience," Tom said without hesitation.

Smith grinned. "Another 'A' for the genius. So why would such patient motherfuckers send tens of thousands to their death against the firepower of the U S of A? They know we'll drop a shitload of bombs on any concentration of troops, be they Cong or NV regs. So why the obvious, blatant, doomed-to-get-your-ass-kicked assault on Khe Sanh?"

"A diversion?"

"That'll earn ya a gold star, buckeroo."

"Do you suppose Westmoreland sees the same thing but plays the dumb American in order to lull the Communists into making an error?"

"You give the 'good general' more credit than he deserves. I've been warning the military that something's up; they treat me like an idiot. 'You CIA always see conspiracies.' The ignorant pricks. Hanoi is starting to discuss possible peace talks, yet the fuckin' generals don't think anything's amiss when Hanoi mentions possible peace talks while at the same time throwing a hundred thousand soldiers at some piss-ass Marine base? They're jerkin' us in six directions at once, and the Einsteins running the war think everything's just dandy.

"So what's the diversion about? What is the real target?"

"If I knew that I'd be meeting with a State Department bigwig instead of sipping a beer with one of its underlings."

"Yeah, but you'd rather have a beer with me than champagne with one of those necktie-wearing uptight peckerheads."

"Damn right. I don't even like champagne."

"Anyway, no point in worrying about it until after Tet."

Tet is the lunar New Year celebrated by Buddhists, a massive holiday when Vietnamese travel throughout the country visiting relatives and paying respect to the deceased.

Smith's eyes narrowed as he looked at Tom. "Right, the Communists have pledged a ceasefire during Tet."

"You sound skeptical."

"It's my job to be skeptical. Besides, I don't believe 'em."

"Because they're godless commies?"

"Naw, I don't believe 'em 'cuz they're too smart to make stupid promises. You know the saying: all's fair in love and war. Well, we in the 'civilized' world don't buy that, what with the Geneva Conventions and our refined sense of nobility. We respect white flags when they're waved and don't torture prisoners and never wage war on civilians. Bullshit! Truth is we're hypocrites, though we take the high ground and claim otherwise. Not so the VC and Northies. To them this is war, and all's fair. We invaded their country and flooded it with our troops and weapons and morality, and we expect them to fight fair so we can whip their asses. That ain't gonna happen. They've assassinated civilians and tortured prisoners and terrorized the people, and they're gonna continue to do so and worse. I sure as hell would do the same if I was in their position. What do you think of this scenario? The VC and army of the North stage a massive diversionary campaign near the border, drawing our attention to the north. At the same time they start to mumble about peace talks so that we think they've had enough of fighting. Now we got Tet. There's a ceasefire—though not in Khe Sanh, you'll note—and every Tom, Dick, and Nguyen is allowed to travel around the country to visit relatives, though their bags are full of guns and bombs, instead of the presents and live chickens you'd been led to believe are in them. The VC have been storing stockpiles of weapons throughout the south for just such an event."

"Fact or part of the scenario?" Tom interrupted.

"Both. I know the VC have been stockpiling weapons. Hell, that ain't no big deal. Any guerilla army with half a brain would do the same. But my sources have been going on about more weapons than usual, more than you'd expect as a big holiday approaches. I've also heard that there have been more communications between Charley and Hanoi than usual."

"I assume you've intercepted some."

"Sure, we always do, but we never know which ones are real and which ones were dropped in our laps to put us on the wrong trail. That's the essence of covert operations, trying to differentiate between the real and the appearance of real."

"Let's say your scenario is brilliant and you've nailed it this time. Now what?"

"Now what, indeed. It's like the boy who cried wolf. If I tell 'em that Charley is about to strike and they put the troops on high alert and nothing happens, then they won't listen to me next time. If I don't tell 'em and Charley strikes, then I've blown it and they'll blame me for not warning them and they won't listen to me next time. "

"So the only way you can win is to get it right, warn the military in time, and smash the Vietcong before they can do any damage. Easy."

"Yeah, a breeze." Smith smiled and shook his head. "You know, this might be a good time for you to sound out your sources, see if you can catch a whiff of what's in the breeze."

Tom winced ever so slightly.

"Look, Tom, I'm not asking you to betray anybody. I'm just asking if you could kinda ask around. I mean, if you don't wanna…" Smith let the words trail off.

"I appreciate that you haven't said, 'I warned your friends two years ago in Hué and you owe me.'"

"Maybe I'm saving up debts for later."

"Maybe you are, but you're too clever to pull a 'you owe me.' You helped me in the past and you know I remember that. If I ever learn anything that can help you, I'll pass it on."

"As long as it doesn't threaten your friends or your friendship with them."

"Exactly. Tell you what, I've been trying to book a flight or train to Hué. No luck so far, what with so many Vietnamese traveling."

"How dare they book up all the seats in their own country," Smith grinned.

"Yeah, the nerve. Anyway, if I manage to get to Hué I'll check around, ask a few questions, see what I can find out. If I learn something I'll call you."

"Thanks, Tom."

"No need to thank me. What are friends for?"

Tom never made it to Hué. He'd never been busier in his entire life. As the troop level approached half a million, the embassy was pressed to find local staff to service the growing American contingent, and respond to the growing number of problems that such a huge foreign presence created. As well, with LBJ looking to the November election and knowing that his chances of reelection seemed to fall as the troop level rose, there was greater pressure to win the war, be it politically or militarily. The result was that Tom could be found at his desk at the embassy seven days a week, from early in the morning until late at night. He hadn't been to Duffy's or talked with Sam Smith in nearly a month. The only thing he had to look forward to was his weekly calls to Anh. They had set up a regular Sunday evening call when Anh would be waiting by the phone. If Tom was unable to call Anh, or she was unavailable to answer the phone, he would try the following night, and if that failed they would have to wait until the next Sunday.

It was the Sunday before Tet that Tom talked with Anh for the last time. During the weekend of the lunar New Year everything would be crammed to capacity: trains, planes, roads, even the phone lines. Anh had warned Tom that he might have trouble getting through to her, so he was enormously relieved when she answered the phone on the first ring.

"Hey, Anh. I've been thinking of you all week. I really missed you."

"Yes, me too."

Tom immediately sensed that something was not right. Anh's voice was strained, devoid of the warmth that normally carried through the phone.

"How are you? Is everything all right?"

He could hear her breathing, could sense that something was not right.

"Tom, you must be very careful this week. Keep your eyes open. Be on your guard."

"Me personally?"

Silence.

"All *farang*?"

Silence.

"There is an official ceasefire for the entire Tet holiday," Tom mentioned, as if Anh didn't know.

"When people are desperate, they do desperate things."

"All's fair in love and war."

"What?"

"It's a saying. When people are in love or in war they do whatever is necessary to win. Somebody said it to me recently while discussing the war. Actually, he was talking about the Tet ceasefire. Said he didn't trust the Vietcong to respect it."

"Who was this man?"

"The same one who warned me about Ky's crackdown on the Buddhists two years ago."

"Will you tell this man about my warning?"

"I love you. I don't love him."

He'd never told Anh he loved her, hadn't felt compelled until that minute. He had a sudden flash that he'd made a mistake by not asking to have his assignment in Vietnam extended a year. Tom had selected career over love; now he was stuck with his choice, separated from the woman he loved at an extremely dangerous time.

"Anh, I'm going to try to get to Hué tomorrow. I'll call and tell them I'm sick and can't work this week."

"No," she said forcefully. "Do not travel. Do not go to work. Call in sick and stay home."

"I want to be with you."

"I want to be with you too, but it is not safe now. Maybe after Tet."

"Will you be safe?"

"Yes, of course."

He didn't believe her. There was something in her voice that carried... what? Fear? Excitement? Determination?

"I'll talk to you next Sunday?" Tom asked hopefully.

"Yes."

"I do love you, Anh."

There was a pause. "I love you too."

Tom put down the phone. Anh's message was unambiguous. Something big was about to go down. Smith had been correct. The Tet ceasefire was a sham. The battle at Khe Sanh was most certainly a diversion. Tom suddenly realized that he faced a dilemma: should he contact Smith and tell him what he'd just learned? It was Smith's tip two years previously that had helped open the door with the Buddhists, that had convinced them that Tom might be a legitimate friend of the Buddhist community rather than an American agent trying to infiltrate their organization. Smith had been the closest thing to a true friend in Vietnam. Didn't he owe Smith a warning? And what of his responsibility as an employee of the State Department? Then again, Smith already knew that something was going on. Hadn't Smith told him that a month earlier at Duffy's? Tom couldn't ignore one other important point: if he told Wayne Glass about Anh's warning, there was the possibility that Anh's life would be in jeopardy.

Sam Smith would have been the first to acknowledge that security leaks were common. Just as Tom and Smith shared information, many US government workers shared information with contacts and acquaintances. Tom could imagine somebody in his own office passing the warning on to a friend or lover, and that person passing the message on until hundreds, perhaps thousands knew. Then it would only be a matter of time before somebody learned that Tom was the source of the information, and somebody who knew of his relationship with Anh would assume that she was the original source of the warning. How long would it take to get back to the Vietcong, thus sealing her doom? Yes, he owed Smith, but he loved Anh, and that, he finally decided, is where his ultimate loyalty resided. Smith was a well-informed guy. He would do fine without a call from Tom.

During the evening of January 30, 1968, the eve of the lunar New Year, all hell broke loose in South Vietnam's cities. Preparation for the Tet Offensive had begun months earlier, when Vietcong cadres started to store weapons in cities throughout the south. Then, under the cover of the Tet truce, the Vietcong moved into those cities, uncovered the weapons, and waited for the prearranged time. Suddenly, the VC ruthlessly assaulted US and ARVN forces, military bases, communication facilities, and—most alarming to Americans who watched the event on the evening news—the US embassy in Saigon.

Tom was in a deep, dreamless sleep when he was jolted back to life by the nearby sound of explosions and shots. He ran into the living room as Stefan Boudreau emerged from his bedroom.

"What the hell's goin' on?" Boudreau asked, his voice elevated and shaky with fear.

"Unless it's the Fourth of July, I'd say there's a firefight going on."

"But it sounds like it's comin' from the embassy. Who the hell'd attack the embassy?"

The question was so stupid that Tom didn't bother to respond. The explosions and shooting continued, and they seemed to grow fiercer by the minute.

"What do you think we should do?" Boudreau asked. "I mean, we're not military. They certainly don't expect us to grab a gun or anything. Do they?"

"With nearly half a million GIs in country I think we'd just be in the way. Sit tight."

Tom went into his room, dressed in his workout clothes, and returned to the living room.

"What are you doin'?" Boudreau asked.

"I'm going to take a look around."

"You're not serious."

"Serious as a heart attack."

"What the hell for?"

"Curiosity."

"Curiosity killed the cat."

"Knowledge brought him back."

On that childish note, Tom walked out of the apartment and into a world he'd never known. It was early in the morning, not yet dawn, a time when Saigon was as close to sleep as a city can be. There were no buses, few cars or motorcycles or people, yet the city was humming with life, and death. The loudest sounds of warfare came from the US embassy, which was a few blocks away. Tom could also hear fainter sounds of fighting coming from the direction of the imperial palace and Saigon's main radio station. He slowly walked toward the embassy, keeping close to the shelter of the buildings and being careful not to make himself too visible a target.

A block from the embassy his path was blocked by a contingent of marines who had just pulled up in jeeps and personnel carriers. They appeared to be preparing to storm the embassy. As Tom approached, one of the marines suddenly turned and leveled his gun at Tom, who instinctively threw his arms up.

"Jesus fuckin' Christ," the marine snapped. "I almost shot you. What the hell are you doing here?"

"I work in the embassy."

"Not today you don't. Get your butt off the street."

Tom backed into the shadow of a building and stood rapt in awe. He had no idea how many Vietcong had attacked the building, couldn't see a single one, in fact, yet over the next hour he watched as hundreds of GIs arrived and leapt into action. The fighting was sporadic, and relatively few shots were fired. When the day had fully dawned he went back to the apartment to shower and change. He ate breakfast, filled Boudreau in on what little he'd seen, then went back to the embassy. By midday the fighting was over and the small band of nineteen invaders had all been killed.

When they declared the embassy compound secure, Tom entered and wandered around in a daze, along with dozens of the embassy staff. At one point he noticed that people were streaming toward a gathering next to the main building. As Tom approached he realized that General Westmoreland was holding a press conference. Tom hovered on the edge of the crowd as Westmoreland blasted the cowardly Vietcong for breaking the Tet truce. He reported that surprise attacks had occurred throughout South Vietnam in more than a hundred cities. Although most of the VC had been killed and most of the cities were now secure, fighting still raged in a few places, particularly Hué. Tom caught his breath when he heard this, but was soon drawn back to Westmoreland's speech, a speech that Tom realized was just a variation on the same bullshit the general had been spouting since his arrival in Vietnam.

Westmoreland was confident that the staggering casualties suffered by the VC indicated a desperate mass suicidal act that meant the end of the guerilla movement. Then again, the general had been forever saying that the VC were an uncoordinated ragtag force that represented little more than an annoyance to the mighty US military machine. He'd been proven spectacularly wrong on that count, and Tom had a gut feeling that Westmoreland was yet again wrong. Constant US claims that the war was nearly won, that they could "see the light at the end of the tunnel," now appeared to be hopelessly optimistic at best, and possibly no more than blatant lies. Sam Smith had certainly known that. Tom froze in mid thought. Would Officer Smith suspect that Tom had forewarning about the assaults? Tom felt a flush of guilt, then he flashed on Anh, and his blood went cold.

His first thought was that he had to get to Hué, then he realized it would be impossible. In the first place, he had duties at the embassy, duties that would assuredly be augmented due to the Tet Offensive. It was also highly likely that all travel would be forbidden until the country was secured, if there was such a thing now. More seriously, with the fighting still raging in Hué, he stood little chance of being allowed near there. Lastly, and perhaps most importantly, he was clueless as to Anh's status. With close ties to the radical Buddhist movement, she might be hiding from possible retaliation from ARVN and US forces. There was even a chance—and this was something that Tom had only wondered to himself, being too fearful to broach the subject with Anh directly—that Anh herself was a member of the Vietcong. If this was the case, she might be dead. Regardless, there was nothing for Tom to do but wait until the fighting in Hué stopped, at which time he would get to Hué as quickly as possible.

Except the battle in Hué raged on, a savage battle that was one of the bloodiest instances of urban warfare during the entire conflict. Tom struggled daily with the urge to hitchhike to Hué, an insane act had he tried it. Fortunately, his colleagues, aware of his relationship with Anh, kept him busy with new assignments and offers of evenings out. Stefan Boudreau was especially thoughtful. Boudreau had requested an additional year in Vietnam. Although he claimed the need to complete research, everybody knew that Boudreau loved the decadent life he was living in Saigon: an endless supply of cheap booze and cheap bar girls. This had added to Tom's dislike of his roommate. Now, he was pleasantly surprised to find that Boudreau had become a friend. Tom brought it up one night over drinks at the Continental.

"Stefan, thanks for what you're doing for me."

"I didn't do nothing 'cept invite you for a drink, and I expect you to pick up the tab."

"Sure. To be honest, I was...how shall I put it...resentful of you during my first year."

"Really? Just because I was ratting you out to Hard Case?"

"Yeah, mostly that."

"And because I was suckin' up to Case and telling him whatever he wanted to hear?"

Tom smiled. "Yeah, that too."

"Now that you're bein' honest, you gotta admit you weren't just pissed at me the first year."

"Well..."

"You have a pretty low opinion of my lifestyle, my whoring to be more precise."

Tom focused on his beer.

"The feeling was mutual. Not that you were whoring—I do believe that you love that gal in Hué. No, I'm referring to your sincere Boy Scout thing. You made me look bad, and I was kinda jealous and figured to take you down a notch or two."

Tom's face registered the shock he felt.

"Yeah, I know, I was being a butthole. Truth be told, I hold you in the highest regard. Your whole act ain't an act; you're the real deal. I even considered trying to be more like you, then I realized I couldn't 'cuz a person's gotta be who they are. Oh, you can change some things, the color of your hair and your weight and your education and such, but ultimately you are who you are, and you're a good man. You're not out for yourself, like I am."

Tom started to protest, but Boudreau cut him off.

"That's OK. I'm not a bad person, not really, just kinda selfish. I think my mamma spoiled me, always telling me I was the smartest and best at everything, even when I wasn't, which was most of the time. I'm OK with who I am, and I know there are no great things in my future, only small achievements. You, on the other hand, have big things ahead of you, and someday I'll be able to tell people that I helped make you what you are."

Tom laughed and Boudreau joined in with a guffaw.

After calling Hué two Sundays in a row, Tom began calling daily. Nobody picked up the phone. His friend at the noodle stall could offer no information, saying only that Hué was cut off from the rest of the country. Tom became so desperate that he even called the Buddhist Community Association in Hué to ask for Nguyen; nobody answered.

The day before his departure for Mali—his next posting—he was walking back to his apartment after work when a familiar voice spoke from behind his left shoulder.

"Weren't you even gonna say goodbye?"

Tom turned and looked at Sam Smith. "It's been kind of busy the past month."

"It might have been a hell of a lot less busy if we'd had some advance warning." Smith's voice carried an edge.

Tom closed his eyes and took a deep breath.

"You got time for a cup of coffee?" Smith asked. The edge in his voice was gone; it now carried more of a tone of disappointment.

"Yeah, sure."

He followed Smith to a hole-in-the-wall coffee shop, the kind of place that doesn't have a sign, just a few tables and chairs set up on a sidewalk and a small wooden counter with a couple of burners on a ledge along the wall. Smith ordered two Vietnamese coffees, then hunkered down across from Tom.

"So how'd you know?" Tom asked.

"I didn't. Not 'til right now."

"Shit," Tom cursed softly.

"I never even gave it a thought, not right away anyhow. When you didn't show up at Duffy's and didn't try to contact me, I started to wonder. I mean, with Hué under siege and communications cut off, I figured you'd be asking for help finding your lady, or at least try to get some info about her and the Buddhists. Three weeks after Tet, I started to contemplate things, over a beer. 'Damn,' I thought to myself, 'something for sure is up with my boy Tom. Maybe he's heard from his little lady.' Then I had another thought: Maybe he heard *before* Tet and didn't tell his ol' buddy Sam, and now he's feeling guilty about having let the side down. Course, when I learned that you were leaving and still hadn't gotten in contact with me, well, I knew something wasn't quite right."

"I'm sorry."

"Are you?"

"Yes and no. Sorry that I let you down."

Sam waved away Tom's concern. "I appreciate that, but we should always try to keep it professional. Stay away from the personal."

"I'm sorry that I ignored a professional responsibility."

"Sorry? Some would call your act criminal negligence."

"You said you'd been warning them about Vietcong activity and they ignored you."

"I'm CIA. I'm used to being doubted. You're a political attaché whose area of expertise is the Buddhist community. Had you told the bigwigs that a very reliable source had warned about hostile activity during Tet, they'd have been a lot more likely to take you seriously. The military might have been put on high alert. You might have saved a shitload of lives."

"And put Anh's in jeopardy."

"Yeah, there is that." Smith shook his head. "Sometimes you got some pretty tough choices to make."

"How do you do make the tough choices? I mean, when lives are on the line."

Smith leaned forward. "Don't kid yourself. Lives are on the line for all of us, all the time. The State Department supported Diem all those years while he was trying to destroy the Buddhist leadership. Besides the flaming monks, there were mass arrests, mass disappearances, military attacks on Buddhist temples. Shit, hundreds died, thousands probably. Lives were on the line every day, yet none of us gave a rat's ass about the consequences." He took a gulp of coffee. "So how do we do it? Same way the State Department does it. Make it impersonal. Claim it's about national security and world peace; eliminate a few in order to save and protect the many. You can't make an omelet without breaking eggs. Bullshit like that."

"What about when it's the life of somebody you love that's on the line?"

"A bright boy like you already knows the answer."

Tom did know the answer. "Keep your personal life and professional life separate."

"Bingo."

"Then why don't you bust me for, what'd you call it, oh, yeah, criminal negligence?"

"For one thing, I have no evidence. You could just claim you haven't heard from Anh for months. For another, you're right about them not listening. You might have told Glass and he would have told the ambassador and he would have told the military and they would have blown him off as some State Department appointment who didn't know shit from shineola. There's one other thing: I like you."

"What about keeping your personal life and professional life separate?"

"Believe it or not, I'm human."

Tom was humbled.

"Look, Tom, no one single incident defines a man; it's his life work that ultimately defines him. You got a long life in front of you—hopefully—so you've got a lot of years to do good things."

Tom smiled ruefully. "A dear friend, the one who's been studying Buddhism in California, encouraged me when I started my career to do good."

"She'd be proud of you, 'cuz I know that's what you've been trying to do. You're also learnin' that sometimes it's not so easy to do good. Sometimes you just try your darnedest and hope for the best. You're new at this. You'll get better."

"Thanks, Sam. Am I going to hear from you again?"

"I wouldn't be a bit surprised. It's a big world, yet the world of politics and espionage often overlap, and you'll find yourself bumping into people when you least expect it."

"Like walking down the street in Saigon."

"A smart guy like you should have been expecting me."

"I will next time."

⤞

"Have a good flight, sir," said the soldier, as he handed Tom his bags.

"Flights," Tom corrected him. "I have four flights and three connections."

"Hopefully it won't all be in the back of military transport planes. There aren't any pretty stewardesses or free booze, just C-rations and warm water."

"I'm told that where I'm heading is not known for its food. Maybe I'll prefer C-rations."

"Nobody in their right mind would ever prefer C-rations. No offense, sir."

"No offense taken. Be safe, soldier."

The soldier looked around the airfield where masses of soldiers and supplies were being unloaded. "Thanks, though somehow since Tet I don't feel as safe, even with the troop buildup."

"Maybe there'll be a diplomatic breakthrough and all this will end."

"Right," said the soldier, "except there always seems to be another Nam."

"I suppose that's what keeps you employed."

"The both of us."

Tom was taken aback. "I'm supposed to be preventing wars."

155

The soldier hesitated.

"Please speak your mind. You're not going to offend me."

"Well, sir, if you don't mind me saying, you diplomats are supposed to prevent wars, but you don't seem to have much luck. I've studied history, doesn't seem like any diplomats ever, anywhere, have had much luck stopping wars. Fact is, they seem to start more than they stop."

"I can't argue with that. Let's hope we learn enough someday to actually stop wars in the future."

"Yes, sir. We can hope."

As Tom walked up the steps to the plane he had one thought on his mind: it's not about luck or hope; it's about people and human nature. He was more determined than ever to be one of those people who made a difference.

CHAPTER 10—1968

Tom sat at his desk on the second floor of the US embassy in Bamako, Mali, and stared out the window at the dusty haze that blew down the street. The light was indistinct, had been since he arrived in the country. Mali was slowly sliding into a drought that seemed to drag the country toward the ever-nearer Sahara desert. More pertinent to Tom's mission in Mali, the country was slowly sliding toward political collapse, which inevitably meant a military coup d'état in this part of the world. It should have been the perfect assignment. Mali was a former French colony; he was a French-speaking diplomat who had spent his Peace Corps years in French-speaking Côte d'Ivoire and had completed his three years in Vietnam, yet another former French colony. The tribal conflicts that exacerbated the myriad problems of Mali's government were similar to those Tom had dealt with in Côte d'Ivoire and not that different from the factionalism in Vietnam. Although just twenty-seven, Tom had the right credentials for his Mali posting. Yet he was struggling. The desert dryness and heat depressed him; Mali food was bland, consisting of yams, rice, millet, and not much else; Malians suffered from malnourishment, malaria, and the effects of long-term poverty. Yet in spite of the grim facts about Mali and its people, the problem was not with Mali. Vietnam had left a gaping hole in Tom's soul.

Part of Tom's sense of loss had to do with his role in the US foreign service. He had lived in Saigon at a time when it was the center of the world. Whether in Washington, Moscow, or Paris, anybody of importance was dealing with the Vietnam War and its effect on international relations. Even when Tom was a lowly novice working under Howard "Hard" Case, he knew that he was working on something that was historically and politically critical. The same could not be said for Mali. Tom would have bet his annual salary that fewer than five percent of Americans could find Mali on a map. He had gone from the top of the international diplomat heap to the bottom in one short hop. Yet Tom's largest loss, the source of the enormous void in his life, was leaving Anh behind. A day didn't go by when he questioned his decision to accept the transfer to Mali without requesting an extension in Saigon. Not only had he abandoned the great love of his life, he was now stuck in a country that offered next to nothing for his career. Unless he could somehow broker a successful election that would allow Mali to continue on the road to democracy, his time in the country would amount to little more than a few lines on his résumé.

His colleagues in the US embassy felt the same way and could offer little consolation. They drank gin and tonics together after work and filled some of the time with poker games, trips out to the desert, and the occasional barbecue, but Tom didn't find a single person he could relate to. The lack of friends only added to Tom's sense of loss. He regularly received letters from Suzie, had even gotten two brief scribbled notes from Ira, yet nothing helped.

In late October, eight months after arriving in Bamako, he was called into Ambassador Howell's office.

"Tom, thanks for coming at short notice."

Caleb Howell was a nice man, the type who never raised his voice or confronted anybody, the kind of diplomat who ended up in nowhere places like Mali. He was the rare ambassador who had actually risen through the ranks rather than be appointed by way of political payback. Lacking the support of a powerful ally in Washington—and not having any significant diplomatic achievements—he was destined to remain in little-known backwaters like Mali.

"It's my job to jump when the ambassador calls," said Tom. "Besides, it's not like I was working on a major position paper."

Caleb Howell smiled. "No, there's not much of that here, though if things heat up Washington will want an explanation about what we could have done differently and how the change will affect us."

"And the report will end up in a box somewhere in the State Department collecting dust until they find oil or gold in Mali, then Washington will dig it out and dust it off."

Howell's eyebrows arched. "You've grown cynical in your short time with State."

Tom was surprised and disappointed to hear the ambassador say it. Surprised because he hadn't realized he had become cynical; disappointed because he immediately knew that Howell was right.

"Sorry. Cynicism is something I've always rejected and found distasteful in others."

Howell shrugged. "It happens in the foreign service. Especially in a place like Mali. I've seen the same thing all over the world: El Salvador, Sikkim, Malta. You spend three years doing what seems to be inconsequential work in places that nobody back home has ever heard of, then you get transferred to a place that isn't any better—it just offers a different climate and another language that you have to learn, though you know you'll never use it once you leave. Then there's the parade of cynical colleagues, the kind who drag you just a little bit lower each day, not that they mean to."

He sounded like he spoke from personal experience. Tom squirmed as Ambassador Howell described just the situation where Tom found himself.

"Can't say as I blame you, Tom, what with you coming directly from the heart of the diplomatic world to the armpit."

"That's a lousy excuse. Thank you for pointing it out."

"I'm sure that your cynicism is a temporary condition."

"I can assure you it is. Thanks for your confidence."

"Don't thank me. I didn't call you in to discuss your personality or conduct. In fact, I called you in to ask a favor. If you agree to it, I'll be the one thanking you."

"I'll do whatever it is you need," Tom assured Howell.

"Once you've heard my request I doubt that you'll be so eager to accommodate me. I got a call yesterday from Washington, somebody close to Secretary of State Rusk. I know you're aware of the peace talks taking place in Paris regarding the situation in Vietnam."

Tom leaned forward slightly, his interest piqued.

"You may not be aware that things are not going well, regardless of what the official statements have been saying. Apparently, your name has been brought up by both sides."

"My name?"

"That surprises you?"

"It certainly does. I didn't make any progress during my first two and a half years in Vietnam, never met anybody of consequence. The last few months, after we got a new ambassador, I was given more leeway and was able to meet a couple of people who were higher up in their organizations, but it still never led to anything."

A wry smile had appeared on Ambassador Howell's face.

"What?" Tom asked.

"You're a natural diplomat. You manage to gently point out that the first ambassador failed to support you and left you to waste valuable time..."

Tom shrugged noncommittally.

"...and you praise the second one without doing so directly or openly criticizing the first."

"They had different styles."

The wry smile remained in place.

"You must have done something significant enough to catch the attention of the Vietnamese as well as some of our people, even though it was your first assignment."

Tom thought about it for a moment. "I cared and I believed. I suppose my sincerity made an impression. Plus I spoke French and learned Vietnamese, and I made a few valuable friends." Calling Anh a friend seemed a lie; she was so much more. Sam Smith, on the other hand, turned out to be a true friend.

"I know what you mean. Sincerity can go a long way, but sometimes one needs friends to succeed. The State Department doesn't appear to agree with us. They think we get farther by throwing our weight around, threatening and making bad deals with the wrong people. That's why I'm stuck in places like Bamako. I'm too soft. Fact is, if I was a hard guy I wouldn't have asked you to my office today. I would have told State to get lost. Flat out refused their request."

"Request?"

"They'd like you to go to Paris and join in the peace talks."

Tom's heart fluttered, and he had to take a deep breath to steady myself.

"I thought that'd get your interest."

There was a note of sadness in Howell's voice. Tom suddenly realized what was happening. Howell knew that he had a star on his staff, somebody capable of making a difference. Now he was about to lose that star.

"Ambassador Howell, I accepted the position in Mali and I'm not about to abandon it."

"That's noble of you, Tom, but it's not like you called Washington and begged to be transferred. It's part of the job. Sometimes you get called away from paradise, and sometimes..." he nodded toward the desolate dust and heat that lay outside the window.

"I get the sense that you didn't tell Washington that I was indispensable."

"No, I didn't. What I did say was that I'd talk with you." Howell stared out the window a minute, gathering his thoughts. "Mali may be a sandpit full of scorpions and warring factions, but for three years it's my sandpit. I'm the US ambassador, and I intend to do my job. The fact is—and this is between you and me—you're the best man I've got. I know you must be frustrated, since it appears that we're just pissing in the wind here, yet I really believe we've made a difference and we can continue to do so. You yourself said you didn't get anywhere in Vietnam the first two years because you didn't have the support of your ambassador. Well, you've got my support here. I have faith in you and I believe we can do good."

That did it. Echoing Suzie, Ambassador Howell's appeal he had struck the right note. Nobody in his right mind would turn down Paris, one of the plums of the US foreign service, yet Tom knew that was precisely what he was going to do.

"I'll stay here as long as necessary."

Howell let out a sigh of relief.

"Thanks, Tom. I really appreciate it. The thing is, this is a critical time. The Chinese seem to be out of favor and the economy seems to be picking up and the military seems to have stopped rattling their sabers and threatening a coup."

"That's a lot of 'seems,'" Tom remarked.

"It is. That's why I think it's so critical to push ahead with diplomacy. If we can keep moving Keita in the right direction, nudge him with aid toward democracy, then we'll have saved Mali from communism and tribalism."

Mali had gained its independence from France in 1960. Modibo Keita, Mali's first elected president, had steered his young nation toward an independent course that favored socialism, yet he accepted aid from all sides. His nationalization of major industries had worried Washington, appearing communist in nature, yet Keita had avoided extremes and now appeared to be leaning toward the West. Or so Washington and Ambassador Howell believed. There had recently been a gradual purge of conservative members of Keita's government, and one of Tom's sources had insisted that members of the military were not happy with the purge. As well, the year's rains had been inadequate and US meteorologists had warned that an extended drought was highly possible. If the drought intensified or if Keita continued the purge or if somebody with a big head in the military decided that eight years of Keita was enough, then things could fall apart quickly.

"Tom, I promise that I won't hold you a day longer than necessary. If things seem to be heading in the right direction, I'll call Washington and tell them you've completed your job."

"What if the opposite happens? What if the situation deteriorates beyond our control?"

"Same thing. I call Washington and tell them your services are no longer required in Mali. You have my word."

Things fell apart quickly, as if Tom's meeting with Ambassador Howell had acted as a jinx for Mali. The drought's toll spread rapidly. An agricultural nation, the drought robbed Malians of their food and major source of income. The farmers were unable to buy even the most basic goods, and their misery rapidly spread to the merchants who relied on their business. It soon became apparent that Keita's efforts at nationalizing Mali's few industries had failed. The industries bled money, and one by one had to close their doors, furthering Mali's unemployment problem and exacerbating the abrupt decline in consumer demand. Aware of the growing discontent of the people, deeply dissatisfied with Keita's continual wavering between allies, and upset with his purge of the conservatives in his government, the military staged a bloodless coup d'état in November. The new president, Moussa Traoré, blamed the United States for propping up Keita's regime for so long and shut down all communications with the US embassy. Concerned with what Traoré might do if he thought the Americans were in any way interfering with his new government, Howell temporarily put a freeze on all diplomatic activities.

When Tom was called to Ambassador Howell's office in early February, 1969, he found Howell sat slumped in his chair, staring out the window.

"Good morning, Mr. Ambassador."

"I wish it was," said Howell glumly. "I sent Washington a cable yesterday asking if they still wanted you in Paris. I received their reply this morning when I got to my desk."

Howell slid a piece of paper across the table. Tom picked it up and read.

It would be beneficial to have Tom Kington join peace negotiations in Paris. Please inform him that he should report to the US embassy, Paris, France, within the week.

"You're booked on Thursday night's flight to Paris. I assume that should be sufficient time for you to put things in order here."

Thursday was two days away. Tom could have caught a flight that evening. He had two suitcases' worth of belongings, lived in embassy housing, and didn't have a bank account or phone line or anything else that needed to be canceled or closed.

"I'm sorry we didn't have a chance to make a difference," said Tom.

"That's life in the world of international diplomacy. You win some, lose some, and sometimes you don't even get into the game." Howell turned and looked Tom in the eye. "Don't let this get to you, make you cynical. The United States is a great country doing great things. We screw up sometimes, but we mean well. Give them a hand in Paris. Make me proud of you. Make your country proud."

Tom stood up, as did Ambassador Howell.

"Thank you, sir. Good luck to you."

They shook hands.

"You're the one who's going to need luck. Mine seems to have run out here. I know you'll enjoy Paris. A marvelous city. Just keep in mind that you have a job to do there, and it's going to be damn tough. The world will be watching. The day may come when you wish you were back in some nowhere place like Mali."

"Maybe." Tom doubted it.

CHAPTER 11—1969

I t was too cold to sit at the outdoor café in the Place des Vosges, yet that is just what Tom was doing on that chilly gray day in Paris in early March. He'd arrived from Mali the previous week, and the extraordinary climate difference between sub-Saharan Bamako and northern European Paris had kept him indoors for the first few days. The tolerance for cold that he'd naturally acquired during twenty-two years in Indiana and New York City—and lost during his years in Côte d'Ivoire, Vietnam and Mali—finally reemerged. Besides, he couldn't wait for a warm May day to do something he'd dreamed about for years. He'd read all the giants of literature while pursuing his minor in French at Columbia, and he knew that many had spent their formative years in Paris, with much of that time spent sitting at outdoor cafés, sipping coffee and chatting.

There was a buzz in the air, a sense of purpose and destiny. The previous year's protests by students and trade unionists had brought down the government of the mighty Charles de Gaulle. The sexual revolution, born in 1967's Summer of Love in San Francisco, and the fashion revolution that started in London's Carnaby Street and followed the Beatles and other British bands around the globe, contributed to Paris's transformation from snobby *haute couture* capital to a city of youth and fun and carefree living. To use one of the hip phrases of the day, Paris was "where it's at."

As the heart of the French-speaking world and a center for international diplomacy for over two hundred years, Paris was the logical place for the Vietnam War peace talks. During Tom's brief time in Paris he had already eaten twice at *Les Deux Magots* (unofficial headquarters for the Lost Generation of American writers who lived in Paris between the wars: Hemingway, Stein, Fitzgerald, and others), and walked the streets until he stumbled back to his apartment exhausted. Every member of every foreign service on the planet dreamed of being stationed in Paris, and Tom Kington was living the dream. Or nearly. All that remained to make this a dream come true was for Tom to achieve something in his capacity as special assistant to the Paris Peace Talks.

Tom had received a warm welcome from the entire staff at the US embassy and had found the atmosphere dramatically different from his previous two posts. His colleagues in Saigon had been frustrated by their limited role, the State Department taking a backseat to the Department of Defense and the White House. Bluntly put, Mali was an unimportant country when it came to America's geopolitical interests, and its staff knew their work was of little value. The US embassy in Paris was an entirely different thing, though Tom discovered early that it was a posting with its own share of frustrations and aggravations.

He'd checked in with the embassy the previous Friday, been given a tour of the grounds and shown where his desk would be, and met his new colleagues in the political section. After a morning of glad-handing and putting a few personal touches on his desk—a photo with Ira and Suzie taken just after Suzie's graduation ceremony, a small bronze Buddha statue, an ebony carving of an elephant from Mali—his two roommates helped Tom move into the three-bedroom apartment they would share. The embassy itself was in the 1st arrondissement, near Place de la Concorde, one of the priciest neighborhoods in Paris. Consequently, staffers, with the exception of the ambassador, lived relatively far from the embassy in more affordable neighborhoods. Tom's apartment was in the 18th arrondissement, north of the famous Montmartre Cemetery. His roommates, members of the regular political staff, were impressed by Tom's special designation.

"What'd you do to get such a sweet title, 'special assistant'?" asked Mark Fensky.

They had dropped Tom's bags off at their apartment and settled down for an afternoon drink at a sidewalk café on Avenue de Clichy. Fensky was in his early thirties, having joined the foreign service after earning a master's in international relations from the University of Southern California. He rubbed his hands together and shivered in the chilly Paris air.

"George here has been in the service for decades, and his only title is one that's not used in polite company," Fensky said with a smirk.

George Newman ignored the apparent dig. "I've only been in for eighteen years, and I'm quite happy with the work I've been doing, title or no title."

Newman looked up at the approaching waiter and began ordering drinks in rapid French. "What would you like?" he asked Tom.

Tom turned to the waiter and ordered a kir in his own fluent French.

"Impressive," said Newman in French after the waiter had left. "You speak very well."

"Not as well as you," Tom replied in kind. "You've got the Parisian accent down pat."

"I should after three years here."

"*Pardonez moi,*" interrupted Fensky in atrocious French, before resorting to English. "If you gentlemen don't mind, could we stick to a language I can understand?"

"That would limit us to English. Spoken very slowly," said Newman.

"If there's something you two need to discuss," said Tom, "I could excuse myself."

"Oh, it's nothing," Newman assured Tom. "We actually get along fine. You know how roommates can be. You spend too much time together and bicker like a married couple at times."

"Though I'd prefer you use a different image than a married couple," said Fensky.

"I'm gay," Newman said. "Mark worries that people will think we really are a couple."

"I'm not homophobic," said Fensky, "it just doesn't do your career any good if the powers that be think you're queer."

Newman flinched slightly at the use of the term.

"Sorry, George. He's been training me on sensitivity. I'm a slow learner, like with French."

"Mark means well. He could have requested a different apartment if he wanted."

"And be seen as a malcontent? No way."

"Mark may be slow with languages and such, but he has a well-developed sense for survival. Many things can impede rising in the ranks, and Mark is careful to avoid them all."

"You have designs on an ambassadorship?" Tom asked.

"Hell, no. I'm not that ambitious. I just don't want to get stuck in some shitty place, a war zone or in some plague-infested country. I figure if I don't make any enemies or tick somebody off, I can continue to land comfortable assignments like Paris."

"Though our friend here would prefer places that speak English," said Newman.

"Why not? It's the number-one language on the planet. Everybody's going to be speaking it sooner or later. What's the point of learning Swahili or Burmese? I'm probably never going to use French again."

Tom had had colleagues like Mark Fensky in Vietnam and Mali, people who had joined the foreign service for some adventure, but not too much of it. They were content to be on the government payroll, expected to be head of a division at some point, and looked forward to a healthy pension courtesy of Uncle Sam. Making the world a better place was not high on their agenda.

"George here is a hell of a lot more serious," Fensky continued. "He was very ambitious when he joined the service."

Tom gave Newman a quizzical look.

"I know what you're thinking," Newman said. "An ambitious man, fluent in French, and working for the State Department for eighteen years, yet still a mid-level flunky living with other mid-level flunkies, rather than somebody important with a residence in the 1st."

"It's the gay thing," said Fensky, as if Tom hadn't immediately grasped the cause of Newman's stagnation. "They won't toss out gay people; they just keep them in menial positions in crummy places."

"I'd hardly call Paris crummy," said Tom.

"You know the rotation," said Newman. "Hardship assignment, nice posting, back stateside, then hardship again, and so on. They can't keep sticking you in disaster zones. That's only Mark's paranoia. Besides, there aren't that many who speak French as well as I do, and there are quite a few French-speaking countries."

"George is lucky. From what he's told me those countries are more gay friendly."

168

"Friendlier than many of my colleagues," Newman concurred. "The titles Mark referred to earlier are courtesy of my fellow State Department associates."

"Like Mrs. Newman," said Fensky.

"Or Mr. Newwoman," added Newman. "Childish, really. By the way, I hope my sexual orientation isn't an issue. I mean, sharing an apartment and all."

"No problem. I had a gay colleague in Saigon, we got along fine. To be honest, I haven't met that many gay people, not ones who openly admit it like you."

"As long as George doesn't peek when you're in the shower," Fensky winked. "Unless that's your preference," he hastily added.

"Mark," Newman started to admonish his roommate.

"No, I'm straight," Tom said, "and I believe it's the right of everybody to be who they are, as long as they aren't hurting others."

"Ah, a liberal," said Newman. He raised his glass. "Here's to good old American freedom of choice."

They clinked glasses.

"Now that we have that out of the way," began Fensky, "we can get to the question of the day. What is so special about Tom Kington?"

Tom felt himself blushing.

"Oh, a humble one," Newman said.

"Not really. I find the whole thing amusing and, well, confusing at the same time."

"How so?" asked Newman.

"We were talking earlier about not wanting to be branded as malcontents, not doing anything to impede our ambitions. My first posting was in Saigon."

"Wow. So Washington tabbed you as special from Day One," said Fensky.

"I don't think so. I had recently finished two years in the Peace Corps in Côte d'Ivoire and my French was pretty good. Somebody in the State Department maybe figured that qualified me for doing grunt work in Vietnam. Only my ambassador didn't want a smartass Ivy Leaguer mucking about, so he tried burying me by assigning me to research the Buddhist community. He thought it was a dead-end assignment since Washington didn't give a damn about the Buddhists. I wanted to contact the Buddhists from the start. They're the vast majority of Vietnamese, yet Washington was ignoring them. I spent two years establishing connections, which didn't mean much until the new ambassador, Wayne Glass, showed up."

"A good man," said Newman. "We were together long ago in Honduras."

"Yeah, a good man and a fine diplomat. He knew I was on to something and making progress, then Tet happened, my time was up, and I was sent to Mali. I was there less than a year. Now here I am."

"You're not special, you're lucky," Fensky said, a hint of admiration in his voice. "Sounds like you angered the first ambassador and were on the way to Shitsville. Three years of dead-end research, no important results to show, and you'd be on the track to nowhere. Instead you land a sympathetic ambassador and look like a star."

"Hardly a star. I failed dismally. Washington never supported a Buddhist government, and I never provided any meaningful information." Tom flashed on his forewarning about Tet, then forged ahead. "I left with my head hanging." He didn't mention Anh.

"I don't suppose by any chance you learned the lingo while in Vietnam?" Newman asked, though the upturn of the corners of his mouth showed that he already knew the answer.

"I had lots of free time, so, yeah, I worked on it."

Newman smiled. "Modest, indeed. After hearing your French I know you have an ear for languages. So now you speak French and Vietnamese, and there just happens to be the Vietnam War peace conference in Paris."

"Bingo," shouted Fensky. "Mr. Special is a linguist."

"No, it's more than that," corrected Newman. "We've got linguists with more experience in negotiations. Our man here must have made quite an impression in Saigon, an impression that made its way to Washington and on to Paris. He's been called in to get the process moving."

"Too bad he's going to be disappointed," said Fensky.

"The secret cynic speaks."

"Secret?" Tom asked.

"There are two Mark Fenskys. The public one is a team player, though a quiet one. He never sticks his neck out too far, never takes too strong a stance—for or against—never does or says anything that will upset the powers that be."

"There's no extra pay for making waves," Fensky readily agreed.

"The private Fensky, the one you're sitting with, is a cynic with a low opinion of diplomacy and career diplomats."

"You must have taken enough history and poli sci classes at Columbia to know the long, depressing history of international diplomacy," said Fensky.

"It could be argued that the world would be a far worse place without the Council of Vienna or the Peace of Paris or the creation of the UN," Tom said. "It's kind of like baseball. You strike out a lot, get on base less than a third of the time, score even less; but occasionally you hit a home run and win the World Series."

Newman laughed. "Strike out or hit a homer, I think I'm going to like having you on the team. Mark, looks like you're going to remain a benchwarmer."

"Fine with me, as long as I keep getting a salary and they don't send me to a war zone."

"Would you mind elaborating on what you mentioned earlier about me being disappointed with the peace talks?" Tom asked.

"I don't mind," said Fensky, "in fact, I enjoy pointing out how screwed up things are."

"Actually, if you're not offended, I'd like to hear what George has to say on the subject."

Newman smiled. "Providing further proof of the wisdom of our young colleague. You're not offended, are you, Mark?"

Fensky shrugged. "I'm used to being ignored. It means less chance of being blamed for something."

Newman wearily shook his head. "I'll give you the short version; you can pick up details over the next few weeks. As you well know, Johnson started the peace process during the final months of his presidency. Not surprisingly, the embassy staff here were used mostly as facilitators: find housing and translators, procure facilities for conferences, issue press releases, the usual mundane chores that always fall to the local staff. The serious negotiations were carried out by heavy hitters brought in from Washington, though there weren't any serious negotiations, since the first year was spent determining the size and shape of conference tables and who would sit on which side and crap like that."

"Now you're sounding like me," Fensky said.

"I never said you were wrong, only that you were cynical. Anyway, when Nixon won the election things began to slide downhill pretty rapidly. Apparently, our president doesn't hold the foreign service in very high regard. There are even whispers that he thinks we're Democratic stooges who would like nothing better than to see him fail big time. I've been told by one of Nixon's own people that he borders on paranoid, wants to use us for cleaning up after conferences and not much else. The result is that he's sent in his own team to do the heavy work."

"The word is that Kissinger is Nixon's point man," said Fensky. "Can you believe it? The president of the United States sends a German to do his negotiating."

"Kissinger is a US citizen," Tom pointed out, "and one of the top diplomats of our age."

"Mark, you'd better treat Tom with respect. He'll be your boss before he gets his first gray hair."

"Maybe," said Fensky, "and maybe I'll be still collecting checks from the State Department when he's teaching high school civics."

Tom laughed. "Highly likely. Two years ago I nearly left the service in frustration."

"Now you're special," Fensky pointed out.

"Special assistant," Tom said. "Whatever that means."

Tom soon learned that special assistant didn't mean a hell of a lot. George Newman had been right; most of the work carried out by the embassy was menial and mundane. He translated and interpreted, helped find housing and arranged schooling for the children of diplomats who moved to Paris for the conference, and attended all-day meetings that did nothing more than determine ground rules. He knew that international conferences could last years and achieve little, yet he hadn't known how little time was actually spent discussing substantive matters. Tom heard more discussions about menus and weekend excursions for delegates than about troop withdrawals and turnover of military bases. And although he hadn't seen the great diplomat in person, Tom continued to hear about Henry Kissinger spottings. If the rumors were true, then Kissinger would do the most meaningful negotiations while Tom and the rest of the embassy staff would continue to arrange dinner parties and museum viewings.

Yet Tom didn't complain. He was in Paris, part of the peace process (regardless how small), and he was even polishing his Vietnamese while dining in the many Vietnamese restaurants that dotted Paris. He'd become a regular at one in the 19th arrondissement, a short walk from his apartment. The place was a bit of a dive, the kind avoided by the French but popular with Vietnamese, some who had lived in Paris most of their lives and others who had only recently arrived as the situation in Vietnam grew more desperate. As in Vietnam itself, Tom had not been welcomed at first. Rather than be pleased with his use of their language, the owners and waiters distrusted Tom. It was only after he had been eating there nearly a month that a waiter had revealed the problem: most still had relatives in Vietnam and they feared for them. What if one of the restaurant staff happened to mention how much he despised the Communists, and Tom mentioned it to some embassy staffer, and the staffer mentioned it to a Vietnamese delegate, who then sent a message back to Hanoi? As well, the United States had failed to defeat North Vietnam and now appeared to be selling out the South to Ho Chi Minh and his hordes. Besides, the restaurant had no desire to add a white clientele, which might drive away their Vietnamese customers. Things changed dramatically, though, one evening while Tom was eating dinner.

"Who is this round-eyed devil who eats and talks like one of us?"

The man stood behind Tom and spoke native Vietnamese with a southern accent. Tom looked up at the waiter who stood still, a shocked look on his face. Tom slowly turned his head, then his jaw dropped. Standing there grinning was Nguyen, the accountant for the Buddhist Community Association of Hué. The two men had shared many meals and intense philosophical discussions that had often lasted long into the night. Tom jumped up, and the two men warmly shook hands and slapped each other on the shoulders. When Tom glanced around he noticed the look of relief on the waiter's face.

"I think the waiter was expecting a fight," Tom said in Vietnamese. "Maybe he thought I would do a John Wayne and bust up the place."

"How could he know that we are old friends?"

"Indeed. By the way, how did you know it was me? Recognize the back of my head?"

"The people here have been talking about you for quite a while, the *farang* who speaks and eats like one of us. When they described you I knew immediately. I was hoping to see you sooner, but I've been quite busy."

"This is fantastic. Please, join me for dinner."

They sat down and Nguyen ordered a 333 beer and dinner.

"By the way, I've only known you as Nguyen," Tom said.

"Van Co Nguyen, at your service."

They shook hands across the table, waited for the waiter to pour Nguyen's beer, then clinked glasses.

"*A votre santé*," Tom toasted.

"To your health also," Nguyen replied, this time in English.

"Am I right in guessing that you're not here as a tourist?" Tom asked.

"I told you I was a simple accountant."

"And I always knew that was a load of *merde*."

Nguyen smiled. "I was an accountant for the BCA, among other things."

"So you're here to cover financial aspects of the peace talks?" Tom asked skeptically.

The smile faded from Nguyen's face. "I wish that was all there was to it. Figuring out the value of military bases and possible compensation would be simple. Instead, we're still trying to establish basic ground rules and starting points for negotiations. It's far safer than what I was doing in Hué; it's also extremely tedious."

"How come I haven't seen you around? I mean, I haven't seen many of your team yet, but I've run into a few. I suppose it's because I'm a lower-level peon and you're in the higher echelons of power."

Nguyen looked uncomfortable and hesitated to reply.

Tom slowly nodded. "I get it. More secret stuff behind the scenes, like in Hué, only without the threat of violence."

"Yes, that is correct. I'm involved in something that is not ready for public display."

It suddenly dawned on Tom. Nguyen must be part of the secret talks that were taking place between Henry Kissinger and Le Duc Tho, the meaningful negotiations. Tom was enough of a diplomat to know that Nguyen was not at liberty to discuss them with anybody.

"I look forward to learning more about what you're doing, whenever you're at liberty to do so. For now, let's forget about our jobs and enjoy this wonderful food."

Nguyen smiled, a look of relief on his face. "You are wise for somebody so young."

"I had good teachers in Vietnam. Speaking of Vietnam, are you in touch with Anh?"

Nguyen froze, the chopsticks holding a piece of roast duck inches from his mouth. Slowly, he put the duck back on his plate. "You really don't know?"

Tom placed his chopsticks across the edge of his bowl. "Know what?" he asked, though he realized he already knew the answer.

"Anh was killed during the first few days of the Tet Offensive."

Tom struggled to take a breath. "Who killed her? I mean, why?"

Nguyen looked into his bowl for a moment, gathering his thoughts, or perhaps trying to figure the best way to explain what had happened. Finally, he looked up at Tom. "It was a frightening time for everybody. I suppose the American government believed all southerners welcomed the offensive and cheered the brutal attack on US forces and their Vietnamese allies. That is not the case. Like all people, we've always wanted one thing: peace. Only it's not that simple." Nguyen shook his head before continuing. "Those of us who knew what was planned were eager to finally take the fight directly to the Americans. We'd been bombed and herded into camps and treated like animals for so long; it was finally time to get our country back. When Tet arrived, hell was let loose across the south.

"Even those of us who dreamed of this day were horrified by the blood that flowed. Yes, we hit your people hard and ultimately we succeeded. After all, your Johnson would not have asked for peace talks had we not struck such fear into the American people." Nguyen was justifying the violence, yet his voice didn't carry the same conviction as his words. "But it's like when you let a dog out to chase away a fox, and the dog ends up killing all of your chickens. Many Americans were killed during Tet, but also many Vietnamese. It was a time of punishment, and of revenge. People who carried ancient grudges used Tet as an excuse to settle old scores. We will never know how many died because they helped the Americans and how many died unnecessarily, for personal reasons."

As Nguyen talked his eyes had drifted downward, unable to look Tom in the face as he described the horror of Tet. He now looked up to see tears brimming in Tom's eyes.

"When I heard that Anh was dead I went to her apartment to find out what I could. The old lady who ran the place told me that the VC had killed Anh for collaborating with the enemy. I became upset and told her how important Anh had been to the Buddhist community, how much she had given of herself to liberate her nation. The old woman said she knew, but everybody also knew that she had a *farang* boyfriend. An American. They said she was a traitor."

Tom pushed back from the table and struggled to get a breath. He wiped the tears from his eyes with the back of his hand. "Anh loved her country. She would do anything for it." He leaned forward and put his hands on the table. "I asked her to come with me when I left. She wouldn't do it. Told me she was Vietnamese and always would be."

"Anh was a hero. She also loved you very much."

Tom's shoulders slumped, and he fell back in his chair.

"She was not a child, Tom. Anh knew what she was doing."

"Maybe, and maybe she made a fatal error because of her love."

"What error?"

"Anh called me a few days before Tet and warned me to be careful."

"Oh. What did you do?"

"Nothing."

"You didn't tell your superiors? Inform the military?"

"No."

"You see, Anh trusted you because she knew you. Her fate was sealed when she fell in love with you. One phone call would not have made much difference."

Tom knew that Nguyen was correct. Anh had been marked as a collaborator. It happened throughout history. When the Germans left France at the end of World War II, French women who had slept with German soldiers were dealt with ruthlessly. Tom had learned this in his history classes, yet he'd been blinded by youth and naiveté and, yes, love. Tom stood and fumbled in his pocket for money.

"Please, dinner is on me tonight," said Nguyen.

Tom nodded, put on his jacket, and started for the door.

"Tom, you know that line from Shakespeare? 'Better to have loved and lost than to never have loved.' If she had it to do over again, Anh would still have loved you. It was meant to be."

"Thanks." He walked out the door into the cold Parisian night.

Dear Tom,

I am so sorry to hear that Anh passed away. When you and I shared that wonderful weekend in Bangkok I knew that you were deeply in love with her, and I knew she must be a special person to have won your heart. If it is any solace, the Buddha taught that all things are transitory: love, hate, pain, life. Although I hope Anh's memory warms your heart forever, it is a thing from the past, and the past can never live again. As Baba Ram Das teaches, Be Here Now! You have people who love you and are here for you. Although I am very busy with work against the war, and have started teaching meditation in the local community center, I would gladly visit you in Paris, if you want. Just call me and I'll be there.

Love, your sister, friend, and lover,

Suzie

Tom,

It's a drag that Anh was murdered, but that's the kind of shit that happens when you get tangled up with United Fascist States of America. I warned you! We go around the globe messing in other people's business, trying to sell them our form of government (even though it favors the haves and oppresses the have-nots) and our religion (which robs the poor to build huge fuckin' cathedrals for the greater glory of a god that doesn't exist), and anything else that enriches us and impoverishes the poor. I know you meant to do good, but you can't do good when you're working for the bad guys. Quit! Now! Come back and teach the truth in some high school, 'cuz you know the truth.

I'm scraping by, though I have to hit up my old man for coin from time to time. The thing at the *Voice* never panned out. I walked away 'cuz I was still emptying trash bins, with the occasional poetry or music review to appease me. I've had a few things published in literary mags though nothing that paid more than a few bucks. I've been thinking of moving out of the Big Apple. Too many bad vibes, too many people who think they know literature when they don't. California's time is past. Paris is definitely where it's at, the happening place, but those fuckin' frogs only speak French. If I can get my dad to buy me a ticket I might visit you, then check out London.

Hang in there. Don't let the bastards keep you down!

Ira

Summer rolled by, and the cold winds of the northern European autumn began to again chill Paris. When Tom wasn't busy with work—meaningless work that offered little challenge but kept his mind occupied—he walked the streets and parks of Paris. He sipped kir and wine at sidewalk cafés, though never to excess. He ate rich and delicious French food, though he never seemed to taste what he ate. He spent hours in the Louvre and other museums, though he never actually focused on the art. Tom had stopped going to Vietnamese restaurants, hoping to avoid Nguyen. Anh's murder threatened Tom's effectiveness as a diplomat and an interpreter. Once, when shaking the hands of a junior member of the Vietnamese delegation, a man with cold, battle-hardened eyes, Tom had fleetingly wondered if this had been the man who killed Anh.

The only person who reached out to Tom, who was there for him during the darkest moments, was George Newman. Tom would usually turn down Newman's offer to go out for dinner, but one night in October Newman insisted, telling Tom that it was a special night and he wanted Tom to share it with him and his French lover, Thierry.

They met at a small restaurant in the Marais at eight o'clock one evening. Newman introduced Tom to Thierry, who appeared to be half African, half European, and fully gay. He spoke no English and clung to Newman while batting heavily made-up eyes at Tom. Newman ordered a bottle of champagne, and when the three glasses had been filled he raised his and made a toast.

"Here's to friends and lovers."

They clinked glasses.

"So what's the occasion?" Tom asked.

"This is the twentieth anniversary of me coming out of the closet."

"Here's to openness, honesty, and understanding," Tom toasted.

They clinked glasses again. Later, after appetizers and polishing off the first bottle of wine, Newman brought up Tom's toast.

"Tom, I'm glad you've joined us here in Paris. I happen to think you're special, though perhaps not for the same reasons you were named special assistant. I also know that something changed in you a few months back. Fensky hasn't noticed, but I'm not Mark Fensky."

Tom smiled. "No, you're definitely not Mark Fensky."

"Back to your toast. I want you to know that I'm here if you need somebody to talk to. I'm not prying. I'm just trying to be a friend. If you want to share what's going on, I'm here."

"So you didn't invite me just to be part of your anniversary. You had ulterior motives."

"Guilty as charged, though I am glad you're sharing this moment with me. With us," Newman hastily added, glancing at Thierry to be sure he wasn't upset. "Thierry, I hope you don't mind, but I'm going to talk with Tom briefly in English. It's a bit of business." Newman switched to English. "I like Thierry, but he's more of a boy toy than a true friend, not that I'm complaining. You, however, if I'm not being too presumptuous, are a soul mate. I relate to you. We're both sincere, and we care about who we are and what we're doing. I could have quit the foreign service since I'm obviously not going to rise in the organization, but I think I'm good at my job. I also believe that things may change someday for people like me, though not for a long time. You, on the other hand, can achieve something important right now. You've got a gift for language; a natural, easy way with people that earns their trust; a passion for your work; a clear vision of what America can do to lead the world. Yet the passion somehow faded a few months back. What happened?"

Tom sat quietly for a moment, then started to speak in French so as not to exclude Thierry. Tom told about his life in Vietnam and his love for Anh, how Anh had warned him about the Tet Offensive, and how she had paid with her life. When he finished they sat silently.

"That explains your change," Newman eventually said. "It must be a heavy burden to feel responsible for somebody else's death."

"I didn't just *feel* responsible. I *was* responsible."

"You said that Anh was very intelligent. Yes?"

"Yes."

"Did you lie to her? Trick her into loving you?"

"Of course not."

"So this intelligent woman, of her own free will, fell in love with you, and because of this love she called to warn you when she thought you were in danger. And you're not even sure if the phone call led to her death."

Tom nodded.

"Then both of you are guilty of falling in love. Do you think Anh regretted loving you?"

"No."

"Then respect her enough to honor her love. Don't turn it into something twisted and sad, something you regret. Take the word of somebody older and wiser in the world of love. Love doesn't come to everyone. Some people spend their entire lives alone. You must cherish what you and Anh had, cherish the memories of each moment you were together. As importantly, devote yourself to your work. From what you've told me, that is one of the things she loved about you, your sincerity, your commitment to doing good. Honor Anh by working to bring peace to her country, the peace she ultimately died for."

A single tear trickled down Tom's cheek.

Thierry raised his glass. "Here is to love. It causes pain and pleasure, often in equal measures, yet without it we are no more than flesh and bone."

The three men raised their glasses and clinked them once more.

Tom threw himself into his work with renewed energy. Rather than avoid Vietnamese delegates as he had after learning of Anh's death, he now sought them out and invited them to lunch or visits to museums. Since George Newman's pep talk he had considered what had led to his limited success in Vietnam, and the answer was obvious: he cared and he was sincere. It was these qualities that had won over Anh, had led to his meetings with Nguyen, and had earned the respect and support of Wayne

Glass. Tom recommitted himself to doing everything he could to keep the peace talks on track, to give them every possible chance to succeed.

Although there was some resentment from colleagues who had been at it longer and didn't think they needed the help of this special assistant, they soon came to appreciate Tom. Meetings were notably more congenial. Tom encouraged, and taught, his colleagues to eat Vietnamese food and to learn basic phrases. He'd tell stories about life in Vietnam, the beauty of the country, and the quality of life when there was no fighting. The Americans gained a greater understanding of their Vietnamese counterparts and the Vietnamese grew more relaxed as they came to believe that the Americans viewed them less as enemies and more as fellow diplomats with a common cause: the end of the war. Small points that had stalled the talks were settled and more substantive matters were now put on the table. However, the fact remained that the most important issues were being discussed secretly by Kissinger and Le Duc Tho, which is why Tom returned to the Vietnamese restaurant where he had dined with Van Co Nguyen.

Tom went there every day for a week, and asked daily if they had seen Nguyen. Finally, when he walked in for dinner on Friday night, Nguyen was sitting at a table, sipping green tea. Tom sat across the booth from Nguyen and ordered a beer.

"Two glasses?" he asked Nguyen.

"Yes, of course. I was only drinking tea because I didn't want to start without you. As you know, we Vietnamese don't hold our liquor as well as you Europeans."

"We certainly wouldn't want an important man like you to appear too drunk in public."

"Oh, I am not so important."

"Important enough to get me transferred to Paris."

"Perhaps it was your Ambassador Glass or your friend from the CIA. Smith, was it?"

Tom smiled in admiration. "I always knew that our people underestimated you."

"That was our greatest advantage. Even though we had stood up to the Japanese and defeated the French, you still saw us as too ignorant to organize and fight the right way, the civilized way. How did you figure I was the one who asked for you?"

"The peace talks are being run by the White House, and they have little regard for the State Department and even less for ambassadors. That's why Johnson used Secretary of Defense McNamara as his point man and Nixon is using Kissinger. Interdepartmental rivalries. Even if Wayne Glass had called, they might not have answered the phone. As to Smith, he has no pull with State or the White House. No, it had to be from the Vietnamese side, and after bumping into you a few months back it all became clear."

"What was it that became clear?"

"The talks were going nowhere because the two sides didn't know how to talk with each other, how to communicate."

"It is always more difficult when one side prefers lecturing to listening. Is that not what you discovered when you urged your government to include Buddhists in the government of South Vietnam? They wouldn't listen to you. It was my hope that they would listen to you now and learn about my people."

"Sorry I couldn't get here sooner. I had a commitment at my last posting."

"That is one of the things I respect about you. You are a committed person."

"One of the things?"

"You are not an ideologue. You are willing to consider new ideas, willing to see things from different perspectives. Also, you respect all people, it seems. Whereas many of your people saw us as gooks and whores, you saw into our hearts. That is why you fell in love with Anh; that is why Anh fell in love with you. That is why you hurt so badly when I told you of Anh's death, because your heart broke. It is also why you are here tonight. Your love of Anh has led you to love Vietnam. You couldn't save Anh, but maybe you can help her people, start the healing."

"So why the secret negotiations? Why not put Kissinger and Le Duc Tho in the public eye and push on with this thing, start the healing now?"

Nguyen sat contemplating. Finally, he spoke. "What I am telling you is speculation. In spite of what you may think, I am only a mid-level cadre. I am not included in creating policy, only implementing it. Just as Nixon is playing politics with these talks, so is my government. They will accept nothing short of a single, united Vietnam, something your government will not allow. We also recognize that we have an advantage. Nixon must produce some results prior to the next election. After all, he did promise to end the war when he ran for president."

"Peace with Honor." Tom used Nixon's phrase.

"Yes, Peace with Honor. It sounds so much better than, 'We were defeated by the gooks and we're getting the hell out of there.'"

The two men laughed.

"We too have political considerations," continued Nguyen, "but we are not a democracy and we have time, though not an unlimited amount. We could continue fighting until you Americans grow tired of the cost, both in dollars and lives. However, whereas we now benefit from international support, that won't last forever if we're not viewed as reasonable. By holding peace talks we show the world that we want peace, and world opinion is on our side."

"So you go through the motions and figure the real pressure is on Nixon, who has to show results before he runs for reelection in '72. So if you think I have a chance of making some progress, even if it's only with the public talks, then why ask for me?"

"A smart young man like you knows the answer."

"Requesting me shows that you are serious, that you want these peace talks to progress. But I'm nobody. I have no track record, nothing to impress those who follow the talks."

"It shows that we Vietnamese are open to trying new things to get the talks moving. You Americans have not requested anybody special from our government, nor any neutral arbitrators. Maybe requesting you is a small thing, but it is something. There is one other thing. I like you, Tom. If I'm to be stuck in Paris, I might as well be stuck with a friend."

"You don't have any friends among your colleagues?"

"Remember, I spent time in America, at USC. Most of my colleagues have never left Vietnam before. They don't want to eat French food or go to museums. I have heard many of them say that you are the first person to introduce them to French culture. You have become a favorite with them. Why should I not also enjoy my time here?"

"Plus, if I am successful to any extent, you might get to go home sooner."

"It is too cold in France. My body is suited to southern California or Vietnam."

"In the meantime, we might as well enjoy ourselves." Tom lifted his glass. "Here's to peace and friendship."

CHAPTER 12—1970

"**O**f course I don't care if he's gay. Half the Beat poets were gay. Some of our finest writers are gay. Homer was gay. I mean, look at all those hot, sweaty Greeks sharing tents for ten years. You think they weren't poking each other?"

"Ira, we don't know for a fact that Homer existed, much less his sexual orientation."

"I notice you're not challenging my assertion about the Greeks."

"I'm not challenging it because it's not worth arguing about."

"Who's arguing? We're having a literary discussion."

"No, we're not. I'm prepping you for my roommates, the ones who are kind enough to let you crash on the couch for a while."

Tom had picked up Ira at Orly airport, and they were riding the bus to central Paris. Ira's father had agreed to buy a ticket to Paris, based on false information, though Ira preferred referring to it as "misleading" rather than false. He'd told his father that *The Village Voice* had authorized him to write a story about the hip scene in Paris, supposedly agreeing to pay when the story was completed. The truth was that Ira hadn't worked at the *Voice* for six months.

Ira had written Tom and him that he'd need his help to get around Paris and interpret for him. Tom told Ira he was out of his fucking mind. Tom would have time for meals and a few walks, and not much else. Rather than be irritated by Ira's presumption that he had plenty of free time to kill, Tom was encouraged that Ira had gotten his shit together to get a ticket, passport, and actually get on the plane. For a man who had done little more than talk in the ten years that they'd known each other, Ira was finally doing something.

They got off the bus and took the Metro to Tom's neighborhood. After dropping off Ira's suitcase, they walked to a local café and ordered coffee. Ira was quiet, something not unusual for a person who had just completed a transatlantic flight, though unusual for the verbose Ira. Tom assumed that Ira was overwhelmed to be in Paris.

"Pretty impressive city, huh?" Tom said.

"It's just another city," Ira replied.

"Don't be an asshole."

"All right, I'll say it if it'll make you happy. This is pretty cool. Lots of trees and parks, fantastic architecture, foxy-looking women; it still ain't New York."

"I'll grant you that you won't find pizzas or corned-beef sandwiches as good as New York's; then again, Paris doesn't have rats as big as cats or thugs who'll rob you for a dollar. Paris also has killer jazz. I got tickets for Dexter Gordon for Friday night."

"In that case I'll stay. So how's life?"

"You'd know if you read my letters."

"I read them; I just didn't reply. Besides, letters only tell what the reader wants to reveal."

"Isn't that the purpose of writing letters?"

"Sure. You write your parents to tell them how happy you are and how much you miss them. You write your buddies to tell them how beautiful the girls are or how good the dope is, and you write Suzie to tell her you're horny and you'd love her to visit as soon as possible."

"You're a real slimeball sometimes."

"Letters rarely reveal what's going on inside your head. That only comes out face-to-face, 'cuz you can't bullshit when you're looking an old friend in the eyes."

"So what do you see in my eyes?"

"Pain."

"I'm getting over it."

"You get over colds and hangovers. Not death."

"What do you know about it?"

"I know that Dylan never fully recovered from Woody Guthrie's death. Folk never recovered from its own death at the Newport Folk Festival when Dylan went electric. The US hasn't gotten over Kennedy's death and the death of the American dream that was killed in Vietnam. You'll never get over Anh's death, which is a good thing."

"A good thing?"

"Death gives you perspective and gives meaning to life. Dylan's music just keeps getting better. Some say it's 'cuz he's living more; I say it's 'cuz he's seen more death. He was shaken by Woody's death, then the death of hope in Nam, then the murders at Altamont. We see things clearer when we understand our own mortality and the mortality of others. I know you feel guilty for Anh's death—you implied that in your letter. See? I do read 'em. Our actions do have consequences, though usually not the consequences we expected or hoped for. What really matters is what you do with that guilt, whether it's deserved or not. You stopped writing for a while, and I knew you were in a funk 'cuz you're a very sensitive guy. Now you're back on the job, a more insightful you, a bit more cautious, though still a do-gooder 'cuz that's who you are in your core. Now you're going be a better diplomat."

"Wow. What have you done with my hopelessly cynical friend Ira?"

"I haven't changed. The US government is still morally bankrupt, and the world is still a dangerous place. What's changed is you, and I know it's for the better. You left Columbia as a naïve kid, still eager to save the world from its greedy, selfish leaders. Now you've lived a little, seen death up close, and you're more ready to do what's necessary."

"More ready?"

"It's an ongoing process. You don't jump from naïve to worldly, unless you're Dylan, and I don't know if he was ever naïve."

"Thanks for your faith, though I'm not sure I've earned it just because I've been in a war zone and suffered loss."

"Like I said, I've always had faith in you 'cuz of who you are. I just thought the system would eat you up and spit you out. That's why I gave you shit when you said you wanted to be in the foreign service. I figured the hick from Indiana—even with four years under my tutelage—would be destroyed by the system. That you've not only survived, but prospered..." Ira pointed his chin around the neighborhood where they were sitting. "I mean, Paris, special assistant to the mucky-mucks. You done good, man."

"I'm lucky. I have an ear for languages."

"Don't give me that 'aw, shucks' modesty bullshit. You don't really believe it, do you?"

"No, I don't. You make your own luck. I worked hard, stayed true to my beliefs, earned the respect of my colleagues. Most of them, anyway."

"You probably scare the shitheads who see that you're the real thing. You tend to make others look bad."

Tom glanced at Ira, then quickly looked away.

"Don't get nervous, Tom. I'm not blaming you for making me look bad. I haven't had your success 'cuz people don't get me yet. Like you, I don't compromise. You caught a hailstorm of shit your first two years in Vietnam with that Hard Core dude."

"Hard Case."

"Whatever. You stuck to your guns. The next guy respected your for it, as did the locals, including Anh. She loved you, man, because you were real. Well, I'm real too, and the day will come when people will see it and respect it, and I'll finally make it."

"They didn't get Van Gogh until he was dead. He only sold one picture while he was alive."

"That's how art works, sometimes. Some people don't get it, others do. Diplomacy is like art in the same way. Its beauty is in the eye of the beholder. Or its ugliness. Say you guys end up letting all of Vietnam fall to Uncle Ho and his minions, with the promise that they won't abuse the losers and will let us Americans leave without killing too many more. To the world that will seem like a sweet deal, even if it's not a masterpiece. The right-wing nuts, on the other hand, will hate it. 'You've sold out to the commies.' 'The dominos will continue to fall.' Crap like that. The South Vietnamese, especially those who openly supported us and our allies, know damn well that they're in deep shit. You've signed their death warrants. See, it's all a matter of perspective."

Tom stared at Ira with his mouth wide open.

"I may be cynical—I prefer honest—but I am your friend, and I've been doing some thinking. I'm a poet at heart, yet I dig Halberstam and those guys who tell it like it is. Poetry will always be in my soul, but the Beat Generation is dead; so is poetry, at least poetry readings. The poetry of today is in the music, and it's alive and well and kicking ass. Heard Buffalo Springfield's "For What It's Worth?" "Feel Like I'm Fixin to Die

Rag" by Country Joe? Sheer poetry with a tune, and each one tells the truth. So how can I tell the truth unless I seek it? That's why I've been doing a lot of reading, a hell of a lot more than I ever did at Columbia, and I started with Vietnam, 'cuz it's happening and—more importantly—you're a part of the story. I used to get on your case 'cuz you didn't know shit and somebody needed to keep reminding you of that fact."

"Thanks."

"You're welcome. Now the hayseed from Indiana is a bit seasoned. You've lived the real life. I was always on your case about Kerouac and doing *On the Road*. Well, you did it, and then some. You cruised to California to, then damned if you didn't cruise all the way to Africa and Asia and now Paris. You took my advice and you're a better man for it."

"Thanks," Tom smirked.

"You're welcome. Now for my next bit of advice: don't let bumps in the road force you to turn back or take detours. Anh's death, asshole bosses, apathetic colleagues, they're part of the journey, the part I see in your eyes. Keep moving, keep growing."

"Thanks." This time Tom meant it. "What about you?"

"It's time for me to heed my own advice. First stop, Paris. I am going to write something that'll knock 'em dead. The *Voice* will have to take me seriously. Then on to London to write lyrics. My stuff'll be so good the public will demand more. Then I'll be on the road to fame and fortune."

"Why don't you pick up a guitar? Do the Dylan thing?"

"Naw, Dylan's already done the Dylan thing. Besides, I don't have tunes in my head; I have words, ideas, concepts. I'm going to be a lyricist, put my poetry to somebody else's music. That's where it's at, man."

Tom lifted his glass. "Here's to poetry, music, and shaking the world by its tail."

"Look out, world."

Tom was revitalized by Ira's visit. He realized that the cynic who had goaded and mocked him during his years at Columbia also believed in him. From the start Ira had pushed Tom to expand his horizons, to spurn the easy path for rougher roads that led to personal growth and greater insights. From Tom's first free-form poetry reading to taking courses that challenged his thinking to the reading list that opened his eyes to what was really happening in Vietnam, Ira had been a guiding force in his growth and maturing worldview. It was ironic that the do-nothing, go-nowhere Ira would be Tom's muse, yet he was just as important as Suzie, who provided the spiritual and calming influence that balanced Tom's life. Or, to use an image from Suzie's world, Ira was yang to Suzie's yin. Combined, these two provided the foundation and support for Tom's life in the foreign service.

Ira spent two weeks in Paris and would have stayed longer, but his New York intensity was too much for Tom's roommates, and Ira decided he'd better split for London before Fensky and Newman booted him out. Ira's time in Paris was not wasted, though. He sent a series of articles to *The Village Voice* that caught the eye of the editor. Ira raved about the energy that emanated from the students and workers of Paris, the same people who had brought down de Gaulle's government. He also scolded America's students and workers, blaming them for allowing Nixon to continue the war in Vietnam in spite of his campaign pledges to end it. Using information gleaned from discussions with Tom, Ira savagely attacked Nixon's stalling. Ira urged the *Voice*'s readers to rise up, take charge of the antiwar movement, and run Nixon out of office, as the French had done to de Gaulle. The series was enormously popular, and the *Voice* asked Ira to keep sending pieces from Europe. Energized in a way Tom had never seen before, Ira left for London with a sense of purpose, a man on a mission to change the world.

Ira's excitement was contagious. After he departed for London, Tom threw himself into his work with renewed vigor. He also continued to dine regularly with Nguyen. In late April, over a French bistro meal and a bottle of cheap red, Nguyen expressed his frustrations with the pace of the Kissinger-Le Duc Tho negotiations. Kissinger had, in fact, been absent from Paris for weeks. Although Tom assured Nguyen that, to his knowledge, nothing was happening, he had to concede that he had been totally left in the dark regarding the Kissinger-Le Duc Tho talks, so anything was possible. On April 30 that "anything" became known to the world.

Nixon and Kissinger had been preparing a military action that was to have dire consequences, though not the consequences that the duo had imagined. Kissinger knew that he held the weaker position, and thus had no real power to negotiate. The US public had grown weary of the prolonged war and rising body count, and a growing number were beginning to demand an immediate end to the war. North Vietnam knew that they had won; it was only a matter of time before US troops withdrew and South Vietnam fell. In order to speed up the inevitable, the North continued the flow of troops and supplies to their forces in the south via the so-called Ho Chi Minh Trail, a rough road hacked out of the jungle that ran south through Laos and Cambodia. On the morning of April 30 Nixon announced that US forces had crossed into Cambodia and Laos to destroy the trail, thus crippling the North's strategy and giving Kissinger greater bargaining power in Paris. Or so Nixon's team thought.

Worldwide outrage was immediate and intense. Rather than end the war as promised, Nixon appeared to be expanding the war into two other countries. Protests erupted in major cities around the world. On May 4, at a protest at Kent State University in Ohio, four protesters were shot and killed by green National Guard troops who panicked and fired into the unarmed mob. The American public turned even more virulently antiwar. Finding themselves in a weakened position, Nixon's team hunkered down for prolonged negotiations, willing to wait as long as necessary for something that would alter the balance. The result was that negotiations ground to a halt.

As 1970 drew to a close Tom's frustration grew. It was one thing to be developing rapport and connections, as he had done during his first two years in Vietnam. He had also been in love with Anh, so there was no sense that he was wasting time. That was not the case in Paris. After two years he had visited all the museums, and was intimately familiar with back-street restaurants that were unknown to tourists. He had also slept with a number of women—French and otherwise—though he was always discreet. A few wanted to take their relationship farther, out of the bedroom; Tom never called them back. Anh's death had left a hole in his heart, and he only shared his feelings with George Newman and Nguyen, and in letters to Ira and Suzie. Paris had lost its magic, and he was considering asking for reassignment when fate stepped in.

Tom occasionally received invitations to attend receptions and dinners at the US embassy. He had been developing a reputation as an up-and-coming star of the US diplomatic corps, and his French fluency meant that he was a ready interpreter at any gathering. People were entertained with his stories from Mali, Côte d'Ivoire, and Vietnam. His good looks and youthful charm meant that he was often placed at the dinner table next to wives and daughters of important diplomats, the better to charm them and win the support of their powerful, influential husbands and fathers.

Such was the case one evening in December. Rather than a State Department dinner for diplomats, this dinner was for wealthy Republican donors who were on a tour of the capitals of Europe. Many were scoping out embassies with the hope of being appointed ambassador sometime in the future as a reward for their considerable donations. Tom had grumbled about having to attend, but Newman reminded him that it was one of his duties as a diplomat. Tom put on his best suit, plastered a smile on his face, and walked into the embassy's ballroom with a clenched jaw. He was halfway through his first drink when he heard a familiar voice.

"I think we had a wonderful time in London, but my jet lag was so bad I hardly remember. I was up all night, then yawned through the day and fell asleep at the theater."

There was a round of polite laughter, and Tom turned to see Barbara Bennett. She was more beautiful than he remembered. Her long blond hair fell upon her deep red dress, and she had gained a few pounds, adding sensuous curves to her once anorexic body. Her laughing lips were the same deep red as her dress, and her blue eyes dazzled the half dozen men who surrounded her. As the laughing stopped, Barbara glanced around the room. When she saw Tom her eyes opened wider in surprise. One of the men, the director of the US Information Service, called to Tom.

"Come over, Tom. You're single, so your wife won't hit you over the head for talking with a pretty girl. My lady's been giving me the evil eye. Barbara Bennett, this is…"

"Hello, Tom."

"Hi, Barbara."

"You two know each other?" the director asked.

"We attended Columbia at the same time," replied Barbara. "You're looking well, Tom."

"Not as well as you."

"My, my. This is a side of Tom we've never seen. A secret romantic," said the director.

"I would have thought that Tom was quite the lady's man in Paris," Barbara said.

"If he is, he's not flaunting it. Tom is a serious diplomat, a favorite with our Vietnamese counterparts with whom he converses fluently in their language, beloved by our French hosts who are impressed by his language and diplomatic skills, respected by his colleagues. Our special assistant to the peace talks has a bright future with the State Department."

"I'm not surprised. Tom was always looking ahead. Most of the time, anyway." Barbara delivered this last sentence with a slight frown.

"Do I detect a hint of dirt about our Tom?" asked the director.

"Care for a drink?" Tom asked Barbara.

"I'd love one."

"Smooth escape, Tom," said the director. "See, I told you he was a diplomat."

Tom offered his arm. Barbara put her arm through Tom's and they walked toward the bar. With glasses in hand they retreated to a quiet corner of the ballroom.

"You really do look lovely," Tom said.

"I've put weight on since Columbia."

"You wear it well."

"The director was right. You have taken your diplomatic training to heart."

"Wasn't I diplomatic in New York?"

"Always, except when you gave your graduation speech."

"A friend challenged me to avoid the usual banalities and to say something memorable."

"It certainly was that. My father's face still turns red when your name is mentioned."

"Is it mentioned often?"

"Not if the person wants to avoid my father's most ferocious glare."

"And do you glare when my name is mentioned?"

"I was angry for a while. Hurt, is more like it. You seemed happy enough to accept my family's hospitality and more than happy to share my bed. Yet you had no hesitation slapping us in the face in front of the entire student body." Barbara took a deep breath as if to calm herself. "Eventually I realized that you were influenced by your friends. I understand that. You were young; insulting the wealthy and privileged is a natural part of youthful rebellion."

"You never rebelled."

"Why would I? I am very fortunate, and I appreciate all that I have. Maybe others have something to complain about. Speaking of which, are you still in touch with those two?"

"Ira was here a few months ago." Tom decided not to mention Suzie's visit to Vietnam.

"It would seem that your ongoing friendship hasn't harmed your career. That man was singing your praise as if you were the next Kissinger."

"I've been fortunate."

"Modesty was always one of your finest qualities. That and your athleticism between the sheets."

"That's the second time you've mentioned our passionate affair."

"Would you rather I dwell on your graduation speech?"

Tom laughed. "No, I'd rather dwell on the good times we had, though I doubt that your father would approve."

He nodded toward a group of men who were looking at them. Barbara's father, Henry Bennett, stood with the ambassador and a few other distinguished, wealthy-looking men. It was clear that Tom was the subject of discussion.

"There go my chances of getting a promotion," Tom said.

"I wouldn't be so sure. My father has a long memory, but he's also a practical man, and he respects nothing more than success. The fact that you're here counts heavily in your favor. Although Daddy may not forget what you said, he'll forgive you if it suits him."

"Let's find out if it suits him."

Tom offered Barbara his arm again and escorted her to the group.

"Ambassador, may I present Barbara Bennett."

"How delightful to meet you, Miss Bennett. I was just complimenting your father on having such a lovely daughter. He tells me you are as bright as you are beautiful."

"I do whatever I can to be of help to him. Daddy, you remember Tom Kington."

Tom held his hand out. "Mr. Bennett, sir."

Henry Bennett hesitated a second before giving Tom a firm, manly shake.

"Tom. I was…surprised to see you. This was not what I expected after our last meeting."

The ambassador chuckled. "Henry was just telling us about your speech. You apparently advocated anarchy among the graduates. Encouraged them to abandon their education and explore the world."

"I tolerated his support of Kennedy and his ilk out of my love for Barbara," said Bennett. "The speech seemed ungrateful."

"Daddy, that was ages ago."

"True. And the ambassador tells me that Tom is a diplomat with a very bright future. Tom, have you reconsidered your Democratic tendencies?"

"There are no Democrats or Republicans in the foreign service. We're all Americans."

"Tell that to the next Democratic president when he gets ready to replace all of us ambassadors with Democratic ones," said the ambassador to much laughter from the group, many of whom had been appointed by Nixon or had donated generously to his campaign.

"I'm a career diplomat," said Tom. "I'll leave party politics to others."

"Said like a true diplomat," said the ambassador. "See? Just like I told you," he said to Henry Bennett. "Plus he's fluent in French and Vietnamese. Tom's been indispensable to our negotiating team."

Henry Bennett looked approvingly at Tom. "I should never question Barbara's judgment. She always said Tom was special."

Tom blushed slightly, flashing on Barbara's remarks about their active sex life. He quickly took a sip of wine to cover his embarrassment. Just then the music stopped and an announcement was made that dinner was ready. Although Tom and Barbara sat at different tables, they looked at each other throughout the meal. After dessert, the music resumed and dancing commenced in the ballroom.

"Care to have a personal tour of Paris at night?" Tom asked Barbara as they met on the edge of the dance floor.

"I'd love to."

"Will your father approve?"

"After what the ambassador said about you? Knowing Daddy, he's probably already trying to figure how much it would cost him to get you an ambassadorship."

Tom looked decidedly uncomfortable, as if he'd just eaten something slightly sour.

"Oh, Tom, don't get upset. Daddy's always looking for angles. That's what made America great, men who did anything necessary to get ahead.

But I don't want to talk about Daddy or politics or business tonight. I'm in Paris."

"The City of Lights. The City of Love."

"Show me the lights." Barbara smiled mischievously. "Maybe I'll show you the love."

They lay in Tom's bed, still sweaty from sex, their breathing slowly returning to normal. Tom fondled Barbara's breast, gently running his index finger around the nipple.

"You don't seem to mind the extra weight I put on," said Barbara.

"You've put it on in all the right places."

"I always suspected that I was too skinny for your tastes."

"Why would you think that? Didn't I always show appreciation for your body?"

"You always made me feel special, and you never left me unsatisfied. It's just that I felt so, well, shapeless next to your friend Suzie. Her body was so voluptuous."

"We were friends. We're still friends."

"I know you fucked her."

"Yeah? How do you know that?"

"We women sense those things. It was the way you felt comfortable with each other, as if you'd spent time in bed together. Was she good in bed?"

"Would you want me to tell others how you are in bed?"

"As long as it's complimentary."

"You were always great in bed."

"You're a liar, though I love you for it. I know I wasn't very adventurous. I bet Suzie would do things that I refused to do. I'm a lot more fun now, Tom. Let me show you."

Barbara sat up and grabbed Tom's limp cock, then placed it in her mouth and gently sucked it until it started to become erect. When they were dating she only reluctantly performed fellatio, and never after he had been inside her. She sucked until he came.

"Wow!" Tom gasped. "You've been practicing."

She lay beside him gently stroking his now flaccid cock.

"Oh, I've had an affair or two, but I never got over you."

"Good girls like bad boys."

"You're not a bad boy, Tom. You're special, and I still want you."

He turned on his side and gave Barbara a long, slow kiss.

"I want you too."

It hadn't been difficult to convince Suzie to meet Tom and Ira in London. The three hadn't been together since Suzie's graduation ten years earlier. Suzie was living in San Francisco with a Chinese-American woman who ran a highly regarded progressive preschool. They had met at a Buddhist retreat near Big Sur and fallen in love before the weekend was over. Although Suzie continued to spend her evenings counseling young men who had been drafted, she started to work full-time at her partner's preschool. In a way, it eased her guilt at not using the education degree she'd earned at Columbia. More importantly, Suzie soon realized she was good at working with preschoolers. Her earth-mother persona helped them feel comfortable away from their own mothers, and Suzie shared with them the thrill of learning. It was the first job at which she truly excelled. Although Suzie was reluctant to miss a week of teaching, her partner assured her that the preschool would survive her absence and encouraged her to join her college friends. In early February she flew to New York to visit her parents, then traveled on to London.

Ira had used his articles about radical Paris for *The Village Voice* to land a job at the London *Free Thinker*, a leftist rag that was created in the hip '60s but was struggling in an England that was growing more conservative by the year. Ira was living happily in a fourth-floor walk-up in Earl's Court, writing scathing articles about the United States and England, and was developing a tiny, though fervent, band of readers. He was also writing lyrics for a guitarist from Manchester who was trying to break into the tough London music scene.

Tom picked up Suzie at Heathrow and took her to an inexpensive hotel that Ira had booked. They checked in together and went up to the room, which contained a double bed.

"Oops," said Suzie upon entering the room. "I guess you ought to go down and get a room with twin beds."

"You think we'll be less likely to misbehave if we're separated by two feet of carpet?"

"I just don't want to feel like I'm leading you to cheat on Barbara."

"She knows we're still friends, and she knows we've slept together."

"Does she knows I'm in London?"

"She knows I'm visiting Ira; I never got around to mentioning that you were coming too."

"Wise decision."

"Does your partner know of our history?"

"She's from San Francisco."

"She's also Chinese."

"True, and her parents are very old world. They think we're just friends. Su Yin is modern, and I've told her everything about my past, and she's OK with it. She's not bi, though, so there's no chance of doing what you and I did with Tony in San Fran."

"Too bad. That was a lot of fun."

"You're a bad boy, Tom."

"Only when I'm with you."

"Isn't that why you like me? Because you can let your hair down and remember when you were still learning about life and sex, and everything was an adventure?"

Tom kicked the door shut. "Let the adventure continue."

Suzie coughed out a lungful of smoke.

"Fuckin' tobacco," she coughed.

"It's the European way," said Ira. "They don't get pounds of weed like we do from Mexico and Jamaica, so they've got to make it last. Besides, I kinda like the tobacco buzz."

"It's nice to see you stepping away from your New York habits," said Tom, "Sort of a new Ira. Suzie and her Buddhism..."

"And lesbian sex," said Ira.

"...you and tobacco in your weed."

"And celibacy," Suzie shot back.

"So how's the music coming?" Tom asked, ignoring their jibes.

"Owen's been playing open mic nights and getting a pretty favorable response."

Owen O'Neil was the guitarist from Manchester who had been putting Ira's lyrics to music.

"Somebody's offered him a paying gig, fifty quid. He said he'd pay me 10 percent."

"Wow. You've got it made," said Suzie.

"Fuck off. The money's not in performing, anyway. It's in selling records. One big hit and we'll be on our way. Besides, it'll help my writing. The *Free Thinker* doesn't pay shit. If I can make it as a songwriter, then I can maybe write for music magazines or review music for one of the big dailies."

"That's great," said Tom. "You've got more going on in London than you ever did in New York."

"See," Ira said to Suzie, "Tom understands what I'm trying to do here."

"Tom's the diplomat. He always says the right thing. I'm just giving you shit, Ira. It's wonderful that you finally took your own advice and hit the road. Don't forget that I was always a big fan of your Beat poetry. You've got a way with words. It's just a matter of time before you find the right audience."

"Thanks, Suze."

"So what's new with you?" Ira asked Tom.

Tom took a small puff from the joint and slowly exhaled, careful not to cough.

"I asked Suzie to join us in London because I wanted to run an idea past you two."

"You're finally chucking in that foreign service bullshit," said Ira.

"No," said Suzie. "It's not about his job." She began to nod her head slowly, as if she'd finally realized something. "It's about Barbara."

A startled look came over Ira's face. "No fuckin' way. You're not serious about Barbie?"

"Cool it, Ira," Suzie cautioned.

"You're not going to ask Barbie to marry you? If you do I'll have to call you Ken."

"First of all, I haven't asked her to marry me yet, though we've been having a nice time together. She's matured since Columbia."

"It's been ten fucking years..."

Suzie glared at Ira, and he shut up.

"She's more open minded, hasn't said word one about me quitting the foreign service and working for Daddy, asks tons of questions about what I'm doing. Rather than figure ways for me to become part of her family, I sense more independence."

"Even though she was in Paris on a trip with Daddy," Ira pointed out.

"True, but she's more of an executive assistant than a fawning daughter. Her mom hates traveling, has a weak constitution, so she's helping her father."

"As he seeks ways to increase Republican power in Europe and enhance his personal wealth at the same time. Take a few more ambassadorships, maybe secure a couple of defense contracts," said Ira.

"I won't deny that Henry Bennett is a rich, power-craving son of a bitch, and to tell you the truth, that's some of the attraction. Not the money part, the power part. Look, you two know how frustrated I've been. You've got to be in the foreign service a long time to have any chance of doing something important. Most of my colleagues have given up. They just go about their jobs as if they were at a factory or working for some giant corporation, which they are in a way. The State Department isn't one of those places where you start by sweeping floors and end up CEO. You can climb, but only so high. The real power, the only power, originates from the top. I've jumped a few rungs, and I'm still a nobody. Like I've told you, the real negotiations are taking place in secret, and since Nixon's invasion of Cambodia they've been put on ice. They may stay that way for a year, maybe more. My colleagues and I are being used to appease the public. That's all."

"I see where this is heading," said Suzie. "You marry Barbara, her father pulls a few strings, and you jump to the top of the pile. Bingo! You're a major player. Aren't you concerned that you're going to piss off some of the people you've left behind?"

"I'm not in it to make friends. I'm in it to make a difference."

"What about when the Democrats return to power? You're out," said Ira.

"Not as long as I stick to my job and stay away from politics. No attending Republican functions, no statements of support for purely political views, absolutely nothing to do with politics. As well, I've got to get to know people from both parties. I still have connections with Kennedy Democrats. I know they'd love to try to lure me to their side."

"That's the Tom I knew so well at Columbia," sneered Ira. "The man who would fuck Republicans and Democrats alike."

"Kind of the same thing," Tom acknowledged. "I didn't care about their politics as long as the sex was good. Now I don't care about their politics as long as the goal is achieved. Ira, what difference does it make who ends the war in Vietnam?"

"Not much, I guess. Whoever ends it will take full credit, win the next election, then find other ways to fuck over the people."

"Speaking of which, Barbara has become much more adventurous in bed since we last slept together. In fact, I'd go so far as to say she's pretty damn good in bed."

"Better than Suzie?"

"This may be a foreign subject to you, Ira, but sex is not a competition. As they say, variety is the spice of life. Wouldn't you agree, Suzie?"

"Absolutely. Take Tom, for instance. He's well endowed, long lasting, always aiming to please, but sometimes gentle female love is preferable. Sometimes combining the two is bliss, though at other times two is too many."

Ira jumped up, grabbed a pad of paper and a pen off the coffee table, and started to write.

"What the hell are you doing?" Suzie asked

"You've just given me the idea for a song, a variation of Mary Wilson's 'I've Got Two Lovers.'"

"Great, just don't use my name," said Suzie.

"Nor mine," agreed Tom. "I don't think Barbara would be amused.

"This Barbie thing reminds me of that new song by Steven Stills, 'Love the One You're With,'" said Ira. "There's this line: 'If you can't be with the one you love, love the one you're with.'"

"That song is about free love, not feeling guilty just because the one you're balling is not the lady you're in love with," said Suzie.

"Well?" retorted Ira.

"It does seem a bit calculated," Suzie agreed. "It kind of feels like you're trying to convince yourself that it's OK, and you'd like Ira and me to tell you it's cool, though you knew coming in that Ira would never approve."

"But I do approve," said Ira.

Tom and Suzie looked shocked.

"Would either of you describe me as a romantic?" Ira asked.

Tom and Suzie raised their eyebrows.

"I'm a cynical bastard. I believe that love only exists in fairy tales and very rarely in real life. Tom and Anh had true love. Chances are very slim that'll happen to him a second time."

Tom nodded.

"I know that two things are important in your life: your undeniable urge to do good and sex, though not always in that order. No matter what I say, you're not going to quit the foreign service, not while you think there's a chance that you can make a difference. Barbie's connections and good looks could be enormously beneficial to your career as a do-gooder. With her WASP power and your intelligence, you could go to the top. And if Barbie has learned to give a good blowjob and is willing to study the Kama Sutra..."

"I'm shocked," said Tom. "What are your thoughts, Suzie?"

"Personally, I'm a romantic, but I'm not a big fan of marriage. I'm never going to get married. Neither is Ira. On the other hand, I see Ira's point. You're ambitious. You always have been. I'll always remember when you ran for student government at Columbia. You connected with just about every group, every clique. You were good and you were going places and you still are. Only you ain't going far without the right wife on your arm. I don't like it, but that's the way our society works." Suzie dropped her voice to a husky male register. "Howdy, this is my little lady. She can cook a meal in thirty minutes, pop out babies like a factory, and still look like Miss America." She shook her head and returned to her normal voice. "It's a fact of life. People like Ira and me, people who don't fit into the family-of-four-with-a-pet-and-a-lawnmower picture, we're nothing. Our best hope is that good people like you keep the assholes from doing too much harm. So go ahead and marry her. Besides, you can always get a divorce."

"I thought the idea of marriage was 'til death do us part," said Tom.

"It used to be. Seen any stats lately? The divorce rate in America is over 33 percent," said Suzie. "'Til death do us part has been replaced with 'til I can't take any more or 'til I find a younger one with firmer tits.'"

"Now who's a cynic?" smirked Ira.

"Yeah, I'm being cynical," admitted Suzie. "I was hoping Tom would find real love again. He deserves it. Tom, do you like Barbara? I mean, really like her? It doesn't have to be love, but I'd be very disappointed if it was only about getting ahead."

"I do like her. I even love her in some ways. She has changed since Columbia, and not just sexually. She's met Nguyen and some of my other Vietnamese acquaintances, and she doesn't talk down to them. She knows I'm still friends with you both and she hasn't said a single unkind word. She moved in with me over the objection of her parents and hasn't mentioned marriage once, unlike ten years ago when it seemed to be her only goal in life. I'm happy with her, and I think she loves me."

"Then you have my blessing," said Suzie.

"Mine too, as long as you name the first kid Ira."

"Right," said Tom. "I'm sure Barbara will go for that."

"I guess that's the end for you and me," Suzie said. "I mean sexually."

"I hadn't thought about it."

"I'm not asking you to think about it. I'm telling you how it is. I may be a free spirit when it comes to sex, but I'm not a cheater, and that's what we'd be. Our relationship has always been based on honesty and mutual respect. That would change after you marry. You'd have to start lying about where you were and why your clothes smell of another woman. We'd turn a beautiful thing into something ugly. I won't do that, not even for you, Tom."

"You're right, of course. I'll miss our moments of bliss," Tom admitted," but it's always been about friendship."

"Always?" asked Suzie.

"Well, not the first night, though pretty soon the friendship was as important as the sex. Some older people have told me that over time, when sex becomes less important, it's friendship that's most important to married couples."

"That's for really old people," said Suzie. "We're not there yet, and you're not married yet."

"Then we'd better go out for dinner," began Ira, "so you two can go back to your room and fuck while it's still kosher."

"Asshole," grumbled Suzie, though with a smile.

Barbara and Tom were married in a church in Washington, DC. With the
Paris Peace Talks stalled indefinitely, Tom had been assigned to work at the
State Department's East Asia section in Washington. Besides, holding the
ceremony in the capital assured that plenty of politicians from both sides
of the aisle would attend. Tom thought that Henry Bennett would object
to inviting Democrats, yet as Barbara had assured him, her father was a
canny wheeler-dealer: Bennett knew the benefits of playing both sides,
hedging his bets as it were. Henry Bennett also proved to be a generous
father-in-law. He bought the couple a three-bedroom townhouse in
Arlington, Virginia, a pricey neighborhood and a safer location for his
daughter than in crime-ridden Washington itself. Tom stayed in a hotel
until the wedding in order not to offend the more morally conservative
members of the Bennett clan.

Tom's family came from Indiana for the wedding, though their pictures never featured in the social pages. He spent a couple of days with
them visiting the Smithsonian museums, as well as touring the White
House and Congress, places Tom had never visited previously. They
enjoyed their time in Washington and were dazzled by the many well-
known politicians they'd met, and they knew they would probably not see
Tom again for a long time.

The wedding was covered by all the major newspapers and magazines, including a few from France that compared him to a young Thomas
Jefferson. Although only two hundred attended the wedding ceremony,
nearly five hundred were wined and dined at the banquet that followed.
The Beach Boys provided the music, and the crowd danced until late.
Quite a few powerful men—Republican and Democrat—asked Tom if he
had considered a career in politics, and, if so, told him he should give
them a call when he was ready to stop working for the government and
start helping to run it. Tom replied that though he was flattered, he still
had a job to do in the State Department and would remain there until the
job was finished. This always brought a knowing, conspiratorial smile and
a promise to be there when Tom changed his mind, which they all assumed he would inevitably do.

Many of the captains of American industry also attended the wedding
and made similar offers. Tom's gift with languages, his good looks, his
international experience and—perhaps most important of all—his new
liaison with Henry Bennett made him an attractive prospect, either as a

lobbyist or a public face for any conglomerate. Tom told them the same thing he'd told the politicians. He wasn't available and didn't expect to be; thanks for the compliment.

Neither Ira nor Suzie were invited to the wedding. Ira acted hurt when he first learned of his exclusion, claiming that he had a few things he wanted to discuss with the politicians and robber barons. Suzie understood why her presence might not go down well. Liberal bisexual Jewish Buddhists were not welcome in Henry Bennett's circle, and even the liberal Democrats who attended were not so liberal as to risk being photographed with somebody like Suzie. Tom promised both of them that they would get together and celebrate his marriage in their own way. Neither Ira nor Suzie expected that to happen anytime soon.

An independent record producer heard Owen O'Neil perform at a small club in north London. Although O'Neil's singing was strong and his guitar playing better than average, it was the songs that grabbed the producer. The music was melodic and memorable, songs you hummed to yourself on the way home. Even better were the lyrics, which alternately made him smile at the clever phrasing and nod his head at the political and social truths they revealed. One song in particular grabbed his attention: "Two Lovers Blues."

I've got two lovers who fill me up inside
Yeah, I've got two lovers who fill me up inside
One serves meat and two veg
The other gives me an opening in which to hide

Two kinds of love, both that I need
Oh there's two kinds of love, both I need
One gives me a hunk to hold on to
The other opens up and lets me feed

Some say it's unnatural, the love I feel
Totally unnatural the love I feel

But whether I'm on top or on the bottom
For me it's all too real

Five years earlier, at the time of the squeaky clean Herman's Hermits and the Hollies and Beatles, "Two Lovers Blues" would have been untouchable. Now, at the dawn of the seventies, after years of protest songs and the rise of women's liberation, the raunchy song struck a chord. The producer signed Owen O'Neil to a recording contract. Within two months O'Neil had completed his first record. Although banned from the BBC, "Two Lovers Blues" was picked up by independent radio stations across Europe and eventually the United States. A small though loyal following grew for O'Neil, and the single and album both sold well. A two-year tour of Europe and the United States. followed. All the songs were originals attributed to Blue O'Neil, which everybody assumed was the singer's nickname. The lyricist, Ira Blue, never revealed the truth, enjoying the notoriety from those insiders who knew his role. He received calls from other musicians and record producers who wanted to hire him to write lyrics. Some of the musicians were famous, and Ira had a chance to make some serious money. He enjoyed receiving royalty checks—physical proof that people finally "got" him—but he had no interest in becoming stuck as a lyricist. After all, everybody knew Frank Sinatra; how many people could name his lyricists? No, Ira had other plans. Bigger plans.

CHAPTER 13—1972

"I am told that you served in Paris," said French President Georges Pompidou, in French.

"It is far too formal to say I 'served' in Paris, Mr. President. Let us say I was fortunate to be allowed to live in Paris for three years."

"A handsome young man like you must have become familiar with the women of France," smiled Madame Pompidou.

"Not all of them, Madame President."

President Pompidou and his wife laughed politely. She gave Tom a coquettish smile.

"What is your opinion of French women?" Madame Pompidou pressed.

"Among the most beautiful, intelligent, and fashionable women in the world."

"Among? Not *the* most beautiful, intelligent, and fashionable women in the world?"

"Madame President, I am a diplomat. Would you have me make a statement that might come back to haunt me someday?"

The announcement was made that dinner was ready, and everybody made their way to the White House banquet room. Tom offered his arm to Madame Pompidou and escorted her to her seat before taking his own at a table for lower-level guests. Tom had been in Washington for six months, and he'd been to the White House seven times. Each had been a social function, and Tom had been charming at each. He had yet, however,

206

to be invited to a single serious meeting at the White House. Had never been asked his opinion on the Vietnam War or the peace talks or anything of substance. Not at the White House. Not at Congress. Not even at the State Department, where he was officially employed. This annoyed him at first, then infuriated him. He'd gone to his immediate superior's office one day and demanded to know why his expertise was being wasted.

"Look, Tom, everybody in Washington is an expert on something. Doesn't mean shit."

"But we're the State Department. We're supposed to be dealing with international relations. Besides, I'm in the political section, not public relations."

"Public relations is an important part of politics, and right now you happen to be doing public relations."

"That's not the title in my files."

"Just the same, it's what you're doing, and you do it extremely well. You're in huge demand. You've become a favorite at the White House. Nixon's daughters appear to be especially fond of you. I wouldn't be surprised if you get invited to a private dinner with the First Family."

"Damn it. They know I'm married. They know Barbara and her father."

"Maybe they regret having missed the sexual revolution. Even Republicans have libidos."

Lately, Tom found himself slipping toward apathy. Things had started off well enough when he and Barbara had moved from Paris and settled into their Arlington townhouse. Tom had never owned any property, had never expected to own any due to the nomadic nature of his job. Up to a point, he'd been caught up in Barbara's enthusiasm for decorating and had participated in most of the decision making. In truth, he'd allowed Barbara the final say on each and every choice, though he was always careful not to make it appear that he was capitulating. He didn't really care what color the curtains were or what silverware pattern they selected. He only wanted Barbara to be happy, especially after she announced that she was pregnant. Though they'd been careful to use condoms when they first started living together in Paris, they had stopped using them shortly before their wedding. Barbara joked that people would think she was white trash if she delivered any sooner than nine months after the date of their wedding.

Although it hadn't mattered to Tom, Barbara was obviously concerned about "doing things the right way," as she was fond of saying. Just as Tom had been caught up in Barbara's enthusiasm for decorating, he got caught up in her excitement at starting a family. Not that Tom wasn't thrilled; he'd simply never given much thought to having a family. He wasn't sure of the benefits of dragging a family from assignment to assignment, though he'd known diplomats with families that seemed well adjusted and happy. He figured he had three years to get used to the family thing and prepare them all for their next move.

Tom was less casual about his problems at work. Actually, there were no problems because there was no work. Not diplomatic work anyway. Besides the White House dinners, Tom showed diplomats and their families around Washington, and helped recently arrived diplomats and their families settle in. Though Tom had accepted that he would be called upon to do this for French speakers, he soon realized that it wasn't about his fluency in French. He also hosted Spanish speakers as well as some who spoke Japanese, Greek, and Swahili, among others. He had assumed at first that this was temporary, that he was being saved for more important things. To fill in his time he began to take Spanish lessons and was soon fluent, so he moved on to Italian. To his dismay, this meant that he was invited to even more functions so that the White House and the State Department could show off their latest star. It finally dawned on Tom that that was precisely what he was: a star, something bright and shiny that was pretty to look at and amusing. He mentioned it one night to Barbara over dinner.

"Well, you are a star," she said.

"Barbara, I'm thirty-one, and I've achieved nothing."

"You're a star of the future."

"I didn't enter the foreign service so that I could chat up world leaders and their wives."

"You're too hard on yourself. You yourself said it's a process that takes time. I can't imagine that Kissinger was negotiating with world leaders when he was thirty-one."

"No, he was a member of the Harvard faculty at thirty-one and a consultant. He wasn't taking families to see the Lincoln Memorial."

"Look at the connections you're making. Daddy says you're the talk of Washington."

"Sure, among his cronies."

It was the wrong thing to say. Barbara was six months pregnant and had grown more emotional by the week.

"So what's wrong with Daddy's cronies?"

"Nothing, per se. It's just that your father's cronies are not the people I care about."

Barbara slammed down her fork. Her lower lip quivered.

"I didn't mean that I don't care about them. They're just not the people who matter to me, people who can help me get to where I want to be."

"Because they're Republicans?"

"It's not about politics."

"It's all about politics in Washington. It's because of Daddy and his friends that you're dining with President Pompidou at the White House instead of eating in the State Department cafeteria with secretaries and low-level flunkies."

"That's exactly the point I'm trying to make. I don't want to be dining with presidents at the White House, not if I'm only there to provide witty conversation. I'd rather be at State working on peace treaties or trade negotiations, anything with substance. I'd rather dine with secretaries and low-level flunkies as long as we're doing it while working toward a valuable goal."

"I thought we moved to Washington because of your goal to rise more quickly to a position of power."

"Not so much a position of power as a position of importance."

"Well?" Barbara asked, as if talking to somebody who was slow on the uptake. "Who's going to get you that position? Secretaries and low-level flunkies or the president?"

"I don't want somebody to 'get' me anything. I want to earn it. I wasn't appointed special assistant to the Paris Peace Talks simply because I knew somebody. I worked my ass off for three years in Vietnam. I earned the trust of people. I earned that appointment."

"So you're earning points right now, only in a more pleasant setting, with more civilized people."

It was the first patrician thing that Barbara had said since Columbia, and it didn't go down well with Tom. It was the first time since their marriage that he sensed a flicker of doubt.

"I loved living in Vietnam. Sure, I was frustrated, but was I happy. I had a purpose."

"You still do, Tom. That's one of the reasons why I love you. You're going to be somebody someday soon. You just need to be patient, and you need to have more trust in Daddy and his friends. They have big plans for you. In the meantime, we'll start our family and build a life here in Washington."

"You do understand that this is a temporary posting."

"Of course, silly. I know it'll be a while before you're assigned to London or Tokyo."

That flicker of doubt grew ever so slightly.

While Tom's life seemed to stagnate in Washington, Ira's became frenetic in London. Although he had nothing substantial to show from his years in New York, he had developed into a formidable writer. Maybe it was his years of reading the sharpest, most incisive minds of the era. Maybe it was the dynamic poetry readings or endless late-night bull sessions in New York's coffee houses and jazz clubs. Certainly it had a lot to do with following Tom's career and reading everything he could that related to it: history, international relations, the role of the US. The result was that Ira had developed a clear view of the world that rose above his usual cynicism and approached fanatical fervor. Ira *knew* what was wrong with the world, *knew* the evil that the US was doing in the name of freedom and democracy, and he believed that his mission in life was to educate the rest of the world and encourage people of every nation to stand up to America and reclaim their rights as sovereign nations. Suzie sensed that Ira was jealous of Tom's success and his belief in his mission to do good. She told Ira that she still knew he was a cynic at heart and that his desire to be the anti-Tom was a way for the mentor to show his pupil that he was still his intellectual superior. Ira had become enraged at the perceived insult and ranted at Suzie until she said goodnight and hung up. They hadn't talked in months.

The success of "Two Lovers Blues" meant that Ira had the money to pursue his dream: to create a newspaper that was as important and as respected as the *Village Voice*. It would be a shoestring operation to start, but it would be a beginning. Thanks to "Two Lovers Blues" he also found a degree of notoriety and became a regular in London's party and club circuit. His name even cropped up in a few hip magazines and the odd society column. "Noted lyricist and American critic Ira Blue was seen last night with members of the Rolling Stones at a wild party in Chelsea that was broken up by police in the wee hours of the morning." "Ira Blue got into a shouting match last night at club in Kensington with two members of the Doobie Brothers regarding his patriotism."

Ira's notoriety led to a marriage proposal, one he eagerly accepted.

Jane Covington came from an English family that traced its ancestry to the Battle of Hastings, 1066. Various relatives proudly flaunted titles, and the entire clan was fabulously wealthy, with land and castles throughout Scotland, Wales, and England. They were also politically and socially conservative to the extreme. Jane, on the other hand, was openly and unapologetically gay. Although she dressed in the latest fashion for London's hippest women, her female companions favored short hair, black T-shirts, and black leather jackets. Jane's grandmother, a cranky old duchess, finally sent the word to Jane via Jane's father: marry a man and stop the lesbian nonsense or be cut off immediately from the family fortune. Though Jane Covington was a rebel and had been a lesbian her entire life, the thought of being made a pauper turned her blood cold—thus her marriage proposal.

Jane was in awe of the fiery American, loved his willingness to say anything and damn the consequences. She also knew—having spent many a boozy evening with Ira at parties throughout London—that Ira had no interest in Jane sexually, or any woman for that matter. Her proposal was mutually beneficial. Ira would marry Jane in a very proper public ceremony. The photos would be sent to the duchess. The duchess would present Jane with a large sum of money that she had been withholding until her granddaughter was married. Jane would give most of the money to Ira. Jane would continue to receive a generous monthly income from the family trust. Lastly, Ira would use his wedding dowry to create a formidable newspaper from the start, rather than the shoestring operation he had originally considered. He would rent a large space, hire qualified writers, and start out with a large print run. Best of all, he would be his own boss and could write whatever he liked. For living space, he and Jane would share a large flat in Kensington, with Ira sticking to his small two-room wing, while Jane and her lovers would have the run of the rest of the flat.

The Handless Monkey, or the *Monkey* as it was usually called, derived its name from the Asian image of three monkeys sitting side by side, each using its hands to cover a part of its face: eyes, ears, mouth. See no evil, speak no evil, hear no evil. Ira romanticized himself as a devilish monkey who would not be muzzled, blinded or deafened to the evil of the world. Rather, he would be a monkey on the back of the corrupt and greedy people who ruled at the expense of ordinary citizens. Although the US was the *Monkey's* primary target, all governments and corporations were fair game. The first issue came out a month before the 1972 US presidential election, and nailed Nixon and his administration without mercy. Ira called Nixon a liar and murderer and any other insult that came to mind. *The Handless Monkey*, like Ira, was driven by emotion, not fact.

In the charged atmosphere of the time, the *Monkey* was a huge success. It never made any money, but copies were mailed throughout Europe and the United States, and demand grew throughout the rest of the world. It was the type of magazine that was read and quoted by the young and the radical, though serious journalists scoffed at it. However, since it was quoted frequently on radio and television, and occasionally by members of various governments, it could not be ignored. Ira began making appearances on the radio and was invited to give talks to liberal groups. The *Monkey's* circulation grew rapidly.

Tom was happy for Ira's success and never gave their friendship a thought until the *Monkey* devoted an entire issue to the stalled Paris peace talks. Tom's name was never mentioned, yet a lot of information that he had told Ira during Ira's time in Paris ended up in the magazine. Although none of it violated national security, much was sensitive, and it was evident that Ira had an inside source. Particularly damning were revelations about the secret Kissinger-Le Duc Tho meetings and the declaration that the public peace talks were a sham. Tom rarely read the *Monkey*, and didn't know about the Paris peace talks issue until he was called into the office of the State Department's director of public relations on a cool late December morning.

"Have you read this?" the director asked, throwing a copy of *The Handless Monkey* on the desk in front of Tom. He glanced at the front page without touching it.

"Not this issue."

"So you do know *The Handless Monkey*?"

Something in the director's tone caught Tom's attention. Rather than his usual personable self, the director seemed tense, his lips set in a rigid frown and his forehead deeply furrowed.

"The editor, Ira Blue, is an old friend."

"So I've been told."

Tom nodded, as much to acknowledge the fact as to confirm that his initial suspicion was correct: the director knew of his connection to Ira.

"We attended Columbia together."

"I understand he visited you in Paris while you were stationed there."

"I see Ira every few years. Like I said, we go back a while. Is there a problem?"

"Since you are aware of this, this rag, you'll understand that the administration is not a fan of it."

"The *Monkey* is certainly not the only publication to criticize Nixon's policies."

"Certainly not. Every president has been attacked by the press. It comes with the territory. However, most magazines don't benefit from having a source within the administration."

Tom's mouth went dry.

"Our discussions tend to be of a theoretical nature. Ira isn't much of a detail man, as you can tell from his writing. Although Ira fancies himself a radical, he isn't a deep thinker and he's never done anything besides talk."

"Until *The Handless Monkey*."

"I've got to admit it took me by surprise. I didn't think Ira had it in him."

"This goes well beyond theoretical. It contains specifics regarding the Kissinger-Le Duc Tho meetings, and it didn't take long for our people to trace the information to you."

"It's not what it looks like."

"What does it look like?"

"I suppose it looks like I've been feeding Ira information. The thing is, Ira visited me over two years ago. I was frustrated with the lack of progress and I was blowing off steam. Ira hadn't started the *Monkey*. He never even talked about starting a magazine. Sure, he'd written some articles for *The Village Voice*, but nothing important, and he never used anything that he might have gotten from me. It was just college friends bullshitting."

I guess some of my bitching came off as anti-American or antigovernment. It was just bullshitting."

"Well, right now you're knee-deep in bullshit. Nixon is seriously upset, and he dumped on Secretary of State Rogers, and Rogers dumped on me."

"Sorry."

"Not as sorry as you're going to be if this happens again. The Kissinger-Le Duc Tho talks were a poorly kept secret from the start. You can't be blamed for leaking the story, only for providing details that are embarrassing to your government. Your friend is now on Nixon's shit list. If you want to keep yourself off the list you'd better distance yourself from him."

Tom squirmed uncomfortably.

"Do you have a problem with that, Mr. Kington?"

"I would like to think that my private life is just that: private."

"That may have been the case before; but by giving your friend privileged information that he published, it's now public. We'll be keeping a close eye on Mr. Blue."

"Who's 'we'?"

"The president has the responsibility of keeping an eye on America's enemies."

"What about the First Amendment? Doesn't the president have a responsibility to respect and uphold the right to freedom of speech and expression?"

"I'm not going to debate the constitutional responsibilities of the president. I'm giving you some friendly advice. Continued contact with Ira Blue could have detrimental effects on your career. You have a bright future with the State Department. Don't throw it all away."

Tom stood up. "Thank you for the warning."

Tom walked back to his desk with a storm of emotions raging in his skull. He was furious that his own government would threaten him over his friendship with Ira. He was equally furious with Ira for using information that Tom had shared during a private moment. When added to Tom's frustration at his limited and seemingly useless role in Washington, it left him in a deep funk. When he reached his desk he discovered that the shit storm hadn't played out fully yet.

As Tom neared his desk he was startled to realize that he knew the man who sat at it. Officer Jones was dressed as he had been when they first met at Columbia a decade earlier: black suit, highly polished black shoes, white shirt, black tie, buzz cut. Officer Jones slowly stood up. He was half a head shorter than Officer Smith and had the same scowl on his face that he'd had when they first met. Tom sensed that it was Officer Jones's only facial expression.

"Mr. Kington, is there some place we could talk in private?"

The shorter Officer Jones had to look up at Tom, somewhat reducing his attempt to be the hardass officer that he had been at their first meeting. Although Tom had been impressed and a bit intimidated at that time, ten years plus his friendship with Officer Smith had eliminated any awe that he might have had of CIA Officer Jones.

"Had you called and scheduled a meeting, we might have had a private talk. Now that everyone on this floor knows we're meeting," he nodded around the room to indicate the dozen workers who were doing a lousy job of trying to look busy while intently watching Tom and Officer Jones, "we might as well talk here."

"Mr. Kington, I must insist that we find a room where we can talk without others hearing us. This is a matter of national security."

Tom glared at Jones for a moment, then stormed off toward an empty conference room. Jones rushed to keep up. When the door to the conference room was closed Tom turned, crossed his arms, and waited for Jones to speak.

"Take a seat," Jones ordered.

Tom sensed that Jones wanted him to sit so that he would have to look up at the officer. He remained standing.

"All right, have it your way. I'm investigating a possibly serious breach of national security."

"Do you mean a possible breach or possibly a serious breach? What I mean is, was there in fact a breach or not, and was it possibly serious or possibly minor? I'm confused, possibly."

Officer Jones's fists clenched at his side, and his face turned a deep crimson.

"I was hoping to do this the easy way, but if you want to play games that's fine with me. I can have you arrested and held in solitary confinement until you're ready to talk."

"You know, I had a lot more fun talking with Officer Smith in Vietnam. He's a good man, the kind you want to have a cold beer with. Heard from him lately?"

"I'm not authorized to discuss fellow officers. I am authorized to get information from you, and I'll do it any way I need to."

"I bet you'd love to get out the rubber hoses and bright lights and get tough with me."

A tight smile crept over Officer Jones's face.

Tom dropped his hands to his sides and shook his head. "I get the feeling that I'm not going to win this pissing contest. Let's get this over with." He sat down. "Please proceed."

Officer Jones smirked for a second, then put his game face back in place.

"We've already established that you've been friends with one Ira Kornblue since 1958."

"Ira Blue. That's his legal name. Let's keep this all legal."

"You remain friends with Mr. Blue."

It was a statement rather than a question, so Tom didn't bother with a reply.

"Mr. Blue edits a magazine,"—Jones said "magazine" like he was saying "dog shit"—"called *The Handless Monkey*. The most recent issue revealed information regarding secret negotiations that are taking place between our government and the government of North Vietnam. Do you know how Mr. Blue acquired this information?"

"It's quite possible that some of it came from me."

Tom thought he saw a flicker of surprise in Jones's face.

"You admit giving Mr. Blue secret information?"

"No. I admit telling Mr. Blue..." Tom smiled a bit, drawing a scowl from Jones. "Sorry, I can't keep a straight face while talking about Ira. You make him sound like a character from the game Clue. 'Mr. Blue killed Miss Scarlett in the bar with a beer bottle.' Everybody calls him Ira. You can call him Ira."

Jones's scowl deepened.

"All right, don't call him Ira. Anyway, I told Ira that Kissinger and Le Duc Tho were meeting in Paris. If the meetings were meant to be secret, it was the worst-kept secret in Paris. There weren't too many people who didn't know about it. The meetings have been the talk of the diplomatic community for years. I also told Ira that I was frustrated, because the Kissinger talks were the important ones and we lower-level diplomats were just pulling our puds for public consumption. As to the content of the Kissinger talks, I have absolutely no idea what they were talking about, so I never told Ira anything that could possibly be construed as sensitive or having to deal with national security."

"It's not your call to decide what constitutes national security and what doesn't."

"Fair enough. I shouldn't have said anything to Ira. Like I said, I was frustrated; that doesn't justify talking about my job. It was an error. I've admitted as much to my director."

Jones seemed disappointed, as if he had been hoping to drag Tom into CIA headquarters for a bit of close interrogation.

"If it was up to me, I'd have you arrested and thrown out of the State Department."

"Apparently it's not up to you."

"Not right now it's not. Officer Smith always thought you were harmless. I even think he respected you, maybe was jealous that you were sleeping with all those college babes. Not me. I think liberals like you are just as dangerous as commies like your friend Kornblue. We've got our eyes on you and your friend. One mistake, one more case of you giving Kornblue information, and you'll find yourself in a world of hurt. You have my personal promise on that."

"Gee, and I thought you were a professional."

"I am. That doesn't mean I can't take personal pleasure in my work."

"You're a lucky man then. To be able to intimidate people and take pleasure in it. That's more than most people can hope for."

Jones turned and walked stiffly out the door.

Barbara gave birth to Keith Kington in September, about the time that rumors started to circulate about a burglary at the Watergate Hotel. Since the burglary was at the headquarters of the Democratic Party, it was assumed that the burglars weren't after diamonds. At Keith's christening party, Tom had asked his father-in-law, Henry Bennett, about the break-in. Bennett had grumbled at what he called a "nonstory" that he knew the liberal media would try to inflate. "Just some poor idiots looking for money. Probably drug addicts," he'd said.

Nixon easily won reelection in November, and Tom continued to press the flesh and smile at White House dinners. Although Tom struggled with his professional frustrations, he loved being a father. With many of his professional obligations in the evenings, he had time during the day to take Keith to the zoo and to stroll around some of Washington's many parks. It was a time of marital bliss, and all appeared to be going well, yet problems lurked that would challenge the nation and their marriage.

The five Watergate burglars had been indicted in September of 1972—along with G. Gordon Liddy and E. Howard Hunt—for conspiracy, burglary, and violation of federal wiretapping laws. All seven were found guilty in January 1973, and jailed. Soon after, the media discovered that all seven were in some way connected to the Committee to Re-Elect the President, CREEP as its detractors began to call it. Rumors began to spread of a conspiracy that possibly reached to the highest levels of Washington. Republicans were often spotted in small groups talking in hushed tones, furtively looking over their shoulders. Liberal newspapers began to investigate the break-in with the fervor of anteaters nosing for ants, led by Bob Woodward and Carl Bernstein of the *Washington Post*. By the end of April the scandal had reached the White House, and Nixon was forced to ask for the resignation of two of his closest aides, H. R. Haldeman and John Ehrlichman.

During this time Tom only saw Henry Bennett at family occasions. Tom noted that his father-in-law was preoccupied and short-tempered. The few times that Tom brought up Watergate, Bennett scowled and cursed the liberal media, calling the whole thing a witch hunt. Barbara's mother also seemed distracted. Tom asked Barbara about it one night after her parents had left their house following a dinner party. They were standing by the sink, drying the dishes.

"Of course Daddy is upset. Those horrid liberals in the media like Bernstein and Woodward are just trying to destroy all the good that Nixon's been doing."

Tom avoided political discussions because of the political gulf that existed between Barbara and himself, so he refrained from getting into Nixon's questionable record as president. He didn't avoid discussing Watergate.

"The *Post* didn't make up the Watergate break-in. Nor did they invent CREEP."

"I don't like it when you use that acronym. It's so vicious and unfair. People like my father believe strongly enough in Nixon to want to see him reelected. Liberals make it sound like it's a crime to be patriotic. There's nothing wrong with supporting your president."

"Depends on what lengths they go to get him reelected."

"I suppose Democrats never use dirty tricks. That Dick Tuck fellow put on a conductor's uniform and got a train to leave while Nixon was giving a speech on the back platform. The media thought it was funny, yet people came for miles to hear the president. Nobody complained about that."

"That was before Nixon was president, and it was a prank, not an illegal break-in and wiretap. And Dick Tuck was acting on his own, not on behalf of the Democratic Party. Watergate has reached the White House. You've seen the list of those who have been indicted so far. How many people knew about this? How many others were involved?"

Barbara's face grew flushed, and she turned away. Suddenly it struck Tom.

"Oh, my. Why didn't it occur to me sooner? Your father is a member of CREEP—oops, I mean the Committee to Re-Elect."

She turned and snapped at Tom. "Of course he's a member. He was one of the founders of the committee. You know he's been a big supporter of Nixon, but you're like everybody else these days. You want to see how many people can be brought down. It's become a game."

"I want to see justice in America. I want honest men to lead my country."

"Daddy *is* an honest man. He had no idea that his money was being used illegally. Now he lives in fear of being arrested. Can you imagine my father led off to jail? Being locked up with criminals? The shame would kill him."

"Your father's a lot tougher than you give him credit for. If he was unaware of illegal activities by the committee, then he has nothing to fear."

"What if he did know? What if he believed so strongly in Nixon that he agreed to let the money be used in any way necessary to help the president get reelected? Sometimes you have to use questionable methods to achieve great goals."

"That may be your father's philosophy; it's not mine. The end never justifies the means."

"You never bent the rules a little bit to do good. Never cheated on a test."

"No. Never."

"Well, well. Aren't you Mr. Perfect."

"I have principles that I live by. That's what civilization is based on, rules of law that apply to each and every citizen."

"So now you're saying that my father is a savage."

"No. I'm saying that if your father put himself above the law, for any reason, then he should suffer the penalty."

Barbara dropped the plate she was drying onto the floor, where it shattered.

"My father is not a criminal. He's a patriot, a greater American than you'll ever be. What the hell was I thinking when I agreed to marry you? You're a do-gooder who has no idea how to actually achieve anything good. That's why you're so frustrated with your job. While men like my father are making America safe against communism, you remain friends with that commie Jew Ira and that socialist Jew whore. You're nothing, and you'll always be nothing, just like your friends."

Tom calmly put down the dish towel. "I'll sleep in the guest room tonight." Then he walked out of the kitchen.

The guest room became Tom's permanent domicile. Barbara and he lived in peaceful coexistence, always being civil and sharing parenting duties. They still attended social functions together and appeared to be the perfect couple. Tom's work continued as if nothing had changed, though their marriage was now one in name only. Tom lay awake many a night considering quitting the State Department and hitting the road. He also thought of visiting Suzie, though he knew he wouldn't. As dear a friend as she was, Suzie lived in another world, one that Tom respected yet had no desire to be a part of. Besides, as long as he was married to Barbara he would never consider sleeping with another woman, not even his friend and longtime sex partner. He was struggling with his thoughts late one night when the phone rang.

"Hello."

"Still sucking on the Republican teat?" came Ira's voice.

"What the hell? It's midnight."

"Not here in London. It's five in the morning and I just got home from a party."

"Good for you, but you probably woke up Barbara."

"Probably? Does that mean you're not sharing the same bed, or are you working late on your grooming for the next White House dinner party?"

"Asshole."

"That's not very diplomatic of you."

"What do you want, Ira?"

"I want to see how my old buddy is doing. I've been worrying about you."

"Bullshit."

"You're pretty foulmouthed for this time of night. What's up? Did I touch a nerve with my remark about not sharing beds with Barbie?"

"Look, this isn't a good time to talk. I don't want to wake up Keith."

"Although I haven't seen your abode—not having been invited—it's probably big enough that neither Keith nor Barbie can hear you. Am I right?"

"Yeah, you're right. I still don't want to talk about my married life at this time."

"Then why don't you fly to London and let's pull an all-nighter. You know, smoke some weed, go to a jazz club, talk, talk, and talk some more."

"Ira, it would be better if you didn't talk about weed over the phone."

"Paranoid?"

"Let's just say it's not a good idea."

"Then let's talk about Watergate. What do you know that's not in the papers?"

"I'm State Department. As you well know that means I'm involved in foreign affairs. Domestic crimes are not my field."

"Right, but you're married to the daughter of a VIP in the Republican Party."

"Oh, what the hell. Officer Jones, I hope you're listening to this. Record it and get the transcript right so you don't have to come to my office again to hassle me."

"Officer Jones? Your phone really is tapped?"

"Thanks to you, you son of a bitch."

"Me?"

"Yeah, you, or more precisely that piece you did on the Kissinger-Le Duc Tho talks, the supposedly secret ones I mentioned to you."

"Those idiots think you leaked the story to me? The same secret talks that everybody in Paris was discussing when I arrived? If that's the state of US intelligence then we're in bigger trouble than even I imagined, and I have a pretty wild imagination."

"Anybody who's read the *Monkey* knows the extent of your imagination."

"You don't have to get nasty just because I called in the middle of the night."

"Not only called, but asked for inside information in the middle of the night. What do you suppose the CIA and FBI will make of that?"

"All right, you've made your point. I'm a fuckup. Arrest me."

"Keep up the seditious writing and your wish will be granted the next time you set foot in America."

"Has the Constitution been rewritten since I left New York? Has the First Amendment been overturned while I was partying in London?"

"Not yet, though I think they're working on it."

"Then tell *Herr* Jones and those other Nazis to go fuck themselves. I haven't broken any laws, either in America or England, and I'm going to continue to write the truth about Nixon and his band of crooks. Sorry if I've gotten you into trouble, Tom. Sounds like things aren't going so well for you."

"Nothing that time and a few changes won't repair."

"Changes? Intriguing. Why don't you fly to London and let's talk where a really loud band is playing so the fascists can't hear us? I could invite a third party—whose name I shall not mention but is very talented as you well know—and she could join us."

"I don't think that's a good idea, though a trip to London is a real possibility."

"Just show up. I'm not going anywhere. Come to the *Monkey's* office."

"Good night, Ira."

"Actually, it's good morning."

"Whatever."

"Hi. I'm looking for Ira."

The long-haired youth with the scraggly beard looked up from his desk. "You must be Tom, the future president of the United States." His accent was northern England.

"Do you think having Ira's endorsement will help?"

"It may help if you want to gain admission to the mental ward."

"Is that where I'll find him?"

"No, he's at the King George. Out the door, turn right, right at the corner, half a block down. Can't miss it. You can smell the stale beer a block away."

Tom glanced at his watch. He'd taken a red-eye and landed at Heathrow at eight o'clock. It was now nearly eleven. "Early lunch or late night?"

"The George is sort of Ira's second office, though he usually spends more time there than here, except the week the *Monkey*'s published—then Ira never leaves this place. Even sleeps on the floor of his office."

"Wow. His professors would be shocked, those who knew who he was."

Tom walked over to the King George. It was an old pub with a dingy exterior and an equally dingy, dimly lit interior. The bartender—a middle-aged man with an enormous gut—briefly looked up at Tom before continuing to dry a glass with a grayish rag. Tom peered around the room until he spied Ira sitting at a corner table, reading a broadsheet newspaper while drinking from an off-white mug.

"I hope that's coffee in the mug."

Ira looked up. "Regardless of what you might think, I'm not drunk all the time. I'm stoned most of the time." He snickered. "Seriously though, I'm drinking coffee, I don't smoke or drink booze until the day's work is done. It's good to see you. Have a seat. Coffee?"

Tom hesitated. "Sure."

"Robert makes a good cup of coffee, appearances to the contrary."

"I'm sure the coffee's fine. Do you always sit at this table?"

"Yup. Plenty of room to spread out, I can watch the door...Oh. I see what you mean. If Field Marshall Jones is any good he'll know I sit here every day and..."

"Maybe I'm being paranoid."

"You should be. Is this the same Officer Jones who talked with you at Columbia? The same wanker who accused Suzie and me of being pinkos?"

Tom nodded.

"I've talked to a lot of people since starting the *Monkey.* Retired MI5 and MI6—British Intelligence—and such. They tell me there's plenty of reason to be wary of bastards like Jones, people who operate with immunity, outside of the law. Seems we'd be wise to watch our asses. Come on."

Ira stood up and walked to the other side of the King George. "Will this do, or should we go to another pub? I know quite a few."

"I'm sure you do. No, this is fine. It's not like we're actually going to discuss top-secret information. I just want some privacy."

Ira shouted for a refill and another cup of coffee.

"So your marriage is down the drain."

"I didn't know you'd added mind reader to your résumé."

"I don't need to be a mind reader. We're friends. When I called that night and you said I'd probably woken Barbie…"

"Maybe I was working downstairs."

"…and you often mention Keith and work, but never your wife."

"Why would I mention her to you? You've never liked Barbara."

Ira sat and stared at Tom. Finally, Tom nodded his head wearily.

"It's not going to work."

"That's it? Finito? Not going to employ your best diplomacy?"

"This may come as news to you: marriage isn't about diplomacy. It's about love and friendship and shared dreams. Barbara and I strike out on all three counts. I thought she'd changed since Columbia; she hasn't. She's not a humanist, doesn't believe in the things I do, and she's definitely not interested in being a diplomat's wife unless I can guarantee Paris or Tokyo or some other 'civilized' place."

Ira raised his eyebrows and continued sipping his coffee.

"Go ahead. Say 'I told you so.' You were right about Barbara from the start."

"I'm not a genius. Well, maybe I am, but it didn't take a genius to see that you two weren't made for each other. At first you were intrigued by her beauty and wealth and her father's power. You got over that, which was a great relief to Suzie and me. When you two met again in Paris you were still recovering from Anh's death. Barbie was safe. Maybe you thought her father could help your career."

Tom frowned.

"You wandered from what made you special in the first place: your determination to do good. You tried taking shortcuts like marrying into power and accepting jobs that were meaningless yet looked good to shallow people. You were seduced by the illusion of power. You're like a really good hitter, a high-percentage guy who strokes a few home runs and suddenly decides he's a home-run hitter. So you start swinging for the fences, the glory, except you strike out more than you whack the ball out of the park. You're not a home-run hitter, Tom. You have a sweet stroke and you could have a long career in the majors. You just gotta readjust your stroke."

"I never heard you talk baseball. Thought you'd rejected it as too bourgeois."

"I loved baseball as a kid and started following it again after I moved to London. It's one of the only things I miss about the States. Let me ask you a question. When were you happiest: struggling to establish sources in Vietnam or working on the Paris peace talks?"

"That's easy. I loved learning the ropes in Vietnam, loved taking chances. Hell, I loved the Peace Corps in Côte d'Ivoire. It was a small nation, ignored by the rest of the world, yet I felt that I was doing something really important."

"Our dear Suzie would tell us it's a waste of time to dwell in the past, that what's done is done, and she'd be right. So things didn't work with Barbie. The question is, what are you going to do now?"

"I have a child."

"You do realize that little Keith won't starve if you divorce Barbie."

"Would you abandon your kid to be raised by the Bennett clan?"

"Obviously I'm not one to make recommendations regarding children or wives. I do know that kids don't thrive in a house without love. You and Barbie bickering all the time and sleeping in separate rooms isn't a healthy environment for a child."

Tom's jaw dropped.

"Lady Jane's parents apparently fought every day of their married lives. Still do. It really fucked her up."

Ira called his wife—Jane Covington—Lady Jane.

"I thought you rarely see her."

"Exactly. The perfect marriage. I've given her a cover and allowed her to continue to receive a small fortune every year. She pays the rent and only bothers me once a year to accompany her to her family's annual gathering."

"I wish my situation was so simple."

225

"Well, it's not. Fortunately, you're a bright guy. You'll figure it out. In the meantime, give me the inside scoop on Watergate for the *Monkey*."

"You're out of your fucking mind."

"No, I'm not. Don't give me anything that will get you into trouble. Nothing top secret. Give me stuff that will piss off the Republicans. That'll end your stint as the host with the most at White House dinners and get you sent some place dark and spooky, the kind of place Barbara will refuse to go. You won't have to ask for a divorce; Daddy'll hire a lawyer and kick your worthless ass out of the Bennett empire, and you'll be free to help the poor natives of some shitty little country far from Washington and Paris."

"Interesting scenario, one I'll have to pass. I can extricate myself from the current dilemma without your assistance."

"You're a noble lad, though I'd still like some inside dirt on Watergate. What about Henry Bennett's role?"

"You're fishing."

"Not for *gefilte* fish. I want to catch one of those big, gentile whitefish."

"Good luck. You'll be doing it without my help."

"This is your chance to get back at that rich motherfucker and his kind. Selfish shits like Henry Bennett are only into it for themselves. Isn't that what Watergate is all about? Nixon and his band of crooks wanted to get re-elected at any cost, the law be damned. They all deserve jail time and public shame. That's where I come in, me and my *Monkey*. We'll get those creeps."

Tom flinched.

"Aha! I've struck a nerve. So Henry Bennett is a member of CREEP."

"I think I need a beer."

"Now you're talking."

"No, I'm not. I'm buying, though."

CHAPTER 14—1973

Tom had been back nearly a month from London when he was called into the office of the director of public relations. When Tom entered the office and saw the director's scowl, he knew he was in trouble.

"Good morning, sir."

"No, Mr. Kington, it is not a good morning."

He threw a copy of *The Handless Monkey* onto the desk in front of Tom.

"I assume you've read this," the director said.

"Which issue?"

The director glared at Tom as if trying to discern whether or not Tom was playing coy.

"Like I told you when this whole *Monkey* thing cropped up," said Tom, "I'm an old friend of the editor, but I don't read every copy and I am not a source of information."

"You said you'd discussed the secret Kissinger-Le Duc Tho talks with this man."

"I mentioned the talks. We didn't discuss them. It was a mistake, and I've acknowledged it as such. It has not happened again."

"So you visited this man in London one month ago, he's now put out an issue about Watergate that carries some damning—and previously unknown—information, yet you're telling me he got none of this information from you."

"That's precisely what I'm telling you."

"Well, I don't buy it for a minute, nor does the president. You've been reassigned to the political section, effective today. Clear out your desk, and check in with them."

Tom stood and wordlessly left the room. He only had a few personal items in his desk at Public Relations, and it took less than half an hour to find a box and load his things. Rather than check in with the political section, Tom left the box at the security desk and informed them that he'd be back to pick up his things. Tom spent the rest of the day walking Washington. He sat on the cold steps of the Lincoln Memorial and contemplated his life—past, present, and future—then walked the Mall before sitting in a coffee shop near the White House. He nursed a cup of coffee for an hour, then resumed his walk. Tom wasn't upset. In fact, he felt more at peace than he had for many years. His days with Ira in London kept coming back to him, and he realized with a start that he and Ira had somehow switched places. Tom was now the one who talked much yet achieved little. If he wasn't doing any harm, he also wasn't doing any good, not for himself, his family, nor for the world. Ira, on the other hand, was doing a lot of good, depending on your viewpoint. Tom scoffed at most of the articles he'd read in *The Handless Monkey*. It was lazy, rabble-rousing journalism that was little more than leftist propaganda, yet it served a vital purpose. Love it or hate it, *The Handless Monkey* stimulated debate and led people to question their governments and themselves. Tom begrudgingly had to admit that he admired Ira's creation.

What to do? As the sun set Tom realized that he had the answer, that he'd always had the answer. Ira had been correct about Tom having gotten off track by marrying Barbara. It was a mistake that had to be corrected. People would be hurt. Tom's career would be set back, perhaps irretrievably. That was the price he'd pay to get back to where he belonged. In a way, he was already back on track. Being relieved of his public relations work and reassigned to the political section was precisely what Tom wanted. It was an opportunity he planned on making the most of. He would not make waves. He would accept whatever shitty diplomatic assignment came his way. He thought about Caleb Howell, his ambassador in Mali. Howell had bucked the system and ended up in a long series of unimportant postings, yet he seemed content. Howell accepted his postings and always did his best at each one. He was respected by fellow members of the foreign service, something Tom could not claim. It was time for Tom to put ego aside and commit himself to doing a good job, whatever and wherever that might be. Dealing with his marriage would be another matter.

When Tom got home he found the place empty. A note was waiting on the kitchen counter: "Moved back home with Daddy. Do not call." Somebody had evidently tipped Barbara off about the *Monkey's* latest edition, and Barbara had jumped at the opportunity. Tom poured a generous portion of single-malt Scotch and put some Beethoven on the stereo. He glanced through the mail until he came upon the latest issue of *The Handless Monkey*. Tom leaned back in his favorite chair and started to peruse the rag. It was devoted to Watergate and mostly rehashed old stories. What was new was an account of the Committee to Re-Elect the President that named "rumored" members, including Henry Bennett. It was crap journalism, devoid of supporting evidence or quotes from reliable sources. It was all groundless speculation, yet written in such a way as to protect Ira from possible legal action. Although Tom's name was never mentioned, the article often referred to anonymous sources within Nixon's administration. Since Tom's relationship with Ira was now commonly known, it was inevitable that Tom would be identified as the likeliest source. A small part of Tom was annoyed with Ira; a greater part silently thanked Ira for giving him a much needed kick in the butt.

The next day he checked in at the political section of the State Department. He was assigned a small desk in a small room crammed full of small desks, where a dozen people spent their days reading memos and dispatches from America's nearly two hundred embassies. As well, they read magazines and newspapers from around the world, gleaning articles for information that related to US foreign policy. It was drudgery, and Tom was thrilled to be doing it. Every once in a while he'd read something that piqued his interest, and he'd smile, realizing he was getting more professional satisfaction from this tedious task than from all the White House dinners he'd attended.

A week after his exile, Tom received a note from Barbara asking him to meet her for lunch at her father's club. Henry Bennett had reserved a private room, complete with a private waiter, to ensure privacy. Barbara was sitting at the table when the maître d' ushered in Tom.

"Hello, Barbara. You're looking lovely."

"I don't feel lovely. I feel fat and ugly. It may take me another year to get my old figure back. You men have no idea of what it means to be pregnant. You think we carry a baby for nine months, pop 'em out, and then it's back to normal. Well, let me tell you, that's not the way it is."

"I guess I never thought through all of the consequences of sex."

"That seems to have been our problem from the start."

They sat in silence for a moment.

"Barbara, you and Keith should move back into the house. It's yours, after all, and you should be there with Keith."

"It's your house as well."

"Not really. I didn't buy it, and I certainly didn't earn it."

"Dear, noble Tom. Actually, I'm better off with my parents. Between Mother, the nurse, and their staff, Keith and I are well cared for."

Tom was on the verge of saying he'd prefer that his children not be raised by a gaggle of servants. Instead he said, "Whatever works best for you, Barbara. If you want to move back or your father wants to sell the house, I'll move out."

"What I wanted was to be happily married to you, to raise a family together, to help your career in any way I could. Now that you've publicly stabbed Daddy in the back you won't have to worry about his connections." The veneer of good manners fell away. "See what your dear friend Ira's connections can do for you."

"Did you read the CREEP article in *The Handless Monkey*?"

"I wouldn't use that horrid article to wrap dead fish."

"Although I'm not a fan of your father's politics, I did not sell him out to Ira. The article is all speculation and innuendo. It's lousy journalism, and it was written without any input from me."

"I find that hard to believe."

"I've never lied to you, and I never will."

"Even if what you say is true, the fact remains that your friend slandered my father and his friends."

"Then your father should sue Ira."

"He might."

They sat and fumed for a minute, then ate their lunch in silence. When their plates were cleared Tom spoke.

"I miss Keith. I'd like to see him."

"That can be arranged."

"Great. Maybe I'll take him to the zoo."

"Keith would like that."

"What's next? Are you planning on filing for divorce?"

"Daddy has urged me to get a lawyer; I haven't done it yet."

"Why not?"

"I don't want to believe our marriage is over. Is it?"

"I don't know. Some days I think it is, and other days I want to give it another try."

"Are you dating anybody?" Barbara asked.

Tom looked Barbara in the eyes. "I'm married to you."

"How silly of me. You're a man of principles. You'd never do anything even mildly immoral. So what should we do?"

"I wish you'd asked that before moving back with your parents," Tom snapped. He let out a sigh. "Sorry. You probably did the right thing. Why don't we just give it time? I'll pick up Keith on Saturdays, if that's all right with you, and let's see where things go."

Summer of 1973 saw an escalation of the Watergate scandal. Nixon had hoped that firing his two closest aides, H. R. Haldeman and John Ehrlichman, as well as White House Counsel John Dean, would appease his critics. It didn't. The Senate's televised hearings because must-see viewing, and the public couldn't seem to get enough news about Watergate. When it was revealed in July that a secret system had been recording all of Nixon's meetings in the White House, public fervor for blood leaped. Loyal Republicans complained that the White House hadn't been under such a serious threat since the British stormed Washington in 1812.

Tom was thrilled to have been exiled by Nixon and the Republican elite, thinking he had avoided being caught up in the scandal. He soon found that he was wrong. A few weeks after the Watergate article in *The Handless Monkey* was published, Tom began to get phone calls at home from newspapers and magazines—mostly liberal to radical—asking for information. At first Tom politely said he knew nothing. As the calls piled up his patience waned. One day after work he was walking toward the bus stop when a pretty young woman walked up to him. She had long black hair, and even though she wore a loose-fitting jacket, Tom could see that she had a dynamite figure.

"Hi. You're Tom Kington, right?"

Tom's first instinct was to refuse to answer and to keep walking, but he'd never been able to ignore a beautiful woman.

"Maybe."

"I'm Ellen Becker of *Progressive Times*."

Progressive Times was a far-left magazine that had been founded in May, 1970, in the wake of Nixon's invasion of Cambodia and the deaths at Kent State. Like *The Handless Monkey*, *Progressive Times* was on a mission to expose moral corruption in government and industry. Unlike *The Handless Monkey*, *Progressive Times* was a magazine that had always been intent on serious journalism. All of its staff had journalism degrees, and every article was meticulously researched. It had a reputation for honest, though blatantly biased, journalism.

"Oh. One of those." He started walking faster.

"One of what?" she said, hustling to keep up with him.

"Some people in Washington consider you the enemy, right up there with *Pravda* and other pinko rags."

"But you don't think that because you're bright and an independent thinker."

"Gosh, thanks." Tom increased his pace.

"Listen for one second, please," Ellen Becker gasped, struggling to keep pace. "I've checked around. You're one of the good guys."

Tom stopped abruptly and turned around. Ellen Becker nearly walked into him.

"If I'm seen talking with you, I'll be an unemployed good guy."

"Whatever happened to freedom of speech and rule by law?"

"You write for the *Progressive Times* and you have to ask that question?"

"Then talk with me—one hour, that's all I ask—and we'll show them that we're not going to be intimidated."

Tom laughed. "You talk pretty tough. Then again, you don't have much to lose. You have a job with a magazine that rewards brave talk. I, on the other hand, work for an organization that frowns upon those who speak independently. Are you married, Miss Becker?"

"I don't know what that has to do anything."

"Any dependents? Any children?"

"No, to all of your questions."

"I have a child and a very angry wife. I also have a career. How would you suggest I support my family and keep the peace at home if I'm fired from the State Department?"

"I'm sure Henry Bennett would help. My sources tell me that your wife is living with her father right now."

Tom glared at the reporter, then turned and stormed away.

A few days after being waylaid by Ellen Becker, Tom received a letter in the mail. When he opened it he found a condolence card. On the cover was a picture of a bunch of limp stems minus the flowers and with the words, "Sorry For Your Loss." The inside of the card showed a brilliant bouquet of roses and the words, "May Love Bloom Again." The handwritten note said, "I was a total jerk and I apologize. I'll be at Jack's Tavern in Georgetown Saturday night at 7:00. Dinner is on me. No RSVP required."

Tom contemplated the card over the next few days and didn't decide what to do until six o'clock Saturday evening. He left work and took the bus to Georgetown. Tom had never been to Jack's Tavern before, and he smiled when he walked in. The place was dimly lit, packed with a Georgetown University crowd; not the type of place that Washington insiders would frequent. It was the perfect place for a clandestine meeting. Tom wove his way through the dense crowd until he spied Ellen Becker sitting at a table for two. She was nursing a glass of red wine and smiled broadly when she saw Tom approach.

"I'm glad you came."

Tom sat down. "I nearly didn't, but seeing as I haven't gone out for dinner in weeks..."

"And considering that dinner's on me."

"I'd have thought *Progressive Times* was picking up the tab."

"This is on me, my way of apologizing for being an aggressive jerk."

"You were being a journalist."

"We can be aggressive without being unpleasant. I went over the line. I apologize."

"Apology accepted."

"Would you share a bottle of wine if I ordered one?"

"Sure."

She ordered wine and appetizers after asking Tom's preference.

"You know, even if you get me drunk it won't help," he began, before hastily adding, "as far as me being a source, I mean."

Ellen Becker laughed. "Men are never good for much when they're drunk."

"What I meant was I don't know anything of interest for the readers of *Progressive Times*. I work for the State Department. I'm not involved in domestic issues, and I don't know squat about Watergate. By the way, I assume your card refers to my separation? I didn't think it had made the society pages, so how did you learn about it."

"A good journalist never reveals her sources."

"Maybe I should order a second bottle and see if it'll loosen your lips."

"I have excellent lip control, and I'm willing to match you drink for drink to prove it."

"We diplomats are trained to avoid dangerous situations."

"Yet you put your life and career on the line in Vietnam."

Tom sipped his wine while looking at Ellen. She had a beautiful face with full lips and deep brown eyes. He was pretty sure she had some Spanish or Italian blood. She wore a low-cut sweater that revealed sumptuous breasts. All of a sudden, it dawned on him.

"Ira."

Ellen flinched ever so slightly. "Ira who?"

Tom smiled and kept his eyes on Ellen's. Finally, she cracked.

"Damn. What gave me away?"

"You have a lousy poker face. You gave it away when I mentioned Ira's name."

"We have sources in London, as we do in many cities. When the Watergate article came out in the *Monkey* we sent somebody over to see what they could get from your friend Ira Blue. He apparently kept his mouth shut until the second beer."

"That shows admirable loyalty. Ira usually tells all after the second sip. So you went looking for Ira's source on Watergate and ended up with a dossier on me."

"I'll be honest. I went looking for the *Monkey's* Watergate source, but your background piqued my curiosity. Then, after I met you for the first time, I was intrigued." Ellen hesitated. "To be honest, I was attracted to you."

"I'm flattered, and I'll be honest with you. I don't know anything vital about Watergate. Really. Since you read the *Monkey's* article you know that Ira doesn't have anything vital either. I should also mention that I've been faithful to my wife, even while we're separated."

"According to Mr. Blue your marriage is over."

"If you'd met Mr. Blue you'd know he's not the most reliable source. Truth is, Ira never liked Barbara and has been hoping for our divorce since the day we were married."

"So your marriage isn't over."

Tom opened his mouth, closed it, then took a sip of wine. "My wife and I have what lawyers refer to as irreconcilable differences."

"Meaning you're an independent internationalist and she's a nativist Republican."

"I see you have done your research."

"I'd like to research you a bit more."

Just then their dinner arrived.

"One course at a time," Tom said.

Tom and Ellen didn't sleep together the first night, nor did they for a few weeks after. They dined together a few times a week and quietly slipped into a couple of movies, though always after the lights were dimmed to avoid being seen. One evening they attended an art opening, arriving separately, only talking briefly, and acting as if they had just met at the opening. Ellen called one particularly hot Sunday morning in June and invited Tom over for dinner on her balcony. They had planned on going out for dinner, but Ellen claimed that her apartment was always cooler than the rest of steamy Washington. She offered a crab salad, chilled white wine, and homemade cherry ice cream, and after his initial hesitation Tom accepted.

Ellen opened the door wearing light cotton shorts and a thin scallop-necked T-shirt. Strands of dark hair stuck to her damp forehead. The front of the T-shirt was moist with sweat and adhered to her chest. It was immediately apparent that she wasn't wearing a bra.

"Damn, I was hoping you'd be half an hour late," Ellen said.

"Have I ever been late?"

"Never. I was just hoping. It's a hell of a lot hotter than I'd expected, and I've been cranking the ice cream, and I was going to shower and put on this slinky short dress and…"

Tom put his arms around Ellen and gave her a long, slow kiss. As their lips parted she pushed him away.

"I'm going to get your shirt all sweaty."

"I can fix that."

Tom pulled his polo shirt over his head, then reached and lifted Ellen's T-shirt over her head. He again wrapped his arms around Ellen and pulled her to him. Her ample, warm breasts pushed against his chest.

"There. No sweat," Tom said. "Is the ice cream in the freezer?"

Ellen nodded. "And the salad and wine are in the fridge."

"Then it's shower time."

"Let's work up a sweat first."

It was the hottest, sweatiest bout of lovemaking that Tom had experienced since being with Anh in Vietnam. Ellen was an enthusiastic, adventurous lover. Tom, who hadn't had sex in months, came quickly. When he started to apologize, Ellen put her finger on his lips and hugged him close. A little later they made slow, intense love until they both came at the same time. Afterward, they took a cool shower together and then sat down on the balcony for dinner.

"I'm sorry if I led you to be unfaithful," Ellen said while they ate the cherry ice cream.

Tom snorted a laugh. "Yeah, you should be sorry. I came here with the most noble of intentions and you met me with those fantastic nipples bursting through that damp white T-shirt. I was powerless."

Ellen laughed.

"When I accepted your invitation I was pretty sure that we'd end up in bed. Wasn't that your intention?"

"Not necessarily my intention. More of a hope."

"You know this can't lead anywhere, not while I'm married."

"I have no secret plans, no desire to get rid of Mrs. Kington. I find you very attractive and I wanted to have sex with you."

"Slut."

Ellen slid to her knees and started to slide her hands up Tom's bare legs to his groin.

"Let me show you how slutty I can be."

Tom had been at his desk less than an hour when his phone rang.

"This is State Department security. You need to come to Room 688 immediately."

"Immediately? Is this an emergency?"

"Room 688." The caller hung up.

Tom turned to the young political officer who sat at the next desk. "If I'm not back by tomorrow just box up my stuff and have it sent to my wife."

The man gave Tom a quizzical look. Tom stood up and walked to Room 688. When he walked in he knew he was in for trouble. At the head of the table sat the undersecretary of state for Political Affairs. Next to him was CIA Officer Jones. Another man dressed in a somber brown suit sat next to Jones. To the other side of the undersecretary was a woman with a notepad.

"Take a seat," said the undersecretary.

Tom noted that it was not a request.

"I've been hearing some distressing things about you, Mr. Kington."

Tom looked around the table. The three men were giving Tom hard looks; the woman hovered over her notepad and didn't look at Tom. If the undersecretary was waiting for Tom to speak he was in for a disappointment. Tom folded his arms across his chest and waited.

"We have evidence that you've been having an affair with a journalist from *Progressive Times*. Officer Jones informs me that you've been warned about talking with the press."

Again the undersecretary waited for Tom to speak, and again Tom sat like a brooding Buddha. The undersecretary continued.

"You've met Officer Jones. This is Officer Johnson of the Federal Bureau of Investigation."

Officer Johnson was a heavyset man with thinning hair. His suit was rumpled, and he seemed to wear the same permanent scowl that Officer Jones always wore. Tom wondered if scowling was part of their training, though Sam Smith never scowled. Officer Johnson leaned forward and put his forearms on the table.

"The CIA has asked the FBI to keep an eye on you. During the past two months we have documented numerous meetings between you and Miss Ellen Becker. Recently your relationship has taken a more personal turn."

An image of Ellen kneeling between Tom's legs on her balcony flashed in Tom's mind. He fought the anger that began to well up within him. There was no way he was going to give Officer Jones the pleasure of seeing him go berserk; nor was he ready to tell the undersecretary to go fuck himself.

"I'm sure this is very upsetting for you," said the undersecretary. "It is not normally our habit to pry into the personal lives of our staffers. However, we would not be investigating you had you not done some things that forced us to act. We accepted you in the foreign service in spite of some questionable acquaintances, and until recently you have performed admirably for your country. Two years ago you met with one," he looked at his notes, "Ira Blue, editor of *The Handless Monkey*. Although the CIA has been unable to prove anything, it appears as if you revealed information about secret negotiations between our government and the government of North Vietnam. You again met with Mr. Blue in London a little under a year ago. Subsequently, Mr. Blue published an article about the Watergate investigation. The article also contained information of a secret nature. Now we learn that you have developed a personal relation with Miss Becker, whose employer, *Progressive Times*, is an opponent of the current government. Mr. Kington, these are potentially serious allegations. What do you have to say for yourself?"

Tom sat silently for a minute, took a deep breath, then lashed back. "You mentioned 'potentially serious allegations,' yet you also admit that the CIA had been unable to prove any wrongdoing. I assume that the FBI has also failed to prove that I have done anything illegal. While we're on the subject of legality, I wonder what a good lawyer would make of the CIA and FBI spying on a government employee who has committed no crimes."

Officer Jones opened his mouth to speak, but Tom silenced him with a raised hand.

"I'm sure you have all sorts of legal explanations for violating my right of privacy, though it might be embarrassing for the press to learn that you spy on journalists during their private time. Besides, I'd guess the president has enough with Watergate and would rather not be dealing with an angry media on the issue of government harassment of that very same media."

This time Officer Johnson opened his mouth, but the undersecretary silenced him with a shake of the head.

"Take all the photos you want. Keep listening to my phone conversations and those of my friends. You may hear some shocking things, but nothing seditious. Truth is, you have nothing on me because I've done nothing wrong. My relationship with Ira Blue is common knowledge, even if the CIA and FBI think it's some sort of major scoop. I'm sure you're also aware of my friendship with a lady in California who attended Socialist meetings over a decade ago and is now a practicing Buddhist. If you think she's a greater threat to national security than the Soviet Union or China then have at her. The bottom line is that I've committed no crimes and I've worked diligently for many years for my country. If you want to charge me with something," Tom looked at the two officers, "do it. If you want to fire me," he looked at the undersecretary, "go ahead, because I'm not going to quit. Of course, if you do fire me, I'll hit you with a wrongful termination suit and we can meet in court. We can set up a trial with State, the CIA, and the FBI, have a public discussion of how loyal government employees are treated."

"Now, Tom," began the undersecretary, "there's no need to get belligerent. These are serious allegations, and it is our responsibility to investigate them."

Tom stood up. "Do what you have to, Mr. Secretary. In the meantime, I'll continue to do the job I was hired to do. Next time you want to have a meeting like this you'll have to give me at least twenty-four hours notice so that I can bring a lawyer with me."

"You haven't been charged with anything," pointed out the undersecretary.

"Let me know when I am. Right now I have some bulletins from Laos I need to analyze."

As he stood to leave he glanced at Jones. The officer wore a smirk that said, "This isn't over yet."

Tom sent Ellen a note at *Progressive Times* telling her that he couldn't see her for a while. He did not give an explanation. For the next month he focused on his work, eating alone at home every evening. He picked up Keith every weekend and made pleasant conversation with Barbara when he saw her, though Keith's nanny was the one who usually handed Keith off to Tom. He never saw Henry or Emily Bennett. One day in mid-October, though, Barbara was waiting for Tom when he came to pick up Keith.

"Hi. Where are you and Keith going today?"

"To the zoo again. Keith can't seem to get enough of the pandas and gorillas."

"Sounds like fun. Mind if I come with?"

Tom was shocked into silence.

"If you don't want me to come with..." began Barbara.

"No, I mean, yes, I'd love for you to come with. I was just caught by surprise."

"I've read that surprises are good for a relationship."

Tom nearly said that it depended on the nature of the surprise.

They spent a lovely day at the zoo, a family day. Tom and Barbara ate hotdogs and talked about nothing consequential. Keith seemed to bask in the glow emanating from his happy parents, and he babbled away, occasionally pointing at the animals and squealing with excitement. Tom couldn't remember a day when Barbara and he had been so happy together.

The next weekend was unusually warm, an Indian summer sort of day, and they took Keith for a picnic on the Mall. Tom and Barbara began to talk almost daily on the phone. The following weekend they went for a drive in Maryland. Tom took Barbara and Keith home that evening, and they put Keith to bed together, each taking turns reading a bedtime story. Afterward they went to the kitchen, and Barbara poured each a cognac.

"That was a nice day," Tom said.

"It's been a nice month," Barbara corrected. "Nearly perfect. Tom, honey, why don't you spend the night? Then it *will* be a perfect month."

"I thought we'd agreed that sex is what got us in trouble in the first place."

"No, we'd agreed that there may have been too little thinking and too much sex. Now we've done the opposite. We've both overthought things and failed to follow our instincts." Barbara ran her bare foot up Tom's leg and started to rub his crotch. "I think we should go up to my room and let our animal instincts loose."

Tom rubbed Barbara's foot, then gently moved it to his thigh.

"Barbara, there's nothing more I'd like to do than have sex with you, but not here, not in your parents' house, not with them at home."

Barbara stiffened and put her foot back on the floor. Tom leaned forward, kissed Barbara, and started to fondle her breast. She sighed and put her hand over Tom's.

"Now you're teasing me. You won't go upstairs, but you'll get my juices flowing."

"Why don't you come over to my place Saturday night and let your parents babysit Keith? I'll cook us a dinner, and you can stay the night. Then we can let all the juices flow."

"I'd like that. Maybe we can rekindle the flame."

"Least we can do is have a great time like we used to. Who knows where it'll lead?"

Tom was intently watching TV when the front doorbell rang. It was Saturday, October 20, a night that would come to be known as the Saturday Night Massacre. Nixon's new attorney general, Elliott Richardson, had appointed Archibald Cox in May as special counsel to investigate Watergate. Nixon had agreed, hoping the investigation would turn up nothing and thus end the entire debacle. Instead, Cox had performed brilliantly; too brilliantly for Nixon. Cox sent a subpoena demanding copies of Nixon's secret tapes. Nixon told Attorney General Richardson to fire Cox. When Richardson refused, he and his deputy were forced to resign. Nixon had never looked guiltier. Tom had a difficult time tearing himself away from the TV to answer the door.

"Did I interrupt something?" Barbara asked coyly.

"Not at all, just watching the news." It was best not to mention what he'd been watching.

"I wasn't sure if you'd remembered I was coming over for dinner."

Tom took Barbara's hand and led her into his apartment.

"For dinner and more," Tom said.

Barbara pulled Tom close and gave him a long, wet kiss.

"If dinner can wait a bit, I thought we'd start by working up an appetite."

"Are you sure?"

"Shut up, Tom. It's been too long, and I'm horny as hell."

The sex was hot, dinner was tasty, and the after-dinner sex was even hotter. Barbara stayed the night and to all appearances their marriage was back on track. Except that in the afterglow of sex Tom felt uneasy, as if he'd committed an error. In the middle of the night Tom went to the living room and sat in the dark. It had been a fun evening, yet images of Nixon, Elliott Richardson, Archibald Cox, and Henry Bennett kept flashing in his mind. He also couldn't stop thinking about Ellen Becker. In fact, during their second bout of sex, Tom had seen Ellen's face superimposed on Barbara's. It had caused him to hesitate, though fortunately Barbara had taken Tom's pause as a sexual tease and had grabbed his butt and forcefully restarted intercourse. As Tom sat in the dark he had an uncomfortable sense that he'd made a big mistake.

Tom was walking up to the house one day when he heard a car door slam. He turned to see a furious Barbara walking determinedly toward him.

"You cheating bastard," she hissed, then slapped him across the face.

Tom opened his mouth to protest, then snapped it shut. Instinctively, he knew that Officer Jones had somehow informed Barbara of the affair with Ellen Becker. He stood and waited for the next assault.

"You said you'd never have an affair while we were still married," Barbara snarled. "You've humiliated me."

"When I told you I wasn't sleeping with anybody it was true at the time. I hadn't planned on having an affair; it just happened."

"You son of a bitch. Nothing 'just happens' with you. You always know exactly what you're doing, especially when you married me as a shortcut to the top."

Barbara's statement hurt more than her slap. He also noted that cars had pulled up in neighboring driveways and people were getting out and watching the battle.

"Do you want to come inside so we can have this discussion in private?"

"No, I don't want to come inside. The damage has already been done."

"Barbara, I doubt that anybody else knows about my relationship."

"You're so naïve. This is Washington. You've really pissed somebody off, and now we're all going to pay, starting with you. I want you moved out of this house immediately."

"Do I have time to find another place?"

"Move in with your whore. From what I saw in the photos I was sent she loves sucking your cock. On the balcony, for god's sake, where people could see you. You, you goddamned..."

Barbara tried to slap Tom again but he caught her wrist.

"Why don't you go home, Barbara? I'll move out this weekend and mail the key to your parents' house. When you've calmed down we can talk about what to do."

"No, we won't talk. We'll never talk again. Oh, by the way, I'm pregnant."

Tom would have preferred another slap. The news was like a kick to the gut.

"Pregnant?"

"Yeah, you know, from all the times you've fucked me the past two months."

She shouted this. Tom glanced up to see neighbors turning away in embarrassment.

"What are you going to do?" Tom asked.

"What am I going to do? You mean should I murder the kid? Have my uterus scraped?

The Bennett family was strictly against abortion. Barbara was going to have their child. It was a bigger mess than Tom had realized, yet there was no turning back. The marriage was over, and most likely so was Tom's career with the State Department.

CHAPTER 15—1974

Tom spent his days at his desk at the State Department doing mundane work. Nominally assigned to the Asian section, he read newspapers from around the world and reviewed dispatches from US embassies. His written summaries were handed in to his immediate supervisor, though he never received any indication that they had been read. It didn't matter. Tom was merely doing time, as if he'd been sentenced to three years in a minimum security prison, one that allowed him to go home each night. In many ways his home life was an extension of his workdays. He'd broken off relations with Ellen Becker the same week that Barbara had confronted him on the front lawn. Ellen was sad yet understood and moved on with her life. Tom moved into a one-bedroom apartment near Howard University, one of the rougher sections of Washington. He shopped at a local market, rarely went out for dinner, and spent his evenings alone watching TV and reading. His weekends were spent walking the city and exploring museums, though he'd visited every museum at least twice. Colleagues who knew his reputation as a future star of the State Department pitied Tom for his dramatic fall from grace.

Tom was reading on the couch one night when the phone rang.

"Hello."

"Hello, lover."

"Suzie! Great to hear from you. How long has it been?"

"Way too long. Wanna meet me in New York next week?"

244

"I'd love to. Visiting your family?"

"Yeah. It's been a long time and my dad's health isn't good. He's a life-long smoker. Speaking of short lives, I understand your marriage had a short life."

"Been talking with Ira?"

"When I can reach him. He never returns calls or responds to my letters. I call every few months to catch up on things, and occasionally he picks up the phone. I talked to him last week. That's when he told me you were divorced."

"It's not official yet. We've signed papers and there's a court date in June."

"Does that mean you're free to meet me or does your moral code preclude meeting female friends until the divorce is final?"

"Barbara and I are finished, and New York sounds perfect. I'm owed weeks of vacation time and I won't be missed in Washington. I'll book a hotel and meet you there."

Tom took the entire week off and arrived in New York a few days before Suzie. He walked Manhattan from upper to lower, explored the museums and Central Park, and was the most relaxed he'd been in months. When Suzie arrived from the airport Tom greeted her in the lobby and carried her bags up to their room. As soon as the door was closed they embraced and started to caress each other. Soon they had shed their clothes and were in bed.

"It's been a long time since I was with a man. You'll have to be gentle."

"We could put our clothes back on," Tom said, stroking her moist mound, "though you do seem to be physically ready."

"I'm physically ready whenever I'm near you, Tom. That's never been a problem. It's my muscles that are a bit tight."

"Then we'd better take it nice and slow. Wouldn't want to hurt anything that might hinder having more fun this week."

Afterward they lay back and breathed slowly in harmony.

"Wow, I haven't come that often in, well, since last time we were together."

"You haven't found any other studs in California?"

"I'm not looking for any studs. I'm happy with my lady friends and my Buddhism. The only cock I crave is yours, and it's because it's attached to you, my best friend. Sex with you is about sharing and love and our souls. When you're inside of me I'm completely happy."

"I feel the same way."

"Do you think it's special because we fuck so rarely or because of our friendship?"

"Both and more. We never make demands, never dwell in the past or worry about the future. Our relationship is physical and spiritual. It touches something magical, yet I don't think it could work on a daily basis. We'd get hung up on mundane things like bills and bosses."

"Is that what happened with Barbara? Were you done in by the mundane?"

"It never really worked for us. We lacked love and respect from the start. It was all about sex and dreams, about what each could do for the other. I thought Barbara and her dad were shortcuts to power. Barbara thought I would be famous and powerful, her father's man in Washington. It was never about love."

They sat in silence for a minute.

"Are you disappointed in me?" Tom asked.

"For what? Not being perfect?"

"I had ideals, a purpose in life."

"You don't anymore?"

"Well, of course I do, but my goals..."

"Stop! Didn't you say that our relationship works because we never dwell in the past or waste our energy worrying about the future?"

"Yeah."

"Buddhism teaches that we should do the same in all of our life. You're feeling sorry for yourself because you sold out in an attempt to find a shortcut. Now you found out that there are no shortcuts. So you learn from your mistakes and move on. As to believing you've somehow blown your future, that's bullshit. Speaking of your future, it must be about time for your next assignment."

"If they give me one."

"There must be some shithole they'd love to dump you in."

"There are plenty of those out there."

"Except there are no shitholes to my friend Tom, only desolate places that need US help. If there's a job to be done, you're the man to do it."

Tom rolled over and kissed Suzie.

"I don't deserve a friend like you."

"You're right. Now it's time to earn my friendship. I could use some oral stimulation."

"Want me to tell you a story?"

Suzie playfully pushed Tom.

"Shut up and lend me your tongue. Afterward you can come with to my parents for dinner."

"There's something wrong with discussing oral sex and dinner with your parents in the same sentence."

"It's all about doing good."

"In that case, I'm your man."

Tom and Suzie's last dinner together was at the same Italian restaurant where they had had dinner to celebrate Suzie's graduation from Columbia. They had already discussed Tom's failed marriage and his affair with Ellen Becker and Buddhist philosophy. It was now time for the last topic of conversation, the one they'd put off all week: Ira Blue. Tom had avoided it because he felt some hostility toward his old friend and he wasn't sure how Suzie would take it.

"So our do-nothing buddy Ira is finally doing something," Suzie began.

"Yeah, much to my regret."

"From what you've told me the problem is not so much Ira's writing as an overzealous CIA officer, and you can't blame Ira for being an investigative journalist. I'd thought you'd be proud of him."

"You glorify Ira by calling him an investigative journalist. He takes information that other people have collected, mixes it with innuendoes and long stretches of the imagination, then calls it news. I wouldn't mind that except Ira is driven by narcissism rather than ideals. He wants recognition and fame; he wants people to fear him, and he doesn't care who gets hurt."

"That's pretty harsh. Besides, what's the big surprise? Ira was always in it for Ira."

"Then why do we remain friends? How can you, a Buddhist, tolerate somebody who's only out for himself?"

"We're all ultimately out for ourselves. The Buddhist quest for enlightenment is a singular quest for individual salvation from endless suffering.

It is the rare person indeed—the bodhisattva—who delays his own enlightenment in order to help others achieve theirs. Let me pose a question: do you know of a case where Ira purposely tried to hurt somebody?"

"Besides Barbara?"

"I disagree. I don't think Ira ever set out to hurt her."

"How can you say that after the nasty things Ira said to her face in this very restaurant?"

"Were any of those things untrue?"

"He nailed her for being a WASP."

Suzie raised her eyebrows as if to say, 'So?'.

"He attacked her blondness, her family's wealth, her lack of social consciousness, her utter lack of ambition."

"You're describing the way that Ira talks to everybody. I was always the overweight slut who lacked self-confidence. You were the hayseed lost in the big city. That's why we liked Ira. He told it the way it was: unabridged, harsh, and in your face. Maybe he did it because by putting us down he looked better. Except I don't believe that and neither do you."

Tom nodded his head. "Yeah, you're right. For Ira honesty is the most important thing. It's what friends owe each other more than loyalty."

"If he didn't care for you he wouldn't bother saying anything to you. It was Ira's love for you that led him to be brutally honest in his assessment of Barbara. What kind of friend would have said you were lucky to have found such a wonderful, perfect woman?"

Tom laughed.

"Was Ira's assessment of Barbie correct?"

"A direct hit."

"And even though you were hurt by his Paris Peace Talks article and the Watergate article, was any of it false or misleading or flat-out lies?"

"Not really."

"Did you expect Ira to write something that would help your career? Something that would make you out to be a hero?"

"Not in a million years."

"So who fucked up? You or Ira? You said things you shouldn't have. Ira incorporated them in articles that enlightened some people. You blame Ira for being honest and direct. That's like blaming a shark for biting off somebody's leg. It's what they do."

"I won't repeat that analogy to Ira. He'd love himself too much."

"Then your choice is pretty clear: drop Ira as a friend or accept him the way he is."

Tom picked up his glass of red wine. "Here's to friends. They may piss you off, but they're always there when you need them."

"Speaking of need, I need one more bout of hot, sweaty love before I return to California. It may be the last cock I have for a long time."

"A friend in need," Tom said, as they clinked glasses.

Later that night, as they lay in bed together, Suzie turned on her side to face Tom.

"You've sprouted some gray hairs."

"Life in Washington. Do they make me look old?"

"Naw, they make you look distinguished, like you've done some living."

"I wish I felt like I'd earned them doing something important."

"You may feel right now like you're wasting your life, but you have to remember that it's a long journey. You can't expect to do good every day."

"From the sounds you were making I thought I did pretty damn good tonight."

"Better than good, though that's not what I was referring to. You might not have saved the world during the past three years, but you've grown as a person. You've taken huge steps toward bigger things. I believe in you, Tom. You need to keep believing in yourself."

Tom reached over and hugged Suzie. They fell asleep in each other's arms.

Tom sat at his desk and stared at the hundred-page report he'd just finished. Nobody at State had asked for the report, so he'd done most of the work at home during his free time. The report, *Limiting Falling Dominos*, summed up the failed US foreign policy in Southeast Asia and warned about dire consequences should the United States continue on its current path. The answer to the problem of stopping communism seemed obvious to Tom: grant the people of Southeast Asia independence and self-determination immediately.

It was too late for Vietnam, but Laos and Cambodia still stood a chance, if a slight one. If the US would agree to free and fair elections within months—as should have occurred in Vietnam a decade earlier—it was possible that the US could salvage something in Southeast Asia. Now if he could only find somebody of importance to read the report. Unfortunately, Tom soon learned that he'd used up all of his goodwill. Nobody at State was interested in anything Tom had to say, and he had no other connections in Washington. His remaining options were few, yet he decided to try each one. He called CIA headquarters and tried to get a message to Sam Smith, hoping that Smith could get somebody at CIA to read the report. After a week of waiting he tried Henry Bennett. Henry refused to accept his calls, so he tried Barbara.

"What do you want?"

"I was wondering how Keith is doing." He was hoping to soften Barbara with family talk.

"You can see for yourself when you pick up Keith next Saturday."

"Right. Um, I actually called for another reason. I want to ask your father a favor."

Barbara's response was a derisive snort of laughter.

"I'm still the father of his grandson."

"He'd change that if he could."

"Maybe you'd prefer that Keith's dad become an alcoholic bum."

"Don't be so melodramatic."

"OK, so maybe that was a bit over the top. I'm not the alcoholic type. I'm ambitious and I'm not going to let our divorce and your family's quest for revenge stop me. If you want Keith to be raised in a domestic war zone with constant sniping and bickering, there's nothing I can do about it. I had hoped you could move past your anger for the sake of others."

Finally, after a long pause, Barbara spoke. "I'll call Daddy and see what I can do. I can't promise anything; you know he never forgets, and he'll never forgive you."

"I just want five minutes of his time."

Henry Bennett agreed to meet Tom at Henry's club Friday after work. When Tom showed up the doorman led him to a small private room. He sat alone for ten minutes before Henry Bennett walked in.

"I've agreed to meet for five minutes, not a second more. I don't like you and I never have. You're a know-it-all liberal who would sell out our great nation to the commies. You attack a great man like Richard Nixon because you don't want him to succeed, even if it means weakening our nation. If I had my way you and your liberal friends would all be thrown in jail."

"I hope that wasn't part of my five minutes."

"You snotty little prick. Have your say."

"First of all, I've never acted against Nixon or my own government. I never told anybody about the Committee to Re-Elect the President, never gave away national secrets. Although you and I don't see eye to eye, we both love our nation. That is why I wanted to meet with you. I have been doing research that leads me to be enormously concerned about what is happening in Southeast Asia."

"You mean communism isn't spreading fast enough for you?"

"I mean the US is losing influence in the region and the results could be dire for us as well as the people of the region. There is a strong possibility that there will be bloodbaths in Vietnam, Cambodia, and Laos shortly after we leave. It is also likely that violence and anarchy could spread throughout the region. The United States must act now to establish unity governments in Cambodia and Laos. It is the only way that we might possibly avoid more carnage."

"So after you liberals destroyed public support for our troops in Vietnam, after you forced President Nixon to capitulate and humiliated our nation, now you want me to help you to 'save' Southeast Asia through your brilliance." Bennett stood up. "You're even more arrogant than I thought. Well, let me tell you something, you hick. You don't belong in Washington, and I'll do everything I can to make sure you spend the rest of your career sitting at some shitty little desk in some shitty little embassy in some shitty little country in the middle of nowhere."

"Fine. I'll get my message out without your help."

"Hi, Ellen, it's Tom."

"Tom, how nice to hear from you. How are you doing?"

"I've been better. How are you?"

"Never been busier. This Watergate thing has kept me busy round the clock. What have you been up to?"

"Trying to stay out of trouble."

"I hope you're doing a better job of it than before."

"Yeah, I really fucked up, didn't I. I hope our affair didn't cause you any grief."

"I lost a few nights sleep after receiving the photo of me giving you head on the balcony, then I decided it didn't matter who saw the photos, since it only showed the top of my head."

"That bastard. He sent you a photo?"

"Yeah. I guess he didn't want us together. Who was he?"

"Some shithead from the CIA who I pissed off. He's been doing whatever he can to wreck my life, and he figured to hit me where it hurts most."

"In the balls."

"I was thinking in more romantic terms, like hurting my love life."

"Same thing."

"So you still have the photo?"

"Yeah, though well hidden. After I realized that it hadn't been sent to my parents and wasn't going to be made public, I decided to keep it for old time's sake. Besides, it's kind of hot."

"I don't think my wife agreed."

"No, I don't suppose she would. So what's up?"

"I was wondering if you'd be interested in meeting for lunch or drinks."

"I'm in a relationship right now."

"I'd still like to meet with you, strictly professional. I might have a story for you."

"In exchange for?"

"Nothing. There's something I want, and I'm not having any luck with State."

"Still in the doghouse."

"Only with the entire State Department, my soon-to-be ex-wife, and her bully of a Republican father. The thing is, I've written a report, and I think it should be read by somebody other than myself."

"How about Monday after work where we met the first time in Georgetown?"

"I'll be there."

Tom was sitting at the bar when Ellen walked in. She was as beautiful as ever, and for a moment Tom regretted that their relationship had ended.

"You're looking terrific," Tom said before kissing Ellen chastely on the cheek.

"I wish I could say the same for you. You're kind of thin and pale."

"Too much time at my desk and not enough outside."

"So what led to the collapse of the golden boy?"

"I think collapse is a bit strong. Let's just say I've been on the ropes."

Tom proceeded to tell Ellen about his run-in with Officer Jones, Barbara's response to the photos, and throwing himself into his work on Southeast Asia. When he finished, Ellen shook her head and gazed into Tom's eyes.

"You've left something out. Something personal."

Tom blushed.

"You look much better with color in your face," Ellen joked. "Now I'm really curious."

"I slept with Barbara again, and now she's six months pregnant."

"Thinking with your dick." Ellen shook her head. "What have you been doing with your brain?"

Tom explained the research he'd been doing on Southeast Asia and his conclusions. He spoke from the heart, passionately, and Ellen was moved by his appeal.

"Certainly your superiors at State would be interested."

"They're so upset with my alleged leaks to you and *The Handless Monkey* that I've become a pariah. I tried a contact at the CIA."

"Jones?"

"No, one of Jones's old colleagues, Smith if you'll believe it."

"From the CIA? I believe it."

"No response. I became so desperate I called Barbara's dad."

"You asked Henry Bennett for a favor?

"Like I said, I was desperate.

"What is it you want from me?"

"Help me get my report out there. People should know that there's an alternative policy."

Ellen sipped her wine and nibbled at her salmon for a few minutes.

"How long before your next assignment?" Ellen asked.

"I expected it a few weeks ago, and, to be honest, I've been a little worried that they may stick me at the same desk in Washington until I either quit or show greater humility. Only I don't know how to be more humble."

"And you think publicly challenging the State Department's Southeast Asian policy will demonstrate humility? Tom, do you want me to talk as a friend or as a journalist?"

"Both."

"Fine. Americans are sick of Southeast Asia. They've lived through two decades in Vietnam and Nixon's invasion of Cambodia and rumors of communist insurgencies in Burma and the Philippines, and they're fed up with it. You'd have a hard time finding a dozen people who give a damn about Southeast Asia. If you try an end run around State and get your paper published, your career as a diplomat will be over. I believe everything you say about Southeast Asia. Sadly, it doesn't matter right now."

"It does to the people of Southeast Asia."

"Even if I could get the entire thing published and get you a lot of publicity, it still won't achieve anything. You think Nixon is going to change his foreign policy because of a paper written by a junior diplomat? Nixon is betting his reputation on China, hoping the history books credit him with normalizing relations while blaming Kennedy and Johnson for Vietnam. I'm sorry, Tom. This isn't your year to be a hero. Hopefully your next assignment will bring you more satisfaction, personally and professionally."

"Thanks, Ellen. Although it's not what I wanted to hear, I know you're right." He looked at Ellen and a smile slowly spread across his face. "This day wouldn't be a total bust if you'd consider coming to my apartment for a nightcap?"

"So you think I'll take pity on you and put out to ease your pain?"

Tom shrugged.

Ellen looked at Tom a moment, then shook her head. "Oh, what the hell. My boyfriend hasn't proposed yet, and you *are* a lot of fun in bed."

"Not to mention the couch, the bathtub, and the balcony."

"Get the check. I'll get my coat."

Tom's divorce from Barbara became official July 14, Bastille Day. Ellen met Tom for a quiet French meal in Arlington, far from where her boyfriend lived. They got drunk on French wine and Calvados, then went to Tom's apartment for a night of celebratory sex. Barbara gave birth to a baby girl on August 9. She named the girl Karen after the singer Karen Carpenter.

Tom suspected that the naming had as much to do with Karen Carpenter's conservatism as to the music. Tom had pushed to name their son Keith after Keith Richards of the Rolling Stones; naming their daughter Karen was a way to stick it to Tom. He didn't care. He liked the name and loved his daughter, whom he got to hold hours after she was born. He walked into the hospital as Henry Bennett walked out. They didn't exchange a single word.

August 9 was also the date that Richard Nixon resigned the presidency. Ellen was too busy working on the story to meet with Tom and have a drink in honor of Karen's birth, so Tom went out and got drunk by himself.

A week after Karen's birth Tom belatedly received his next assignment: Paraguay. It was one of only two landlocked countries in South America, a poor mountainous nation that had been under the iron-fisted control of Alfredo Stroessner since 1954. The United States had supported Stroessner's dictatorship from the start because he was anticommunist. He was also a serious abuser of human rights. It was a lousy assignment, one guaranteed to bury Tom in thankless, hopeless work. He was thrilled with it. Paraguay would give Tom a chance to master Spanish. He also hoped that three years in Paraguay would give his enemies time to forget him and allow for a new administration to replace some old State Department hands. If he could keep his nose clean for three years, quietly do his job without making waves, he might be able to recommence his climb up the State hierarchy. Tom put his Southeast Asian notes and his position paper into a cardboard box, sealed it with tape, and stuck it in the bottom of a friend's closet. For the next three months he studied Spanish, and the history and culture of Paraguay. He drove to Indiana in early October to say goodbye to his family, then flew to Miami for a few days on the beach before boarding a flight to Asuncion, the capital of Paraguay. As the plane took off he let out a long, loud sigh.

"Nervous about flying?" asked the businessman sitting next to Tom, who had apparently misunderstood the sigh.

"Not really. Just expelling some bad air."

"Well, they got good air in Paraguay. That and tropical fruit. Eating and breathing are two things that you can do well in Paraguay."

"Sounds like there are some things that aren't done well in Paraguay."

"Freedom of speech. Freedom of political thought. Treatment of the poor. Spend enough time there and you'll have a new appreciation of the good ol' U S of A."

Tom smiled. "Sounds like there's work to be done in Paraguay."

CHAPTER 16—1977

T om sat on the front porch of his small house in Asuncion, Paraguay, and watched torrents of rain crash onto the sodden ground. It was late February and nearing the end of a long, steamy, tropical antipodean summer. Though he had loved the tropical climate of Vietnam, basking in the perpetual warmth and humidity, there was something about Paraguay that drained a person's energy, leaving one listless and unmotivated. Some of the difference was cultural. The Vietnamese were an industrious people; they were always working in the rice paddies or tending gardens or traveling to shrines or visiting relatives. Paraguayans exhibited stereotypical Latin American traits. They believed that things could always wait until *mañana*—tomorrow. They took long siestas that often stretched until the next day. Little in their lives aroused passion except soccer and perceived insults to the Church, their manhood, or their women. Even more debilitating than the climate was the twenty-three-year rule of General Alfredo Stroessner. Elected president in 1954 (he was the only candidate), he had added commander-in-chief of the army and head of the powerful Colorado Party to his official titles. There was no end in sight to Stroessner's reign, nor was there any hope of political, economic, or social growth for most Paraguayans, thus their bone-deep apathy. As a result, Tom had not fallen in love with Paraguay as he had most other countries in which he had lived.

Not that Tom complained. He was still in the foreign service, still wrote reports regarding the political situation, still felt that he was doing something meaningful with his life, even if it wasn't as meaningful as he had hoped. He was thirty-six years old and still had decades remaining to achieve greatness. Or at least goodness. He had one year remaining in Paraguay, and he hoped that his next assignment would be some nation that was more unstable or more dangerous. More anything besides boring.

Tom hadn't been back to the States since departing under a cloud. He talked with Barbara every few weeks to ask about the kids, and sent letters and pictures to Keith and Karen, though he never got anything in return. He tried not to dwell on what he was missing: first words, first steps, first friends. When he began to slide into a funk he called Suzie and was always encouraged by her positive attitude and unconditional support. His occasional calls to Ira were never as pleasant. Ira was often too busy to talk or too drunk or stoned, and when he did have time and was clearheaded enough, he spent most of the conversation berating Tom and the US government for propping up a dictator like Stroessner. Tom would listen until he had enough, then cut the call short. It usually took a drink or two before Tom could stop cursing his old friend and finally shrug off his annoyance. Eventually, Tom realized that he was better off focusing his energies on Paraguay and pretending that the rest of the world didn't exist.

Asuncion, like the rest of Paraguay, was distinctly divided between rich and poor. Those in favor with President Stroessner—a small, powerful elite—reaped the benefits of Paraguay's natural resources. Whatever wealth that could be extracted from the ground went into the pockets and foreign bank accounts of this oligarchy. The have-nots scratched out a subsistence living from marginal soil. Paraguay was one of the poorest countries in Latin America with little hope of ever climbing out of poverty. It would have been poorer still, except for one thing: President Stroessner was virulently anticommunist. This meant a constant flow of military and economic support by the United States, which assured that Stroessner would always live well, his armies would be equipped with the latest weapons, and the president and his nation would remain safe from invasion or revolution. The transfer of so much wealth and power could not be left to foreign service grunts like Tom. Rather, all important decisions and communications were carried out in Washington by top White House and national security officials. The result was that the US embassy in Asuncion only dealt with low-level diplomacy such as visa and customs issues. Tom's main occupation was attending official functions and assuring that American businessmen were left alone and allowed to extract as much wealth as Stroessner allowed. If an American weapons dealer or mine owner killed a Paraguayan in a traffic accident or got into a barroom brawl, a call was made to Washington, then Washington would inform the embassy that it was their task to get the bigwig out of jail immediately. It was unfulfilling, humiliating work, yet Tom did it without question. It was all part of paying his dues.

Unlike his previous assignments, where he quickly earned a reputation as a lone wolf, Tom made a point of being part of the team. This proved easy for two reasons: there was a limited social scene and he liked his fellow diplomats. Whereas in Saigon, Paris, and Washington the social opportunities were vast, there were few options in Asuncion. Wealthy Paraguayans had no interest in partying with poor American diplomats, and poor Paraguayans were not allowed to socialize with foreigners. The members of the business community were a closed lot who looked down on civil servants. Not surprisingly, diplomats ended up socializing with fellow diplomats. Tom played doubles tennis with British, Spanish, and French diplomats. He went to bars and restaurants that were frequented by diplomats from dozens of countries. He met aid workers and a few Peace Corps volunteers. Tom even developed a close relationship with one of his first overseas roommates: Stefan Boudreau.

Boudreau had left Saigon shortly after Tom and had been stationed in Jordon, Poland, and New Zealand. He arrived in Asuncion six months after Tom, and they had quickly resumed their friendship, falling into that camaraderie that develops between people with shared experiences, particularly those who were together in war zones or disaster areas. The last time Tom had been with Boudreau had been during the Tet Offensive, an event that had seared distressing memories in both of their minds. The night of Boudreau's arrival in Asuncion, Tom had taken his old roommate out for drinks and dinner. Boudreau seemed mellower than when they had lived together in Saigon, drank less, and didn't ask about where to get laid.

"Hey, what ever happened to your Vietnamese girlfriend," Boudreau asked while sipping an after-dinner drink, "the one you almost chucked your career for? Didya stay in touch?"

"She was killed during Tet."

"Oh, gawd, I'm so sorry. I wasn't exactly supportive of your relationship."

"You mean like ratting me out to Hard Case?'

Boudreau started to bluster a protest, then shook his head. "I've spent a lot of time regretting those years. I was a shallow prick and I resented you. Yeah, I tried sucking up to Hard Case, and I was willing to sell you out. I've thought about you often and I've tried to be more like you. Now that I learn about your lady's death it makes me think I still haven't done enough."

"We're both still young. There's plenty of time left to make a difference."

"I'm glad to hear you haven't drowned trying to swim against the bureaucratic tide."

"I've swallowed a few gulps of sea water over the years, not enough to drown, though."

"I always thought you'd either be a top dog, maybe somebody high up in State, or you'd be out of government, you know, working for some NGO like CARE or the Red Cross."

"You were nearly right on both cases."

Tom explained how he'd rapidly climbed the diplomatic ladder and become a semi regular at the White House, and how he'd then fallen just as rapidly.

"I'm not all that surprised," Boudreau said. "Hard Case almost tossed you out 'cuz of your gallivanting around Nam, then you became Glass's darling. It would appear that you've continued on that path: either star of the future or disgraced diplomat of the past."

Tom smiled at the image.

"So that's how you ended up in the purgatory of Paraguay."

"Yeah, messed up by one of my oldest friends."

"Like they say, with friends like that, who needs enemies."

"Ira also helped me to develop a conscience."

"Otherwise you'd be just another foreign service hack like me."

"I thought you've been trying to be more like me, the man with a conscience who wanted to save Vietnam."

"Sure, I've been trying. Doesn't mean I've been succeeding. Most of the time I just feel like a clerk, filing reports and meeting with my local counterpart and making visa decisions. You know, Tom, I sometimes wonder if we've already had the most important assignment of our career. Vietnam may have been our one chance at stardom."

"Every day offers us a chance to do good, even if it's only a tiny bit of good at the local level. Maybe you granted somebody a visa to study in the States, let's say the nephew of President Stroessner. He gets out of Paraguay, sees democracy in action, returns home, and convinces his Uncle Alfredo to hold open and fair elections. The nephew even runs for president against his uncle, gets elected and brings peace, prosperity, and freedom to his fellow Paraguayans. See, one tiny action could lead to benefits for hundreds, thousands even."

Boudreau grinned. "It sure makes my heart beat with pride to know that a decade in the foreign service hasn't diminished your idealism. Damn, I'm happy as a hound dog in heat that we're going to be working together."

"I'm not sure about your reference to a hound dog in heat. You're not going to start humping my leg are you?"

Boudreau howled with laughter, imitating a horny hound dog. "Nah, I'll leave your leg alone, though I sure as hell look forward to seeing what we can accomplish in this landlocked dictatorship."

Tom looked around anxiously to see if anybody was listening.

"We'll start tomorrow to change things; for now we'd better be careful of what we say or else our careers may be over sooner than we think."

Boudreau glanced nervously around. "You're right. I'd better watch my mouth. Places like this can be dangerous to more than your career."

Stefan Boudreau was not the only old colleague to join Tom in Paraguay. At the start of his second year in Asuncion, Tom had greeted Caleb Howell as the new ambassador. Although Howell had only been Tom's ambassador for a few months in Mali, Tom had enormous respect and admiration for him. He was a selfless, hardworking man who was given one thankless, insignificant ambassadorship after another. Howell had also allowed Tom to take the Paris Peace Talks assignment when he could have insisted that Tom complete his three years in Mali. At that time, eight years earlier, Tom appeared to be on his way to the top of the State Department. Now they found themselves together in Paraguay.

"Tom, it's great to see you again. Please take a seat and make yourself comfortable."

The ambassador had asked Tom to join him in his office at the start of Howell's first day in Asuncion.

"Thank you, Mr. Ambassador. I look forward to working with you. Hopefully it'll last longer than our stint in Mali."

"I'd like that. By the way, please call me Caleb. I never liked to stand on ceremony, always thought it sanctimonious to have some millionaire who bought his ambassadorship expect people to bow and call him Mr. Ambassador. We're all doing the same work, promoting America's interests, and we should do it as a team."

"All right, Caleb."

"Now that we have that settled, I hope you don't mind if I ask a question that might be sensitive."

"You can ask anything you want. I'm not easily offended."

"Good, I like straight shooters. So what's a star like you doing in a pit like Asuncion?"

Tom delivered an honest appraisal of the past eight years, neither glossing over his failures and errors nor asking for pity.

"A lot of people would have left the foreign service," Glass remarked. "Quite a few have. Sounds like you're committed to starting over here in Paraguay, to continuing the work you set out to do."

"I still feel that it's what I'm supposed to be doing. A friend has helped me to understand that dwelling in the past is foolish."

"That's a smart friend."

"She is indeed."

"A bright guy like you understands that there aren't many opportunities for us to do good here in Paraguay, unless you've found some areas since your arrival that might benefit from our services."

Tom smiled wryly. "You've been doing this longer than I have, and I assume you've been fully briefed on the situation here. There is no democracy, no personal freedoms, no economic hopes for the masses, and Stroessner means to keep it that way, with the blessing of Washington. I know you'll be presenting your credentials to the president this week; don't expect to see much of him afterward, except at his lavish parties. President Stroessner loves to have a slew of ambassadors on hand, makes him appear more statesmanlike. He does meet regularly with Americans, but not from the embassy. My sources—and they are few and unreliable, since most live in fear of the government and have nothing to gain by talking with us—tell me that Stroessner's door is open to the CIA, weapons dealers, American businessmen eager to hand over large sums in exchange for exclusive concessions, and Washington insiders who don't bother letting their own embassy know when they're in town. Caleb, we're out of the loop, and we're virtually powerless."

Howell smiled. "Frustrating, yes; hopeless, no. Remember, I've spent my entire career in tiny backwaters like Paraguay. You'll never read about any of my achievements, but that doesn't mean there aren't any. I suspect you already know what we're able to do."

Tom nodded. "Small things to us, yet things that help the little people. We've gotten scholarships for young Paraguayans to study in the States. I was able to make a few calls to people with money in Washington and found funding for some schools and clinics in the countryside. We've smoothed the way for a gradual Peace Corps expansion that's improved sanitation and reduced infant mortality in some villages. Like you said, nothing that will make the news or history books, but things that make a difference to people who had resigned themselves to quiet lives of desperation."

"I knew I had you pegged right. Being a good judge of character is one of my better qualities. Some in State would say it's my only good quality." The ambassador shrugged off the implied criticism. "To hell with them. We're going to achieve some good here, you and me and anybody else willing to do what they've been hired to do. Speaking of the Peace Corps, there's a new director for Paraguay showing up next week. It would be a good opportunity to have a gathering of Americans and the foreign service community, a way of thanking the outgoing director for his service, greeting the new director, and establishing a spirit of cooperation."

"Terrific idea."

"Would any Paraguayans be offended if we kept it to foreigners?"

"On the contrary, I think it's the only way to start. The wealthy and powerful wouldn't waste their time coming here for hotdogs and beer. They prefer eating lobster and drinking champagne with fellow millionaires and foreign power brokers. If you invite the intelligentsia—what few exist—or working-class or common people, Stroessner will brand you a socialist and some of our guests might end up in jail. No, you're smart to play it cool. As long as we stick to foreigners, we'll be left alone."

"I know it's not part of your job description, but would you mind organizing the event? Keep the food simple, remind people to dress casually, let's set the tone for a cordial working environment."

"My pleasure. I'll recruit an old colleague from Saigon to help, Stefan Boudreau. He's a good man and far more sociable than I am. As well, Stefan is one of the good guys. He's taken the lead in raising money to help some of the villages. Last week he got one of our Paraguayan drivers out of jail, not an easy task."

"Sounds like we've got the makings of a pretty good team. Thanks, Tom. I'm encouraged."

The US embassy party was held on a pleasant March evening. Stefan had hired a jazz combo, and there was enough barbecue and booze to sate any appetite. As Ambassador Howell had requested, it was a relaxed atmosphere conducive to casual talk. There were guests from a few dozen embassies, the Peace Corps, and other nongovernmental organizations. Caleb Howell was a congenial host, and Stefan and Tom made sure that things ran smoothly. After dinner Tom found himself talking with the outgoing Peace Corps director, who coincidentally was a graduate of Columbia. The two hit it off well and began to reminisce about favorite and least favorite overseas postings. It soon became evident that both were humanists who struggled to make the world a better place against overwhelming odds.

"Sometimes I think the Peace Corps is frivolous," said the director, "teaching sanitation and birth control while dictators plunder their nations' wealth and the two superpowers threaten us all with nuclear annihilation."

"I know what you mean, yet the Peace Corps serves a double purpose. You not only help people who desperately need the help, but you're also creating a cadre of young Americans who develop a broader, more humane, worldview. Fifteen years after the creation of the Peace Corps there are now thousands of Americans who have taken their knowledge and empathy, and are now rising up in the ranks of government and industry. We may not know how meaningful their experience is for decades. I do know this, people like you are doing something concrete while most of the world only complains."

"That's kind of you. It's encouraging to meet somebody in government who is a realist *and* an idealist. Maybe you can mentor my replacement, help her see things the same way."

"You apparently have some concerns about Mary."

Mary McNeil, was the new Peace Corps director for Paraguay. A graduate of Boston College, she had served four years in Sierra Leone, then worked for the Peace Corps at their headquarters in Washington, DC. Paraguay was her first posting as country director.

"She's bright and idealistic. That's the problem. We've been meeting since she arrived a few days ago and I'm concerned that she lacks the realism that is an essential element of what we do. She seems to believe that we can achieve anything with hard work, determination, and conviction. I told her that whatever the Peace Corps attempts to do in Paraguay will have to succeed in spite of the Paraguay government, not because of it. She's implied that maybe I wasn't determined enough, that somehow I don't have what it takes to get the job done."

"Ouch. How did you respond?"

"I tried patience, then she accused me of being condescending because she was younger and a woman. She said she would not be deterred from making changes in the country. She intends to demand—that's the word she used—demand a meeting with president Stroessner and inform him that he needs to spend more money on his people and less on the military."

"I was Peace Corps in Côte d'Ivoire, and I know the Peace Corps counsels its volunteers to use diplomacy and leave coercion to the State Department. You are, after all, guests of the host country."

"Of course, and she's been told that many times. I suspect that the powers that be in Washington see a lot of promise in Mary and are willing to let her learn the facts of life on the job. As well, in this age of women's liberation, placing women in positions of responsibility is expected. You and I know that Paraguay would not be our choice for putting a woman in charge, not yet anyway. Paraguay doesn't have a large Peace Corps presence and it's never been easy to deal with Stroessner." He glanced around to see if anybody was listening, then lowered his voice. "He only tolerates us because it makes him look good to the world community, and he probably thinks that by accepting the Peace Corps he has some leeway in abusing his people. He's a son of a bitch, but he's willing to let young Americans dig latrines in the poorest villages."

"It won't take Mary long to figure out what she can and cannot do. It'll be frustrating."

"Keep an eye on her, Tom. I don't want to see her get hurt."

Later in the evening, as people said their farewells and thanked Ambassador Howell, Tom found himself standing next to Mary McNeil. She was a head shorter, yet presented herself in a way as to appear taller. She stood straight and proud, pushing out her meagerly endowed chest and looking people directly in the eye. Her dark red hair was cropped short and stood up, and she had a pretty face, yet it was her proud bearing that struck Tom first.

"Hi, I'm Tom Kington."

"Mary McNeil." She gave Tom a firm handshake. "I've heard good things about you."

"Really? It couldn't be my backhand in tennis."

"You have time to play tennis?" she asked, clearly scornful that anybody in Paraguay would have time for games.

"Over the years I've found that too much work can lead to burnout."

"Too much work? How can you work too much when you're trying to help others?"

"I'm not a priest. I allow myself some personal pleasure from time to time."

"Is that a crack about me being Catholic?"

"I didn't assume you were Catholic. Aren't there protestant McNeils?"

"Well, I happen to be Catholic, and I don't appreciate your remark."

"My apologies." Hoping to change the subject, Tom said, "You know, I was in the Peace Corps for two years, in Côte d'Ivoire. Somebody told me you volunteered in Sierra Leone."

Mary McNeil glared at Tom a moment, trying to decide if she wanted to let him off the hook for his priest comment. She apparently decided to let the comment go for the time being. "Sierra Leone changed my life. I'd partied pretty hard at Boston College and didn't have much direction. I mean, what was I going to do with a degree in sociology? Teach? Work with inner-city kids? Nothing grabbed me, so when a professor suggested the Peace Corps, I applied. Boy, were my eyes opened."

Tom nodded enthusiastically. "I know what you mean. As a kid from Indiana, I'd never been further than New York. Wow! The world never looks the same as after a couple of years in west Africa."

"That's the truth."

Tom sensed that Mary had thawed a bit and might actually be somebody he could talk to.

"Why don't you drop by the embassy some time? Let's see if we can't be of help to each other."

"The last thing I want is for the Peace Corps to be associated in any way with the federal government. As an ex-Peace Corps volunteer I'd have thought you'd know that."

"What the hell are you talking about? The Peace Corps *is* a US federal program."

"Legally, yes; in spirit, no. We volunteer to help people in need. We serve people, not governments. The fact is, time and again governments are the problem, not the solution. Paraguay is a perfect example. The government extracts the wealth of the soil, sells it, then divides the spoils among the elite, who build enormous ranches and mansions and fly to Europe to shop, while the people work every day of their lives to eke out a living. And what does our federal government do about it? They supply Stroessner and his goons with enough weapons to pacify the people and destabilize the entire region. You're one of the bad guys. Why would I want to be associated with you and your cohorts?"

"In town nearly an entire week and you're already an expert on Paraguay. I'm so lucky to be in the presence of a true genius, one who openly criticizes the president of our host nation while surrounded by Paraguayans."

"These Paraguayans are poor workers and musicians. They agree with me."

"So there's no way one would turn you in to gain points with Stroessner and protect his family from future abuse."

Mary McNeil looked around anxiously, trying to determine whether any Paraguayans may have heard her outburst. "I trust these people more than I trust my own government," she declared, though a hint of doubt had entered her voice.

"If the police bring you in for questioning, see what the people are able to do for you. When Peace Corps supplies are held at the airport while local officials try to squeeze a bribe, see what the people are able to do for you. Paraguayans are a good people, but they won't be of much help getting visas for Peace Corps volunteers or expediting the delivery of medicine and farm supplies."

Mary's backbone stiffened and she stood as tall as possible. "When I need something done I'll tell you. In the meantime, you continue sucking up to the elite while I help the people."

"While *you* help the people? Not the Peace Corps but Saint Mary of South Boston? Praise the Lord for blessing the people of Paraguay with *your* presence."

Mary turned and stormed out of the party, nor stopping to say farewell to the ambassador.

"I see you've met the new director," came a voice from behind Tom.

He turned to see the outgoing director standing next to Ambassador Howell. Both were smirking.

"Seeing as how you've already started a dialogue with Miss McNeil," began Caleb Howell, "it seems proper that I appoint you embassy liaison with the Peace Corps." Howell struggled to suppress a full-blown grin.

"I accept the appointment on the condition that I never have to actually talk with her. I just want to be on hand to escort her to the airport when the authorities throw her out of the country, unless I am fortunate enough to be allowed to bring her food while she rots in a Paraguayan jail." Tom glared at the doorway that Mary McNeil had passed through. "If you two gentlemen will excuse me, I need to wrap up this affair."

The outgoing director turned to Ambassador Howell. "That relationship should provide some much-needed entertainment in your mundane life."

"Then my gratitude to the Peace Corps. I could use a little entertainment."

Unfortunately for Caleb Howell, 1977 would not prove to be an entertaining year. Instead, it was a year of turmoil and tension due to the election of Jimmy Carter as president of the United States. Since 1947 the US had been supplying Paraguay annually with an average of $750,000 worth of weapons. Those thirty years had also been marked by political repression, intimidation of opposition parties, and economic stagnation for the masses. Jimmy Carter was a man of principles who was elected as a direct response to Richard Nixon's unprincipled presidency. When Carter was inaugurated in January, 1977, he took office with the intention of altering US foreign policy to reflect those principles. Paraguay would be one of his earliest targets.

A month after taking office, Carter instructed the State Department to serve notice to all nations that the United States would not tolerate dictatorships, especially those who deprived their citizens of their natural rights. Caleb Howell had in no way approved of Stroessner's dictatorship, but his style had always been one of constructive engagement rather than confrontation. He regularly attended presidential functions, and he and his wife were even invited to the presidential ranch on a few occasions. Howell was able to use his connections to help American business interests and to get the odd American out of jail, usually for public drunkenness or some other minor infraction. To avoid antagonizing the president, Howell never openly criticized Stroessner and was therefore viewed by many as a Stroessner supporter. The president even once told a visiting American journalist that Ambassador Howell was like a member of the president's cabinet. The remark caused a stir in the American liberal media and caught the eye of Jimmy Carter. Rather than recall Howell to Washington for talks, Carter began to look for a hardnosed liberal to replace him.

In the midst of this turmoil Tom flew to Washington to spend two weeks with his kids. Barbara was going to Europe with her father, and Tom had volunteered to babysit. Keith was now five and Karen three, perfect ages for trips to the zoo and children's museums. Tom never called Ellen Becker, choosing to be a devoted family man for his entire stay. His children were a bit standoffish at first, though Keith—who vaguely remembered trips to the zoo as a toddler—warmed up by the second day, and by the middle of the first week Karen was crawling into Tom's lap to be read to. By the time Barbara returned from Europe, Tom had established warm ties with his children, and he went to the airport with a heavy heart. His spirits took another beating when Stefan Boudreau picked him up at the airport.

"What a pleasant surprise," Tom said when he saw Boudreau waiting at customs.

"You won't think it's so pleasant when I fill you in on the news."

"Shit."

"You got that right."

"What, no driver?" Tom asked as they climbed into the embassy car. The embassy employed Paraguayan drivers for two reason: to provide work for locals and to prevent US nationals from having to drive in a country full of horrible drivers who ignored all rules of the road. Apparently, a third reason had recently been added.

"We're starting to get the feeling that Stroessner and his people are hearing what's going on at the embassy."

"Bugging devices?"

"That's possible. Spies are more likely or, to be more precise, Paraguayan workers who keep their ears open."

"I thought most of the Paraguayans working at the embassy lacked sufficient English to eavesdrop."

"We're reevaluating that opinion. I understand you were with the new Peace Corps director at our party in March when she blasted Stroessner and his cronies."

"That wasn't all she blasted."

Boudreau chuckled. "I do remember you telling me she accused you and everybody else at the embassy of sucking Stroessner's dick."

"She said we were sucking up to the president, not sucking his dick."

"Close enough. Well, it appears that one of our workers reported her remarks to somebody who got word to Stroessner. Not surprisingly, he blew a gasket. We've been unable to get visas for the newest crew of Peace Corps volunteers, and their supplies have been growing mold at the airport."

"I warned her, goddamned know-it-all. Maybe it wasn't Paraguayans who told tales. Maybe the Russians or Poles or even the French ratted her out, you know, earn some Brownie points with El Presidente."

"We thought of that too, but there've been other developments that lead us to believe the leak is within the embassy itself. Word has gotten around that Carter is preparing to cut military deliveries to Paraguay until Stroessner delivers free and open democratic elections."

"As if that'll ever happen here," said Tom.

"Everybody was talking about Carter's new policy, it being the hot topic. All of a sudden, Howell is ordered—not invited—to meet with

Stroessner, who proceeds to read Howell the riot act. Threatens to throw out the Peace Corps and shut down the embassy. Said maybe the Brazilians or Russians might make better trading partners."

"What did Caleb say?"

"You know Howell. He hates confrontations. Told El Presidente that it was only rumors and that he'd had no word of a change in policy toward Paraguay. Reminded Stroessner of our long and steady history of friendship and mutual support. Howell believed he'd placated Stroessner, though the Peace Corps visas have yet to be issued. Anyway, we're all being a lot more careful about what we say and where we say it. Which is why I picked you up, that and because I enjoy your company and I missed you."

"Aw, shucks, thanks."

"I also wanted to be the first to wish you good luck."

"Good luck with what?"

"Dealing with Mary McNeil. She's been calling or stopping by nearly every day to demand action. I keep telling her you'll be back soon."

"Bastard."

"You seem to have become more foulmouthed during your time in Washington. Was that something you picked up from the politicians?" Boudreau grinned.

"I was with my kids, as you well know, and the worst word they know is 'poopy.'" Tom wearily shook his head. "I told McNeil when we first met that Paraguay was a difficult assignment and that we should work together. She told me to fuck off."

"Maybe you ought to remind her of your offer and her response."

"I should, though it hardly seems diplomatic."

"No, I would not describe 'I told you so' as diplomatic. Then again, she's been a first-class pain in the ass; it might do her good to learn something about diplomacy."

"You think Mary McNeil would be an eager pupil?" Tom asked with a frown.

"No fucking way."

"Now who's foulmouthed?"

"Miss McNeil seems to bring that out in people."

"It's about time you got back to Asuncion," Mary McNeil grumbled. "Maybe something will finally get accomplished."

"I'm glad you have so much faith in me."

"I don't have any faith in you. I'm just hoping you're not as incompetent as that worthless Boudreau."

Tom nearly laughed at the jab at his friend, yet knew that McNeil would go berserk. He had no desire to deal with an irate Peace Corps director. She had stormed into his office and had refused the seat he'd offered.

"Stefan Boudreau happens to be a very competent diplomat. He's also very busy. Besides, I'm the embassy's liaison with the Peace Corps."

"Lot of good you've done the past two weeks."

"I was caring for my two children in Washington."

McNeil seemed taken aback. "Oh, I didn't know you were married."

"Divorced, and I haven't seen my kids since arriving in Paraguay two years ago. If my timing was inconvenient for the Peace Corps, I'm sorry."

McNeil regained her fury. "You mean that southern-fried hick Boudreau can't cover when you're gone? Things grind to a halt when Tom Kington isn't around?"

"Mr. Boudreau can cover quite well, when necessary. I could also have returned on twenty-four hours' notice, if there was an emergency. This is not an emergency. Your visa problem and the issue of supplies stuck at customs have been going on for over a month, and it's a political problem that may take many more months to crack. My absence in no way affected the situation."

"So I'm stuck waiting for you politicians while you pull your puds."

This time Tom couldn't hold in the laugh.

"You find this funny?" McNeil shouted.

"Laughing is preferable to telling you what I really think."

"Don't you dare be condescending. I'm not some ditsy little intern or secretary. I'm the director of the Peace Corps for Paraguay."

"Then act like it," Tom snapped. "Be passionate, but be professional as well. We're not politicians; we're diplomats. A graduate of Boston College should know the difference. And how dare you accuse us of 'pulling our puds.' Do think you're the only person who cares? The only professional in this country? If you want to be treated with respect, treat others with respect. Want to get things done in Paraguay, learn how things are done in Paraguay. You've been in the Peace Corps for nearly a decade, and you still think we should go into a country and tell them how to do things? You think you're being a hero; all I see is another ugly American."

Mary McNeil looked as if the air had been let out of her. Her shoulders sagged, and she grew pale.

"I'm sorry if I was rough," Tom said, moderating his voice.

"No, you were being honest." She began to sway slightly.

"Please sit down, Miss McNeil. Let me get you some water."

Tom ran out and got a glass of water. When he returned Mary was sitting in a chair with her head in her hands.

"Here, take a sip."

Mary McNeil drained the entire glass.

"It looks like you haven't been drinking enough liquids."

She let out a weary sigh. "I've been so wrapped up in my work, so...so damn frustrated, sometimes I forget to eat or drink."

"Look, Miss McNeil..."

"Mary, call me Mary."

"All right, Mary, we got off to a bad start."

She glanced up at with a wry smile. "You're a natural diplomat. 'We got off to a bad start.' Fact is, I gave you shit the first time we met."

Tom shrugged.

"I'm sorry," Mary said, words Tom never expected to hear. "When I jump into something I go all the way. I never accept excuses, not from myself or from others. I always believed that 'being diplomatic' was another term for compromising your principles."

"Diplomacy is often exactly that. Diplomacy means weaving idealistic principles with reality. Like the Stones said, "You can't always get what you want, but if you try sometimes you'll find you get what you need.'"

Mary's wry smile spread into a grin. "I'm a big Stones fan. Saw 'em in DC last year. Yeah, I see your point. I've been demanding action, and I've achieved nothing, except driving myself to the point of collapse. I knew what was happening, but I've been a stubborn asshole."

"I wouldn't say that."

"What would you say?"

"I'd say you've been observing how things work—or don't work—in Paraguay, and now you're ready to formulate a plan of action, with the assistance of the US embassy and its Peace Corp liaison."

Mary nodded.

"I'd also recommend that we continue this discussion at a nearby restaurant where we can both get something to eat and replenish the bodily fluids that are essential for good health and clear thinking."

Mary McNeil stood up and started to say something when a sob escaped from her. She quickly covered her face and fought back a second sob.

"I've got to meet with a colleague for a minute," said Tom. "I'll be right back. Oh, and there's a bathroom down the hall on the right if you want to freshen up."

He knew that a proud person like Mary wouldn't want him to see her crying, so he hustled out the door. When he returned five minutes later Mary was looking out the window. She turned to face him, and Tom could see she'd scrubbed the tears from her face.

"Mr. Kington, I owe you an..."

"You owe me nothing, and please call me Tom. As Peace Corp director you owe the people of Paraguay your best effort, and you've given it. Now it's time to bring in some allies. Our first official meeting starts in five minutes at Juanita's Cantina." Tom hesitated. "I hope I'm not being too pushy or condescending."

"Not at all. You're being patient and helpful. Let's go. I'm thirsty."

Fifteen minutes later they'd ordered their second iced lemonade and were munching on a plate of fried plantains.

"Tom, it's obvious that I'm a demanding person, and I know I can drive people crazy."

"Everything you've done, you've done for others."

"That's not entirely true. I'm driven by ego as well. I'm one of the youngest country directors ever, and I wanted to show people that I deserved it, that I wasn't appointed because I was a woman who benefitted from the women's liberation movement. Instead, I've come off as just another overly emotional female frustrated by my dealings with a male-dominated society. I fucked up. Sorry about my language. I swear a lot when I'm upset or excited."

"That's all right, I'm not offended, though if I may make a suggestion..."

"Please."

"You might refrain from swearing in front of Paraguayans. They're serious about their Catholicism. They won't give you any respect if you swear like some cheap whore."

Mary's eyes opened wide in shock.

"Now I've offended you."

"No, I was just surprised. You've always been so careful with language."

"My years as a diplomat. I thought you'd prefer that I speak honestly, using words we're both comfortable with."

"I do."

"Good, then you understand that I'm not calling you a cheap whore. I'm sure you'd be very expensive."

Mary's eyes bulged, and then she burst out laughing, spitting lemonade across the table.

"I think I've misjudged you," she said.

"We're out of the office. We can be ourselves. Personally, I find it draining to always struggle to find the right phrase, to use the proper diplomatic terms."

"Oh, god, I know exactly what you're talking about."

"I respect your desire to be true to your ideals, but you certainly must use different language when talking with your priest, especially during confession."

"Of course."

"Same thing here. You don't want your priest to think you're a cheap whore; you don't want the Paraguayan military and government to think you're a cheap American Peace Corps whore."

"I see your point. When I'm on Peace Corps business I should watch my fucking mouth."

Now it was Tom's turn to spray lemonade across the table.

"Thanks, Tom. Now let's get down to business."

CHAPTER 17—1977

It took all of Tom's diplomatic skills to negotiate some action from the Paraguayan government regarding the Peace Corps. He tried to assure Stroessner's men that Carter's election did not necessarily mean a change in US policy toward Paraguay, though it was evident that was the case. He gave personal assurance that even if Ambassador Howell was replaced the United States would still support President Stroessner and his fight against communism. Tom knew this to be false. Dramatic change was coming soon. So why put his political head on the line?

"I do believe my old friend Tom is in love," Boudreau joked over a cold beer late one afternoon.

"Mary McNeil and I are fellow Americans who happen to be working toward the same goal: improving American relations with the rest of the world, thereby moving closer to world peace and American security."

Boudreau guffawed.

"We have also become friends, something you seem incapable of being to a woman."

"I like many women. I've just never had the opportunity to become friends with one."

"That's because you're too busy trying to get them in bed. Women know when you're more interested in their tits than their minds."

"If women want me to focus on their minds, they ought to cover up their tits better. I never got those women's libbers. They stop wearing bras to show their freedom from male bondage, then they get angry when I look at their nipples peeking through their shirts."

"Mary wears a bra, dresses modestly, and has one of the keenest minds I've come across. She's hotheaded, to be sure, yet she usually loses her cool while she's struggling to help others. She's a good woman. No, let me correct that: She's a good person. I'm proud to be her friend."

"I'll never understand you liberal Ivy Leaguers. You're going out of your way to help Mary and the Peace Corps, which may get you laid, but it'll also put you in the doghouse with El Presidente. What do you suppose is going to happen to you and Mary McNeil when Howell is shipped out and replaced by a fire-breathing liberal who suspends arms deliveries to Stroessner and demands political and human rights for all Paraguayans?"

"We'll both be run out of the country."

"If you're lucky. Most likely you'll both end up in one of El Presidente's dungeons and we'll never hear from you again."

"It's a risk I'm willing to take. Besides, my days are numbered here anyway. I have less than a year remaining; hopefully I'll get transferred before the shit hits the fan."

"In the meantime, maybe Mary will find a way to show her gratitude for your assistance. She's a bit skinny and muscular for my tastes, though I'm sure she'd give you a hell of a horizontal workout."

"You're a sleazy prick, Boudreau, but I'll forgive you if you're able to get the Peace Corps supplies out of customs."

"Almost done, boss. I had a case of Johnny Walker delivered recently to the head of customs, and he assures me that the goods should be available for pickup by the end of next week. That is, as long as Miss McNeil doesn't personally come to pick them up. The men at customs have had their fill of McNeil's foulmouthed badgering. They refer to her as the red-headed bitch from hell and have a strong desire to send her back to the blazing netherworld."

"I hear what you're saying. The men at the visa office have expressed similar views, though they used more diplomatic terms to describe her."

"Well, I kinda encouraged them to speak freely, you know, entered into good-natured male bantering with 'em, loosened 'em up a bit. Let 'em think we're of a like mind."

"So you called her a redheaded bitch from hell too."

"It's gonna get the Peace Corps shit cleared through customs. It ain't much worse than you telling Stroessner's people that America will always remain allies of El Presidente. We're both trying to get something done in a country where it ain't easy to get any action without a huge bribe or giving a blowjob to one of Stroessner's men. Besides, I kinda like Mary. She's got fire and integrity, and I hope you get in her pants soon."

"Peckerhead."

"I do believe it's your round."

"*Dos cervezas, por favor.*"

Tom and Boudreau were eventually able to get all of the supplies for the Peace Corps released from customs and visas issued for all the volunteers. Mary McNeil had been visiting volunteers around Paraguay and had only recently returned to Asuncion, where she met Tom for dinner at a quiet restaurant frequented by diplomats. They ordered a bottle of Chilean red wine and sat back to chat. Tom began by telling Mary about what he and Stefan had achieved.

"Thanks, that's great news," though Mary didn't sound encouraged.

"I thought you'd be thrilled," said Tom, disappointed by Mary's lack of enthusiasm.

"I'm sorry, Tom, I know I sound like a bitch."

"I never called you that."

"I'm sure some have."

"There are some men at customs feel that you've tried to emasculate them."

"Those goddamned jerkoffs. They expect all women to shut up, fall on their backs, and spread their legs."

"It does seem to be the dominant national view toward women."

"They're going to learn that I won't stand for their archaic attitudes."

Tom silently contemplated his wine. After a prolonged silence Mary uttered a deep sigh.

"Sorry, Tom."

"Yeah, you've said that already."

Mary raised her hands in exasperation, then let them fall heavily on the table.

"I'm so damn frustrated."

"Understandable."

"As if you could understand how I feel."

"You're right, I've never been a woman, but I was a white Christian in Buddhist Vietnam, and it took me over a year to make any meaningful connections. I was never accepted or gained access to the people who mattered. I was also in Côte d'Ivoire and Mali, and I've been here for two years, so I know what it's like to be an outsider and what it's like to be so frustrated that I wanted to scream or quit. Sure, being a woman makes it harder for you, especially in a Catholic Latino country, but you're not making the situation any better by demanding that Paraguayans change their views overnight to suit you. I thought you were going to practice some diplomacy."

Mary drained her wineglass and slammed it on the table, causing other diners to look over. Mary cringed slightly under their gaze.

"I'm not cut out for this job. I'm not a natural diplomat like you are."

"Oh yeah, I'm a master of diplomacy. That's why I'm a junior staffer in Paraguay after ten years in the service."

"You expected to be higher up by now?"

"You became country director in a shorter time."

"That's the Peace Corps: liberal equal-opportunity employers. It's not an old-boy network like most government agencies. If I was in the foreign service I'd have probably been tossed out by now."

"That's true, as I've been close to."

"Really? Mr. Diplomat has a checkered past? I'd love to hear about it."

It took Tom over an hour, and a bottle of wine, to tell his story.

"I'm afraid I've misjudged you," Mary said. "I assumed you were just another one of those government workers who views his job as financial security for life."

"You think we make that much money?"

"No, I never credited government workers with that much ambition. Most seem content to get a regular paycheck and know their retirement is paid for."

"That's pretty cynical."

"Is your experience different?"

"Not really. I've met too many who fit your description. I've also met some good men who are trying to make a difference in the world."

"Good 'men.'"

"It is an old-boy's network, as you correctly pointed out. The State Department reflects society. As society changes, so will State. Still, it's not a reason to condemn the entire foreign service. We may not be able to boast about immediate achievements like the Peace Corps, yet I'd like to think we're working toward a safer, more peaceful world."

"I wouldn't have agreed under Johnson's or Nixon's presidencies, but I believe Carter is trying to work for lasting world peace."

"Which I'm happy about, though it'll mean problems for us in the short term."

"Like the situation we're dealing with. I've heard that Carter is planning to replace Ambassador Howell and make dramatic cuts in military aid to Paraguay."

Tom looked around to be sure that nobody was listening. He leaned closer to Mary. "The word is that Stroessner is pissed off and is taking it out on Americans in Paraguay, especially the Peace Corps. You've managed to make your organization a prime target. That's why it's been so difficult getting your supplies and visas. We've had to use all of our diplomatic training."

"Which means?"

"We've lied and made veiled threats and false promises."

Mary laughed. "I'm grateful. Let me buy dinner."

"That's very kind, but I know what the Peace Corps pays. Let me stick our Uncle Sam with the bill. This was, after all, business."

"Very pleasurable business. Tell you what: you pay for dinner and I promise to work harder on my diplomacy. The least I can do is not to make your job any more difficult."

"Sounds like a good deal to me. Come on, I'll take you home."

Tom settled the bill, and they walked outside and located a taxi.

"I'll be OK from here," Mary said.

"I was raised to see a woman to her door, especially in a country where the locals don't respect foreign woman. Unless that's being sexist."

"It is sexist, but you're right. Paraguayan men creep me out."

They got into the taxi and drove in silence to Mary's apartment. Tom escorted her to her door. Mary turned and looked into Tom's eyes.

"I find you very attractive, Tom, but I think it would be a big mistake to get involved. I mean, we're both professionals and under close scrutiny and..."

"You don't have to explain. The attraction is mutual, I assure you. Besides, as I explained earlier, I'm coming out of a rough marriage. We'd be smart to keep things professional, though that won't stop me from thinking about you."

Mary smiled. "Me neither."

They kissed briefly, stared into each other's eyes, then said goodnight.

When President Stroessner received official notice that Robert White—a known liberal— would be replacing Caleb Howell as ambassador, the ex-general was furious. It was rumored that he briefly considered tossing out the entire American community. When Stroessner calmed down he reconsidered the situation. Tossing out businessmen would be foolish; it might take years to build up new business alliances, and in the meantime he and his cohorts would suffer economically. Throwing out the entire US embassy staff was tempting, yet it might have serious long-term consequences. Although it was rumored that President Carter intended to drastically cut military aid, it was still only a rumor. Even if Carter cut weapons deliveries by half, it still left a considerable amount. Stroessner considered contacting other countries such as France and England, but he knew that the Carter administration might make far more trouble for Paraguay if Stroessner tried to procure weapons from another nation. Although Stroessner was corrupt and brutal, he was not a fool. It would be better to wait and see what Carter actually had in store before deciding his next course of action.

Another factor had to be considered. After years of negotiation, Brazil and Paraguay had recently hammered out an agreement to build an enormous dam across the Paraná River, which separated the two countries. Construction on the Itaipu Dam Project had started in January, 1975, and a major phase was due to begin the following year. This necessitated the relocation of thousands of poor Paraguayans, a move that was proving vastly unpopular to human rights organizations around the world. Stroessner knew that 1977 was not a good year for getting into a diplomatic battle with the United States—over the dam or any other matter. That wouldn't, however, stop some people from paying dearly for his anger.

In particular, Stroessner's wrath was focused on Mary McNeil. Stories had been reaching the president about her conduct, her profane berating of Paraguayan officials, her predilection for dressing in pants and T-shirts like a common male laborer, her love of peasants and disdain for the wealthy. Stroessner had no doubt that she was a communist, which was to be expected from the Peace Corps. At least her predecessor had showed proper respect for the Paraguayan authorities. He never raised his voice, never swore, and always had a good time at presidential parties. The president had also learned that two embassy staffers—Tom Kington and Stefan Boudreau—had helped expedite official matters for the Peace Corps. Recently, a source claimed that McNeil and Kington had gotten drunk together and that Kington had escorted McNeil home. If immoral conduct could be proven, then heads would certainly roll. The president prided himself on being a patient man. He would wait, knowing that sooner or later these Americans would pay for their arrogance.

Tom was working at his desk at the embassy one morning in June when Boudreau rushed into the room.

"We've got a serious problem near Itaipu."

Tom felt his stomach contract. Mary McNeil had gone to check on the Peace Corps volunteers living in the area. Tom had been concerned about Mary's planned visit because every time the dam came up in conversation her face turned red and profanities spewed from her mouth. Each time Tom attempted to pacify her, reminding her of the necessity to remain professional at all times, to sublimate personal feelings. He never succeeded in cooling her passion.

"Mary's in jail, charged with assaulting a police officer."

"Damn. Any airports nearby?"

"There's one under construction, though last I heard it wasn't completed. Contractors for the dam have been using military airports."

"Would you check with our military contacts to see if they'll allow us to land at their airport?"

"Sure."

"Have you told Caleb yet?

"Naw, I thought you'd want to hear right away."

"Thanks. You check on the airport; I'll talk with Caleb. How'd we get the news?"

"One of the Peace Corps volunteers called. Mary's apparently been in jail for a couple of days. The volunteers have been looking for her and only found her this morning."

Tom went to Caleb Howell's office and shared what little information he had. Ten minutes later Boudreau walked into the ambassador's office shaking his head.

"No go on using the military airport. In fact, according to my source in the Paraguayan army, nobody is to provide any assistance of any kind to the Peace Corps or the US embassy. It's all unofficial, and my guy said the government will deny any charges of obstruction, but the message is clear: El Presidente is furious and it's payback time against Carter, McNeil, all of us."

"What do you think we should do?" Tom asked.

Ambassador Howell thought for a minute before speaking. "You two go home and pack your bags. Don't forget your passports and all official documents. I'll order a car and driver to be ready in one hour. Drive to Itaipu as quickly—and as safely—as possible. Evaluate the situation and call me as soon as you can. I know I don't need to say it, but be very careful not to exacerbate the situation. Mary has stirred up a hornet's nest, and it may take a while to calm things down a bit. I'll request an immediate meeting with Stroessner and try to determine how much trouble we have here. If they plan on slapping Mary's hand, we may have to roll with it. If, however, Stroessner does have it in for Mary and plans to make an example of her, we'll have to see where Washington wants to go with this. I know one thing: we'd better clear this up before Bob White takes over for me next month. If Mary's in jail when White starts to cut military deliveries and presses Stroessner for greater human rights, then she's going to be in for a long, ugly stay in a Paraguayan jail."

After further discussion, it was agreed that Tom and Boudreau should take as much money as they could gather. Ambassador Howell took all the embassy cash available, then went to the bank and arranged for a personal loan. Tom and Stefan also withdrew all the money in their accounts. Although it wasn't much, they knew it would appear more impressive to the poor people who inhabited the Itaipu region. They didn't hit the road until midday, and it took a day and a half to reach Itaipu. The roads were unpaved and deeply rutted, and an avalanche cost them several hours while men with shovels cleared boulders and dirt. Tom wanted the driver to continue through the night, but Boudreau wisely counseled caution. They wouldn't be of much help if a sleepy driver rolled down a ravine.

When they arrived at the small town—really just a village with a single road running through—it was late afternoon, and Tom and Stefan were exhausted. The driver located the police station and parked in front. It was a grim, dirty, two-story wooden structure that hadn't been painted in years. They walked in to find three policemen slumping in metal folding chairs behind a scratched wooden counter. The room smelled of stale coffee and soiled clothes. A mound of dirty plates and cups sat in the sink, a cloud of flies buzzing slowly around it. None of the policemen spoke a word of English, so the initial discussion was held in Spanish with Pedro, the embassy driver, helping translate when necessary.

"We are here to inquire about an American who may be in your jail. Miss Mary McNeil."

The two younger policemen looked over to the third policeman, a short, squat man with a thick, graying mustache. The man slowly stood up, stretched, and shuffled over to the counter. His uniform was wrinkled, and a brown stain dribbled down his shirt front.

"Who is inquiring?" the policeman emphasized the last word, scoffing at its formality.

Tom introduced Boudreau and himself. Both men pulled out their passports and letters of introduction and laid them on the counter. The senior officer—Sergeant Lopez according to the tag on his uniform—gave the documents a cursory glance.

"Yes, we have an American in our jail."

"May we see your prisoner?"

Sergeant Lopez hesitated. "I will need to call the district headquarters to ask permission."

Tom opened his mouth to protest, but Boudreau put his hand on Tom's shoulder and spoke first.

"Is there a hotel nearby?"

"It is very far from here, nearly an hour by car," replied Sergeant Lopez.

"Perhaps there is some place we could wash up?" Boudreau asked.

"Yes, down the street," he nodded to indicate the direction. "There is a cantina. You can clean up and get something to eat. Come back in one hour."

When they reached the dirty street, Boudreau turned to Tom.

"I kinda sensed you were about to jump down Señor Lopez's throat."

"Very perceptive. Thanks for stepping in."

"I thought it better to be diplomatic. Don't want to piss off these local officials; not yet."

They washed up, then ordered coffee and lunch.

"What do you think, Pedro?" Tom asked the driver when they were all seated at the table.

"I think we are very far from Asuncion."

"What does that mean?" Boudreau asked.

"It is not good. We are far from other diplomats, far from the eyes of the world."

Tom and Stefan shared surprised looks. Pedro continued.

"President Stroessner is careful not to appear too brutal to foreigners. You've noticed that people are treated gently in Asuncion. The police do not beat people, and they do not burn down houses or demand large amounts of money for traffic offenses. This place is far from the capital. The police and military here are not so careful." Pedro glanced around to be sure nobody was in hearing range. "We must watch what we say and do."

"So why did Lopez put us off?"

Pedro shrugged. "To have the time to consider what to do. Maybe he wants to clean up the prisoner. Maybe he needs to call somebody higher up, to get instructions. He is in no hurry. He will be here tomorrow, next week, next year. Maybe the prisoner too."

They returned to the jail an hour later and were confronted by a radically different scene. Windows had been opened and a fan turned on to dissipate the odor of filth and mildew. The dirty dishes had been cleared from the sink. One of the junior policemen was sweeping a pile of dirt out the door, narrowly missing the two Americans and their driver. When Sergeant Lopez approached the counter it was apparent that he had put on a clean shirt, though it was as wrinkled as the other had been. Mary could be heard shouting from the back of the building, though her words were too muffled to be made out.

"We are preparing the prisoner, but she is not being cooperative."

"Maybe if I were to go back to talk with her..." Tom began.

"That is not possible. We do not allow visits in the cells. You must wait here. Also, Captain Melendez is on his way from district headquarters. He should be here soon."

"Will we be able to see Miss McNeil before he arrives?"

"Only if she cooperates."

"Could I have a piece of paper, please?" Tom asked.

Sergeant Lopez ordered the sweeper to get Tom some paper and a pen. Tom wrote a simple note: "Cooperate! I am here with Boudreau. Tom."

The policeman took the note and carried it through the door that led to the back of the building. Five minutes later, he emerged, followed by Mary McNeil and the third officer. Mary's face was streaked with dirt. Her red hair was crusted with muck, as were her blue jeans. She was wearing an oversized white T-shirt that hung to mid-thigh. As she approached the counter, Tom noticed that her right eye was nearly swollen shut and her bottom lip was split. As Mary reached the counter she tried to pull away from the policeman who was holding her arm. When he yanked her back Tom saw that Mary's hands were cuffed behind her back.

"Would you please remove her handcuffs?" Tom asked Sergeant Lopez.

"Absolutely not," Lopez replied, shaking his head emphatically. "She is a dangerous prisoner. She should not even be out of her cell."

"With three policemen and three of us," said Boudreau, "I'm sure we can keep Miss McNeil under control."

Sergeant Lopez again shook his head.

"How are you, Mary?" Tom asked.

"How the fuck do you think I am?" she snarled before turning and glaring at Lopez.

Tom stood and looked her in the face, silently demanding that she look back at him. When she finally turned back Tom held her gaze until she calmed down a bit.

"You've got to get yourself under control," Tom cautioned. "Now."

Mary glared for a second, closed her eyes, took a deep breath, then opened her eyes.

"You're right, but..."

"No 'buts.' Self control. Now."

Mary took a few more deep breaths, then nodded. "OK. All right."

Tom looked around and saw a shabby wooden bench in the waiting area.

"May we sit down?" he asked Sergeant Lopez.

Lopez nodded his approval. Mary had a hard time sitting with her hands cuffed behind her back. Tom helped her.

"How about cuffing one hand to the bench," Tom suggested.

After some hesitation Lopez ordered the policeman to do as Tom had requested. The junior officer kept a wary eye on Mary as he unlocked her cuffs and relocked her left hand to the arm of the bench. Tom noticed that the wary eye of the officer was puffy, though not as swollen as Mary's. With her free right hand Mary rubbed her hair, dislodging bits of dirt.

"This may seem like a stupid question," Tom said, "but how are you?"

Tears began to form in Mary's eyes; she wiped them away with the back of her hand. "Pissed off. Frustrated. Humiliated. Scared."

"Physically?"

"Filthy, otherwise I'm OK."

"You are a sight. How did you get so dirty?"

"Wrestling with the fuckin...sorry, wrestling with the police."

"I suppose this would be the time to ask what happened."

"We have two volunteers in a village near the border, a husband-wife team. I was visiting last week when they got word that the village was going to be destroyed in order to build housing for the workers who're going to build the new dam. The government hasn't offered to pay for their land or their houses or to move them to new land. Just ordered them off it. I agreed to be there on the date of their eviction. We organized the villagers and instructed them on nonviolent disobedience, a sit-down strike in the path of the bulldozers. The volunteers and I sat with them."

"Oh my," muttered Boudreau.

"I know it's not what the Peace Corps is supposed to do, but I couldn't do nothing."

"Go on," said Tom.

"The police gave the order to start the bulldozers and began to drag away my volunteers."

"They wouldn't hesitate to bulldoze the villagers," Boudreau pointed out, "though they were smart enough to know that squashing foreigners might cause problems."

"That's why we sat with them; we were the only hope of saving the village."

Boudreau rolled his eyes.

"We had to do something," Mary snapped at him.

"So when the police grabbed your volunteers, you grabbed the police," summarized Tom.

"I pushed one away; I didn't slug him as they're saying I did. Not at first, anyway."

"Oh. That came later?" Tom asked, trying to remain calm.

"The guy I pushed came at me and tried to grab my hair. When he couldn't get a grip, he grabbed the front of my shirt. I think he was trying to cop a feel, so I slugged him. Next thing I knew a couple of them jumped me and knocked me to the ground. We wrestled for a bit, and then they pinned me down and cuffed me. Bastards. I got slapped and groped all the way to this shithole of a jail. Just bars, no privacy. I sleep on the concrete floor and have to use a hole in the floor as a toilet. Goddamned pervs. Every time I squat I have an audience." She shook with rage, and tears formed again in her eyes. "A little while ago they brought me a bucket of water and this T-shirt; must have wanted me to clean up because of your arrival. I refused."

"That explains the yelling that took place after we arrived."

"I planned to stay filthy and bruised, to show people how I was treated."

"You cooperated when they gave you my note."

"They threw water on my face," Mary said, explaining the streaked dirt on her face, "but I wasn't going to change my shirt. I wanted you to see the blood on it from my nose and lip."

"I'm glad you finally cooperated, to the extent that you did," Tom said.

"Now what?" Mary asked.

"A Captain Melendez is on his way. Sergeant Lopez tells us we need to deal with Melendez."

"Probably looked for a bribe," said Mary. "My volunteers tell me the police and army are always looking for bribes."

"I wish it were that simple," said Boudreau.

Mary shot him a challenging look.

"I'd listen to Stefan," said Tom. "He's been our man in the countryside, and he knows how it works."

"We've gotten a few Americans out of jail with well-placed bribes. You're right, that's how it's usually done here. The police and military are poor. They assume all Americans have money; it's only natural for them to expect some financial remuneration. Only this is different."

"Because it's me," Mary said glumly.

"Yeah, partly. Lopez probably called Melendez 'cuz he was dealing with a foreigner and because you're a VIP, Peace Corp director. Melendez probably called somebody higher up—to protect his ass or find out if he could profit from it—and that person called somebody until the word reached the president himself, and El Presidente is apparently not pleased with you."

"So there may be orders to fuck me up good," Mary said.

"Well, not literally," Boudreau said. "If you'd been Paraguayan you'd most likely have been raped many times by now, unless they'd decided to dump your body in the Paraná River."

Mary clenched her fists in fury.

"The problem we have," Boudreau continued, having made the point to Mary that she was in an extremely dangerous situation, "is that you don't have any friends in Asuncion. Worse, you've made a lot of enemies. Pardon my bluntness, but you're in some serious trouble."

"Thanks for being straight with me," Mary said.

"From what I've seen, that's the way you like it. No bullshit."

"I'd rather know the whole truth than be treated like some powder puff."

"Believe me, nobody who's ever met you would think of you as a pow- der puff," said Boudreau. "I do respect you, though I wish you'd have been a little bit more diplomatic."

"That what Tom's been telling me since I arrived."

"Our Tom is one smart cookie."

Just then the door burst open, and a Paraguayan police officer came storming in. The middle-aged, stocky man with a thick black mustache glared around the room before fixing upon Mary McNeil.

"Is this the prisoner?"

"Yes, captain," Sergeant Lopez answered.

"Why is she not in her cell?"

"She is handcuffed to the bench so that she can talk with these two men from the American embassy."

The senior officer glared at Tom and Boudreau, then turned on Sergeant Lopez. "Return her to her cell at once. She is a dangerous prisoner who will remain in jail until her trial."

Lopez shouted orders at one of the junior officers, who unlocked the handcuff from the bench and again cuffed Mary's hands behind her back. For the first time Tom saw fear in Mary's eyes.

"We won't leave without you," Tom told Mary.

Mary opened her mouth to speak, but nothing came out. After the door shut behind her Tom turned to the senior officer.

"May we speak with you, please?"

"Of course." He barked orders to one of the policemen who had entered behind him, then said something to Sergeant Lopez. The officer spoke too rapidly for Tom to follow his Spanish. Seeing the questioning look on Tom's face, the man now spoke slower and more deliberately. "I have ordered my man to find a private place where we can talk. I told the sergeant not to let anybody else talk with the prisoner. This is a police station, not a social club. You understand."

The officer's words were neither angry nor menacing. Rather, he seemed to be establishing the fact that he was in charge, not Sergeant Lopez or Tom.

"I understand completely. I am Tom Kington, political attaché at the US embassy. This is Stefan Boudreau, also a political attaché. We appreciate that you are a busy man and are grateful that you have taken the time to meet with us."

A tiny smile curled up the ends of the officer's lips. He nodded his head slightly at Tom's acknowledgement of his control of the situation.

"I am Captain Antonio Melendez. Come, let us sit down and discuss this problem."

Tom, Boudreau, and Pedro followed Captain Melendez to the cantina.

"Who is this man?" Melendez asked, nodding toward Pedro.

"He is our driver and interpreter," Tom answered.

"He will wait outside. We can call for him if he is needed."

The three sat down around a rickety wooden table. After coffee was served, Captain Melendez told everybody else to clear the room. When they were alone he got down to business.

"It will be best if we keep this discussion just between the three of us. You understand?" Tom and Boudreau nodded. "This region, Itaipu, is nowhere and has always been nowhere. We are an isolated region of a landlocked country, with no economic opportunity. I am not from here, but I have been stuck here for many years. I arrived as a private, a small fish in a small pond. A few years ago, when talks between Paraguay and Brazil began regarding the building of an enormous dam across the Paraná, I was promoted to captain and ordered to maintain order and eliminate smuggling. After all, if this region was to become a vital part of the Paraguayan economy, it could not be lawless. I have worked very hard to create and maintain order; there were hundreds of criminals who grew wealthy from the lack of law. It was not easy to put things right, and it cost many lives. In the end, I was the big fish in this small, yet safe pond.

"Now they are ready to begin work on the dam, and soon this small pond will become a very, very big pond. More police will be needed and more officers. I should become a lieutenant or major, maybe even a colonel some day, but I won't because I do not have the proper connections. I came from a poor family in a poor region and I've risen as high as I ever will. Asuncion will send their own lieutenants and majors. Even worse, as the dam nears completion, our president will worry about security and will sooner or later order the army to take control of security. I will then be a very small fish in a very, very big dam. You understand?"

Tom now understood why Pedro had been dismissed. Captain Melendez assumed— probably correctly—that Pedro provided inside information to President Stroessner. If they were going to figure out how to liberate Mary, it would have to be done under the table.

"Yes, we understand. You have spent your life working for your country, and you would like fair compensation for that work. Also, Miss McNeil has made your job more difficult."

Captain Melendez wearily shook his head. "You have no idea what headaches she and her people have caused. It is relatively easy to deal with smugglers and communists. You pay bribes for information—or use extreme methods to convince people to provide the information— then you set up ambushes and eliminate the problem. It is dirty work, yet necessary. Your Peace Corps and other international organizations complicate things. They cry about human rights and the abuse of peasants, failing to see that it is these supposedly innocent peasants who are spreading communist beliefs and smuggling guns and drugs. In the past we ignored these do-gooders. Now, with reporters from international newspapers coming to write about the dam, we are in the spotlight and must be more… careful about our methods. This difficult situation has reached a critical point because we have been given a deadline to clear large areas of land to build barracks for soldiers and housing for workers. Except your Peace Corps people are organizing peasants to resist moving from these areas. Now we are struggling to meet the deadline. I thought we had convinced the Peace Corps volunteers to stick to farming and sanitation. Then this woman whipped the peasants into greater resistance. What are we to do? If I were to use our usual methods, your Miss McNeil would disappear."

Tom felt a chill run down his spine.

"Normally, that would not be an option. President Stroessner would not dare risk the anger of you Americans. Everybody knows that you provide the weapons and money that keep the president in power. However, now that your President Carter has made it known that he opposes Stroessner's methods and his very presidency, Stroessner has become enraged. I have been told by my superiors that I no longer need treat Americans so gently. In fact, I have received word that President Stroessner would not be unhappy if some Americans were punished in order to teach Mr. Carter a lesson. In truth, all I have to do is tell Sergeant Lopez that he is free to treat Miss McNeil as he would a local and…"

Again, the threat was clear.

"Captain Melendez, we understand your frustration," said Tom. "You've worked hard to establish and maintain order in the Itaipu region. We are also aware that police are paid little and must find other means to supplement their income. When the army arrives, along with police lieutenants and majors, it will be extremely difficult to find sources of new income for a man such as you. Perhaps we can be of some assistance in helping you to prepare for this change."

"Don't get me wrong," said Melendez, "I am very happy that my country will have a new source of energy and income. It will lift many people out of poverty."

Including the captain, thought Tom. A man of his resourcefulness would certainly find many ways to profit from the building of the dam, regardless of how many senior officers competed to suck cash from international contractors.

"Yes, of course, it will be good for all Paraguayans," Tom agreed, "which is why Miss McNeil's obstruction of the work has been so upsetting. We apologize for her actions. However, by solving one problem, another one may have been created."

"What problem would that be?" asked the captain.

"Whether President Stroessner likes it or not, the fact remains that the United States is the most powerful nation in the western hemisphere. Furthermore, as is becoming evident, President Carter is a moral man who insists on a moral foreign policy."

"Indeed," agreed Melendez. "He is willing to destroy a thirty-year alliance with Paraguay because of alleged human rights abuses."

"Exactly. President Carter will use any means to promote what he believes is right. It is also apparent that he will do whatever is necessary to correct any wrong. If Miss McNeil is harmed, it would mean a great deal of trouble for many people. Carter could use US power to obstruct construction of the dam, then nobody would profit."

"I see your point," said Melendez. "By arresting Miss McNeil, Sergeant Lopez may have created an international incident."

"One that you have the power to defuse," said Boudreau.

Tom nodded his agreement. "Truth is, you are the only person in a position to keep the peace and assure prosperity for all the Paraguayans of Itaipu. If we put our heads together, we can all come out ahead."

"Do you have any ideas?" Melendez asked.

"Well, it seems obvious that Miss McNeil has to get out of jail. You could order Sergeant Lopez to release her, but that would get you into trouble with President Stroessner. If, on the other hand, she managed to escape...We're how far from the border?"

"Brazil is just across the river, only a mile or so."

"Would it be difficult to find somebody who could get her across the Paraná?"

"I know some people who could do so, though it would not be cheap," said Melendez.

"No, I don't suppose it would be," Tom agreed. "We'd need to find a way to get Miss McNeil out of jail and a way to get her across the river. If it could be done, you would be doing your nation a great service. Sadly, nobody will ever know—in order to protect you—though I'm sure we could find a way to thank you for your trouble."

"I don't suppose you brought any money with you?" Melendez got to the point.

"In fact, we did."

"How much?" the captain asked eagerly.

The next hour was spent in negotiations. Captain Melendez asked for an outrageous sum, far more than Tom and Boudreau had brought, and Tom responded with a ridiculously low offer, far less than they had brought. Melendez eventually agreed to accept all of the money Tom and Stefan had, though the captain didn't know it.

The next topic was trickier: how to exchange the money. Boudreau surprised Tom with his grasp of the intricacies of such an exchange. He told Melendez that the problem was one of trust. If they gave the captain all the money up front, he might not spring Mary from jail. If he gave half with the promise to give the other half when they reached the Paraná, there was a chance that their guides might simply kill them, take the money and leave their bodies to rot. There was even the possibility that their guides would kill them and then carry their bodies back to Itaipu and ask for a reward for their capture. Boudreau's solution was to return to Asuncion and write a detailed report of the entire deal, naming names and figures. He would then give the report to Ambassador Howell in a sealed envelope with instructions not to open it unless something happened to Mary or Tom. Nobody would want the envelope opened, as it would reveal details of the jailbreak and the bribing of a Paraguayan policeman by US officials. If the escape worked, the envelope would be burned and everybody would come out a winner: Captain Melendez would have a pile of cash, Mary would be free, and Tom and Boudreau would have the satisfaction of being heroes. If things went without a hitch.

"I don't feel so good about leaving you here alone," Boudreau said.

"I'm not alone. I have Captain Melendez," said Tom with a wry grin.

"Yeah, that's what I'm worried about, that and thinking about all that could go wrong."

"Then stop thinking. Look, you've got to get back to Asuncion to set this up. You have four days, and if you fuck up, Mary and I will be stranded in the Brazilian jungle."

"As if I needed more pressure."

"Let's go over this one last time, so there's no chance of confusion."

"All right," agreed Boudreau. "Pedro and I hustle back to Asuncion. Pedro is told that I'm going back to meet with the president and plead for Mary's release, which I will do in order to lure them into complacency. We don't want 'em to transfer Mary to some high-security prison fearing US action. In the meantime I contact security at our embassy in Brasilia and request a rescue operation at the place designated by Melendez. Then I hunker down and wait for all hell to let loose. In the meantime, Ambassador Howell works behind the scenes to prepare Washington for Stroessner's fury, though there's nothing El Presidente can do. He may kick out Howell, but Howell only has a month remaining anyway. I'll have my bags packed in case they drive me to the airport, and I'll meet you in Washington for drinks."

"Sounds easy."

"It is for me. You, on the other hand..." Boudreau shook his head.

"I kind of welcome the excitement. This has been a particularly boring posting."

Boudreau shook his head some more.

"We agree that this is our best chance to get Mary out, and there's no way a southern gentleman would allow a lady to languish in a Paraguayan jail while sleazy cops drool at her."

"I'm no gentleman, and she's no lady."

"That may be true, but we're still springing Mary and heading to Brazil in four days."

They had been standing in the shade of a large tree about fifty feet from the car. Now they walked to the car and warmly shook hands before Boudreau climbed in the passenger seat.

"Good luck," Boudreau said.

"You too. Drive swiftly and safely, Pedro. *Via con dios!*"

Tom walked to the cantina. The owner had agreed to rent out a room for his stay, though "room" was a bit grand. He'd actually cleared a space in an upstairs storeroom and put a dirty mattress on the floor. Tom was content with the basic space, it reminding him of his Peace Corps years in Côte d'Ivoire. He worried about Mary and the escape, yet felt strangely calm. Although he hadn't joined the foreign service to play commando, neither did he join to write and file reports. During the next four days he planned to visit Mary as often as he was allowed, to meditate as Suzie had taught him to do over the years, and to consider what he would do after he was kicked out of the State Department.

It was a cloudy, mild day. There was nothing ominous in the air, nothing that foreshadowed what was about to happen. The only street in town was as quiet as a graveyard. A few trucks rumbled through. A couple of dogs scratched fleas in the sun. It was just another day in Itaipu. Except that Tom Kington awoke knowing that it was a day that would change his life forever. He had slept surprisingly well, perhaps because he knew there was nothing more to be done than to follow Captain Melendez's lead and hope for the best. He had met with Melendez the day before, and they had gone through the plan one final time. The captain had assured Tom that all contingencies had been covered and nothing could go wrong. Tom was a realist who knew that there was always something that could go awry. After a full breakfast—possibly his last decent meal for days—Tom walked over to the police station. After his initial insistence that Mary stay in her cell, Melendez had relented and allowed Mary to sit with Tom on the bench in the front room of the station. Melendez had also convinced Sergeant Lopez not to handcuff Mary. She pledged not to try to escape or to hit any more policemen.

Tom and Mary were attempting to appear relaxed as they talked, though Mary kept glancing toward the front door. At ten o'clock on the dot, Captain Melendez walked in, followed by two other policemen.

"Sergeant Lopez, I am here to take the prisoner," Melendez commanded.

"I have not received any orders from Asuncion."

"That is because Asuncion doesn't know what I know. Last night one of my sources informed me that a plan is in the works to attack your jail and free the prisoner. I will take her to a more secure jail."

"Where? Which jail?" asked Lopez.

"That is not your concern. If I was you I'd be preparing for the attack."

"Preparing? I have two men and only a few weapons."

"Fortify doors and windows and have your weapons ready and fully loaded. I am waiting for more information. When I know more I will send more men to reinforce you."

Sergeant Lopez looked skeptical.

"This is no time for debate," thundered Captain Melendez. "I am taking the prisoner."

Melendez spoke briefly to his two policemen, who each took Mary by an arm and led her to a waiting car.

"I would like to come with," said Tom. "Miss McNeil is a US citizen, and I'd like to see where she's being taken."

Captain Melendez hesitated a moment, nodded his approval, then turned and walked out the door followed by Tom. A policeman sat on either side of Mary in the back. Tom took the front passenger's seat while Melendez slid into the driver's seat.

"Where are the transfer papers for me to sign?" asked Sergeant Lopez, who had followed them out of the jail.

"I did not have the time to have them typed up. I will send them tomorrow."

As they pulled away Tom glanced over his shoulder to see Lopez glaring at the car.

"That went pretty smoothly," Tom said, "though for a second I thought that you weren't going to let me in the car."

"I had to make it look real, not as if we had planned the whole thing," said Melendez.

"You would make a fine actor."

"If only Paraguay had a film industry," Melendez smiled.

They had only driven fifteen minutes when Melendez shouted, "Hold on," and stamped his foot on the brakes. The car skidded before sliding to a halt, leaving deep marks on the dirt road. Melendez turned toward Tom.

"It needs to look as if I really did have to hit the brakes. Let's get out."

As they climbed out of the car there was a rush of activity from the edge of the jungle. Half a dozen people dragged a felled tree across the road so that it sat a few feet in front of their car. The people then rushed back from where they had emerged and reemerged moments later carrying weapons. A young man with a scraggly mustache walked up to Melendez.

"Get your people away from the car," the man said.

Captain Melendez ushered his group away from the car, and one of the new arrivals stepped forward and fired half a dozen shots from his rifle into the front of the car.

"Make it look like an ambush," Tom informed Mary.

"Exactly," agreed Melendez. "It must look like they blocked the road, destroyed our engine, and took the prisoner. I'll tell them that you insisted on escorting her."

Suddenly, they heard the sound of an engine rapidly approached.

"Hell!" cursed Melendez. "I bet it's that damned Lopez."

He rushed over to the group of six and said something to the young man who appeared to be their leader. He then turned to Tom and Mary.

"Quick, we must hide in the jungle."

Just as they were safely hidden behind a large tree a car pulled to a halt behind Melendez's car. It was immediately met with a hail of bullets that seemed to go on forever, though it was only a minute. The color drained from Mary's face, and Tom heard her mutter, "No, oh, no."

When the silence settled over the jungle Melendez said, "Stay here." He and his two men walked back to the road.

"My god, Tom, they've killed people in order for me to escape. I can't do this. I have to go back."

She took a step toward the road before Tom grabbed her arm and forced her to face him.

"It's too late, and it's not your fault. Nobody was supposed to get hurt. This wasn't part of the plan."

"But it happened."

"Yes, it did, and it can't be undone. If we go back now, we'll all face a firing squad."

Captain Melendez walked back with a grim look on his face. "It was Sergeant Lopez and his men. It seems that he didn't believe my story and followed us to see what we were up to. It is a shame. He was a decent policeman, but he left us no choice. I ordered the band of smugglers to ambush them. That way, should somebody investigate, they won't find Paraguay police bullets in their bodies."

Mary began to shake and appeared ready to fall. Tom put his arm around her waist and held her close. The band of smugglers approached.

"Garcia, come here," Melendez ordered.

The leader walked over.

"Garcia, this is Mr. Tom and Miss Mary. You know where to take them."

The young man nodded.

"First, step over there." Melendez pointed toward a clearing.

When Tom, Mary, and the smugglers had gathered in the clearing, Melendez and his men walked back to the two cars, turned, and opened fire westward into the jungle. After a few minutes of firing, Melendez rejoined the group.

"It must look as if we were involved in a serious battle. I will report that when we stopped because of the tree in the road, communist rebels opened fire. You two escaped while we were pinned down. When the valiant Sergeant Lopez arrived to help, he and his men were killed by the rebels. I will perhaps be reprimanded for not pursuing you, but I will point out that there were a dozen heavily armed rebels and only the three of us. I could not ask my men to commit suicide to capture an American who had slapped a policeman. Now you must go. Garcia will take you to your meeting place in Brazil."

They walked silently for hours along narrow trails that had most likely been used by smugglers for years. When they reached the Paraná there was a small motorboat waiting to take them across. Garcia and two of the rebels went with them. When they landed, Tom and Mary were led to a clearing a hundred feet from the river, where two men waited. One stepped forward.

"*Senior* Kington?"

"Yes."

They shook hands.

"Come, we have a long way to go," the man said.

Tom thanked Garcia and his band. Then he and Mary followed the man down the trail.

CHAPTER 18—1977

T om lay on his side and smiled at the peaceful look on Mary's face as she slept. He had so rarely seen her at peace that he marveled at the change in her appearance. Usually tense with anger or frustration, her face now seemed almost angelic. Her short red hair highlighted her tanned face and ruddy cheeks. The full lips gently parted as she breathed. Tom wanted to reach under the covers and pull her lean, warm body to him, wanted to hug and caress her and be one with her. Instead, he was content watching Mary get the sleep she so desperately needed.

The trip from the Paraná River to Brasilia, Brazil's capital, remained a blur. There had been a long, exhausting day of walking along smugglers' trails, followed by a sleepless evening lying on the floor of the jungle. The next day had started with a difficult walk, a slow drift in a canoe down a narrow river, and a ride in a small plane that took off from a short, rough runway hacked out of the jungle and that landed, finally, at a military airport in the capital. Tom and Mary were taken to a nondescript apartment complex where many of the US embassy staff were housed. Tom was given a spare room in an apartment of male staffers, while Mary was put up in a small one-bedroom apartment of her own. Both slept through the night and past noon of the following day, and awoke to find clean clothes and toiletries waiting them. They remained in Brasilia a week while the State Department tried to settle the diplomatic turmoil that had resulted from their escape. Issuing new passports was a simple matter. A photographer came to the apartment complex to take their photos, and the next day Tom and Mary were presented with new passports. Dealing with the Brazilian government proved to be a far more difficult matter.

Understandably, Paraguayan President Stroessner was furious. He ranted to the international press that his entire country was in an uproar about the brutal murder of three policemen. Paraguayans knew that what really upset the president was that the escape made the police—and by extension the president himself—look incompetent. The enraged leader called in the Brazilian ambassador and demanded the return of the two fugitives, threatening to halt all work on the Itaipu dam.

Although the Brazilian ambassador expressed his outrage at the murders and pledged Brazil's undying support, he knew that the two Americans would not be returned to Paraguay. With the loss of Carter's support, it was apparent to the Brazilian government that Stroessner's hand was considerably weakened. It was also obvious that the dam was far more important to Paraguay than to Brazil, as the dam would generate revenue that Paraguay desperately needed, while Brazil had a healthy economy. Still, it was important to show regional solidarity, so the ambassador expressed his sympathy and outrage, and the US ambassador to Brazil was called into the foreign minister's office and reprimanded for violating Brazilian sovereignty.

Diplomatic notes flew back and forth between Washington, Asuncion, and Brasilia, and the international media closely followed each exchange, hoping for a war that would attract more readers and viewers. Stroessner kept stirring up things by first expelling all Peace Corps volunteers from the Itaipu region and threatening the end of the entire program, then by ordering the expulsion of Ambassador Howell and Stefan Boudreau, who was accused of being an accomplice in the escape. By the end of the week the story had faded from view, and the world moved on to the next crisis.

When things died down, Tom and Mary were flown on a US military transport plane to Washington. As the State Department wanted to interview both of them regarding the affair, they were put up in a hotel nearby. Mary was grilled on Paraguay's treatment of the rural poor, her treatment in jail, and details of the escape. When they finished with Mary, they grilled Tom for two days. He told the entire story, leaving out no details and accepting full blame for the diplomatic row that had ensued. By Friday evening Tom and Mary were exhausted and had accepted that their chosen careers had ended.

Tom knocked on Mary's hotel room door around seven o'clock that night. She opened it wearing a hotel robe.

"You don't look like you're ready to go out for dinner," Tom said.

They had met most nights for a quiet meal at some local, forgettable restaurant.

"I'm going to take a warm bath and go to sleep."

"No, you're not."

Mary's eyes opened wide in surprise.

"We've spent enough time feeling sorry for ourselves. Sure, it's been a tough road, but we survived. I'm taking you out for a special dinner, and we're going to celebrate being alive."

Mary hesitated, nodded her head slowly, then more emphatically. "You're right. Fuck Stroessner and the Peace Corps and the State Department. Let's get hammered."

Tom smiled. "That's the feisty Bostonian I met in Asuncion. I'll be back in half an hour."

He went to the lobby and had the concierge book a table at a small French restaurant near Dupont Circle. When Tom again knocked on Mary's door, she answered wearing a simple, short black dress that highlighted her bright red hair. She had even put on some lipstick and eyeliner.

"Wow, you look terrific. When did you pick up that dress?"

"A few days ago, while you were being grilled at State. I'd finished my last debriefing with the Peace Corps and was feeling low, so I thought I'd try some shopping. Some women tell me it raises their spirits."

"Did it work?"

"No. I hung the dress in the closet and went to bed early."

"I'm glad you saved it for tonight. The first night of your new life."

"Whatever that might be."

They took a taxi to the restaurant and ordered a hearty Bordeaux before opening their menus. Tom waited until the waiter poured the wine and left, then he lifted his glass.

"To the future," he toasted.

"To the future." Mary and he clinked glasses.

"How are things with you and the Peace Corps?"

"Oh, they were supportive and assured me I would be welcome when I was ready to return, but I got the sense that they blamed me for what happened. And, you know, they may be right. I lack the patience necessary for Peace Corps volunteers, not to mention diplomatic skills."

Tom raised his glass again. "Fuck the Peace Corps. They don't deserve you."

"Fuck the Peace Corps." Mary and Tom clinked glasses again. "Time to move forward. What about you, Tom?"

"I assumed I was done. I've caused some problems in the past, though never an international incident. Turns out that Carter thinks I'm some kind of hero, not that he can say so in public. The undersecretary of state for Latin America told me that Carter is under the impression that I risked life and limb to save an American citizen."

"You did," said Mary, "and I've never thanked you properly."

"Aw, shucks, ma'am, I just did what any man would do."

"Normally I'd slap you for that sexist comment," smiled Mary. "However, considering what you risked, it would seem ungrateful." The smile faded from her face. "I've never had a man put his life and career on the line for me. I'll never be able to thank you enough."

"You never have to thank me. It was my job."

"Tom Kington, you're full of shit."

"All right, you caught me in a lie. I was trying to keep things strictly professional."

"By inviting me out for dinner and plying me with wine?"

"Yeah, I admit it's not standard diplomatic training. You just seemed distraught and we've had a couple of tough weeks and...and I've fallen in love with you."

Mary leaned forward and slowly kissed him.

"I'm in love with you, too," she said.

"What do you think we should do about it?" Tom asked.

"I think we should have a terrific meal, drink another bottle of wine, then go back to my room and fuck like rabbits."

They were so drunk when they stumbled into Mary's room that they had trouble undressing each other. After a few minutes of struggling they fell onto the bed naked and held each other so close that they had trouble breathing. They fell asleep before making love.

Now Tom was awake and looking at Mary's calm face. Slowly, she opened her eyes.

"Good morning," Tom said.

"Mmmm. Good morning."

"How's your head?"

"It feels surprisingly wonderful. I haven't felt this relaxed in years."

Tom lifted the covers and slid next to her. He caressed her butt with one hand and one breast with the other while he kissed her.

"Wow, what a great way to wake up," Mary murmured. She pulled Tom close and started to run her hand over his body, when she suddenly stopped.

"This is a silly question, but did we, um, did we make love last night?"

"Not that I remember."

Mary smiled lasciviously. "Then it's about time. I've been waking up nights thinking about you, wondering if we'd ever end up in bed together."

"And here we are."

"Indeed, here we are."

The State Department granted Tom a one-month leave of absence to recover from his ordeal. Mary decided to resign from the Peace Corps. They spent the first week of their newfound freedom in Washington taking care of Tom's kids. It hadn't taken much for Tom to convince Barbara to treat herself to a spa retreat in the Bahamas. She seemed genuine in her concern for Tom after hearing about his escape, and even congratulated him on having a new lover. Barbara revealed that she had been dating a soon-to-be-divorced congressman and hoped to be a congressman's wife within a year or two. The congressman was spending twelve to fourteen hours a day working on new legislation and had told Barbara he wouldn't be able to see her for a while, except for late-night sessions of wild sex, she had told Tom with a grin. It meant she was free to fly to Barbados and leave Tom in charge of Keith and Karen. She even allowed Tom and Mary to stay in the guest bedroom while she was gone, though Barbara wasn't interested in meeting Mary and made it clear to Tom that Mary needed to be gone when she returned.

It was a wonderful week. Tom grew closer with his children, and they bonded as a family. Tom sensed that Barbara didn't spend much quality time with them. In fact, he learned that Barbara didn't spend much of any time with them. The nanny woke and fed them, they spent their days at preschool, and the nanny fed, bathed, and read to them at bedtime. Keith and Karen often spent weekends with Barbara's parents or were tended to by the weekend nanny. As Tom had suspected from the start, Barbara wasn't that interested in being a parent.

Mary, to her great surprise, loved being with Keith and Karen. She'd never had the urge to have kids, assuming the maternal instinct would kick in later, if at all. Now she found herself snuggling with the kids and reading stories and tending to scraped knees, and enjoying every minute. When the week was over Mary teared up when she said goodbye to the children and promised to visit again soon.

Tom bought a used Chevy Impala, and the two lovers set off on a road trip. They took two days to drive to Indiana and spent a couple relaxing days with the Kington family. Mary, who had never been west of Worcester, Massachusetts, embraced the simplicity of middle America. She loved the red barns and corn silos and the smell of fresh-cut hay. She even put ten pounds on her lean frame from eating hearty Midwestern meals packed with meat, starches, and fresh vegetables slathered with butter. They then meandered west, stopping to hike the Rockies in Colorado, explore Canyonlands in Utah. and descend the Grand Canyon.

It was while watching a magnificent sunset over the Grand Canyon that Tom was struck by a desire he could no longer resist. He turned to Mary, put his arms around her, and pulled her close.

"Mary, would you do me the honor of being my wife?"

She squeezed him until he gasped from lack of oxygen, then passionately kissed him.

"I'd be proud to be Mrs. Thomas Kington."

They hugged and kissed and drew smiles from other tourists who walked by and basked in the glow that emanated from the lovers.

"My parents attended my first wedding," said Tom, "but if you'd like a big one..."

"No, I don't want a big wedding. My parents couldn't afford it, and that's not their thing. My dad would drink Irish whiskey until he fell over and Mom would cry because her parents have passed and wouldn't be there. Let's drive to Vegas for one of those quickie weddings."

"You deserve something more special. I have an idea, if you're comfortable with it."

"That's intriguing."

"I told you we were going to visit my friend Suzie north of San Francisco."

"The one you claimed was just a friend," Mary teased.

Tom cringed slightly. "She is a friend, one of my best friends, though I need to be totally honest with you."

"Aha! The truth is finally coming out."

"Mary, I don't want to risk your love, but…"

"You're afraid I'm going to freak out because you slept with her in college."

"Not only in college. We've, uh, had relations on and off ever since."

"By relations, do you mean you've been in and out of love with her or that you've continued to have sex with her?"

"I've loved Suzie as a friend ever since I met her. We've never been romantically in love, but, yes, we've had sex every few years."

"Had? As in past tense?"

"I'll never cheat on you. You're the woman I want to spend the rest of my life with."

"That's good enough for me. If you're suggesting that we get married at Suzie's in California, I'm all for it."

Tom grabbed Mary's face and kissed her.

"I want you to catch a flight tomorrow for San Francisco so you can be at my wedding."

"Why should I?" Ira asked. "I wasn't invited to your first."

"That's because you and Barbara loathed each other. You're going to love Mary."

"Mary what?"

"Mary McNeil from South Boston."

"Why in the world do you think I'd love some Southie *shiksa*?"

"Because she was jailed in Paraguay for assaulting a police officer and we had to bust her out of jail and flee across the border to Brazil, leaving dead bodies behind."

"You lucky son of a bitch. You finally found yourself a good one."

"Ira, I'm at a payphone in Needles, Arizona, and I'm running out of coins. Call Suzie. She's going to arrange everything, find a Buddhist monk or somebody to do the service."

"Probably serve vegan food and herbal tea," Ira grumbled. "Planning to tell your Irish lass about your sordid past with Suzie?"

"Mary is American, not Irish, and my past with Suzie was never sordid, and I've told Mary everything about my relationship with Suzie."

"Everything?"

"Are you going to make it to San Fran?"

"You think Suzie can score some weed for me?"

"I'll see you this weekend, Ira."

"Yeah, maybe."

Suzie Chomsky had moved to a small community northeast of San Francisco three years earlier and opened The Children's School, an alternative early education center. Its reputation for attending to the emotional, developmental, and educational needs of each student rapidly spread. After six months, there was a waiting list for students and a stack of applications from young teachers who wanted to do something special. By the end of the second year, articles began to appear in national early childhood education magazines about The Children's School. Suzie was invited to speak at seminars and workshops, invitations that she mostly turned down. She loved her life, continued to study Buddhism and meditate, and had no desire to franchise The Children's School or to gain national recognition. Rather, as a good Buddhist, she supported the needs of her community. She bought a large house and turned the basement into a meditation center. She cooked meals for the elderly and needy. Ten percent of the students at The Children's School attended for free.

Tom and Mary parked in front of Suzie's house as the sun was setting. Suzie gave them both warm hugs, then they settled in the living room with a bottle of Napa wine and a bong.

"You're still smoking?" Tom asked.

"Only in the evenings and only naturally California grown. How about you two? Are you a smoker, Mary?"

"I smoked a lot in college, not much since, but seeing as how this is a festive weekend..."

"It's been a while," said Tom, reaching for the offered bong. He took in a long pull and slowly exhaled. "Last time was with Ira in London. What's the word from the old radical?"

"He arrives tomorrow evening. I have the ceremony set up for Sunday morning. You need to sign papers with the justice of the peace tomorrow, and a minister from the Universal Life Church has volunteered to perform the ceremony. His daughter attends The Children's School. If you'd like, she can be the ring bearer."

"I'd love that," said Mary.

"It's supposed to be a beautiful day. I thought we could hold the wedding out back. There's a creek and lots of trees for shade. I've been planting flowers since I moved in."

"Wonderful. A real California wedding," Mary said, taking a hit off the bong.

"Sorry you didn't invite your parents?" Tom asked.

Mary coughed up a cloud of smoke and doubled over in laughter.

"I can see Michael McNeil standing in the backyard, a glass of whiskey in his hand and a scowl on his face. 'Where's the priest?'" she said in a thick South Boston Irish accent. "'Where's the lord's holy bible? Mother of god, what is this shite?'" Mary wiped the tears that streamed down her face.

"I like this woman," Suzie said to Tom, then she turned to Mary. "Welcome to the family, sister. You're marrying a great guy. No, let me correct that. You're marrying a great human being."

Suzie leaned over and gave Mary a hug and a kiss on her cheek.

"Mind if I kiss the groom?" Suzie asked Mary.

"I wouldn't want to come between bosom buddies."

Suzie froze, a surprised look on her face, and then Mary burst out laughing again.

"Sorry, I couldn't help myself."

Suzie looked over to see Tom grinning.

"Mary McNeil, you are a naughty woman. See, Suze, I told you you'd like her."

"You told her about...?" Suzie began to ask before stumbling to an awkward halt.

"I've told Mary everything about my past. It's a long drive from Washington, and we started talking. By the time we reached California we had nothing left to hide. We think it's the basis for a sound marriage."

"My parents never really communicated," said Mary. "They always had their little secrets. They've always loved each other, yet I never felt that they were friends. Dad talks to his drinking buddies, and Mom talks with her childhood friends from the neighborhood. Tom and I want to share everything."

"Including old lovers?" Suzie teased.

"Mary did confess to a few lesbian affairs in college."

"At Boston College?" Suzie said in mock horror. "Did that come out in confession?"

"I had stopped going to confession years before."

"I think I'd better put dinner on the table," Suzie said. "This is turning into a far more interesting weekend than I could ever have imagined."

They spent the next day showing Mary around San Francisco and Berkeley: walking, eating, laughing, holding hands. It remained to be seen how Ira would fit into the mix. An hour after Ira's plane landed all four were driving toward Suzie's home. She handed Ira a joint as they exited the airport.

"This should help with the jet lag," said Ira. "I hope you brought a joint for yourselves."

"Don't be an asshole, Ira," Suzie reprimanded. "Pass the joint to Mary."

"That's all right," said Mary, "I know about jet lag; Ira needs it more than me."

"I already like you better than Barbie doll."

"Ira..." Suzie growled.

"That's OK," said Tom. "I've already prepared Mary for Ira's shtick."

"It's not a shtick. It's who I am. You're Miss Natural," he said to Suzie. "I thought you'd want me to be myself."

"I was kind of hoping you'd be somebody else for a change."

"Don't be a pussy, Ira," said Mary. "Give me the full treatment."

"Wow! The anti-Barbie," said Ira. "Here." He passed the joint to Mary, who took a deep toke and blew the smoke out the window. "Tom, I think you finally found the right woman. What do you think, Suze? Honestly."

"I think I'm jealous."

"Maybe our Mary is a liberal type. You know, willing to share all." Ira emphasized "all."

"Ira, smoke some more dope and shut up," said Suzie.

After an enormous Italian dinner they drove to Suzie's, rolled another joint, pulled the cork from a bottle of wine, and sat down to talk. It didn't take long for Ira to stir things up.

"What are your plans after getting hitched? You both still going to shill for Uncle Sam?"

"I was under the impression that we were doing good," said Mary.

"Tom continues to think he's doing good, yet the government puts him in situations where that's impossible. I mean, he helped to prop up that bastard Stroessner for three years."

"He also risked his career and life to save me," Mary pointed out.

"Tom's a good man; he's just not critical enough," Ira said. "That makes him a good match for you," he nodded toward Mary, whose mouth dropped open. "I don't mean his choice of marrying you. I wholeheart-edly approve. You're pretty and apparently hot in bed. Otherwise Tom wouldn't be marrying you. What I meant was that you're not very criti-cal in choice of careers either. I know, everybody thinks the Peace Corps is wonderful, helping the poor and underprivileged and all, but let's be honest. The Peace Corps is just a public relations wing of the federal gov-ernment. We prop up dictators who brutalize and virtually enslaves their citizens, then we send Peace Corp volunteers to show the peasants how to clean their water supply, and we pat ourselves on the back. It's people like you," he pointed at Mary, "who give the US government the legitimacy they crave."

"What the hell have you done?" Mary challenged.

"I'm educating the people, delivering the truth that the mass media refuses to do 'cuz they're afraid of losing advertising money."

"A concern that you don't have, since you married for money," Tom pointed out.

"At least we were honest about it," Ira replied. "You both lie to your-selves, try to believe that you're making a difference. What you're really doing is living off the taxpayer's dollar. You're not producing anything. Not really helping anybody."

"You, on the other hand, think you're doing something productive?" Tom asked.

"I'm forcing people to consider the consequences of their actions. If you had read the *Monkey* about Paraguay I put out two years ago—written in your honor, Tom—you would have asked for an immediate transfer."

Mary shot Tom a look that said: "Is this guy serious?"

"Oh, yes, he takes himself seriously," said Tom. "Ira always believed that he was one of the only people on the planet with perfect understanding of everything."

"It's a curse," said Ira, taking a toke on a joint. "It drove me crazy that people couldn't see what I saw, couldn't appreciate my poetry or my writing. Now they're catching on."

"Ira, the only people who read the *Monkey* are radicals like yourself. I haven't heard any serious people quote the *Monkey* or cite it as cause for changing viewpoints," Tom said.

"That's because you read straight magazines like *Time*. They don't get me. They never will."

"What's your circulation?" Mary asked.

"Circulation is meaningless. The *Monkey*'s the kind of paper that gets passed around and discussed. It's well known throughout England and its former colonies. I'm told I have many important readers in India."

"How many?" Mary asked.

"Don't get hung up on numbers."

"The number that matters to me is two o'clock in the morning, which is the current time," said Suzie. "You two are getting hitched in eight hours. I'm going to bed."

Wedding day was cool and clear. Birds filled the trees and chirped merrily, providing the music that accompanied the ceremony. The minister from the Universal Life Church had graying hair hanging halfway down his back, a long, gray beard, and silver studs in both ears. He wore white pants and an embroidered Pakistani *kurta* that hung to mid thigh. He was soft-spoken and performed the brief ceremony with dignity. Suzie had invited a few close friends to share in the festivities, and each brought a dish for the buffet that followed. While they ate organic vegan food, Ira brought up Tom and Mary's future.

"You know, there are nongovernmental organizations in London that could benefit from your international experience. Oxfam has worked for thirty years to feed the hungry. They operate throughout the world."

"I'm shocked," said Suzie. "I would have thought that a cynic like you would scoff at do-gooders who give food to people who are doomed to die in poverty anyway."

"I reserve my cynicism for governments and corporations. NGOs have earned my admiration. Most, anyway. The American ones tend to be headed by wealthy white men who fly in private jets, never seeing the irony in raising money for the poorest while living like one of the richest. I happen to know some of the people who run Oxfam and some of the other British NGOs, and they've impressed me. They live modestly, and a vast majority of the money they raise is actually used to reduce suffering."

"Maybe you're not a lost cause after all," Suzie said.

"The question isn't about me," said Ira, "it's about Tom and his lovely bride. Have they finally seen the light and decided to stop being a whore for Uncle Sam?"

"I should have known you wouldn't be able to remain civil for long," said Suzie. "Sorry, Mary. Ira is incorrigible."

"Don't apologize, I've been having similar thoughts."

"Really? My little talk last night touched a nerve?" Ira puffed up with pride.

"Sorry to burst your bubble. Tom knows I was reconsidering my career choice before I was jailed in Paraguay. I hesitate to admit it, but my beliefs run a lot closer to yours than to Tom's and Suzie's."

"Wow! You really are the anti-Barbie. Why don't you two move to London, and I'll introduce you to some people."

"Thanks for the offer," said Tom, "but I have to report back to Washington in a week."

"What's Mary going to do when they post you to Ouagadougou?"

"Ask Mary."

"Well?" Ira asked.

"I've thought a lot about my future, our future." Mary smiled at Tom. "I just haven't found anything that grabs me, though your talk about NGOs intrigues me."

"Have you ever studied Buddhism?" Suzie asked.

"I read a few things in college. Baba Ram Das and things like that."

"What did you think?" Suzie asked.

"Thought-provoking."

"Exactly. Buddhism never tells anybody what to do. It helps them to consider choices and consequences."

"Sounds like just what I need. What do you recommend?"

"I'd love to give you some of my favorite books, as a wedding present."

"You've already given us so much."

"One can never give too much love."

"Fucking California," muttered Ira.

Tom and Mary took five leisurely days to drive back to Washington. Mary read Buddhist philosophy much of the way, which led to long talks about the meaning of life, their purpose on earth, and their immediate future. They basked in each other's love and realized that neither had ever been happier. By the time they unpacked their suitcases at their government-owned apartment they had made their decision: Tom would accept his next diplomatic assignment and Mary would join Tom with the idea of working for an NGO in whatever country they landed. She would start anew to help others, and would do it without ties to any government agency.

After putting away their clothes and washing up, Tom turned his attention to the small pile of mail that awaited them. He glanced at the envelopes before settling on a thick one from the State Department.

"This is it. The envelope, please," Tom said, mocking the Academy Award ceremony. "And the winner is..." he tore open the envelope, "Afghanistan."

"I know it's in Asia," said Mary, "otherwise I don't know much about it."

"Nor do I, though I'm pretty sure you won't need to bring a bathing suit." Tom closed his eyes and conjured up a map of Asia. "It's landlocked, has rugged terrain, is on the southern border of the Soviet Union, and its people are serious Muslims. We leave in two months."

"That'll give me plenty of time to refresh myself on Islam. Catholicism in Boston and Paraguay, Buddhism in California, Islam in Sierra Leone, though I understand it was a moderate version. If we keep this up I'll be able to teach a religions course."

Tom pulled Mary toward him. "That's my wife. We're going to make a great team."

"Two ought to be able to change the world more than one."

They spent New Year's Eve with Keith and Karen, who slept over while Barbara partied with her congressman boyfriend. Tom had spent every free moment of the past two months with his children, though little free time remained after his long days of briefings, research, and studying Afghanistan's two main languages, Pashto and Dari. Mary also studied Pashto and Dari, along with Islam, and bought a few modest outfits that would hold her until she could purchase Afghani clothing. She also contacted NGOs with operations in Afghanistan and interviewed with the few that had offices in Washington. By the time Tom and Mary boarded their flight for Kabul, they were excited and ready for a new adventure. The goal, as always, was to do good and make the world a better place. What they didn't know, couldn't possibly know, was that they were flying into a tempest.

CHAPTER 19—1978–1979

They sat around the table in the US embassy courtyard and listened to the eerie silence. Kabul, Afghanistan, wasn't as jammed with honking cars and screaming motorcycles as many Asian cities were, yet there was always the sound of some type of engine that reminded a person that they were in a large city: the occasional motorcycle that whined in the distance as young men sped to meet friends, old buses that rumbled and creaked and belched dark clouds of smoke, well-tuned embassy and government cars that hummed contentedly. But not tonight. Kabul was silent with anticipation, as if the entire city was holding its breath.

Although Afghanistan had a long history of invasion and warfare—Alexander the Great conquered the region three centuries before the birth of Christ—and the many ethnic groups that comprised the Afghani people had been fighting each other for even longer, Kabul was generally an island of calm in a sea of strife. In fact, the entire nation had been blessed with relative peace and stability from 1933 to 1973 under the benevolent rule of King Zohar Shah. Even the coup of 1973 that brought the king's brother-in-law, Mohammed Adour Khan, to power had been bloodless. That peace, which continued until 1978, was now under threat. A prominent member of the People's Democratic Party of Afghanistan (PDPA), a legal opposition party, had been assassinated and many of the PDPA's leadership arrested. It appeared as if Khan's government was trying to eliminate any threat to its leadership. The night before, a cool April evening, the PDPA had launched a counterattack. All foreign nationals had been urged to stay indoors until the situation had settled down and security could be determined.

Since most US embassy staffers lived near the embassy compound, nearly all of them moved temporarily into the compound, which was surrounded by high walls topped with shards of broken glass and protected by a team of marines. Wayne Glass, Tom Kington, Mary McNeil, and Larry Daniels sat around the table in the courtyard sipping mint tea late in the evening. Glass had been Tom's second political head in Saigon, having replaced Howard "Hard" Case during Tom's third year. They had gotten along well, and Tom was thrilled when he learned that he'd again be working with Glass. Larry Daniels was from the other end of the experience spectrum, having only arrived in Afghanistan the previous month for his first diplomatic post. Tom got along well with the young diplomat, as they both had much in common: Daniels was also a Midwesterner, hailing from North Dakota, and he too had headed east for an Ivy League education, graduating a year earlier from Brown.

"Saigon was never this quiet," Glass commented.

"War or peace, that place was jumping twenty-four hours a day," Tom agreed.

"Though there's a similar feeling in the air, like just before Tet," said Glass.

Tom nodded. "As if everybody knew a storm was coming."

"The quiet kind of reminds me of North Dakota," Daniels said.

"This has got to be as far from North Dakota as you can get," said Mary. "Have you been smoking some of the local hash?"

Daniels laughed. "The last thing I need is to be stoned. I think I'd freak out. You know, Afghanistan does remind me of home from time to time."

"They cover women from head to toe in black cloth in North Dakota?" asked Mary in mock horror.

"Let the man talk," said Tom

Daniels was intimidated by the strong-willed Mary McNeil, which only encouraged her to kid him more. Mary was, actually, fond of the young man. She pretended to zip her mouth shut.

"I don't mean the people, though North Dakotans have the same sense of pride in community and culture. No, I'm talking about the land. An April day in Bismarck isn't that different from Kabul. The evenings are cool and the stars are brilliant. Both places have huge tracts of open land dominated by mountains and threatened by harsh winters. It's not easy to make a living in either place, and in both you get a sense that you're far from the rest of the world. Bismarck seems as far from New York and Washington as Kabul is from London and Tokyo. I suspect that I was sent here because it might remind me of home."

"You're giving the State Department more credit than they deserve," said Glass. "You're new, and nothing much is happening in Afghanistan. That's why you were sent here."

"Tom's first assignment was Vietnam," Daniels pointed out. "He scored a hot spot on his first posting."

"I was fluent in French and had some knowledge of Buddhism."

"With those qualifications, I'm surprised they didn't send you to the Congo," chuckled Glass.

"Don't listen to Wayne," Tom said. "He's gotten a little cynical over the years."

"You haven't?" Glass asked.

"It's impossible not to become a bit cynical. I'm just trying to set an example for our young colleague."

"Larry, you're lucky to be learning under these two guys," said Mary. "They have the three things necessary to survive and succeed in an overseas posting: idealism, experience, and a sense of humor. I lacked the last two, which is why I failed in Paraguay."

"It's going to take a lot more to succeed here," said Tom. "The more I learn about Afghanistan the more I wonder if we'll ever get a handle on this place."

"It's sure quiet right now," said Larry.

"Yeah, but for how long?" Tom asked.

The quiet only lasted a few more hours. The Great Saur Revolution— Saur is the month of April in Pashto—began early the next morning with the arrest of Mohammed Adour Khan, his family, and members of his government by the military wing of the PDPA. Within days it was learned that Adour Khan and his family had been murdered, along with many supporters. The foreign community was horrified, yet could do nothing more than wait until there was a new government with whom they could file a protest. Everybody remained indoors, and all work by embassies and NGOs was suspended. On May 1 Nur Mohammad Taraki was named president, prime minister, and general secretary of the PDPA. The nation was renamed the Democratic Republic of Afghanistan, marking the end of the monarchy. As was befitting a group that called itself the People's Democratic Party, Taraki's government announced a series of progressive reforms that included religious freedom, land reform, and greater freedom and rights for women. Although the US ambassador still filed a formal protest over the killings, he privately assured President Taraki that the United States wholeheartedly supported the proposed reforms.

Mary cheered the reforms, particularly those that proposed to radically improve the lives of women. She was sitting with Tom and Larry Daniels one day after work, sipping mint tea, when Larry mentioned those changes.

"Eliminating arranged marriages, relaxing strict dress codes, promoting voting and economic rights, heck, won't be long before the government is packed with women."

"It hasn't happened in the States yet, and women have had the vote since 1920," Tom pointed out.

"Yeah, but the US government is an old boys' club," Mary replied. "We'll never see a woman president until the old boys die and are replaced by progressive thinkers. Things will happen faster here because Taraki supports women's rights."

"Looks like I may have arrived at the right country at the right time after all," said Daniels. "Being here to watch the start of a social revolution will be interesting."

"Are you familiar with the ancient Chinese curse, 'May you live in interesting times'?" asked Tom.

"No."

"You may soon become intimately familiar with it."

"Things seem fine in Kabul," Daniels said. "The Afghani women I've talked to are excited about the future. The city is coming to life, tourists are interacting more easily with locals, the atmosphere is almost festive."

"Not among the few supporters of Daoud Khan who remain alive. Mary, you went out to the countryside yesterday. What's your take?"

Mary had gone to work for Oxfam and spent most of her professional life in the countryside setting up networks for distributing food. The previous day had been her first out of Kabul since The Great Saur Revolution.

"The village I visited hasn't changed since Alexander the Great was passing through."

"That's just my point."

"It's the same everywhere," said Daniels. "Change starts in urban centers that are magnets for intellectuals. It'll take a while longer for reforms to reach the villages."

"Maybe," said Tom, "and maybe reforms will never reach the villages. Remember the Scopes Monkey Trial? Scopes was busted for teaching evolution in rural Tennessee in the 1920s. Big-city journalists covering the trial laughed at the ignorant hicks who still believed in creation. Fifty years later and they're still teaching creation in Tennessee. You think a village that hasn't changed in three thousand years is going to liberate women just because a Marxist president in Kabul tells them to? I don't see Taraki's government winning support for progressive changes from the *mullahs* in the countryside, and without the support of religious leaders I don't see things working here either."

"But Taraki is not a Marxist," Daniels protested.

"Have you studied his background?"

"Not yet."

"You ought to. It'll enlighten you. Taraki studied Marxism at Columbia and Harvard, and the PDPA is rife with Marxists. I might also remind you that Marxism is atheistic. Personally, I have no problems with Marxism. Like most philosophies it has its good points and bad points. However, Marxism is just about as far as you can get from fundamentalist Islam. I have some serious concerns about the future of Afghanistan."

"I hope you're proved wrong," said Mary.

"So do I."

Tom and Mary had honeymooned in Paris for a week before flying to Kabul. They stayed at a romantic little hotel in the Marais that had been recommended by a Parisian friend from Tom's days in Paris. Tom had shown Mary around his favorite museums; they had walked the narrow streets of the Left Bank, peering into shops and chatting with shopkeepers; and each night they had dined at small, intimate restaurants, followed by strolls along the Seine and passionate sex.

Kabul had been a dramatic change from Paris, though not an unpleasant one. Whereas Paraguay had offered a certain familiarity in terms of religion and dress and European orientation, Afghanistan was a different world. The only women on view were either prepubescent or menopausal. Every Afghani woman of fertile age was shrouded in the omnipresent black *chador*, the garment that covered women from head to toe, exposing no skin to the eyes of men.

As Tom and Mary soon learned, Afghanis were not from a single ethnic group. Rather, they were descendants of the original inhabitants as well as remnants of invaders and traders who traversed the region: Persians, Greeks, Uzbekis, Turks, Mongols, and more. The result was that each Afghani reflected his ancestry. Hair ranged from black to dirty blond, eyes were black or brown or even brilliant blue. A man's ethnicity was immediately apparent from the clothing he wore, which varied by group. Added to the mix were the hundreds of young overlanders who wandered around Kabul. Some, the most recent arrivals from the United States or Europe, were dressed as if they'd just walked off college campuses. Others, those who had been traveling on the cheap for months or even years, were clothed in a hodgepodge of garments from India and Nepal and Afghanistan. For Tom and Mary—two people who relished new experiences—being in Afghanistan was like youngsters visiting Disneyland.

Mary had been disconcerted to see all the women in *chadors*, even though she had been prepared for it. Soon, though, she had the opportunity to talk with Afghani women in private settings where they were able to remove their *chadors*. The women, nearly all young and educated by teachers at home, had put Mary at ease. They didn't mind being protected from the lascivious looks of their uncouth countrymen, and they had many opportunities to wear nice clothes and talk with educated young men at private gatherings. As importantly, they saw hope for a more progressive future. Even before The Great Saur Revolution, the PDPA had been advocating social liberalization. Mary soon realized that, rather than be stuck in a medieval country where women were no better off than goats, she would be witness to the start of a new era for women in Afghanistan. Although Tom had been concerned that Mary would revert to her radical self and start agitating for immediate emancipation for her fellow women, Mary was admirably appropriate in her views, eager to facilitate change yet willing to accept the necessarily slow pace dictated by Afghanistan's long history of conservatism.

It only took a few days for Tom to realize he'd landed a gem of an assignment. Most diplomats would have scorned the assignment as a fruitless, thankless job in an unimportant country. There was no Cold War battle raging as had been the case in Korea and Vietnam. There were no critical negotiations like the Paris Peace Talks or the Yalta Conference. Afghanistan did not contain vital mineral wealth like Saudi Arabia with its oil, nor did it sit astride a strategic trade route as Egypt did the Suez Canal. Yet Tom saw a nation divided into hostile ethnic factions that always seemed to be on the verge of an outbreak of violence, creating the sort of constant tension that made Tom feel alive as a diplomat. As well, Afghanistan was surrounded by nations that *were* vital to the health of the world. To the west lay Iran, a wealthy oil producer and US ally. To the east and south was the ever-volatile Pakistan, which had waged wars against India, Afghanistan, and the breakaway East Pakistan, which became Bangladesh. Of greater interest from a US viewpoint was Afghanistan's northern neighbor, the USSR. Thus, Tom would be dealing with domestic tensions as well as Cold War and regional conflicts. It might not have been a plum assignment for a State Department star; for a serious diplomat like Tom it was a rich vein.

It also soon became apparent that the State Department was starting to take Afghanistan more seriously. Soon after becoming president, Taraki began a series of meetings with the Soviet government, and he let it be known that he favored closer ties with their giant neighbor to the north, both for ideological and security reasons. Alarmed, Jimmy Carter sent a new ambassador to Afghanistan. Adolph "Spike" Dubs was a longtime diplomat who had served as charge d'affaires at the US embassy in Moscow and was fluent in Russian.

Whereas 1978 proved to be a professionally and personally fulfilling year for Tom and Mary, 1979 got off to a horribly inauspicious start. Tom was working in his office on February 14 when Wayne Glass burst into the room.

"Ambassador Dubs has been kidnapped. Help me pass the word. We'll all meet in my office in five minutes."

Five minutes later the ten Americans who worked at the embassy were jammed into Glass's office. A few sat in chairs, though most leaned against the walls or stood awkwardly.

"Here's what I know, and it isn't much," began Glass. "The ambassador and his driver were pulled over by the Afghani police, though it now appears they weren't real policemen. They took the ambassador and left the driver, who immediately drove back here. I've ordered the marine guards to close the gate and admit nobody unless they have information about the ambassador. I've also called Washington. There's nothing else to do but wait. Any ideas?"

"We should inform the other embassies," Tom said, "in case this is the start of something."

"Good point," agreed Glass. "When we're done let's divide the task so we can get it done as quickly as possible."

"What about informing US citizens?" Larry Daniels asked.

"Right. I'll get my secretary to make a list of all the Americans we have phone numbers or addresses for and get him to make the call."

"Maybe they should hear from a fellow American," Tom said. "Some of them may flip if a man with an Afghani accent calls and tells them Ambassador Dubs has been kidnapped."

"Good point. We'll divide that task as well."

"What if the kidnappers are trying to call us?" somebody asked.

"Damn, you're right," said Glass. "OK, let's personally go to the embassies; most are within walking distance or you can hire a car for the day. Anything else?" After a pause he continued. "Let's get to it. Tom, would you stay behind for a minute?"

When everybody had cleared out, Tom sat down facing Wayne Glass.

"There's no official pecking order here, but since I have seniority I've gone ahead and assumed temporary leadership."

Tom nodded his approval.

"You have experience under stress, what with Vietnam and your recent adventure in Paraguay. I'll need to meet with somebody from Taraki's office and be on hand here to oversee things. I want you to be our point man when the kidnappers get in contact. Any meetings, exchanges, whatever, I want you to handle it. Are you OK with that?"

"Of course."

"I don't want you to think I'm afraid or anything." Glass was pale and sweating through his shirt. "It's simply that I don't have experience and..."

"It's the right choice, Wayne. I do have experience, and I'd go nuts sitting behind a desk when something's going on."

Glass smiled weakly. "I remember your stories about sneaking off to Hué for secret meetings." His smile faded. "I feel terrible about asking you to put yourself at risk—I mean, after what you went through in Paraguay. It's just, well..."

Glass had three grown children living in the States and five grandchildren. Tom wondered if they were on his mind.

"Wayne, you need to be here. As soon as the call comes in I'll grab Sergeant Wisniewski, and we'll handle it, always checking with you first."

Glass exhaled slowly and seemed relieved. "Thanks, Tom. I knew I could count on you. When Dubs's driver told me the news, you were the first person I thought of."

"Thanks for your confidence."

The call came half an hour later. The Afghani receptionist answered the phone, took notes, then ran up to Glass's office.

"Mr. Glass, they are holding the ambassador at the Kabul Hotel. They demand the release of two political prisoners in exchange for his release." He handed the note to Glass.

"Thank you. Call President Taraki's office and request an immediate meeting."

Glass got up and walked into Tom's office.

"You're on. Is Wisniewski ready?"

Sergeant Wisniewski was head of the marine guards.

"Yup. He's got his men stationed around the embassy walls, and a car and driver ready."

"Copy the names of these so-called political prisoners and take them with you to the Kabul Hotel. Find out who's negotiating and make sure they don't do anything stupid. What little I know about negotiating is that you're supposed to try to engage the kidnappers in dialogue, build a rapport. Don't let the Afghanis rush into anything."

"I'll do what I can, and I'll keep you informed."

The driver parked the embassy car near the Kabul Hotel, where a large crowd of Afghanis stood around and gawked. Sergeant Wisniewski pushed his way through the crowd, and Tom followed with the driver close behind. Tom spied a group of senior men in uniform, and he asked the driver to find out who was in charge. After a few minutes the driver returned and asked Tom and Sergeant Wisniewski to follow. The driver wove his way through a mob of soldiers and policemen until they stood in front of a man who appeared to be directing things.

"I am Colonel Motamedi of the Afghan Security Force," the man said slowly in British-accented English.

"Tom Kington. This is Sergeant Wisniewski, head of the marine guards at the embassy."

Tom shook the colonel's hand, and the two soldiers saluted.

"There are four kidnappers. They are holding your ambassador in Room 117. It is the third window from the end on the second floor." Colonel Motamedi pointed to the room.

"Have there been any other kidnappings?" Tom asked.

"None. This appears to be an isolated case."

"So what do we have here?"

"The kidnappers have demanded the release of two 'political prisoners.' These men are in fact Islamic militants who have plotted attacks on the Afghani government. They are dangerous criminals and will not be released under any circumstances. It is the policy of the Afghani government not to negotiate with terrorists and kidnappers."

"May we offer any assistance?" Tom asked. "We have had some experience with similar situations."

"That will not be necessary. Everything is under control."

"I'd like to be consulted before any military action takes place."

It was something that Tom had discussed with Sergeant Wisniewski on the way over. Wisniewski was concerned that the Afghani military would shoot first and ask questions later. The sergeant had been trained to talk with kidnappers and to try to achieve a nonviolent solution rather than to blast away.

"Mr...."

"Kington."

"Mr. Kington. I appreciate your concern for your ambassador. However, this is an Afghani matter, and we will deal with it as we see fit.

If we have time to consult with you, we certainly will. That may not be possible."

Tom was tempted to push his case, but before he could speak Colonel Motamedi had turned and walked back to where the other Afghani officers stood.

"I'm not getting a good feeling about this," said Sergeant Wisniewski.

"Nor am I. Unlike liberal democracies where people like to discuss and seek solutions, third-world governments prefer to send messages."

"Yeah, like, 'Mess with us and you die.'"

Shortly after noon a battle erupted on the second floor of the Kabul Hotel. Some in the street ducked, others stared openmouthed as shots rang out, though all the firing took place within the hotel. Suddenly, the windows of Room 117 burst outward, and everybody hit the street or sought cover. In a few minutes everything was eerily quiet. People stood up and started talking animatedly, gesturing and pointing at the blown-out windows. Tom and Sergeant Wisniewski looked at each other, grim looks that spoke volumes. They watched as heavily armed soldiers stormed in through the front door. Finally, half an hour after the shooting had commenced, Colonel Motamedi emerged from a crowd of officers and beckoned Tom and Sergeant Wisniewski to join him.

"I am sorry to inform you that there are no survivors."

Tom struggled to keep all emotion from his face. "What happened?"

"Our men attempted to free the hostage. The kidnappers refused to lay down their weapons, and we were forced to shoot."

There was no point in asking who shot Ambassador Dubs, and it didn't really matter whether the kidnappers had executed him or he'd been caught in the crossfire and shot by the Afghani Security Force. The message had been delivered: Mess with President Taraki's government and you will die. Tom nodded, turned, and walked back to the waiting car.

Jimmy Carter sent a personal note of protest to President Taraki regarding the apparent disregard for Ambassador Dubs's life. The State Department's form of protest was the decision not to send a new ambassador to Kabul. The message was unequivocal: if you don't value and respect the life of the US ambassador, then you can deal with a lower-level representative.

Perhaps the United States expected an apology and an attempt to make things right. Instead, the already leftist Taraki sought closer ties with Afghanistan's northern neighbor, the USSR.

Mary remained above the political mud, much to Tom's relief. Since most of his time was spent dealing with the tense political situation, he liked that he could go home and discuss a different topic. Getting supplies for Mary's relief work was even more difficult in Afghanistan than it had been in Paraguay, yet Mary handled the hassles in a calm, professional manner. She was also patient and diplomatic in dealing with the patriarchal society that reigned over the countryside. Mary discussed education and women's rights with women, yet she never preached or pushed for change, which she understood would only occur slowly. In the meantime she could improve the lives of the rural poor of Afghanistan by improving their nutritional intake. Much to Tom's surprise and pleasure, Mary also slid comfortably into the role of a diplomat's wife. She was still outspoken with Westerners, but she bought some nice clothes—including dresses—hosted dinner parties, and accompanied Tom to all official functions. She also acted as a sounding board for Tom's ideas and helped him to write policy papers, and was always eager to distract him in the bedroom after particularly tough days. As importantly, Mary discussed what she was learning about the people of rural Afghanistan. Tom had learned in Vietnam that urban centers only reveal a partial view of a nation's people. He sensed that a similar dynamic was occurring in Afghanistan, and Mary confirmed his belief.

She returned one evening after four long, dusty days in the countryside. Tom made her a gin and tonic, then sat on the toilet seat sipping his own while Mary ran a cool bath and stripped off her filthy clothes.

"Boy, oh, boy, does this bath look good."

"Should I have Ahmed burn your clothes?"

Ahmed was an older Afghani who had worked for embassy personnel for years. His English was excellent; more importantly to Tom and Mary, he was a terrific cook, meticulous house cleaner, and washed and pressed clothes as well as any fancy American laundry.

"Ahmed would freak at the waste. Besides, they're only dusty and sweaty, and Ahmed takes such pride in making them look like new."

"Think we can take Ahmed with to our next assignment?"

"Even if we could, Ahmed wouldn't want to come with. You know, in Paraguay it seemed like everybody wanted to come to America. Hardly a day went by when somebody didn't ask about the size of American houses or if I'd been to Hollywood and seen any movie stars. Nearly all the young people wanted to move to the States and make millions, and the young men all wanted to marry blondes with big boobs. That's not the case here. We've been here over a year, and I've yet to have one person ask any questions about America except about religion. Nobody envies me. They're proud of three things: their village, their ethnic group, and Islam. I've never heard one person call himself an Afghani. Ask them who they are and they say they're Pashtun or Tajik or Hazari. As to their religion, nobody needs to ask. They're all Muslim fundamentalists, though not in a hostile way. The fact is that their lives are totally governed by the Koran and their *mullahs.* Tom, that's where the real power lies. Those bearded guys decide everything: when and whom to marry, what aid to accept or reject, how to bury somebody, everything. Most of the people I talk with don't even know who the president of their country is, and they don't care. They have no idea what the difference is between communism and democracy, but they know the rulers in Kabul are not good Muslims. They tolerate me because I bring food and supplies and I'm going to leave some day. That's not how they feel about Taraki and his government. I'm starting to get an uncomfortable sense that opposition to the government is growing, and these are not the kind of people who debate politics. They're warriors."

Tom trusted Mary's judgment. Her most recent assessment of the mood in the countryside left him concerned.

Tom had gotten into the habit of wandering the streets and neighborhoods of Kabul, an activity that only Mary knew about. Wayne Glass would probably consider it a foolish risk in this time of social and political upheaval, especially in light of the kidnapping and killing of Ambassador Dubs. He was sure that Sergeant Wisniewski would order him to restrict his walks to the more secure Wazir Akbar Khan area, where most embassies were located, or take a marine along for security, which would have defeated the purpose of the walks. He liked seeing things for himself, absorbing the local culture in order to better understand the people. Now, inspired by Mary's time in the countryside and her growing firsthand knowledge of Afghani society, Tom rededicated himself to learning Pashtu and Dari, as well as getting to know the different ethnic groups that comprised the nation. Tom would go home after work, change into local clothes—baggy pants, a long, untucked shirt, and a dark vest—and spend hours wandering Kabul. He knew he didn't blend in any more than he did in Vietnam, yet in a country comprised of so many diverse ethnic groups, each dressed differently, Tom didn't stick out that much. Besides, with so many tourists and overlanders passing through Kabul, the sight of a Westerner dressed in local garb rarely elicited a second glance.

A couple of months after ambassador Dubs's death, Tom was walking along the Old City Wall, which ran south from the Kabul River. As he walked, he would occasionally stop to chat with shop owners, first determining which language they spoke, then exchanging pleasantries before moving on. He'd started to recognize ethnic groups by their clothes and skin, hair and eye color, and had started to offer greetings in the proper language before needing to ask. When Tom guessed correctly, the shopkeepers would respond with praise and invite Tom in for sweet tea. Although he was far from being able to manage political discussions as he had been able to do in Vietnam, he felt that he wasn't far from it. After walking for over an hour, Tom decided to stop at a tea shop. He immediately identified the shopkeepers as Pashtun and greeted them in Pashtu. Soon he was sipping from a chipped ceramic cup and discussing the weather with the owner.

They had only been talking a few minutes when a tall, thin man walked in. It was immediately apparent that the man was a Westerner. He wore dark-gray khakis, an untucked olive-green shirt, a floppy tan hat, and sunglasses. It was a drab outfit, which is one of the reasons the man caught Tom's attention. Most tourists either dressed in a weird mishmash of embroidered Indian clothes or colorful Nepalese outfits, or they dressed as if going to the mall in Des Moines. This man seemed intent not be noticed. Tom instinctively knew that this man was not a tourist. There was also something familiar about him, something vaguely military in his bearing, though the scruffy sandy-blond hair that hung halfway down his neck softened his military posture. Tom was trying to be nonchalant in his assessment of the man, doing his best not to look directly at him, when the man removed his sunglasses and hat and turned to face Tom.

Tom gasped. "If it isn't my old drinking buddy Officer...I mean, Sam Smith."

"*Salaam Alaykum.*" Smith fluently said the Arabic greeting.

"*Alaykum Salaam.*" Tom gave the standard reply.

The shopkeeper smiled, apparently pleased that these two foreigners would choose to give each other the respectful Muslim greeting. He told Smith in Pashtu that he would bring him some tea, and Smith thanked him in Pashtu. The man scurried to the back to get the tea.

"How's life been treating you?" Tom asked. "You got a new employer? I wouldn't have thought the CIA allowed that type of haircut."

"My bosses give me some leeway so that I can fit in a bit better."

"Yeah, a buzz cut sort of shouts military or CIA, and I assume you'd prefer anonymity."

"You got that right. In Nam it was easy 'cuz there were thousands of us white guys with military haircuts, even those not in uniform. Nobody asked if we were out of uniform or retired or independent contractors. Hell, nobody asked much of anything. Here things are different. There's only hippies and diplomats, and ain't none of either group with buzz cuts. Besides, I kinda like the shaggy look. I even find the occasional hippy chick givin' me the onceover."

"Grow another inch or two and you might get laid."

"Oh, I do all right regardless of the length of my hair. Some women like variety, you know, something different from the usual long-haired guys. Others find me exotic, sense I'm a man of action. What they don't realize is that everybody's in costume. Some of them longhairs are ex-military who've seen a hell of a lot more action than I have, and sometimes mild-looking types are in reality ass kickers. Like you."

Tom frowned.

"I was damn proud when I heard of your Paraguayan adventure, almost called to tell you."

"What stopped you?"

"You do remember who I work for. We're not supposed to get personally involved."

"Officer Jones must have missed that memo."

Smith chuckled. "You sure pissed him off, and he wasn't the only one. There was a fairly hot debate about whether you should be brought in for questioning regarding your ties to pinko commies like your newspaper friend in London. You were this close," he held his right thumb and pointer finger about a quarter inch apart, "from trading in your desk at State for a jail cell. Jones kept mumbling about cattle prods and sleep deprivation."

"Bastard."

"Jones is a good officer and a good American. His problem is he takes himself too seriously and he lacks a sense of humor. It was also my impression that you took pleasure in pushing his buttons, which is not the best idea."

"I was going through a rough stretch, personally and professionally."

"I understand, which is why I went to bat for you. They brought me in from the field—thanks, by the way, I am not a big fan of sand fleas and heavily armed tribesmen—and asked my opinion. I told 'em you were a first-rate American, somebody I trusted 100 percent."

"Thanks."

"I meant it. I've followed your career since Nam, and you have earned my respect, even if you are friends with commies and you married a troublemaking radical who distrusts her own government." Smith smiled. "By the way, congratulations. Your wife is not only pretty, she's smart and feisty and dedicated. I should be so lucky as to end up with a fine woman like her."

"Want to come over for dinner some night to meet her?"

"I wish. It's been a long time since I had a home-cooked meal and sat down with normal people for a normal dinner."

"There's certainly nothing normal about Afghanistan. Anyway, I doubt that you're here for the social scene. Nor do I believe that you just happened to drop by for a cup of sweet tea with an old buddy."

"You're right about me not being here for the social scene, though you're wrong about me not dropping by for a cup of tea with a buddy. I like you, Tom, and at times I crave talking with somebody I like, somebody I can be honest with."

"Careful or people will think you're human."

"I trust you not to tell anybody. The CIA is no different from any other security organization. Fear is our greatest ally, and you don't generate fear by being sweethearts. When we bring in somebody for questioning, they know we'll do anything to get what we want. Half of what we're accused of doing—spying and assassinations and organizing coups—isn't true, though you notice we never deny any of those accusations, 'cuz it adds to the fear. I'm not crazy about being seen as a boogeyman, but it helps me get my job done."

"It also makes you a social pariah. 'Dad, Mom,' Tom mocked a young woman's voice, 'this is my boyfriend Sam. He's a spook for the CIA, though he's really a sweet guy and a hell of a cook.'"

"Yeah, it does kinda limit my social life."

"So if not for the social life, why are you here, and why talk with me? You're not in Kabul to catch up on old times."

"No, I didn't think you'd buy that." Smith drained his tea and asked for more in Pashtu. When the shopkeeper had refilled both their cups and returned to the back of the shop, Smith got down to business.

"I believe in what I do. Otherwise I wouldn't be doing it." Smith looked into his teacup and appeared to be gathering his thoughts. "I know in my heart that democracy and capitalism are systems that work best for the most people. When I believe in the program—as I did in Vietnam and as I do here in Afghanistan—I'm a good soldier; I do as ordered and don't ask questions, regardless of the outcome. Now, however, you and your lovely wife have added a new equation.

"I'm sure this guy Taraki means well for his nation, but, like they say, the road to hell is paved with good intentions. Taraki has good intentions, but he's leading Afghanistan down the road to hell. He's getting in bed with the Soviets, which never has good outcomes. Ask the Hungarians or the Czechs what happens when you let the Soviets into your tent. And he's out of his fucking mind if he thinks the *mullahs* are going to embrace Marx and Lenin. Some people think, 'What the hell, it's only a bunch of camel jockeys. Who cares what happens?' You're a diplomat and an intelligent person. You know different. Afghanistan may not have any economic significance, but in geopolitical terms it's potentially vital. That's why I'm here."

Tom nodded to acknowledge the basic truth of Smith's statement.

"I'm struggling with something, though. I said I do as ordered and don't ask questions, regardless of the outcome. Well, I'm worried about the outcome. Specifically, I don't want to see you or your wife end up as collateral damage."

It was a nice, clean phrase. Collateral damage refers to those are not the target of an operation yet suffer just the same. Like when you drop a bomb on a military headquarters in order to kill a general, and six people cleaning the building are killed.

"I see your dilemma." Tom said. "Do you believe what you're doing here is right?"

"Of course not. You know as well as I do that we have no way of knowing what the consequences of our actions will be. I can honestly say that what I've been asked to do appears to be the best option available. Turning Afghanistan into a Soviet ally would be bad for the Afghani people, bad for the United States, bad for the world. Will my actions make the world a better place? Who the fuck knows? It's a huge gamble, and I think it's the best choice available."

"But it's possible—even likely—that it's going to lead to bloodshed."

Smith smiled grimly. "It's a shame that my colleague Jones is such a hardass. He'll never have a chance to know what a pleasure it is to talk with a man of your intelligence and insight."

"It doesn't take that much intelligence to know that almost any action will lead to bloodshed in Afghanistan. Just look at the history of this place. It's not a nation; it's a conglomeration of warring factions, and that's without including outside factors. Throw in the Cold Warriors from DC and Moscow, stir in Islamic fundamentalism, and you've got a highly volatile mix. If the CIA intends to drop a lit match..."

"Nobody wins if this place explodes. You can't accurately direct the force of a huge blast. We'd simply like to see a change of government."

"Simply?"

"Bad choice of word. Nothing's simple or sure. That's why I'm talking with you. You need to be especially vigilant, and you gotta tell your wife to keep her eyes and ears open. I'm sorry I can't be more specific. I do know that Paraguay was a walk in the park compared to this place. If it was me, I'd ask for a transfer or at the very least send my wife back home."

"If you'd been following my career, you know Mary McNeil."

"I do, and I know she'd only dig her heels in deeper if she was urged to leave."

"Then you do know Mary. Thanks for the warning."

"Least I could do."

"Is there a way I can contact you if I need to?"

"Unfortunately, no. If I were to give you my contacts, then my people would know I'd talked with you. That's not a good idea. I'll keep an eye out and contact you when I can."

"Is there anything you can tell me?"

"We subscribe to the philosophy of my enemy's enemy is my friend."

Tom laughed without mirth. "Since everybody in this place is everybody else's enemy, that doesn't give me much to go by."

"You're a smart guy. Chew it over with your wife, and see what you come up with."

"My enemy's enemy is my friend." Mary repeated the phrase while emphasizing different words. "Smith works for the CIA, and America's number-one enemy is communism and the Soviet Union, both of which are being embraced by Taraki and the PDPA."

Tom nodded.

"Could he be referring to tribal enemies? Taraki is a Pashtun. Maybe the CIA is arming Tajiks or Uzbeks or other Pashtun factions."

"I sure hope that's not the case. The US wants a stable ally on the Soviet border. Ethnic warfare would divide Afghanistan, destroy any unity and stability, and make it easy pickings. No, it has to be a unifying element, something that overrides factions."

"Islam."

Tom nodded. "If I was a betting man, I'd put all my chips on an Islamic insurgency."

"But to fundamentalist Muslims, we're no better than the Soviets."

"That doesn't matter. With no allies here, the best we have is our enemy's enemy."

"Aha! Now I see what you're getting at. There's never going to be a democratic government in Afghanistan. Nor capitalism nor equal rights for women, which is fine with Washington as long as there isn't a communist state either. Washington won't tolerate the spread of communism, but it doesn't have anything to fear from Islamic states. We do business with Saudi Arabia and Iran, why not with an Islamic Afghani nation."

"I think you've hit the nail on the head. Washington would consider it a victory if Afghanistan became united under Islam rather than under communism."

"But Taraki's Marxism offers the chance for a better life for women and children, greater equality for all ethnic groups, better health care. Maybe even more stability for the region. The CIA's scheming could lead to a repressive Islamic state. Who wins then?"

"I can't answer that. Nobody can."

"So you're left trying to deal with Taraki's government—without an ambassador or a mandate from Washington—while the CIA plays deadly games behind your back. What the hell are you doing here, Tom?"

"The same as wherever I am stationed. I try to promote American interests while protecting American lives."

"How are you supposed to do that when you don't know what the CIA is up to or what Washington's real intentions are?"

"Damned if I know."

CHAPTER 20—1979

O nce again, Tom sat on the toilet sipping a gin and tonic while Mary soaked off the dirt in the bath. It had become a weekly routine, one they both enjoyed tremendously. Mary would recount how her week had gone in the countryside, teach Tom new words and phrases she'd picked up, and share observations about life in rural Afghanistan. Tom would then discuss the latest political intrigues, which faction appeared to be gaining strength, the latest coup rumors, meetings with diplomats from other embassies. As summer waned, both of their reports revealed seeds of doubt and concern. Mary talked of growing discontent with President Taraki's government and rumblings about a possible *jihad*, a holy war against the heathen Marxist. Tom grumbled about working in the dark, about not knowing what Carter's game was or who was actually formulating America's Afghan policy.

"I had lunch with Jean Guy yesterday," Tom said, referring to his counterpart at the French embassy. "He said his government was growing frustrated with our secret policy toward Afghanistan and asked if I could shed some light on it. I said I'd love to shed light on it, but that Washington hadn't bothered to send me a flashlight. He didn't think it was very funny."

"Understandable. From what you've told me, the other embassies don't see a point in formulating foreign policy if it might be contrary to ours."

"They're right, too. They'd like to engage Taraki in dialogue, try to steer him away from Moscow. Meanwhile, we still don't have an ambassador and Wayne isn't authorized to speak for the US. It's fucked up."

"Maybe even worse than you think."

Tom sat up. "More grumbling from the *mullahs* about Taraki?"

"That's old news. You know I've developed good relations with some of the women in the villages. Most are afraid to talk politics with me, but a few open up when we're alone. A couple have mentioned visits from Americans."

"What Americans? Tourists?" Tom asked hopefully, knowing it wasn't.

"Men who walk like soldiers."

"Smith."

"I described him, and one of the women said the description fit one of the men. Same color and length of hair, same height. She said he visited a month ago and left a large duffel bag. Last week a truck turned up, and the men unloaded crates into an unused hut. The women were told to go inside while the truck was unloaded and warned to stay away from the hut."

"Did she have any idea what was inside the crates?"

"No. She said they appeared to be very heavy. They were weapons, weren't they?"

"That's not my field, but it doesn't sound like seeds or used clothing."

"Maybe Wayne should call Washington and try to find out what's going on."

"If Washington wanted us to know they would have told us. In some ways it's better this way. Next time Jean Guy asks what we're up to I can honestly tell him I don't know."

"Will Washington tell us if they're planning something?"

"Nope. Besides, whatever they have in mind won't include US personnel. That way nobody can lay the blame on Washington if it all goes wrong. The same kind of thing was going down in Southeast Asia when I was there. Americans without uniforms—CIA, special forces—would slip across into Cambodia and Laos, arm the anticommunists and occasionally perform black ops—that's black operations: terror tactics, assassinations. Completely off the books and illegal violations of national sovereignty of those two countries. Nasty work."

"Was Smith part of it?"

"Maybe. I don't know. I don't have any doubts that he's doing something similar here, though I haven't heard anything about assassinations. Hell, there's no need to get blood on American hands. Give the fundamentalists guns and money, pledge US support for the overthrow of the atheists, then let them do what comes naturally in Afghanistan."

"Which means waging war against their enemies, including nearly everybody who wasn't born in their village. That would lead to chaos and anarchy."

"Maybe, though only for a short while. Somebody always rises to the top and grabs the reins for a while. The only question is who—and what they will do when they take over. Typically, it's one of the Pashtun factions. I'm getting an uncomfortable feeling that Smith and his boys have something different in mind, something with potential for really serious trouble."

"The *mujahideen*?"

The *mujahideen* were Muslim militants who had been spreading from the Pakistan-Afghani border and rapidly gaining adherents from the villages of eastern Afghanistan. Nobody from the diplomatic community had taken them seriously because the concept of a unifying force went against the deeply embedded tribalism that was the heart of Afghani society.

"Yeah. Maybe the CIA are more clever than we give them credit for. If the *mujahideen* can get Afghanis to rise above tribalism, they could be a potent—and extremely dangerous—force. You've spent time in dozens of different ethnic villages. What do you think?"

"I think the village elders don't like the *mujahideen*, who they see as a threat to their feudal power, but if they have to choose between the *mujahideen* and Taraki's government there's no choice. Taraki's people have been telling the elders that things are about to change. Telling, not asking or suggesting. That doesn't go down well in the villages, especially when they're being told to educate their women, remove the *chadors*, and allow the women to participate in political discussions. Taraki's either suicidal or a complete idiot."

"Neither. He's an ideologue, and like most ideologues he's blind to anything that doesn't fit into his framework of knowledge. He doesn't seem to care that he has enemies within his own party, among his ethnic group, in the villages, and in Washington."

"Things are going to get ugly, aren't they."

"Without a doubt. The only question is who's going to strike first."

In March, Hafizullah Amin, an ally of Taraki's and a member of the PDPA, took over as prime minister, while Taraki remained president, leader of the PDPA, and head of the army. On September 14, Amin staged a successful coup in which Taraki was killed. The political situation rapidly deteriorated, with rival factions plotting to overthrow Amin while the *mujahideen* began to gain control over the countryside through a combination of appeals to religious fervor and threats of violence. If Jimmy Carter thought the overthrow of Taraki's Marxist government would remove the threat of communist expansion and bring stability to the region, then he was even more naïve than his critics believed. Maybe Carter believed that the Soviets had learned from America's horror show in Vietnam and would never invade Afghanistan, preferring to let their Muslim neighbors murder each other rather than risk the lives of young Soviet men.

Frustratingly, the people who manned the US embassy in Kabul had no idea what Carter was thinking, since they were not in the loop. Repeated pleas for information, guidance, a strategy for dealing with the unknown, all went unanswered, which is why Tom had mixed feelings when Sam Smith knocked on his apartment door a couple of nights before Thanksgiving.

"This is a surprise," said Tom, holding the door open, though not inviting Smith in.

"Not a pleasant one, I suppose. Mind if we talk inside? I feel kinda exposed out here."

Tom hesitated, then nodded and stepped aside to let Smith enter.

"Mary's home."

"I know," Smith said, reminding Tom that he was dealing with a CIA officer. "I want to talk with both of you."

"Let's go to the living room. Can I get you something?"

"I wouldn't say no to a cold beer, if you got one. The places I've been don't go much for beer, and even if they did they don't have fridges. Hell, most don't even have electricity."

"Mary," Tom called to the bedroom. "We've got company."

Mary had returned that afternoon from three days in the countryside and had just gotten out of the bath.

"I'll throw something on and be right out," she shouted from the bedroom.

A minute later she emerged wearing faded blue jeans and a baggy black T-shirt. She was drying her hair with a towel.

"I hope this isn't a formal call because I'm hardly dressed for..." She stopped in her tracks when she saw Smith.

"Mary this is..."

"I know who he is." Her voice had an edge to it, as if she had a lot more to say and was struggling to keep her mouth closed.

"Ma'am," he nodded a greeting. "I'm sorry to barge in unannounced."

"It's my impression that the CIA doesn't usually call ahead to announce their visits."

"Now, Mary, Sam's stopped by because he wants to talk to us."

"So it's Sam?" she sneered

"You can call me Officer Smith if you prefer," Smith said with a tight jaw.

"There are other things I'd like to call you."

"Stop it!"

Startled, Mary looked at Tom.

"Sam is a friend of mine. If you can't be civil, get back in the tub until he's gone."

"That's all right," said Smith. "I've had far worse welcomes. Besides, I would have been disappointed if she'd put on airs. I prefer honesty." He turned to Mary. "Ma'am, you've lived up to your reputation: beautiful and tough as nails. Tom is a very fortunate man."

The fury seemed to drain out of Mary and her shoulders slumped slightly. "I'm sorry. It's been a tough few weeks."

"I understand. It's been tough on everybody. I can't imagine how much harder it must be for a woman in this country."

Mary nodded, then pulled her shoulders back. "Can I get you a beer?"

"Yes, ma'am, you sure can."

"Only on the condition that you call me Mary."

"Thank you, Mary. That's kind of you."

When they were seated in the living room sipping cold beers, Smith got to the point.

"I assume that Tom has told you all about me."

"He has, though I must admit that I thought he was out of his fucking mind. Oops, sorry."

"That's OK, Mary. I'm not a *mullah*. So Tom's told you that I'm not some dumbass soldier who just follows orders. I study, I consider, and when I act it's from conviction."

"Have you ever refused to carry out an order?" Mary asked.

"Most of my superiors respect me enough to know there are some things I'll do and other things that require them to ask somebody else to do."

"You can get away with that?"

"I'm very good at what I do. When I'm ordered to do things, they get done. If my heart's not in it, they find somebody else who'll do it."

"Somebody without a heart?"

Smith shrugged. "Yeah, we got some of those. It's a tough world out there. There are those who don't play by civilized rules. Ask Ambassador Dubs's widow."

"Have you made any widows?" Mary asked, though not unkindly.

"Mary," Tom snapped.

"I don't mind her asking. There are some things I've done that I'm not proud of, but they had to be done and I don't lose sleep over them. It's like people who criticize hunters for shooting Bambi, yet you never hear them complain when they tuck into a bloody steak or chew on a chicken wing. Somebody has to work in the slaughterhouses."

Mary seemed to be staring into the distance, as if the discussion had taken her to a different place. Then she began to talk. "When Tom and I were fleeing from that jail in Paraguay, Captain Melendez and his men ambushed the sergeant who was coming to get me. They waited for the car to stop, then opened fire and blew them apart." She took a deep breath. "I didn't shed a tear and I haven't lost a minute's sleep over their deaths."

Smith silently nodded his understanding.

"So what brings you here, Sam?" Tom asked.

"Concern for you two. I know that you're not getting squat from Washington; I suppose they have their reasons for keeping their cards so close to their vests. I figure you ought to know the score so you can make an informed decision regarding what to do. Mary, you know the situation in the countryside."

"Tense. Everybody's wound up as if they're waiting for something big to happen. The men are preparing for action, though I've got the sense they're up to something a hell of a lot bigger than a hunting party or raid on another village."

"So what is going down here?" Tom asked.

"The *mujahideen* have risen above tribalism and embraced all groups and all villages, regardless of ethnicity. That may be a good thing for Afghanistan, though that's a call for diplomats and for history to determine. When the time comes—and it'll be damn soon—they'll gain control of the countryside, encircle Kabul, and squeeze the life out of Amin's government. Or at least they'll start to squeeze."

"Moscow won't go for it," Tom said.

"I thought you said the Soviets would let Afghanis kill each other rather than risk Soviet lives," Mary said to Tom.

"That's what Wayne and I guessed that Carter believed when he came up with this plan. The other scenario we considered is that Moscow would worry about a rapid growth of Muslim fundamentalism. Remember, the Soviet Republics just north of Afghanistan—Turkmenistan, Uzbekistan, and Tajikistan—are heavily Muslim."

"You mean there's a chance that the Soviets might invade? But that goes against Carter's apparent goal of stopping Afghanistan from sliding into the communist camp."

"Regardless of what you may think of the CIA, they're not idiots." Tom said. "This is like a chess match. You have to be thinking five moves ahead. If your opponent does one thing, you have to be ready to respond. Do I have it right, Sam?"

"Yeah, we think we're pretty clever, though we find ourselves in check occasionally."

"Like the Bay of Pigs," Tom said. "So how do you figure this'll play out?"

"If the *mujahideen* succeed, then Marxism is dead in Afghanistan. Sure, Islam may threaten our interests next door in Iran, but the Shah seems to have things well in hand. We're getting signals, though, that Moscow isn't about to let the *mujahideen* succeed. As you rightly pointed out, Moscow isn't keen on having a full-blown Muslim insurgency in their

Asian republics. The latest intelligence we've gathered points to a gradual buildup of Soviet troops in Turkmenistan, Uzbekistan, and Tajikistan."

"So what is Carter going to do?" Mary asked.

"Nothing. Our advice to Washington is to let the Soviets invade."

"You want the Soviet Union to spread south?" asked Mary, incredulous.

"We'd like 'em to try 'cuz we don't think they stand a chance in hell of succeeding."

"A Soviet Vietnam," said Tom. "Let the Soviets get bogged down in Afghanistan."

"What if they succeed?" Mary asked. "They'd add Afghanistan to the USSR."

"That ain't going to happen, in my opinion," Smith replied. "These Afghanis are tough motherfuckers, pardon my language. They know the land, and they know how to fight."

"Like the Viet Cong and the North Vietnamese Army," said Tom. "Plus, like the NVA, they'll be armed with the latest from America's arsenal."

"It would be a bloodbath," said Mary.

"Unfortunately, yes," Smith replied.

"And nobody will know the role we played in arming the *mujahideen* and destabilizing the country," Mary added.

"Not if I do my job correctly," said Smith, "though I would contend that Afghanistan has never been stable."

"So what are we supposed to do?" Tom asked. "You know damn well that Mary and I are not going to request transfers."

"No, I know you too well to believe that, but like they say, forewarned is forearmed. Mary, keep your eyes and ears open, and don't take unnecessary risks. You're smart; you may even sense things going down before I do. If the *mujahideen* start to get bold, to operate openly, and villages bristle with weapons, get your ass back to Kabul. Don't get cut off in some faraway village. You may be safe as an American, and then again, you may not be. Anybody not a Muslim may be a target. As for you, Tom, share this info with Glass. He's a canny guy. Beef up security, keep the marines on their toes, have an exit strategy ready. When I learn more I'll let you know. Well, I better be off." Smith stood and drained his beer. "Thanks for the cold one. It may be a while before I have chance to sip another."

Mary and Tom saw Smith to the door.

"Thanks for the warning," Mary said.

"Wish I knew more; I'm not a fortune-teller. Take care."

When the door closed behind Smith, Mary turned to Tom.

"Now what?"

"We do as Sam suggested: keep our eyes and ears open, don't take unnecessary risks."

"Some would say staying in Afghanistan is an unnecessary risk."

"Think we should bail out?"

"Absolutely not."

Tom pulled Mary toward him and kissed her.

"I love you, Mary McNeil."

"I love you too, Tom Kington."

By December 1st there was no longer any doubt that war was imminent. The Afghan armed forces were on full display as planes were rolled onto runways and tanks began to appear throughout the city. Although it was not unusual to see some military operations around Kabul, they were usually restricted to a few units parading down main streets. Now it appeared as if the entire armed forces was geared for action. As well, communications with rural Afghanistan began to be cut, though nobody knew for sure whether it was Amin's government that was doing the cutting or the *mujahideen*. Mary made fewer forays to rural villages and stayed away for fewer days at a time. Tom tried to convince Mary to take along Afghan security, but she refused. It was essential, she felt, that Oxfam not be associated with the imminent fighting. Tom reluctantly agreed and worried the entire time she was away.

Tom and Mary were attending Christmas dinner at the embassy when the situation took a drastic turn. There were twenty Americans sitting around the table, enjoying a turkey dinner with all the trimmings, a treat sent by the State Department. Wayne Glass had dryly noted that the secretary of state must be feeling guilty at keeping them in the dark, and had sent them what felt like the last supper of the condemned. Glass's remark had been met with an uncomfortable silence. As the diners were reaching for seconds, Sergeant Wisniewski appeared at the door. Glass started to get up.

"Sit down, Wayne," said Larry Daniels. "I'm on duty. Just leave me a turkey leg."

Daniels conversed with Wisniewski for a moment before following him down the hall to the communications room. Fifteen minutes later he returned, grabbed a turkey leg, and sat down. Every eye was on him while he tore out a chunk of turkey with his teeth.

"You might as well share the news with all of us," said Glass.

Daniels chewed a moment, then swallowed. "Two planes loaded with Soviet troops landed about an hour ago. At the same time Amin moved into the Tajbeg Palace."

"That's believed to be a more secure building," Tom said.

Daniels nodded and continued. "A truck filled with Soviet troops arrived at the Tajbeg Palace about an hour ago. Another group has surrounded the communications ministry, and a bunch have dug in at the airport."

The rest of the dinner was mostly eaten in silence. When Tom and Mary got home it was obvious that Mary had something on her mind.

"Speak up," Tom encouraged.

"You're not going to like what I'm going to say."

"That never stopped you before."

"You remember that young pregnant Hazari girl I've told you about?"

"The one in the village about two hours from here?"

"That's the one. She's due next week, and I promised I'd bring some extra supplies to help her, food and baby clothes and medicine; give the kid a chance to survive."

"Mary, it's going to be tough for a lot of people soon."

"I know. It seems foolish to take a big risk for one pregnant girl, but she's so frightened and helpless, and I thought that before the fighting really gets going...Things are going to get pretty nasty, aren't they, Tom."

"Yeah. Moscow didn't send those troops in today just to give Amin some moral support."

"You've said that Wayne has an evacuation plan. All nonessential personnel will be flown out first. That's me. Tomorrow may be my last chance to get supplies to her village."

Tom thought about Mary's request for a minute. "OK, but I'm going with."

Mary put her arms around Tom's neck and squeezed. "You've always been there for me."

"And I always will be."

They were at Oxfam before sunrise and had the truck loaded and fueled by first light. Although one of the Oxfam directors voiced concern, everybody understood that the job always carried some risks. The director also knew Mary well enough to know she wouldn't change her mind. Tom and Mary assured him that they would turn around and race home at the first sign of trouble. Only there was no sign of trouble, just a single, deafening, blinding explosion. They had been driving an hour, heading eastward into the blinding sun, and had slowed to a crawl as the truck labored up a steep incline. Tom thought he detected movement in a cluster of massive boulders on the hillside to the right, but he couldn't see clearly because of the glare. Suddenly there was a flash followed by blackness.

Tom awoke to the jabber of strange voices. He knew they weren't speaking English, yet in the haze that enveloped his brain he couldn't focus on their words and had no idea what they were saying. He felt nothing, though a remote instinct told him he should be feeling something. Pain? Fear? He looked up and saw a bearded man wearing white robes and a white floppy turban. The man had a rifle, and he began to lower the rifle so that the muzzle pointed directly at Tom's chest. A man's voice barked, and a hand reached out from the periphery of Tom's vision and pulled the rifle's muzzle away from Tom. The hand released the gun, and Tom realized he understood a few words that the man was saying. Something about "good" and "woman" and "American." Tom closed his eyes and tried to concentrate, to will away the haze that enveloped his brain. Suddenly it hit him: Mary. He struggled to sit up, but his body wouldn't cooperate. He looked up at the man with the rifle and implored him with his eyes to help. The man simply said, "*Allahu Akhbar*," then turned and walked away.

Tom faded in and out of consciousness. Every time his eyes opened the sun was higher and the day hotter. His thirst was intense, yet he was unable to move. At one point he tried to call Mary's name, yet he could only manage a croak. Finally, at what seemed like midday, he felt himself being lifted. Then he blacked out. When he awoke, Sam Smith was sitting in a chair next to his bed. The room was dark and cool. The only illumination came from narrow beams of sunlight that snuck in through gaps in the black curtain that hung over the window. As Tom's head cleared he began to remember what had happened.

"Mary," he croaked through dry lips and a raspy throat.

"I'm sorry, Tom. She was killed instantly."

Tom knew it. Had known it as soon as he opened his eyes and saw Smith. Had known it while lying in the burned-out wreck of the truck. He didn't know who had attacked them or why, and he didn't care. Mary was dead.

The next few days were a drug-induced haze. Tom received hundreds of stitches in his face, arms, hands, and chest. His collarbone was broken in two places, and he had three broken ribs and a fractured jaw. The vision in his right eye remained blurry. Wayne Glass and Larry Daniels visited often, as did Sam Smith, though his visits tended to be late at night when nobody else was there. The last time he saw Smith was the night before they evacuated him to Germany for medical treatment.

"The invasion's complete. Soviet forces have taken over all key buildings in Kabul, and thousands of troops are crossing the border daily," Smith said without emotion. "I've heard that the fighting's pretty fierce and the *mujahideen* are really giving it to Ivan. They're gonna curse the day they stepped into this shitty country. I know it won't surprise you to hear that Amin is dead. Maybe he wasn't Marxist enough for them or they blamed him for letting the *mujahideen* get control of the countryside. Maybe they were just sending a message. Who the fuck knows. They've set up Babrak Karmal as the new president, but everybody knows he's just gonna be Moscow's puppet and he'll never have the support of the people. There's sure as hell gonna be one motherfucker of a shitstorm here. Things are gonna get real nasty."

They sat in silence for a couple of minutes.

"Tom, I'm sorry about Mary. I can't help but feel that I played some role. I mean, the rocket that hit your truck..."

"Stop!" Tom managed to croak. His heart was racing, and it took him a moment to get his breathing under control. When he spoke his voice was raspy. "You were doing your job. Mary was doing hers. We all knew the risks. We're all responsible."

Smith nodded. "Yeah, you're right. Doesn't make me feel any better. Mary was a great woman, a great person."

Tom didn't respond.

Smith slowly stood. "I gotta go. Catch you down the road." He gently tapped Tom's hand before turning and walking out the door.

CHAPTER 21—1982

"Good morning, Tom. Come on in and take a seat."

"Thank you, sir."

Tom eased himself into the chair facing the desk of the undersecretary of state for the Middle East. Although the two men had never worked together, they were both veteran State Department personnel who had met many times over the years. Tom remembered a dinner party many years earlier when they had ended up at the same table at a White House function. The undersecretary had been chief political officer in Berlin while Tom had been in Paris, and the two chatted about being stationed in Europe versus other, rougher assignments that they had experienced. Coincidentally, both men had attended Ivy League schools and joined the Peace Corps after university. These shared experiences had led to a sense of camaraderie that seemed to have deepened over time. They bumped into each other every few years and always made a point of getting together for a drink and a chance to catch up on each other's lives. The undersecretary had been on a gradual, uninterrupted march to the top, and rumor had it that it was only a matter of time before he became secretary of state. Of course, Tom's story was well known throughout the State Department. Some wrote him off as a tragic figure who had long ago lost the chance to be a major player. Others held Tom in the highest regard, seeing him as a man who had risked his life for his country on more than one occasion. The undersecretary's view was that Tom was an extraordinary individual whose principles were both an asset and a serious liability.

"You know you don't have to call me 'sir.'"

"I've spent the last three years trying not to make waves."

"I don't mind a splash or two, not from you."

"Thanks."

"How are the kids?

"Terrific. I used to see them once a year or so and I'd be shocked by how big they'd become. Seeing them after growth spurts heightened the feeling that I'd missed key points in their lives. It's one of the things I like about being stationed in Washington: I get to see my kids every week, be on hand for parent conferences and things like that. I've really gotten to know them, and they've gotten to know me. I'll miss them when I go back overseas."

"Oh, so you've got a new assignment?"

"Actually, no, I don't. That's why I asked to see you."

"I assume you've requested an assignment through the proper channels."

"Of course, and I've gotten nowhere. I receive letters that inform me my request is being processed. I meet with people from personnel who assure me that my name has been considered for various posts, yet nothing suitable has been found so far. I'm starting to think that my 'proper channel' is a loop. Maybe I'm being paranoid, but it seems that the powers that be wouldn't be upset to see me retire from public service. The thing is, I'm not ready to retire. In fact, I'm ready and eager for another posting."

"I won't bullshit you Tom. We've known each other too long for that. Some people think you're a loose cannon. You've got to admit, you've left some carnage behind, through no fault of your own," the undersecretary quickly added. "Your lady friend in Vietnam, the escape from Paraguay, Mary," he paused, looking uncomfortable at the mention of the deceased, "not to mention your problems with the CIA. Most embassies prefer somebody who fits in better."

"I've always done my best for the country, and like you said, most of the drama in my life has not been of my choosing."

"Passion for your work and bad luck, that's how I see it, and I'm not alone. Some think you're one of the finest diplomats we've produced in a long time. You're dedicated, knowledgeable, and willing to put your life on the line. Those are rare qualities."

"Then use them. I want to be posted to Lebanon."

The undersecretary's eyebrows rose. "Tom, you've already done more for your country than most will ever do."

"It's the life I chose, and I'm perfect for Lebanon. I speak French and have been studying Arabic for two years. I know as much about Islam as anybody at State, and I have abundant experience dealing with conflict and conflict resolution. My kids live with Barbara, so I'm unattached. I'm the right person for the job."

"I don't know if anybody's the right person for that mess."

Civil war had been raging in Lebanon since 1975, with so many factions that few could keep track of them. Christians, Shi'a and Sunni Muslims, Palestinians, nationalists and pan-Arabs, pro-Syrian and pro-Israeli, the Lebanese Army and private militias, so many factions that the country had degenerated into a political, economic, and social hell. Hundreds of thousands of Lebanese had fled the country, and there appeared to be neither a solution nor an end in sight to the bloodshed. Nobody at State could remember any nation that was a bigger quagmire.

"Maybe there isn't anybody alive who can get a handle on Lebanon, but I'd like to give it a try. I've put in my three years in Washington, and I'm ready for an assignment. For those who wonder how Mary's death has affected me, tell them that Mary would kick their ass if they tried to stop me from doing what I do best."

"OK. I'll talk to some people and see what I can do. In the meantime, let's do dinner."

"I'd like that. I know a small Middle Eastern restaurant where I've been practicing Arabic. They do a fantastic lamb kebab with fluffy rice and a potent Lebanese coffee."

The undersecretary smiled. "I get the feeling that if we don't assign you to Lebanon you'll go on your own."

"Would I do that?"

"I don't doubt it for a minute."

Tom sat in front of the gorilla's enclosure with his children. Keith was ten, quiet and intense. He had a close relationship with his maternal grandparents and was enamored of Ronald Reagan. Karen, age eight, was a daddy's girl and not happy about Tom's imminent move to Lebanon.

"Can we come and visit you, Daddy?"

"Not right now. Lebanon is having problems, and it wouldn't be safe."

"Mother says it's as dangerous as Afghanistan where Mary was killed," said Keith.

Karen's eyes grew misty, and her lower lip began to quiver. Tom put his arm around her.

"I'll be extra careful," Tom reassured his daughter. "You know, Keith, as the big brother, you might consider reassuring your sister rather than frightening her."

"I'm just being honest. Besides, it's an important job, and Mom says you're one of the best at what you do."

"What *do* you do, Daddy?" Karen asked. "I know you live in other countries and talk to people from those countries. Teachers are always asking what our parents do. What do I say?"

Tom had explained his job on a few occasions to both kids, but Karen had either been too little or not interested. With Tom living in Washington the past three years Karen had been content to spend time with her father; details about his work seemed unimportant. Keith had been the one to ask questions about the State Department and foreign affairs and life in other countries. Karen had mostly sat on Tom's lap and enjoyed the closeness of her father. Now that Tom had been assigned to Lebanon, Karen felt the need to know more.

"Dad is a diplomat," Keith said, sounding confident and proud. "He represents the American government, and he tells other countries what they have to do."

"Keith's right that I'm a diplomat, though I don't tell other countries what to do. Honey, do you ever get into an argument with other kids at school?"

"Yes," Karen answered. "Robby keeps bugging me and calling me names."

"What did you do about it?"

"I told the teacher, and she talked to him and told him to stop it."

"Well, I do something similar. If two groups of people in a country are arguing, I try to help them settle their argument. Sometimes other countries get into arguments with the United States. I try to settle those arguments as well."

"So you're kind of like a teacher."

"Sometimes."

"Mom says America is like the world's policeman," said Keith. "If people are fighting or hurting each other, we send our army."

"We only send soldiers when we have to. Most of the time we try to settle things by talking. Do you kids ever have to deal with bullies?"

"Jack Monaghan," Keith grumbled. "He's always trying to pick fights because he's bigger than the other kids."

"What do you do about it?" Tom asked.

"Other kids tell the teacher. I stand up to Jack."

"Have you two gotten into a fight?"

"No. He's not really that tough, just big. If you don't act scared he leaves you alone."

"Well, that's what we try to do at the State Department. We stand up to bullies and try to protect weaker people."

"Why do we do that?" Karen asked.

"Because we can," Keith answered. "Grandpa Bennett says we're the most powerful nation in the world, which means we have a responsibility to keep the peace."

Tom smiled. "Grandpa Bennett is right. The United States is the richest, most powerful nation in the world. When people need help, they come to us."

"Isn't that dangerous?" Karen asked. "Is that why Mary was killed?"

They were back to where they had started.

"Mary was trying to help a young woman who was going to have a baby. Mary put her life on the line for others. That's one of the many things I loved about her."

"Do you put your life on the line?" Karen asked, the quiver returning to her bottom lip.

"I'd rather live for my country than die for it. Besides, I'm a diplomat, not a soldier. I work for peace."

"President Reagan says that the only way to have peace is to be strong, so others won't try to hurt you," said Keith.

"That's one way to look at it. Another way to achieve peace would be if everybody put away their weapons and worked to feed the hungry and build houses for the poor."

"Grandpa Bennett says people are poor because they're lazy and don't work hard enough." Keith held his head up as he'd apparently seen Henry Bennett do many times.

"Let's walk over to the polar bears," said Tom, changing the subject. He had worried that his prolonged absences would give Barbara and her father time to indoctrinate Keith and Karen with a right-wing philosophy. It looked like Keith had already started in that direction. Tom had become so concerned that he called Suzie the year before to ask her view as an educator and a wise person. Suzie had calmed his fears.

"Kids check out a lot of things as they grow up. You know, they want to be ball players, soldiers, priests, whatever attracts them at that age. What's important is the values they learn, and I know that Keith and Karen have learned the right values."

"Even though they've spent so much more time with Barbara and her dad?"

"From what you've told me, Keith is a bright kid. He knows you're not hanging out on some beach, and he knows you didn't abandon him. Keith will grow to respect you and the work you've done, and he's going to have your values because they're noble and good."

"I sure hope you're right."

Although Tom had serious doubts, he knew that Keith spoke with pride of his father. In what little time he had spent with Mary, Keith had grown to like her and had been saddened by her death. Tom also knew that in spite of the personal problems and philosophical differences that existed between them, Barbara was proud of Tom, and she conveyed that pride to her children. The bottom line was that Tom had chosen the life of a diplomat, so his time with Keith and Karen was limited and precious. Rather than worry about their political views, he simply enjoyed being with them. Maybe someday, when they were older and he had a safe posting, they could live with him and go to an international school. Someday. Right now, Lebanon beckoned.

Tom had made the best of his three years in Washington. Much of the first year was spent recovering from the injuries he had sustained in Afghanistan, though like the physical scars he would bear for the rest of his life, Tom would always carry the emotional scars. During that tough first year Suzie had visited twice and had stayed for a month both times, renting a short-term apartment close to Tom's. He had also spent a month in Indiana at the family farm.

For the past two years Tom spent most of his time at a desk at State reading and analyzing dispatches, foreign newspapers, and position papers that attempted to define and guide US foreign policy. It was dull work, similar to what he had done during Officer Jones's investigation, when Tom had been accused of leaking information to Ira. Now, rather than be treated like a person of questionable loyalty, Tom was treated as a tragic figure, one who merited pity. He hadn't minded at first and was content to keep occupied with intellectual challenges and policy formation. Eventually, though, his innate ambition and pride had resurfaced, and he craved a return to the field. Lebanon was the logical choice, and State had finally granted his wish. He had said his farewells over the phone to his family and Suzie, taken the kids to Disney World for a long weekend, and had a farewell dinner with Barbara. After years of on again–off again hostility, they had become friends and collaborated on raising Keith and Karen. His final stop before flying to Beirut was London.

Tom hadn't heard from Ira in over a year. Suzie had told Tom that Ira had closed *The Handless Monkey*'s office and now worked out of his apartment. He was still married to Jane Covington and still rarely saw her. While Ira was hammering out the latest edition of the *Monkey*, Jane was traveling the world with various lesbian lovers, which was fine with Ira as long as Jane kept depositing money in his bank account. The *Monkey* had never paid for its own existence, and now it was selling even fewer copies than it had at its peak in the mid-seventies. Ira had let the entire staff go when the lease ran out on the office, and had continued to publish the *Monkey* from the second room of his minisuite. When Tom had called to say he was going to visit, Ira had grumbled about being busy and it not being the best time. Tom had told Ira that he'd skip the visit, at which point Ira grudgingly agreed that he would take half a day off to see his old friend.

Tom took a taxi to Ira's flat and knocked on the door. After waiting a few minutes he knocked again. Finally, assuming Ira had run out for something, Tom grabbed his bag and started to walk to a coffee shop down the street. He'd walked about fifty feet when the front door opened and Ira stuck his head out.

"Hey, Tom."

Tom turned and walked back. "I didn't think you were home."

"I was trying to finish an article about American interventionism in the Middle East before you arrived. Come on in."

They didn't exchange hugs, nor did Ira ask about Tom's flight. Then again, Ira always made a point of not following social conventions. When they got upstairs Ira pointed down the hall that led to the main part of the flat.

"There's a guest room down there. Make yourself at home."

Tom knew from his last visit to London that the hall led to Jane Covington's section of the flat. He walked down the hall and found a bedroom that was furnished with cozy furniture yet didn't appear to contain any personal affects. Dropping his bag in a corner, Tom washed up, then joined Ira in the kitchen.

"I thought you and Jane kept a strict division in the flat," Tom said, taking a seat next to the window.

"Fuck her. She's off with one of her rug munchers on some island, Ibiza or Majorca or one of those ritzy places, so we've got the run of the place. Besides, I've been given my marching orders, so it doesn't matter what I do."

"Jane's throwing you out?"

"It's mutual. I've had my fill of her rich bitch attitude, her lack of social consciousness. She was only using me to get her inheritance. Now that her granny is dead and Jane's income is secured, she's told me to fuck off."

"Won't she miss your charming personality?"

"She doesn't deserve my charming personality. She never had the brains to understand what it was I was doing, and she never will. I was just somebody she could brag about to her pseudo-intellectual friends, as if she had something to do with the *Monkey*."

"She did pay all of the *Monkey*'s bills."

"That's bullshit. The *Monkey* brought in a lot of money. This flat is Jane's, but the *Monkey* is mine, always has been, always will be. I don't need fuckin' Lady Jane to get the truth out."

Tom knew that it was Jane's money that had kept the *Monkey* alive. In the old days he would have enjoyed nailing Ira, as Ira had done to him for so many years. That had been the basis of their relationship: put-downs and challenges. Ira had always criticized Tom's choice of career, and Tom had responded by criticizing Ira's lack of career. It had been good-natured, though always with an edge. In recent years their banter had lost its good-natured quality and the edge had grown sharper.

"So what are your plans?" Tom asked.

"Plans? Plans are for geeks and bureaucrats. I'm going gonzo. I'll publish the *Monkey* from wherever I happen to be. Maybe I'll stay in London. Maybe Berlin. Maybe I'll even grace the Big Apple with my presence. Rather than sit in London and nail people from afar, I'll show up in a country and hit 'em where they live. It'll have immediacy, credibility."

"Plus, it'll give you a chance to write about each country's prison system, from within."

"They wouldn't dare fuck with the press. The pen is mightier than the sword."

Tom wasn't surprised by Ira's naïveté. He had only lived in New York and London, cities with the freest presses in the world. Ira had no concept of what happened in some countries to people who voiced opposition views. Publishing *The Handless Monkey* in Paraguay or Vietnam would have resulted in jail, beatings, and worse. Tom knew people who had stood up to governments and were never heard from again. There was no point in telling this to Ira.

"I'm glad you've retained your passion for exposing the truth. Good luck."

"It's not about luck. It's about hard work, and I'm the hardest-working bastard in journalism, even if I don't get credit for it." Ira had been rummaging around the kitchen and slammed a cabinet shut. "No fuckin' coffee. Let's go get some java. I could use a pick-me-up."

Tom had been with Ira for fifteen minutes, and so far they'd only talked about Ira, which wasn't necessarily a bad thing. When Ira talked about Tom it was usually the same old criticism. Tom had always known that narcissism was one of Ira's defining qualities, yet for some reason

Tom was more painfully aware of it than ever before. That Ira had never called to offer condolences for Mary's death was something Tom accepted, though it had been nagging at Tom for a long time. Other omissions had begun to irritate Tom. Ira never asked about Keith and Karen. Never asked about Tom's work. Never asked if Tom was happy or sad, lonely or angry. Ira never asked Tom any questions, only berated his career choice. Tom's mantra had always been: Ira is an old friend, and a friend is somebody you know very well and like anyway. Tom again recited the mantra to himself. This time it sounded hollow.

"Ira, do you know the name of my kids?"

"What?"

"What are my kids' names?"

Ira stared at Tom. "What the fuck is this about?"

"You never ask about my kids. I was just wondering if you even knew their names."

"Hell if I know. Look, if you can't remember, call Barbie or Suzie. They'll know."

"They'll know because they care."

"How long have we known each other?"

Tom considered the question. "Twenty-four years."

"During those twenty-four years have I ever asked you personal questions?"

"Never."

"Then why would I now? That's not who I am. I'm not the person who sends toys to your kids. I don't send silver platters when you get married or flowers when you're in the hospital. I'm the guy who keeps you honest, who reminds you what's important in life, and it's not birthday parties and weddings and knowing kids' names. I'm the one who reminds you that it's a shitty, dangerous world out there and if we don't watch the crooks who are running the show they're going to get richer and make the world shittier. I'm the one who turned a farm boy into a world-class diplomat. If not for me you'd be kissing Henry Bennett's fat ass and vacationing in Gstadt and the French Riviera."

Tom slowly shook his head. "You really believe what you're saying."

"Of course I do. I always speak the truth, always have, though you obviously haven't been listening very well. You keep working for those motherfuckers and doing their bidding. I don't hold it against you. There's still a large part of you that's the Indiana farm boy, the kid who had never heard of Miles Davis or the Beat Generation or free love. I'm the one who gave you your soul, though a huge part of the conservative Christian Midwesterner remains."

"My parents are liberals who always vote Democrat, though you don't know that because you've never bothered to ask about my family. If you feel a need to see yourself as my Henry Higgins, go ahead. Sure, you opened my eyes to a new world, but you weren't the only one. Suzie did more to shape my character than you ever did."

"Is that what you call it? Shaping character? We used to call it 'giving head.'"

Tom stood and glared at Ira for a moment, then slowly let out his breath. "You're pathetic. You're still looking at things from the view of an angry midcentury beatnik. You still quote Dylan and Ginsburg. You still think you're relevant, though you haven't been for decades. Truth is, you weren't even relevant back then, which is why *The Village Voice* was never interested in your writing. You're a legend in your own mind, not in anyone else's."

A smirk had spread across Ira's face. "The truth finally comes out. All these years you've put up with my shit, and I thought it was because you lacked balls. Now I see what's really been going on. I'm the one who pushed you to do something important, and you're pissed off that you owe me. Now you resent me and feel a need to cut me down. Go ahead, I can handle it. I've had bigger, badder dudes try to put me in my place. They failed because I'm smarter than all of them. Someday people will write about me and what I've accomplished with the *Monkey*. Like you, they'll resent me, but they'll still have to give me the credit that's due me."

"I'm going to get my bag and check into a hotel," Tom said.

"That's right, go ahead and leave. You can't stand the truth. You never could."

"The truth is that I've had my fill of Ira Kornblue. It's always about you, Ira, always about your brilliance and your opinions and your life. You never acknowledged my achievements, my losses and struggles. You never cared about my children, my work, my feelings. No wonder you're alone. I'd wish you luck, though like you said, it's not about luck. No matter what luck you have, you'll always be the same bitter person. Goodbye."

Tom arrived in Beirut with mixed feelings. Part of him was exhilarated to be back in action in a diplomatic hot spot. Another part of him was deep-down frightened, the kind of fear that twists your guts. The other hot spots he'd been in had not appeared dangerous at first. Saigon was an island of relative tranquility when he'd arrived. Paraguay was totally safe until Mary dragged him into conflict that led to bloodshed. In both cases he'd had a chance to gradually find his way and have his feet somewhat firmly planted on the ground when danger struck. He was now landing in a country deep in civil war, a nation where nobody and no place was safe. Murder, assassinations, bombings, and open warfare existed in every corner of Lebanon: rural and urban, Christian and Muslim. Tom had requested Lebanon because he desperately needed meaning in his life. Now he began to think of Keith and Karen and all he had to lose. He was deep in thought as he walked down the stairway from the plane to the tarmac when he was startled to hear a familiar voice call his name.

"Tom, *assalaam alaikum.*"

George Newman, his colleague and roommate in Paris, stood at the foot of the stairway.

"*Wa alaikum salaam,*" replied Tom, giving the proper Arabic response. They warmly shook hands.

"Welcome to Lebanon," Newman said. "Stefan wanted to greet you himself, but his schedule is pretty full."

"I'm still having a hard time picturing Stefan Boudreau as head of the political section."

"He thought you'd say that. Stefan won't give details, but he acknowledges that he was a real slacker when you two met in Vietnam."

"Slacker? He's being too kind to himself," Tom laughed.

"You'll be proud of him. He's well respected by the entire staff, including Ambassador Dillon. Come on, let's grab your bag and I'll get you through customs, then you can see for yourself when we get to the embassy. I hope you're not too tired; we've got a full day planned."

"I'm ready and eager. I've spent enough time sitting at a desk in Washington."

"Brace yourself. I promise you will not be bored in Beirut."

Newman took Tom to an apartment that wasn't far from the embassy. Unlike earlier in his career when he shared apartments with other young embassy staffers, Tom was given a one-bedroom place with a view of a park. He dropped off his bags, then Newman drove him to the embassy where he was given a tour. He was pleased to find that he had a small office to himself as well as a personal secretary, a middle-aged Lebanese woman named Labiba Shihaa. Finally, they went to Stefan Boudreau's office. Boudreau's secretary told them to enter immediately. The chief political attaché jumped up as soon as Tom and Newman walked in.

"Damn, it sure is good to see you," Boudreau drawled.

Tom and his former roommate shook hands, and Boudreau clapped Tom on the shoulder.

"It would appear that your new position hasn't altered your accent," Tom said.

"I continue to speak with a Louisiana accent as a show of southern pride."

"Though the accent softens when he wants the Lebanese to understand what he says," Newman said.

"Apparently, your southern-fried shtick hasn't impeded your rise to the top."

"You know damn well it's not a shtick, just as you know I was never aiming for the top."

"When we met in Saigon you were more than happy to be wallowing on the bottom."

Boudreau winced.

"Don't worry," Tom said, "I'm a diplomat. I know when to keep my mouth shut. Besides, after seeing my beautiful apartment and my own office—with a personal secretary—it would appear that a down payment has been paid on my silence."

"You've earned the apartment, office, and secretary, otherwise Ambassador Dillon wouldn't have approved them. As to buying your silence, George will attest that I've already confessed my sins—to George, anyway. I didn't see any point in revealing all to the ambassador or the local staff. I am in a position of authority, after all, and it wouldn't do to reveal what a sleazy, worthless son of a bitch I used to be."

"You weren't a worthless son of a bitch in Paraguay," Tom pointed out. The levity instantly evaporated.

"I am real sorry about Mary," Boudreau said. "She was an amazing woman."

"That's not the description you used when she was busting your balls in Asuncion."

"If I remember correctly, you weren't exactly singing her praise at the beginning."

"Stefan has told me about your time together in Paraguay," said Newman. "He said Mary was part saint, part warrior; sort of a blend of Mother Teresa and Attila the Hun."

"Though I did say she was far better looking than either," said Boudreau.

Tom smiled.

"We'll continue this discussion later this evening at a local restaurant where I've booked a table," said Boudreau. "Right now we'd better get down to business."

Tom gave Boudreau an admiring look.

"Don't look so surprised," said Boudreau. "Hopefully George will confirm that I'm not half bad at my job."

"I'm not surprised. You were pretty impressive when the shit hit the fan in Paraguay."

"You shamed me in Vietnam into taking my job more seriously, and in Paraguay Mary and you both taught me about commitment, about truly caring for others. I'm a better diplomat because of you, Tom. Truth be told, you and George deserve this job more than I do. If not for George's...sexual orientation and your amazing ability to spontaneously self-combust, you'd both be in line for section head or even ambassadorship."

"Maybe," began Tom, "but George and I are who we are, and George tells me you're a fine section head."

"I try. So let's get down to business. I assume you've read everything on Lebanon and the region, talked to anybody in Washington who's ever been here, and speak fluent Arabic."

"Yes on the reading and talking with people, almost on the fluency. Nothing beats being at a place to get the true picture, as well as to pick up local idioms."

"I can help with the Arabic," said Newman.

"I'd appreciate any and all help. In Vietnam I had the luxury of time. I could spend hours at a noodle stall picking up the language. That doesn't appear to be the case here."

"Yes and no," Boudreau began. "The situation deteriorates more each day, so, yes, there is a sense of urgency. On the other hand, it is such a convoluted mess with so many factions and conspiracies that this thing isn't going to get fixed any time soon. If it takes time to master Arabic or establish connections, it won't make a huge difference. Let's jump right into the quagmire, then. Secretary of State Schultz and his people are dealing with the international aspect, meaning mainly Israel, Syria, and the PLO. That's a good thing, 'cuz the situation is bad enough without Israel and Syria invading and making things worse, and Lebanon sure as hell doesn't need the Palestinians to stir up the septic tank. So, we're left with only a couple of dozen militia and factions. I deal with the Maronite Christian majority since constitutionally they run the country. George has been ever so delicately working with the Phalange militia since it's the biggest and most powerful, and he's also been keeping in contact with some of the other, larger militias. It's a hell of a job, kind of like trying to reason with a room full of vicious, rabid rats."

"I try to use more diplomatic terms when discussing the militia," said Newman, "though Stefan's colorful description pales next to how the militias describe each other."

"We've had a few people deal with the Muslim factions, none with any success. We've never had anybody who spoke fluent Arabic—except George—and nobody who seemed to understand Islam well enough to make headway with the Lebanese Muslims. That's why I was so thrilled to hear you were coming to Beirut."

"I naturally assumed you missed me."

"The part of me that missed you didn't want you to come here because of the danger. It was in my capacity as chief political attaché that I was thrilled. You have a knack for connecting, for empathizing. I want you to use those skills to establish contact with the main Muslim factions and to get them to agree to work with the Christian majority."

"Is that all?"

"That will do for starters. Next week we can deal with world peace.

Tom had arrived in Lebanon in March, at a time when some in the White House and State Department still believed that Lebanon could be saved from a protracted, bloody civil war. Many people thought the root of the problem was not so much with the Lebanese themselves— after all, different religions had coexisted in Lebanon for centuries—but rather with three groups of outsiders: Israel, Syria, and the Palestinian Liberation Organization. With three hundred thousand Palestinians living in Lebanon and the PLO committed to destroying Israel, instability and violence seemed inevitable. Lebanese Muslims were emboldened by the belief that their powerful Muslim neighbor—Syria—would support them in demanding greater political power in Christian-dominated Lebanon. Many observers believed that Syria was secretly supplying Muslim militia with weapons and encouraging an escalation of the civil war. As well, it was assumed that Syria was also supplying weapons to the PLO in order to weaken Israel and instigate another Arab war against the Jewish nation.

In June, in spite of US attempts to keep peace through discussions, Israel had invaded Lebanon in an effort to stop PLO attacks. Israel drove tens of thousands of Palestinians out of Lebanon and forced thousands more into refugee camps. Not surprisingly, this harsh treatment created more anti-Israeli terrorism and increased the tension between Lebanese Christians and Muslims. Matters took a nasty, irrevocable turn on September 14 when President Bashir Gemayel—a Maronite Christian as stipulated by the constitution—was assassinated along with twenty-five other Maronites in a massive bombing. Tom met the following day with a representative from the Shi'a Muslim community, the largest Muslim sect in Lebanon.

"*Assalaam alaikum*," Tom said upon entering the coffee shop in West Beirut.

"*Wa alaikum salaam*," replied Mohammed Hussein Yermani.

Yermani was a respected scholar who had friends in nearly all of Lebanon's Muslim camps. A Shi'a married to a Sunni, he had Palestinian colleagues as well and was often asked to moderate discussions on Islam in Lebanon. Yermani cautiously avoided involvement with any religious group, always being careful to maintain neutrality. Tom, as he had done in Vietnam when trying to earn the trust of the Buddhist community, had taken a slow, gradual approach to meeting Yermani. He spent a month at a coffee shop in a Shi'a neighborhood sipping coffee, eating sweats, and practicing his Arabic. Nobody spoke with Tom for the first two weeks. Eventually he earned the limited trust of the owner, who would sit with Tom during slow periods and discuss mundane topics such as the economy, Lebanese customs, food, and sports.

When Tom inquired about finding a teacher, the coffee shop owner at first said he couldn't help. Eventually, after Tom gently repeated his request a few times, the coffee shop owner provided the number of an old man who agreed to tutor him. Tom met with Ameen Khuri for three months during which they developed an easygoing friendship. The old man—a retired high school teacher who had taught history and politics— not only didn't avoid talking politics and religion, he loved a good, heated debate. The lessons, which were supposed to last only one hour, usually went on for two to three, and Tom was often invited to stay for dinner. It was Khuri who introduced Tom to Mohammed Hussein Yermani.

Yermani didn't want to meet Tom or any foreign official, for that matter. He only did so out of respect for Ameen Khuri, his friend. Tom understood Yermani's concerns. A private meeting would lead to suspicion once it became public, which would be inevitable. Meeting in a busy, public place would rapidly lead to speculation and, once again, loss of credibility for Yermani. Yermani had come up with a plan that might protect himself while satisfying his friend's request. Rather than meet at Khuri's apartment for a lesson, Tom and Khuri met at the coffee shop where they had been introduced. The lesson was nearly over when Yermani strolled in. Khuri glanced up and did a passable job of looking surprised.

"Well, well. Look who's here."

"Ameen, how nice to see you out of your apartment. I thought you'd become a hermit."

"How would you know what I do with my days? You're too busy to visit an old friend."

"These are busy days, my friend. Not many have time for leisure as you appear to."

"Leisure? Can't you see that I'm working?"

Yermani looked from Khuri to the coffee cups, then glanced at Tom and back to Khuri. "I should have such a job," he smiled wryly.

"I am teaching Arabic. Please, join us. I'm sure my student has grown weary of my voice after all this time. It would be good for him to converse with another Arabic speaker."

Not wishing to appear too eager, Yermani paused as if to consider the invitation. Finally, he slowly nodded. "All right, though I only have time for one cup. I'm on my way to a meeting, and have just a few minutes to spare. I stopped in to drink one cup, for energy."

Khuri asked the shop owner to bring tea for Yermani. The owner had been closely watching the exchange and hesitated. He knew Yermani, as did most Lebanese, and he knew him to be a good Muslim and a spokesman for the Lebanese Muslim community. He wondered why such a man would sit with a representative of the United States. It slowly dawned on him that Yermani didn't know Tom and so didn't know he was American. Besides, Ameen Khuri was a good Muslim and a respected man, so there was nothing to be concerned about. The shop owner nodded his assent and went to get the coffee. Yermani pulled up a chair and Khuri made the introductions in Arabic, then switched to English so that there would be no misunderstandings. The three men spoke in full volume so as not to appear to be hiding anything.

"Mohammed Hussein Yermani, this is Tom Kington. Tom, may I introduce Mohammed Hussein Yermani. My friend is a scholar, one of world's leading experts on the history of Islam in Lebanon. Although he is a Shi'a, as I am, he is respected by all Muslims."

"You flatter me. I am merely a man who has spent too much time in libraries and talking as if I knew everything. If you act as if you're an expert, people will really believe that you are, evidence to the contrary. What brings you to Lebanon?"

"I'm a political attaché at the US embassy."

"So you've come to help us savages learn how to live in peace as you Americans have for two centuries."

"Two centuries of peace, if you ignore our own brutal Civil War as well as wars with Mexico, Spain, two world wars, police actions in Korea and Vietnam, not to mention conflicts with a dozen or more countries in Latin America. Until recently, it was the Middle East that set the example for living in peace. Muslims, Christians, and Jews lived harmoniously as neighbors for centuries. There were few problems until this region was divided after World War I."

"I see that I'm not the only historical scholar in the room."

"I did teach history for forty years," said Ameen Khuri, acting offended, "even if it was only high school."

"My apologies," said Yermani. "Your scholarship was never in question. After all, we have discussed history together for nearly as long as you have taught it. I was surprised at the knowledge of our American guest. In my experience, few Americans have taken the time to learn anything about what they view as inferior civilizations."

"Then I'm glad we've met so I can have the chance to show you that not all Americans are ignorant regarding the Middle East."

"I'm sorry that I have to run. It would have been interesting to learn what it is you know, or think you know."

"I am here most afternoons after five o'clock. I hope we have the opportunity to get to know one another better."

That first meeting had taken place in July. By September 15—the day after President Gemayel's assassination—Tom and Yermani had met half a dozen times. The first meetings had lasted less than an hour. Their last meeting had stretched on until bedtime, with dinner being brought in from the restaurant next door. Although many knew of their meetings, nobody ever suspected that their initial meeting had been set up. They had been careful to avoid any talks about politics or the Lebanese Civil War. That was about to change. Both men waited until they had been served cups of thick, sweet coffee. They skipped the usual pleasantries.

"This is a grim day for all Lebanese," Tom said in Arabic, the only language they spoke at the coffee shop.

Yermani nodded. "Some Muslims will celebrate, but an assassination is never something to celebrate, regardless of religion or politics."

"Especially regarding religion and politics. There will be accusations, reprisals, an escalation of violence. Will Shi'as and Sunnis draw closer together in solidarity against the inevitable Christian response?"

"Perhaps, though it will only be temporary. As you well know, Shi'as and Sunnis will never work together for long."

"Is there any chance that you can convince Shi'a or Sunni leaders to denounce the bombing and pledge to seek those responsible?"

"Can you convince the Maronite Christians not to retaliate against Muslims?"

"My colleagues are attempting that as we speak."

"And?"

"My hope is that the Maronite Christian response is mild and doesn't lead to escalation."

"I will do what I can," conceded Yermani, "though the more violence that occurs, the less people will be inclined to listen."

The next day Phalange militia—a wing of the dominant Maronite Christian sect—entered two Palestinian refugee camps, Sabra and Shatila. Three days later nearly eight hundred Palestinian refugees lay dead. The Lebanese Civil War had entered a new, devastating stage.

CHAPTER 22—1983

1983 got off to a vicious start and then got worse. As expected, the Sabra and Shatila massacres led to an outburst of death and destruction between Christians and Muslims. Those who hoped that the fighting would soon exhaust both sides and lead to a negotiated peace were sadly disappointed. The fighting escalated and spread so that Christians fought Muslims and fellow Christians, Shi'as fought Sunnis, Israel and Syria increased their military presence, and the PLO seemed to be fighting everybody. The US embassy staff carried on with their efforts at diplomacy, refusing to give in to the crippling pessimism that hung in the air.

"*Assalaam alaikum*," Tom said to Labiba Shihaa, his secretary.

"*Wa alaikum salaam*, Mr. Kington," replied the Lebanese woman. "You have a meeting with the political section today at eleven o'clock."

"I always have an eleven o'clock meeting with the political section on Mondays."

"It is my job to remind you of all meetings."

It was a game they had played since first meeting the previous year. Labiba had worked at the embassy for thirty years, landing the job shortly after graduating from Beirut University with a degree in English literature. A short, stout woman with a pretty face and keen mind, she had quickly risen from part-time receptionist to full-time secretary in the political section. Labiba had worked for Tom's predecessor, a humorless man of rigid views who left Lebanon believing there would never be peace in the region. The contrast to working with Tom was enormous. Labiba prided herself on her professionalism, which meant calling her bosses "sir" and maintaining a somber look. Tom had requested—unsuccessfully—that Labiba call him Tom and drop the "sir." He had also tried telling jokes in Arabic. Most of the time she nodded her head and corrected his pronunciation; only on a rare occasion would she actually smile, and even then she would deny that she was amused. Finally, after a year together, Tom had broken through her professional façade. He had insisted on taking Labiba and her family for a Sunday lunch to celebrate the anniversary of their working together. Labiba, who was not married, came with her parents and her four siblings and their families, a total of twenty people. The lunch had been a huge success in which much food was consumed and everybody laughed until their sides hurt. The next day Labiba was her usual professional self, yet she now had a twinkle in her eye and allowed herself to laugh at Tom's Arabic jokes.

"Would you remind me at 10:55 so that I'm not late?"

Tom was never late and never needed reminding, yet Labiba always reminded him five minutes prior to any meeting.

"Yes, Mr. Kington," she replied.

Tom walked to his desk and started to sit down when a massive explosion blew him against the wall. He lay in a crumpled heap. A pounding emanated from within his skull, yet no distinct sound reached his brain. After an undetermined length of time, Tom opened his eyes and attempted to peer through the dust that filled the room. Slowly, sounds began to penetrate his stunned senses: moans and cries, shouts for help, the sound of a distant siren. Tom sat up and waved his hands in front of his face in a futile effort to clear the dust. He took a deep breath and coughed, waved away more dust, and finally took in a lungful of air, then another. When he was no longer disoriented, Tom stood up and staggered toward the door. Except the door was missing, as was half the wall. Stepping over the rubble, Tom looked toward Labiba's desk. It wasn't there. He took another deep breath, closed his eyes for a second, and listened. A weak moaning emanated from a mound of rubble to his left. Tom rushed over and started to carefully pull off pieces of wall and ceiling and splintered furniture. An arm was revealed, then a shoulder, and finally the bloody face of Labiba Shihaa. Tom carefully cleared the rubble from her face and blew off most of the dust that coated it. Labiba moaned again, then slowly opened her eyes.

"Praise be to Allah, you are alive," Tom sighed with relief.

Although Labiba tried to focus on Tom's face, she remained disoriented.

Tom held her hand. "It's Tom, Tom Kington. There has been an explosion. You are alive. Help should arrive soon. I need to see if anybody else is injured, but I'll remain close."

The suicide bomber—disguised as a delivery man who in reality delivered four hundred pounds of explosives—had been brutally successful. Sixty-three people died that day, including seventeen Americans. Labiba Shihaa survived, though she lost one leg and spent a month in the hospital and another three months recovering before returning to her job. A group named Islamic Jihad claimed responsibility. Whether they were supported and encouraged by Iran and Syria as some claimed or simply an independent group of crazies didn't matter. The result was the same. The American people, who had supported President Reagan's efforts at Middle East diplomacy, quickly grew disenchanted with their nation's presence in Lebanon.

Although embassy staffers put on determined faces for the public, they were deeply shaken by the bombing. A few requested transfers. Tom continued to meet with Mohammed Hussein Yermani, though not as frequently and only for a single glass of tea. Yermani had offered his condolences for the loss of life. He did not offer apologies for the bombing itself.

"People do what they must to achieve just ends," Yermani said. "As you say in English, the ends justify the means."

"Even if it means the death of innocent people?"

"Who is truly innocent? Those who work in your embassy choose to do so. Besides, Lebanese Muslims cannot stand up to the American firepower that backs the Christians. Did you Americans not use so-called guerilla tactics in fighting the British for independence?"

"We targeted soldiers and government agents, not civilians."

"Not all of our people are so civilized, to no fault of their own. If you take away rights and treat people like savages, don't be surprised when they act like savages. You must also acknowledge that bombings and assassinations are not the Muslims' only means of warfare."

"Yes, we're keenly aware of a recent spate of kidnappings."

"What is your view of that method?"

"Certainly preferable to bombings. It's a targeted action, though the targets are not always political. The kidnapping of the American University of Beirut professors seems unfair."

"You don't think that working at the *American* University would make somebody an obvious target?"

"I would hope that academics received more respect."

"That would depend on where they teach and what they teach. By choosing to teach in Beirut at the American University, they have sided with the nation that arms the Maronites."

"What about the kidnappings of French, British, Swiss, and Germans?"

"All are colonizers or supporters of colonization, all Christian, all people who are unwelcome. They are fortunate that they were not the targets of those who prefer bombs to the diplomatic pressure that is the aim of kidnapping."

"I suppose if the kidnappers' demands are not met, they too will face death."

"We all face death. That is the inevitable outcome of living."

"True, but some deaths are preferable to others."

"May yours be swift and merciful," Yermani intoned. "The longer you remain in Lebanon, the less chance there is of that occurring."

Tom wasn't sure if Yermani was stating a fact or issuing a warning. Either way, Tom left the tea shop with a sense of foreboding.

"Tom, I think it might be time to suspend your meetings with Yermani."

Tom was sitting in Stefan Boudreau's office with Boudreau and George Newman. The rebuilding of the US embassy was nearly complete, stepped-up security measures had been added, and Ambassador Dillon wanted operations to return to their pre-bombing state so as to deliver the message that the United States would not be intimidated.

"What's the point of being here if we're going to hide behind barricades?" Tom asked.

"At least we remain alive and at liberty behind the barricades," Newman pointed out.

"Limited liberty. I can't do my job sitting at my desk."

"I understand, but with the kidnapping of government agents, journalists, and educators, there are already too many targets," Boudreau argued.

"The journalists and educators came here not knowing they'd be targets. I did know the risks, and it's my choice unless the ambassador issues orders to the contrary."

"He hasn't yet. I'm talking to you as an old friend."

"Thanks, Stefan. All the same, I'm going to continue to meet with Yermani."

"Are you making any progress?" Boudreau asked.

"None that I'm aware of."

"I suppose the good news is that you've been doing this for nearly a year and nobody's kidnapped or shot you yet," Newman said.

"In spite of the fact that there must be a few thousand Muslims who know where you hang out," Boudreau added.

"Then I must be doing something right."

"Maybe," Boudreau said, "or maybe they just haven't gotten around to you yet."

Boudreau's gloomy words took on added weight on October 23 when a massive truck bomb destroyed the headquarters of the US and French forces, claiming 298 lives. Citizens of both nations began to clamor for withdrawal of their armed forces from Lebanon. Rumors abounded that President Reagan was considering just such a withdrawal. It was with that in mind that Tom met Mohammed Hussein Yermani at the tea shop. Tom was now a Monday fixture at the tea shop, although Yermani only showed up a few times per month. Officer Smith, had he been in Lebanon, would have reprimanded Tom for putting himself in obvious danger. It was a risk Tom was willing to take. He returned regularly to the tea shop to show that he was committed to maintaining open communications with the Muslim community through Yermani. Their conversations covered religion, politics, human rights, and a slew of other topics. Voices were never raised in anger nor lowered in conspiratorial whispers. Although there was never any mention of Tom being introduced to key players in the

Muslim hierarchy, he sensed that he was getting closer to making contact with important people in the Muslim community.

"*Assalaam alaikum*," Tom greeted Yermani when the Muslim entered the shop.

"*Wa alaikum salaam*," Yermani replied, "though the likelihood of peace seems remote."

It was one of the rare times that either man mentioned the violence that surrounded them.

"We do seem farther from our goals," Tom concurred.

"To what goals do you refer?"

"Peace for all Lebanese."

"How does the presence of so many foreigners such as you help us to achieve peace?"

Tom was taken aback by Yermani's directness. "Clearly it doesn't."

"Then perhaps it is time for all of you to leave us Lebanese to deal with our own issues."

"If we Americans and Europeans leave, will the Israelis and Syrians also leave?"

"That is no longer your concern."

As they talked Tom became aware of movement around him. He casually looked up and noted that half a dozen men had entered the tea shop. Four had fanned out across the entryway, and two more stood behind him at the entrance to the kitchen. With a sigh of recognition, Tom realized that his diplomatic efforts had just run out of time.

"I'll convey your message to the US government," Tom said.

"I wish that was possible." Yermani's sounded tired. "May Allah give you strength."

The six men converged on Tom. Two of the men facing him parted their robes to reveal pistols that were trained on him. The two men behind Tom grabbed his arms and roughly pulled him to his feet.

"May peace reign next time we meet," Tom said to Yermani.

"*Inshallah*," Yermani replied. "If God wills it."

Tom was dragged into the kitchen, where a rough burlap sack was pulled over his head and tied firmly across his chest. His hands were yanked behind his back and tied with rope so tightly that he grunted in pain. He was dragged out the back door where he heard the trunk of a car opened, then he was roughly tossed into the trunk and the lid was slammed shut. Tom began his yogic deep breathing, willing himself to remain calm. His life was now in the hands of others.

Tom sat on the floor in the dark room with the burlap sack still over his head and his hands secured behind back. He knew the room was dark because light had penetrated the burlap when he had been yanked from the trunk and dragged indoors. The ride had lasted about fifteen minutes, though with all the twists and turns he had lost sense of direction. He assumed he had been taken to one of the Muslim neighborhoods, but it was impossible to determine which one. It didn't matter. He was the latest kidnap victim, the room he sat in was stuffy and smelled of mold and rot, and he was in serious trouble. As with the bombings and assassinations, the goal was the same: to make life in Lebanon so horrendous that foreign governments would have no choice but to depart. There would be no negotiations with his captors, no hope of talking his way out, and the chances of being rescued were so slim as not to be worth pondering. For the time being, his only wish was that his kidnappers would loosen the ropes that numbed his hands. Tom gently flexed his hands and wrists in order to ease the binding and allow the flow of blood. When a hint of feeling—and pain—returned to his hands, he let out a sigh of relief. Next, Tom used his untied feet to push himself until his back touched a wall, then he leaned back and tried to remain calm.

He passed in and out of consciousness, sometimes meditating, sometimes remembering moments in his life, sometimes sleeping. Hours passed, a couple of days without any visitors. He couldn't be sure how much time had gone by, and he was determined not to dwell on time, a concept that no longer had the same meaning as before his kidnapping. Tom knew that if he thought about how long he'd been captive or how long it would continue he might break down. At one point, when he realized his bladder was full, he simply let go and soaked his pants. At a later point he noted that his pants were dry, though the smell of urine remained. Finally, he heard somebody unlocking the door, and it opened. Two people stood in the doorway and talked quietly in Arabic.

"It smells of piss in here," said one, a young man.

"What did you expect?" asked the second man, who sounded older, his voice rough and deep as if he were a lifelong cigarette smoker.

"I did not know what to expect."

"The smell will become much worse if I am forced to crap in my pants," said Tom in fluent Arabic.

"Aiyee," gasped the young man. "He understands Arabic."

"Of course, I forgot. We were told that he has been taking lessons from an old teacher and conversing with Mohammed Yermani at the tea shop."

"Please, give me a bucket so that I may relieve myself," Tom said.

"Shut up. You are not to talk unless we ask a question."

Tom nodded, though he wasn't sure if the men could see the movement in the dark room.

"Come," said the older of the two. "We will discuss this with the others."

The door slammed, and Tom heard a click as the door was locked. He returned to his meditation. Sometime later—an hour? two?—Tom heard the door being unlocked and opened.

"We are going to untie your hands," said the man with the smoker's voice, "and allow you to crap in a bucket. You are not to talk. I have a gun, and it will be pointed at your head. Should you make a sudden movement I will scatter your brains against the wall. If you understand, say yes and no more."

"Yes."

Tom was roughly dragged away from the wall. Hands fumbled at the ropes.

"I cannot untie the knot," grumbled the young man.

"Go get a knife," said Smoker.

A few minutes passed before Tom heard Young Man reenter the room. Young Man began to saw at the rope, occasionally cutting Tom's wrists, causing him to flinch.

"If you're not careful," said Smoker, "you will slice his arteries and we will lose our hostage."

"You do it, then," Young Man snapped.

"Shut up and do as you are told. Turn him so that you'll have more light."

Young Man finally managed to cut the rope. Tom slowly flexed and rubbed his hands together. They were damp and sticky from blood, but the cuts were superficial and it felt fantastic to have his hands free, even if more feeling meant considerably more pain.

"Here is a bucket," said Smoker.

Tom slowly stood. His legs were shaky from inactivity, but he managed to stand and reach out to receive the bucket. He lowered his pants and squatted, placed the bucket under his butt, and tried to defecate. Nothing happened at first.

"Hurry," growled Smoker.

"May I say something?" Tom asked.

After a brief hesitation, Smoker said, "What?"

"It has been a while, and I am...what is the word in Arabic? It is difficult to crap."

"Constipated," Smoker said in Arabic.

"May I move a little in order to make it happen?"

"Do not move from that spot."

Tom did a few knee bends and touched his toes and squatted a few times. Finally, feeling the urge, he squatted over the bucket and vacated his bowels. When he was finished he pulled up his pants, not bothering to ask for the toilet paper that he sensed would be denied.

"Take the bucket out and dump it," Smoker ordered Young Man.

"Why me?"

"Do as you are told," Smoker ordered.

When Young Man returned, Smoker told him to retie Tom's hands.

"I've cut the rope. I'll have to get more."

Tom considered promising not to try to escape in the hope that his hands would not be retied, then decided against it. He might need to talk later, and he didn't want to push his luck with Smoker. Young Man left the room, returned shortly, and tied Tom's hands behind his back. Tom flexed his hands and wrists, keeping some space between them as Young Man tightened the rope. He grunted in mock pain to give the illusion that the ropes were too tight.

"Be sure that they are tight," Smoker said.

"You do it if you don't trust me."

When the job was done the two men left the room and locked the door.

Time dragged on. Tom replayed his life, trying to form sharp images of long-ago events and people. He saw Ira and Suzie at Columbia, tried to remember Ira's Beat poems and Suzie's voluptuous body. Neither aroused any emotion. He felt nothing, which is why he tried so hard to conjure up images and emotions. Tom thought that by connecting with feelings from the past he would maintain his sanity in the present. He was replaying his escape through the Paraguayan jungle with Mary, when the door to his cell opened. It opened twice a day, always by Smoker and Young Man, once to empty the toilet bucket, once to bring him a plate of cold Lebanese food. He was allowed to face the wall and lift his hood just enough to eat. It was tied back in place when he finished, then his keepers would depart. This time was different. Two men entered. Tom had grown familiar with the steps of his two minders. Smoker walked slowly, carefully, deliberately. Tom imagined that he wore sandals with black socks. Young Man shuffled as if his shoes were too big or he had crushed the back of his shoes and wore them like slippers. One of the new men walked heavily, as if he were a big man wearing heavy shoes. The other had a lighter step; he seemed to float over the dirty concrete floor with barely a whisper. It was the latter of the two who spoke in English.

"We are here to ask you questions. You will only talk to answer those questions." The man spoke in American English, as if he had studied in the States or spent considerable time there.

"May I ask a question?" Tom asked in Arabic.

Heavy Shoes stepped forward. A fist came crashing down on the left side of Tom's head.

"You will only talk to answer our questions, and you will speak in English," Floater said calmly. "Arabic is for Arabs, not foreign agents. Nod if you understand."

Tom's head throbbed from the blow. He took a deep breath to gain control and nodded.

"What is your question?" asked Floater.

"Could my hands be tied in front of me rather than in back, please?"

"We will discuss your request. Now it is time for you to answer our questions. How long have you worked for the CIA?"

"I don't work for the CIA. I work for the State..."

Wham! Heavy Shoe's fist landed another stunning blow that knocked Tom onto his side. He lay dazed for a moment before struggling to sit up.

"Answer the question. Add nothing."

"I don't work for the CIA."

"Why do you speak Arabic? Is it so that you can listen to our conversations and report to your CIA masters?"

"I always learn the language of where I am stationed."

Heavy Shoes stepped forward, and Tom braced himself for the blow, but Floater said "no" in Arabic.

"Where have you been stationed?"

Tom told him.

"All places where the CIA have operated and caused misery," Floater said. "Why are you, a Christian, trying to gain favor with Mohammed Hussein Yermani?"

Tom had given some thought to what his captors might ask—assuming that they'd do more than simply hold him hostage—and he had decided to be totally honest. He had nothing to hide and everything to lose should he anger his captors. Telling lies would eventually catch up with him as he grew more exhausted and would inevitably slip. The only thing he would refuse to do was reveal the names of the few CIA officers that he knew in Lebanon, and he was confident that he could believably deny knowledge of the CIA.

"I talk with Muslims like Mohammed Hussein Yermani because I want to understand the view of Lebanese Muslims. We have no Muslims on our staff, no native Arabic speakers other than support staff."

"Why do you speak with Yermani?"

"I speak with Yermani because he is wise and knowledgeable."

"What has he revealed about the Muslim leadership?"

"Nothing."

Wham!

"What has he revealed about the Muslim leadership in Lebanon?"

"We have never talked about the Muslim leadership in Lebanon. Ask the owner of the tea shop. He will tell you that we talk about religion, customs, culture, and such."

"What about when you talk in English, a language the shop owner does not speak?"

"We never talk in English. My goal is to learn Arabic and better understand the Lebanese people."

The interrogation continued for over an hour, with the occasional punch to the side of the head. By the time Floater and Heavy Shoes departed, the right side of Tom's head was swollen and sore. Over the next few weeks Floater and Heavy Boots interrogated Tom more than a dozen times. Floater remained calm yet insistent. Heavy Boots continued to slug the left side of Tom's head, indicating that Heavy Boots was right-handed. The interrogations always lasted about an hour, and the methods and rhythms never changed. His treatment by Smoker and Young Man—the two people who were most important to Tom because they were his daily minders—gradually improved. It was obvious that Smoker and Young Man disliked their assignment, particularly Young Man, who had to empty the toilet bucket every day, a task that he constantly whined about. It was Smoker who told Young Man to retie Tom's hands in front of him rather than behind him. It was Smoker who allowed Tom to remove his hood, though with strict instructions to have it back in place every time the door was opened. He warned Tom that there would be dire consequences, fatal consequences, should Tom ever be caught not wearing the hood. Tom was encouraged by this because it meant he was not marked for death unless he saw his captors' faces. There was a possibility that Tom would survive this ordeal.

One day Tom decided to risk engaging Smoker in conversation. Neither Smoker nor Young Man appeared to be militant, and both complained frequently about their job, though with different tones. Young Man exhibited the petulance that was not uncommon for young men anywhere in the world. Then again, anybody would be petulant if stuck with dumping toilet buckets and being the low man on the totem pole. Smoker exuded a certain world-weariness, a recognition that his was a lousy job, though it was a job he seemed committed to fulfilling. When Tom had first asked if he could remove his hood when alone, Smoker had refused. A week later he had relented. The pattern was evident: Smoker was not a hard case, yet he didn't want to seem a pushover. The following week, Tom decided to try communicating again. Smoker had delivered Tom's meal and had reached the door when Tom spoke.

"Sir, may I say something?"

Smoker hesitated. "What?"

"Thank you for allowing me to remove my hood when nobody is present."

Smoker grunted.

"Sir, may I be so bold as to ask another favor?"

"Only if you stop calling me sir. We are about the same age. You need not show deference."

"Thank you. What I want to ask is, may I remove my ropes when I am alone? The sores on my wrists are most painful, and I fear they are becoming infected."

"Remove your ropes?"

In fact, Tom had been slipping his hands out of the ropes for some time now. Young Man had grown careless and hadn't bothered to tighten them the few times he had untied them. Tom had continued to flex his hands and wrists, the result being that the rope was never actually tight. He often sat with the rope dangling from one forearm, keeping it close so that he could slip it back on when he heard somebody approaching. The raw wounds had healed somewhat and were not infected. Tom now took a big gamble and told Smoker a partial truth.

"The rope has been loose for some time, but I never dared remove it."

"So you could have been waiting behind the door and jumped me."

"I am not a soldier; I do not know how to fight."

"Then you are a coward who deserves to be a hostage."

It sounded more like a statement of fact than an insult.

"Perhaps, though if I had jumped at the first person to enter the room and it had turned out to be two armed men instead of one carrying food, then I would have been a dead fool."

Smoker's grunt carried a hint of amusement.

"Also, I came to Lebanon to learn about the Muslim community. Am I not doing that?"

This time Smoker issued a short bark of a laugh.

"I think maybe you are correct. You may not be a coward, but you definitely are a fool."

"A fool whose Arabic is improving, I hope."

"You may remove the rope, though as with the hood it must be in place when the door is opened. To be caught without the hood and with your hands free would not only be fatal to you."

"Thank you. I understand."

Another week went by before Tom attempted to engage Smoker in conversation again. Tom mentioned that Smoker's job must be very tedious and they ended up talking for fifteen minutes about Smoker's job, which mostly consisted of listening to the radio, smoking cigarettes, and napping. Over the next few months Smoker's visits became more frequent, his stays longer, and the subjects of conversation more varied. Although Tom was never so bold as to ask what was happening in Lebanon or how long Smoker thought he might be kept captive, the discussions broke up the numbing monotony for both. Tom also realized that, gradually, his meals became more diverse and more nutritious and that he was given more water to drink. Smoker also delivered a clean set of used clothes, including underwear, telling Tom that his old clothes were unbearably stinky. Unfortunately, as Smoker became kinder, the visits from Floater and Heavy Shoes became more brutal.

Tom began to get the sense that Floater wasn't really interested in extracting information. The interrogations only occurred every three to five days and never with a sense of urgency. At one point Floater seemed determined to unearth the names of CIA officers. Heavy Shoes slugged Tom's head repeatedly as Floater demanded names and details about the CIA's operations. Then, having gained nothing, Floater seemed bent on getting Tom to admit that the US was waging a crusade against all Islamic nations. Tom began to play a game where he guessed which day Floater and Heavy Shoes would arrive and what the topic of interrogation would be. It was a game Tom rarely won, and it became apparent that the days and topics were random. Tom played an imaginary conversation in his brain between Floater and his superior.

"This American is worthless," Superior would say. "He knows nothing, yet he continues to eat our food and occupy the valuable time of our brave fighters."

"We feed him leftover shit that dogs won't even eat," remarked Floater. "And Smoker and Young Man aren't good soldiers. Neither knows how to shoot a gun or make a bomb, and neither is very bright. They are only good for emptying shit buckets and serving slop."

"What about you?" Superior would ask.

"Me? I don't have much to do except shoot the occasional Christian and beat my children. Interrogating the American is the only fun I have.

The difficult part is trying to come up with questions. I don't know what to ask."

"I suppose you could just stop by once in a while so that Heavy Shoes can get his jollies by slugging him. Like you, Heavy Shoes has nothing better to do."

Tom played variations on this conversation, trying to find humor in his predicament. He felt that if he made light of his captivity then he would avoid slipping into abject fear and stop himself from going mad. From time to time, though, the reality of the horror that surrounded him surfaced. He was sitting one day, his mind wandering somewhere in Indiana, when he was startled to hear somebody insert the key into the lock. With a start, Tom realized that his burlap hood was in a heap on the floor with his hand binding. He pulled the hood over his head and had just managed to slip the rope over his wrists when the door was thrown open. It was a close call. Tom gasped as he tried to slow his heart, which was beating wildly.

"Have I interrupted something?" Floater asked. "You seem surprised to see us."

"I was having a nightmare," Tom said. "And I can't see you. The hood, you know." He tried a bit of levity to cover his anxiety, though he braced himself for the expected blow.

"Ah, some humor. Let's see if you find the news funny. This morning two brave Muslim warriors drove trucks packed with explosives into the buildings that housed US and French soldiers. I hope my English is correct. Housed—past tense—since the buildings are no longer standing. Hundreds of your invaders are dead. It will take weeks to dig out the bodies, though I suspect that few are still in one piece. Identification of the dead will be most difficult."

Floater paused, perhaps waiting for a reaction from Tom.

"I think this may be the event that drives you from Lebanon. You people don't handle such defeats well. The massacre at Dien Bien Phu drove the French from Vietnam. The same thing happened at Khe Sanh to you Americans. I expect your President Reagan to come up with an excuse to withdraw all US forces. They will leave you behind."

"May I say something?"

"Sure, I am in a generous mood."

"Khe Sanh happened in 1968. The US didn't withdraw all troops until 1973."

"You had better hope it doesn't take your government that long to realize that they have nothing to gain and everything to lose in Lebanon. Five years is a long time to sit in the dark and shit into a bucket."

Tom sat silently.

"You have nothing more you wish to say? Fine. In celebration of to-day's wonderful victory for all Lebanese Muslims, I will not bother interrogating you."

Tom heard Floater say mutter something, though he couldn't make it out. All of a sudden he heard Heavy Shoes coming toward him. Tom braced himself as Heavy Shoes's fist came crashing down on the left side of his face. He began to relax—Heavy Shoes always struck a single blow at a time—when a second blow landed, this time on the right side of Tom's face. The fist didn't have the same power and landed awkwardly, glancing off, yet the shock stunned Tom.

"Caught you off guard, didn't it," Floater said with obvious satisfaction. "Our friend has decided he should develop power in both fists. The surprise is in honor of the surprise attack this morning on the military barracks. I think we were all growing a bit bored with the same routine: I ask a question, you don't answer it to my satisfaction, my friend hits you with his right hand. Now we will try things differently, to make it more interesting. You may be hit with a right hand or a left hand. Maybe he will try kicking you with those solid shoes of his. Maybe I won't even bother asking any questions. Who knows, maybe you will decide to tell us something of value and you won't be struck any more. Or maybe we will end this game. Permanently."

Floater and Heavy Shoes left the cell and locked the door. Tom's head slumped forward.

Some days Tom woke angry. This hadn't occurred during the first few months of captivity, but once the anger started he had trouble containing it. Floater and Heavy Shoes were obvious targets, as was the always whining Young Man. Sometimes Tom found himself dwelling on old adversaries like Howard "Hard" Case, his political boss in Vietnam who tried to stifle

Tom's initiative. President Stroessner of Paraguay was another regular target. He blamed Stroessner for putting Mary's life in danger with his ruthless exploitation of the land and people. Tom fixated on the Afghani *mujahideen* on some days, cursing the rabid fundamentalists for taking the life of his beloved Mary. Officer Jones was a regular target of his anger. He wanted to strangle the man who had tried to end his foreign service career and exposed his affair with Ellen Becker. Other days Tom had trouble finding somebody to hate. He grew bored of raging against the same figures, replaying the same scenarios of vengeance, clutching his fists, and imagining his hands wrapped around the same throats. The focus of Tom's fury changed, but one constant target was Ira Blue.

A friend should support you, right? A friend should always be there for you and heap praise upon your every effort. Instead, Ira berated Tom, criticized his idealism and selfless devotion to his country and mankind. Hadn't Tom risked his life in half a dozen countries? Wasn't he sitting in a dark room, a prisoner whose life might be snuffed out any minute, because he was trying to bring peace to Lebanon? Suzie would give her blessing and show proper respect for Tom's commitment. Ira would tell him what an asshole he was for agreeing to go to Lebanon in the first place, then insult him for making it so simple for the kidnappers to capture him. "Why not just wear a sign around your neck: 'I'm a stupid American who deserves to be held captive and tortured. Please take me!'" That's what Ira would say. And maybe he was right. That's what really irked Tom. In his lowest, most enraged moments he agreed with Ira. His entire career had been a failure, as Ira so often pointed out. Peace in Vietnam? Failure. Successful role in the Paris Peace Talks? Failure. Happy marriage to the conservative Barbara Bennett? Failure. Helping the poor of Paraguay? Failure. The list ran on and on, and at every step Ira was there to taunt Tom, to rub salt in the wounds of his failures.

During the months of rage, Smoker kept his interactions with Tom to a minimum. Tom stopped asking favors, stopped trying to engage Smoker in conversation. Smoker had responded by sending Young Man to bring food most of the time. Eventually, deprived of contact with the only person who showed any compassion, and drained by his fury, Tom fell into a deep, dark depression. He began to dwell on his failures. He calculated how many days he had spent with his children since their birth, and the number was like a kick in the gonads. The faces of women he'd loved and lost haunted his waking hours. Anh—dead. Barbara—divorced. Ellen—gone. Mary—dead. What happened to the ambitious, bright lad from Indiana? He would never be an ambassador, never advise presidents, never formulate vital international policy. His captivity didn't put a serious dent into his career because his career was shit. If Floater were to walk in and put a bullet in his brain, nobody would mourn him.

Ironically, it was Floater who snapped Tom out of his depression. Tom no longer feared Heavy Shoes's beatings, having grown numb in body and spirit. He had traveled from fear to fury to numbness that began to feel like a permanent condition. Then Floater walked in one day in a joyful mood. Tom had come to understood Floater's moods. If Floater arrived in a rage, it was probably because the Muslims had suffered some defeat or humiliation, and Tom knew he was in for a brutal beating. Other times Floater seemed bored and allowed Heavy Shoes to beat Tom out of boredom. These beatings lacked rage and power. Then there were the days when Floater seemed to emanate pure joy. Mere happiness meant something nasty had happened to Lebanese Christians. Pure joy meant Westerners had suffered.

"I hope you've been resting well," Floater taunted. "Too bad you can't enjoy the sunshine that blesses Beirut, as it does every day."

Tom waited for the grim news.

"Have you, by any chance, met Malcolm Kerr, the president of the American University of Beirut?"

"Once, at an embassy party. He is a nice man, obviously very smart."

"Was a nice man," Floater corrected. "And he wasn't smart enough to know that it was time to leave Lebanon. Now he will be leaving in a box."

"He was dedicated to providing an education to all people, regardless of religion or sex." Tom knew that he would be beaten, but if Kerr had indeed been murdered then Tom could not remain silent. "Kerr was a brave man who risked his life to help others."

Heavy Shoes took a step in Tom's direction, but Floater barked an order to stop.

"Courage, stupidity, so little separates the two. Personally, I believe that assassinations run the risk of creating martyrs. A car bombing spreads terror as well, yet it has the advantage of not putting a single face in the news. Somebody in America will see Kerr's face and read his story and perhaps be determined to fight to honor his death. A bomb that wipes

out hundreds is far more terrifying because of the numbers and random-
ness of the killing. Even a common person, a cleaner or a secretary or a
gardener, can be blown to pieces. That has the power to invade the mind.
Then there is the taking of hostages, in my opinion one of the most effective methods for putting fear into the enemy. Anybody can be taken, even
low-level government workers. It is the uncertainty that eats at the spirit.
Take you for instance. Oh, we already did."

He chuckled at his own joke.

"Your colleagues are wondering if you are still alive. Are you being
tortured? Starved to death? Beaten daily and left to rot in your own shit?
It is the uncertainty that always sits in the back of their minds. Except
for the ambassador, they are pretty sure that they will not be targets of
assassination. But if we took you, we can take them as well. So they will
stop going out for dinner and drinks. They'll cower in their rooms, afraid.
Soon your government will have trouble finding people willing to come
to Lebanon."

"So you don't agree with those who assassinated Malcolm Kerr."

"We have our disagreements, though they are not as serious as you
Americans might hope. Why? Because we share a common goal: driving
all of the invaders out of Lebanon. Enough talk for one day. I've left you
with enough to think about."

Tom braced for Heavy Shoes's inevitable bashing.

"You can relax," said Floater. "I'm in a good mood today. I wish you
could see my friend's face. He is quite disappointed. Maybe I should allow
him a single hit."

"As long as you don't have to get blood on your own hands," Tom said.

Heavy Shoes rushed forward and buried Tom under a barrage of
punches and kicks.

"I must have touched a nerve with my news," said Floater. "You are
usually so polite. It would appear that these many months in captivity
have stripped away some of your diplomatic skills. This may turn out to
be more interesting than I had anticipated."

The last thing Tom heard before passing out was the sound of the
door being locked.

Tom awoke in pain, yet strangely alive, vibrant, as if released from
the cocoon that had enveloped him for so many months. He had entered
captivity as a passive, patient diplomat, followed by periods of anger and

depression. Now, a new Tom Kington emerged. He had closely followed the Iranian hostage crisis that helped to bring down Jimmy Carter's administration. The US embassy workers had been held for 444 days. During the crisis Tom had read as much as he could about hostage taking, and he knew it was a mixed bag. Some hostages benefitted from Stockholm syndrome, where a bond developed between captors and captives. He knew that this was occurring with Smoker. Most hostage situations weren't so friendly. Many hostages were kept for years. Quite a few were never recovered, their bodies never found. There was no consensus as to what to do in such a situation, whether to cooperate or struggle to achieve freedom. Tom spent days evaluating his options, trying to be rational, to control the occasional flash of anger or anxiety or desperation. Finally, lying awake one night, Tom made his decision. He was going to escape or die trying.

CHAPTER 23—1984

O nce Tom made his decision to escape his waking hours were spent analyzing the situation and formulating a plan. He broke the escape into two parts: escaping from the building where he was held and finding his way to safety. Although the first part appeared to be the most dangerous, he realized that fleeing from the building would not necessarily mean immediate rescue. When he was tied up in the trunk after his capture, the car had driven neither far nor fast at any time. This meant they had not taken a major road out of the city, so he was probably being held in one of the Muslim sections of Beirut. Assuming this to be the case, he would not find a welcoming community upon exiting the building. Some might tackle or shoot him. Most would be too afraid to offer assistance. That would mean having to run a gauntlet through a hostile neighborhood without even knowing which direction to flee. He could end up going deeper into hostile territory. It was a dilemma he would have to chew on for a while.

Obviously, the main problem that confronted Tom was how to escape, and again the greatest obstacle was lack of knowledge. Even if he could overcome one of his captors—a long shot considering his weakened condition due to lack of food and exercise—he had no idea what it would take to get out of the building. If he was really lucky the exit would be nearby and unlocked. But what if the building contained the headquarters of the group that had kidnapped him and the building was swarming with armed radicals? What if the exit was locked and the key was held by an armed man sitting in a room of armed men? Everything pointed to the need for a weapon. He could take the weapon from the guard he overpowered, except he had no idea if Smoker and Young Man carried weapons. Having worn a hood whenever anybody was in the room, his captors could be naked for all he knew. Or Young Man might like the feel of carrying a weapon, might crave the opportunity to blow away an enemy. He knew he would not attempt an escape against Floater and Heavy Shoes. They always showed up as a pair, and he had no chance of overcoming two people, especially when one was as strong as Heavy Shoes. The good news was that Floater and Heavy Shoes never came two days in a row. In fact, for the past few months, there was never less than three days between their visits and usually as much as a week. The best chance would be for Tom to make his move the day after one of the duo's visits. As importantly, it would have to occur after one of their "friendly" visits, such as after the assassination of Malcolm Kerr. After a nasty beating Tom was in no condition for action. He would have to be sure not to antagonize Floater so that Heavy Shoes would be kept on his leash.

Planning turned out to be therapeutic. Thoughts about taking action helped keep depressing thoughts at bay, and Tom spent all of his waking hours planning. He repeatedly went over every scenario, trying to imagine every possible variation and obstacle. Occasionally other voices would distract him. When he contemplated how to take out the guard, Suzie's sultry voice would mildly scold: "remember Buddha's teachings about Right View and Right Action. Are you making the situation in Beirut worse? Are your actions going to cause lasting harm?" At other times Ira's New York know-it-all critic would poke him: "I warned you, but you never listen. Your self-righteous do-gooder shit has put you in the crapper, and it's only a matter of time before somebody flushes." Tom would shake off the voices and resume his planning. One thing he could do to prepare was try to get Smoker to provide more nutrition. Tom attempted subtlety and appealed to Smoker's humanity.

"In my short time in Lebanon I developed a fondness for dates. They grow the sweetest dates here," Tom said one day when Smoker delivered his food.

"Lebanese dates are among my favorites as well."

"I know it's asking a lot, but if you happen to come across some, I would appreciate a handful. If it wouldn't cause a problem for you."

Dates began to appear on Tom's plate a couple of times a week. He also gently asked personal questions about Smoker, careful to sound genuinely interested in where he was raised and what life was like in Lebanon for a Muslim. Gradually, the amount and quality of food improved. Tom also started to exercise. Not so much that he would burn calories and drain his limited energy, but enough to tone his flabby muscles and restore flexibility. Tom did pushups and sit-ups, deep knee bends. He spent an hour each day stretching and tensing various muscles. He walked back and forth like a caged beast. Gradually, he began to feel better, stronger. Some of the improvement was due to the physical exercise and improved diet. Tom sensed that most was mental, as his focus and determination grew. Still, months dragged on. Doubts nibbled away at his resolve. Some days he felt weaker. Other days he felt discouraged, especially after long, brutal interrogations. There were days after Floater and Heavy Shoes's visits when he felt strong and ready, yet couldn't muster up the courage. Finally, triggered by a visit from his interrogators, Tom knew that the time had come.

It had been obvious for a long time that Floater was a sadist, though one who liked to keep his own hands clean. For months Floater's visits had featured few questions and Tom's answers never mattered; he was going to be beaten regardless. The beatings didn't bother Tom that much, though. He realized early in his captivity that they weren't going to do anything truly brutal like cutting off fingers. Besides, it wasn't the beatings that got to Tom, it was the visits when Floater gloated over some atrocity. Today was such a day.

"It's another glorious day for Lebanon," Floater announced as he entered the room. "Perhaps you'd like to play a game."

Tom didn't respond.

"Don't be such a bad sport. You must certainly be bored. You get so few visits, and you do nothing all day but sit with that filthy hood over your head. Here's the game. Guess what glorious event happened yesterday, and I'll have your guards bring you a special treat. Perhaps you'd enjoy some fruit."

"All right, I'll play. Let me think a moment. Ah, I've got it. Muslim and Christian leaders got together and agreed to respect each other, to live in harmony, and to work toward permanent peace and prosperity for all Lebanese. Am I close?"

"You are a funny man. Wrong answer, not even close."

"Darn. Do I get a second chance?"

"I think this time we'll do one of those multiple-choice questions that you Americans are so fond of. What glorious event occurred yesterday in Lebanon? Was it A, another foreign dog was assassinated? B, another CIA operative—disguised as a minor embassy staffer—was kidnapped? Or C, more invaders were destroyed by an ingenious bomb? For an entire plate of dates, which answer is correct?"

A number of snappy, snide remarks raced through Tom's mind, but he managed to choke them off before muttering, "I'll take D, none of the above."

Floater laughed without humor. "I forgot about the ever-popular none-of-the-above. Normally, I would allow my friend to punish you for your insolence. However, I'm in a good mood, so I'll give you the answer. The correct answer was C, brave Muslims have once again struck the US embassy. Scores have died, and they are still pulling more bodies from the rubble."

Tom felt sick to his stomach. Grim images ran through his mind: the torn body of Labiba Shihaa, his secretary who had been injured in the last embassy bombing; bloody bodies scattered around the streets of Saigon during Tet. He again summoned the willpower not to respond.

"No comment? Well, I'm sorry, no fruit for you today. On the other hand, no punches or kicks either. I imagine it's painful enough to sit in the dark and wonder which of your CIA colleagues are now dead or maimed."

"Last time it was my Lebanese secretary who was maimed," Tom said.

"A Lebanese whore who worked for the enemy is not a real Lebanese. She wanted to earn American dollars; she deserves the same treatment as the invaders she served."

"And yet, in spite of your hatred for Americans, you lived there many years," said Tom, referring to Floater's American accent.

Floater muttered something. Heavy Shoes walked over and slugged Tom's head.

"My time in the United States taught me to hate you Americans. Your wealth and military power have made you arrogant and stupid. It is that same arrogance and stupidity that led you to be captured and keeps you in captivity when you could easily tell me what I want to know. You could be a free man today, on a plane back to America. Instead you insist on being kept like a dog and beaten. There, you've managed to upset me, but I won't let you ruin my good mood. I'll leave you to imagine the bloody mess that was the US embassy. Oh, and one for the road, as they say."

Heavy Shoes slugged the other side of Tom's head before the two men left. Tom noted that Heavy Shoes was getting more power into his left-handed punches. It was time to act.

The only qualms Tom had regarded Smoker. Although their discussions had been brief, there had been many over a wide variety of subjects: Lebanese music and poetry, both of which Smoker was passionate about, Western culture, women, food, and more. Tom was careful to avoid politics and religion, not wishing to touch a nerve that might damage their genial relations. Smoker was not an ideologue or fanatic, but rather somebody who was caught up in events. He occasionally made comments about "doing what was necessary" and "being a loyal member of his community," yet his speech was never strident; he never ranted or threatened. Rather, he seemed intrigued by the United States and often asked how Americans lived, how they dealt with discrimination, what they aspired to. Tom hoped that he wouldn't have to hurt Smoker, though the Lebanese had chosen sides and had earned whatever came his way.

After Floater and Heavy Shoes left, Tom began to prepare himself mentally for what lay ahead. He ran through his plans and all the possible options. His heart raced as he envisioned freedom. He avoided all negative thoughts, aware that fear might rob him of the courage needed to succeed. When Young Man came to pick up the toilet bucket, Tom thanked him. Young Man cursed Tom in Arabic. Smoker brought a generous plate of food, perhaps showing guilt over Floater's grim news and Heavy Shoes's latest punches. Tom thanked him as well and received a "you're welcome" in return. When Tom lay down to sleep, he was ready to act. No matter what the outcome, this would be his last night in captivity.

Tom awoke the next morning feeling strangely calm. It was time to stop thinking and start doing. Violence went against his nature and his training, yet he knew that he would do whatever was necessary to end his captivity. He sat up, pulled off his hood and the rope that hung loosely around his wrists, and stood up. Tom spent the next fifteen minutes stretching and focusing on the first step of his plan. His mornings always began with Young Man picking up the toilet bucket, going out and dumping the contents, then returning the bucket. This occurred about an hour or two after Tom awoke. Tom walked over to the corner where the toilet bucket sat, pushed it away, and crapped into the corner. He then took the bucket and sat just behind where the door would swing when it opened. The first step was simple: Tom would smash the tin bucket into the face of whoever opened the door, which is why he had crapped into the corner rather than the bucket. If there were two people, Tom was fucked. If he missed his target or didn't do enough damage, he was fucked. Tom shook his head to clear out the negative thoughts. *Focus on the task. Visualize successful actions. Believe,* Tom thought. He lost track of time. Then he heard somebody put the key in the lock.

Tom stood and held the bucket near his right shoulder, his arms coiled to strike. The door opened, and Young Man took two steps, clearing the doorway, before Tom struck. He slammed the thick, heavier bottom of the bucket into Young Man's nose. The Lebanese instinctively pulled his arms up to belatedly protect his face, and Tom drove his right knee into Young Man's gut. Young Man let out a groan and doubled over. Tom slammed the door shut, then beat Young Man over his head with the bucket until he stopped moving. Tom stood over the inert body, panting and shaking. Young Man was breathing, but didn't move, even when Tom kicked him in the stomach. Tom quickly checked the body for weapons, but found none. Now for the unknown.

Tom grabbed Young Man's keys, slowly opened the door and peered out. He looked left and saw a long corridor. He looked right and saw a short corridor that took a ninety-degree turn to the left. Still holding the blood-covered bucket, Tom headed right, took the turn, and immediately came to a door. It was locked. From the light that streamed under the door Tom could determine that it led outside to freedom. Tom tried all of Young Man's keys, but none fit the outer door. He tried pulling it open, rattling the handle with a slowly growing panic. Finally, he acknowledged that he would have to turn around and find the key. Of course, finding the key meant he'd probably find whoever else was in the building. Although he didn't relish the thought of battling Smoker, it was too late for second thoughts. He turned and crept silently down the corridor, passing his cell and finally reaching a door at the end of the corridor. He put his ear to the door and heard a muffled news report in Arabic that sounded as if it was coming from a cheap radio. Steeling his courage, Tom slowly opened the door.

"How is our guest this morning?" Smoker asked in Arabic.

Smoker was sitting in a chair with his back to the door. He exhaled a lungful of smoke and took another drag. Sitting, he appeared to be of average height, a lean man with thinning hair and a bald spot the size of a large coin. Tom quickly glanced around the room. To his left was a table. On the table was a plate of food, presumably Tom's. There was also a pistol, and leaning against the table was an old rifle. Tom dropped the bucket and picked up the pistol. He saw that the safety was on, and he snapped it off. The sound of the bucket hitting the concrete floor caused Smoker to turn in his chair. His eyes and mouth opened wide in surprise. Then the look was immediately replaced by one of faint amusement.

"Well, well, well. The cat is out of the bag and he has become a lion."

"A lion in a bad mood with a shaky hand."

"Perhaps your hand would shake less if you had some food in your belly. It might also improve your mood."

Tom glanced at the food, then back at Smoker.

"Eating a meal might also take enough time for others to arrive. I want you to slowly turn your chair so you're facing me. If you reach for a weapon, I'll shoot you."

Smoker did as he was told. Tom saw that Smoker wore a five-day growth of beard. He had no outstanding features, the type of man you would pass on the street and fail to notice. Tom took a step closer and looked for a weapon, but saw none. He also checked the table in front of Smoker. On it were two cups of tea, two partially eaten plates of food, one full plate of food, and the radio. No weapons. When Tom was sure that he was safe for the moment he reached and picked up a piece of pita bread from the plate that was meant for him.

"I want you to take the front-door key out of your pocket and toss it on the table. Slowly."

Tom took a bite of the pita while keeping his eyes on Smoker. The Lebanese did as he was told, a faint look of amusement still on his face.

Tom used the pita to scoop up some hummus and chewed it slowly. He picked up the key, keeping the gun trained on Smoker.

"Kareem was not a very bright boy, plus he complained all the time. Did you kill him?"

"I'm not a killer, though I will kill if I have to," Tom added hastily.

"I believe you, and I am not in a hurry to be killed, not over this...this situation."

"Good. I don't want to kill you. You've always seemed a reasonable man."

Smoker shrugged. "I believe in what I am doing, but I am not a fanatic. I have no interest in being a martyr. You, my friend, have a problem, though."

Tom's heart skipped a beat. "Are Floater and Heavy Shoes coming?"

"Floater? Oh, Ahmed." He smiled. "Ahmed does sort of float across the floor. A good name for him. No, I do not expect Ahmed today. The problem is that you'll never get out of the neighborhood. You are in, what do they call it in the movies? Ah, yes, you are in hostile territory. Dressed as you are, looking as you do, it will be obvious to all that you are not one of us. A good Muslim, I mean. There are many people with guns who hate foreigners in this neighborhood. You will not be able to shoot your way out."

"I've thought about that, and I have a plan."

Smoker watched Tom chew some pita.

"Would you like some tea to wash that down?" Smoker asked.

Tom nodded. Smoker pushed his chair further from the table. Tom walked to the table and drained the cup of tea that must have belonged to Kareem.

"I've been meaning to tell you how good your English is. How did you learn it?"

"School, books, music, movies. The usual. I've been a tour guide and held other bilingual jobs. I am a bit embarrassed to admit that I have always loved everything American. I have a distant cousin who moved to America years go. Denver, in the Rocky Mountains. I've dreamt of visiting him there."

"Yet you have waged war against America."

"Waging war. That is a bit strong. I did what I had to do."

Tom thought of Anh and the many Vietnamese who fought against the United States. It was not because they hated America and Americans; it was what they were driven to do by a bad government backed by foreign invaders. Tom understood and nodded his understanding.

"Will my escape put you in a bad situation?"

"Some will not blame me. Others will." Smoker shrugged again.

"What is your name?"

"My name is Omar. What is your name for me?"

"Smoker."

Omar smiled.

"Want to move to America, Omar?"

"Permanently? Become a citizen?"

"Yes. I could make that happen," though he had no idea if it was actually possible.

"So my choice is stay and hope my Muslim brothers don't execute me or help you escape and move to America. Denver?"

"Sure, why not."

Omar nodded without hesitation. "Let's go."

Tom didn't know if Omar was playing him, but it was worth the gamble.

"How do you think we should play this?" Tom asked Omar.

Omar thought a moment. "We are a few blocks from a busy street where there are taxis. We walk there and take a taxi to the US embassy. What had you planned?"

Tom hesitated, not sure if he wanted to show all his cards, especially since his cards were shit. He finally decided to trust the only man who had shown compassion during his captivity.

"I was going to find a telephone and call the embassy, request a rescue."

"Not even knowing where you were?"

"Yeah, that was a problem. I figured there would be signs with addresses or I'd grab some mail from a counter or..." It was Tom's turn to shrug. "The main thing was to escape and hope for the best. It was better than waiting for the next beating or my execution."

"I see your point." Omar looked around the room and his eyes settled on a rifle next to the front door. "I have an idea."

Omar started walking toward the rifle.

"Stop," Tom barked. "What are you doing?"

"If you walk out of here looking like you've been held hostage," he gestured toward Tom's ratty clothes, his long stringy hair, and shaggy beard, "and I'm walking unarmed next to you, what will people think?"

"You carrying a rifle won't attract attention?"

"Not in this neighborhood," Omar said ominously.

Tom thought about it, then picked up the rifle and handed it to Omar.

"Remove the bullets, slowly, without pointing the barrel in my direction."

"You are being cautious, I understand, but what if we are attacked?"

"Try and make sure that doesn't happen."

Omar ejected the bullets and placed them on the table. Tom looked around the room and saw a faded tan cotton jacket hanging over the back of the chair that he assumed was Kareem's. He walked over and put it on. It was snug, and the arms were a couple of inches too short, yet it would do. He then put the bullets in the jacket pocket.

"Are there more bullets?"

"In that drawer," Omar motioned toward a table by the door. "I'll get them, if you wish."

"OK, but slowly, and remember I've got you covered."

Omar walked over and opened the drawer. He gestured for Tom to look in the drawer, which Tom did. There were two boxes of bullets; no weapons.

Tom loaded one jacket pocket with rifle bullets and the other pocket with bullets for the pistol. Then both men headed toward the front door.

When Omar opened the front door the light hit Tom's eyes. He staggered back like a vampire struck by sunlight. Had Omar decided to flee, this was his opportunity.

"We weren't thinking," Omar said, looking back at the cringing Tom. "Wait a minute."

He started to walk back down the corridor.

"Where are you going?" Tom asked.

"Here." Omar handed Tom the rifle, then hustled down the hall. He returned with a baseball cap. "It's Kareem's."

Tom pushed his long hair behind his ears and yanked the hat down low. Keeping his head down, he followed Omar out of the building. They emerged into an alley and stood silently in the shade of a small overhanging roof for a minute, allowing Tom's eyes to adjust to the light, then they started walking. Tom walked with the pistol in his belt, covered by Kareem's jacket. He stumbled a bit, but the exercise he'd done in captivity meant that he was soon able to walk in a relatively normal fashion. Next to him walked Omar, the rifle held unobtrusively at his side in one hand, the barrel hanging along his right leg. At the intersection of a modestly sized road they turned right and continued walking down the side of the street. There were only a couple of cars on the road, and the few pedestrians seemed intent on getting to the market. Tom avoided eye contact, fearful of eliciting a hostile response. As they approached the next intersection Tom looked up and saw a busy street with cars rolling in both directions and throngs of people.

"Almost there," Omar whispered in English.

Parked at the corner were four taxis. Tom and Omar walked up to the first in line, where a short, solidly built man leaned against the driver's door. Omar opened the back door and nodded for Tom to get in.

"What are you doing?" asked the driver in Arabic.

"I am taking this man somewhere," Omar answered.

"Not in my taxi you're not."

"You don't wish to help the Muslim cause?" Omar challenged in a low growl.

"I don't wish to be shot full of holes. Since when did you people start taking taxis?"

"What do you mean 'you people'? You are not a good Muslim? You do not want to help us force the invaders out of Lebanon?"

The other taxi drivers gathered around and a crowd formed. People started to mutter and ask questions: "Who is this man?" "Where are you taking him?" "Why are you transporting him in the middle of the day?"

The crowd was turning on Tom and Omar. Omar grabbed the rifle with both hands and aimed it over the crowd.

"Everybody step back." He looked over his shoulder at the taxi driver. "You can drive us, or I'll take the car myself. It's your choice."

"Fuck you," the man snarled. "Nobody's taking my taxi, and I'm not driving you anywhere. In fact, you're not going anywhere until we find out what the hell is going on."

The crowd began to surge forward when Tom pulled the pistol from his belt and fired twice in the air. There were shouts and people dropped to the ground, but the taxi driver held his ground, blocking the driver's seat. Tom pointed the gun at him and ordered him in Arabic to move. The man stood defiantly, his chest puffed out.

"Fuck you," the driver snarled again.

"Quickly, follow me," Omar said in English.

Tom turned and followed Omar into the dry goods store on the corner. People moved out of the way. Some looked on with curiosity, others with animosity. None tried to stop them. They halted next to the counter behind which sat an old man wearing a haji hat. Omar turned to Tom.

"Can I load the rifle now?"

"That would be a good idea." He gave Omar a handful of bullets.

Omar turned to the old man behind the counter.

"Uncle, may I please use your phone? We mean no harm. We only wish to go in peace."

The old man silently reached under the counter and handed Omar an old, black phone with a rotary dialer.

"Bless you." Omar turned to Tom. "Do you know the number of the US embassy?"

"Yes."

"You better make the call. I'll tell you the intersection when you reach somebody. I hope you'll tell them it's urgent."

Tom called Stefan Boudreau's direct number, and Boudreau's stunned secretary immediately put Tom through.

"This is Stefan Boudreau."

"It's Tom, and I need help now!"

"Kington? Is that really you?"

"Write this down and send in the marines. Got paper and pen?"

"Ready."

Tom told Boudreau the neighborhood and intersection, then explained his precarious situation. He knew that Boudreau had many questions and appreciated that he only asked one."

"Are you all right, partner?"

"I will be when the troops arrive. I gotta hang up—the hostiles may rush us any minute."

"Hang in there. I'll chill the beer."

Tom had just hung up when something flew past his head and slammed into the shelf behind him, breaking glass.

"Get down," Omar shouted.

A barrage of rocks and bricks filled the air. The old man cowered behind the counter while Tom and Omar crouched behind shelves.

"I'm going to check to see if the back door is secure," Tom said over the din.

He raced to the back of the store and found the flimsy door ajar, probably left open for ventilation. Tom slammed it shut and was glad to see that the door was set up for security, with a metal bracket on each side and a two-by-four leaning next to it. Tom secured the door with the two-by-four, then checked and saw there were no windows or any other way to enter from the rear. As he reached the front of the store he heard a familiar voice shouting to Omar.

"Give us the American and we will forgive your unfortunate act." It was Floater/Ahmed.

Young Man/Kareem must have called Ahmed when he awoke, and now Tom's main tormentor stood in front of him. Ahmed was tall and thin with a close-cropped beard and neatly combed hair. He was well dressed with a brown sport coat and pressed tan trousers. He could have been a professor or economist. Tom fought the urge to step forward and shoot the man.

"I think we've done enough to this man," said Omar. "It is time for him to return home. That is what we want, is it not? For the invaders to return to their homes?"

"That is not for you to decide."

Tom stepped forward. "It was my decision," he said in Arabic. "I've also decided that you have ten seconds to disappear. If you're still here in ten seconds, I will shoot you."

"You'll never leave here alive, neither of you."

"Maybe not, but we will not be the only ones to die."

Tom shot a few feet in front of Ahmed. The bullet hit the sidewalk and ricocheted. Somebody yelped in pain and the crowd fell back. Ahmed stood his ground for a few seconds, but when Tom stepped forward the Lebanese slowly walked backward, his eyes fixed on Tom.

"I hope help arrives soon," said Omar, worry in his voice. "Ahmed isn't going to let you go without a fight. It is now a matter of pride."

Ten minutes later Tom and Omar were still standing behind shelves, watching the street in front of the shop. People stood across the street, though none appeared hostile. The silence was eerie. Tom glanced over at the old man, who still crouched in fear behind the counter. Tom apologized for the damage to the shop and told the old man he'd better leave while he could. The old man stood up and walked to the front of the shop, shouted that he was coming out and not to shoot, then scurried out of the building. Omar looked over at Tom.

"Even with your life in danger, you think of others."

"No reason to put him in danger."

"You also had the opportunity to shoot Ahmed."

"He had the opportunity to kill me. He didn't. By the way, what's the date?

Omar told him. Tom quickly calculated the days.

"Ten months. Shit."

Out of the corner of his eye Tom saw something sail through the air and land at the entrance to the shop. There was a soft explosion, then a burst of flames.

"A Molotov cocktail," said Omar. "They're going to burn us out."

Two more missiles exploded, one against the counter and one closer to the shelves that Tom and Omar stood behind.

"This would be a good time for the marines to arrive," said Tom.

Suddenly somebody came rushing in the front of the building, a coat pulled over his head to protect him from the flames. Tom and Omar raised their guns.

"Don't shoot, Tom. It's your old buddy."

Tom nearly dropped his gun when Officer Sam Smith whipped off the coat that covered his head and raced behind the shelves.

"What the hell?" Tom gasped.

"Is that any way to say hello?"

"What are you doing here?"

"Getting you out. Who is this?" Smith nodded toward Omar.

"Omar is a friend."

"Of course he is," Smith smirked. "Let's get out of here."

Smith led the way to the back.

"Any idea what's outside the door?" Smith asked.

"I only got a brief glimpse," said Tom. "There's an alley."

"Any doors across the way?"

"I might have seen one. I'm not sure."

Smoke was billowing in from the front of the shop, and the temperature started to rise.

"We'll find out soon enough. Tom, I want you to take off the two-by-four and get ready to open the door. We'll assume there's company waiting for us on the other side. I'll step left and scan left and up to the roof. Friend," he nodded toward Omar, his voice laced with sarcasm, "you step right and scan right and up to the roof. We've got to cover each other's backs. Tom, look for a door across the alley. When you find one, let us know, and we'll cover you while you run across and make sure the door is open. We'll hope the fire will keep shooters off the roof over this shop. I'll try to check it out if I can, but be ready to duck for cover if somebody shoots from behind. Most people have trouble hitting a moving target, so keep moving. Ready?"

Tom and Omar nodded. Tom looked over at Omar and saw fear in his eyes. When Omar glanced over, Tom said, "We're going to make it."

"*Inshallah*," said Omar."

Tom lifted off the two-by-four and grabbed the handle with his left hand, his right still holding the pistol. Smith pulled a pistol from a shoulder holster and nodded. Tom opened the door, and shots immediately rang out. Splinters flew from the doorjamb and chunks of concrete burst from the floor. Smith stepped out and left and started shooting, followed by Omar, who stepped right and blasted away with his rifle. Tom stepped forward, saw a door across the alley, and ran for it. Bullets whizzed by. He kept his head down and reached the door untouched. The door was locked, but the knob was loose and wiggled feebly when Tom shook it. He took a step back, lowered his shoulder, and slammed into the door, which swung open. Tom turned and backed in.

"The door's open," he shouted. "Come on."

Tom saw movement on the roof over the shop next to the one ablaze. He fired twice, then looked right, where he saw somebody crouching in a doorway down the alley. Tom fired twice at the figure, who ducked back under cover. Smith and Omar broke for the open door. Tom saw Smith stagger halfway across, then the officer stumbled and fell. Omar had just passed Smith when he too fell forward and shouted out in pain. Tom fired a shot to the left and one to the right, then jumped forward, grabbed the collar of Omar's shirt, and dragged him through the doorway. When Tom looked up Smith was crawling in behind him. Smith grunted in pain as a bullet hit his body. Tom grabbed Smith's collar, dragged him inside and tried to slam the door, but Smith's foot was in the way. Bullets started to whistle by Tom. He pushed Smith's leg out of the way and finally slammed the door, then fell on his butt and sat panting.

"Better reload your gun," Smith gasped.

Tom did as he was told. He looked over at Omar, who was groaning in pain.

"Where are you shot?" Tom asked.

"My leg."

"Then you can load your rifle," Smith managed through his pain.

Omar took a deep breath, groaned, sat up, and started to load. Just then they started to hear more shooting, though it wasn't from the alley. The shooting increased.

"The cavalry," said Smith. "About fucking time."

After five minutes the shooting became sporadic, then stopped. Gripping his gun, Tom slowly opened the door. Everything was quiet in the alley. He carefully stuck his head out and looked around. He stood there a minute, peering left, right, up, and around. Tom was aware that he was shaking and gasping. Suddenly, he saw movement at the end of the block. He stepped back, then peered out again, slowly, cautiously. There was one person, then two more. They ran from doorway to doorway, covering each other. When Tom saw that they wore US Marine uniforms, tears welled up in his eyes. He choked back a sob.

"I'm a US citizen. I'm over here," he shouted.

He stuck out his hand and waved frantically. He heard the sound of running feet, then an American voice barked out.

"Who's in there?"

"Tom Kington, US embassy."

"Are you alone?"

"No. Two others. Officer Smith, CIA, and a Lebanese friendly. They've both been shot."

"Put your weapons down, and don't move."

A marine stepped into the doorway, his gun raised and ready. He took a quick look around to be sure it wasn't a trap, then stepped in, followed by two more marines. The other two immediately set up defensive positions.

"Are you the hostage who escaped?"

"Yes."

The marines pulled out a walkie-talkie, gave their location, then looked at Tom.

"They're coming with an armored vehicle. You're safe now."

Tom sat down heavily, put his face in his hands, and started to cry.

The last time Tom had been in a hospital with Sam Smith was in Kabul shortly after the *mujahideen* missile had taken Mary's life. That time Tom had been in the hospital bed and Smith had paid him a visit. This time Smith lay in the hospital bed while Tom sat in the chair next to the bed waiting for Smith to wake up. Stefan Boudreau had filled Tom in on how Smith had miraculously been the first rescuer to show up. Smith had been working in South America when word had reached him of Tom's kidnapping. Smith had finished his assignment, then asked to be transferred to Beirut to search for Tom. From what Boudreau had learned via another CIA contact, Smith's request was more like a demand: he was going to Beirut whether his superiors agreed or not. Rather than let Smith go rogue, the CIA had allowed him to establish a network dedicated to seeking and freeing hostages. Smith was allocated a small office in the US embassy from which he put together a team of sources and contacts. They had followed Tom's trail to the neighborhood in which he was held, but could not determine the building or who actually held him. Smith had been working in his office when Boudreau ran in and gave him the news. Rather than wait for the military to organize the rescue mission, Smith had jumped into a taxi and directed it to the scene of the standoff.

Tom, who had been slouching in the chair, sat up anxiously when he heard Smith moan. The CIA officer moaned again, then slowly opened his eyes. He blinked a few times, peered around the room, opened his mouth, but only managed to rasp out a few sounds. Tom looked at the table next to the bed and saw a cup of water with a straw sticking out of it. He picked up the cup and guided the straw into Smith's mouth. Smith took a sip, waited a moment, then took another.

"Thanks," Smith managed to croak.

"No, thank you."

Smith tried to sit up.

"Hold on a minute," Tom said.

He stuck his head out into the hall and called a nurse. A Lebanese woman dressed in white scurried in.

"He's trying to sit up. Is that all right? I mean, will it open his wounds?"

"If we raise him slowly it should be all right, but he should be resting quietly."

Tom and the nurse gently raised Smith and slipped two pillows under his back. Then the nurse left the room, reminding Tom not to stay long. Tom helped Smith sip some more water. Smith swallowed, sat back and let out a sigh, then looked at Tom.

"You look a hell of a lot better than last time I saw you. Mighty thin, though."

Tom had shaved his beard and his hair had been trimmed. He had spent the last forty-eight hours eating and sleeping and didn't feel too bad, all things considered.

"I'll put the weight back on, now that I can eat three meals a day instead of one. Thanks for coming to my rescue."

"Hell, it was you that escaped. I just helped you complete your journey."

"You could have waited for the rest of the troops," Tom said.

"Sure, and you could find a job that's a hell of a lot safer, except that's not who we are. Fact is, with all the action you've seen, you might as well join the CIA."

"Right. Though I suspect that Officer Jones might raise some objections."

"It was Jones who told me you'd been taken hostage."

"The same Jones who tried to get me booted out of State?"

"The same. I was in deep cover on a mission when you were taken. Jones heard about it and went to a lot of trouble to get word to me. He knew about your troubles in Paraguay and Afghanistan. Called you a tough son of a bitch. Seems like you've earned his respect."

"Well, I'll be."

"Speaking of old friends, how is your new Lebanese 'friend' doing?"

"Omar was shot in the leg. They treated and released him. I've been working on getting him a visa to the States."

"Even though he was one of your kidnappers?"

Tom didn't bother asking Smith how he knew. Smith was a smart man.

"He was the only one who treated me well, and he helped me escape."

"Your 'friend' had a guilty conscience."

"Whatever the reason, I wouldn't have made it without him. Nor without you."

"I was doing my job."

"Bullshit. From what I've learned you made it your job."

"Most of the time I'm working for something vague: liberty or democracy or whatever. You're a good man, somebody worth risking your life for."

Tears welled up in Tom's eyes. "And you're a friend. I'd like to buy you dinner back in the States some time."

"I'd like that."

Tom stood up and put his hand on Smith's shoulder. "Get some rest. I'll stop by tomorrow."

Smith closed his eyes. Tom walked out of the room.

CHAPTER 24—2007

om sat in the rocker and let his mind wander back twenty years, to when his career in the foreign service ended and his new life began. He had returned to Washington after ten months as a hostage to find his face plastered on the front page of nearly every newspaper and magazine in the country. The major television networks wanted to do stories about his captivity and daring escape. At first he refused to grant interviews, then reluctantly agreed in order to give some hope to the families of those still being held hostage in Lebanon and elsewhere. Tom downplayed his own courage, credited Omar and an unnamed CIA officer with aiding his escape, and insisted that his treatment had not been that horrible. Tom's modesty and message of hope, as well as his rugged good looks, made him an even bigger media star. Offers of book and movie deals flooded in. He declined them all. Instead, he drove to California and moved into the spare bedroom in Suzie's house.

Although they occasionally slept together, sex was no longer the vital element it had been between them years earlier. Suzie was Tom's therapist, guru, friend, all of which Tom needed at that moment. During the three months he spent with Suzie, Tom walked two to three hours each day, regardless of the weather. He cooked natural food and read Buddhist philosophy, though he declined to attend meditation sessions with Suzie. Finally, Tom decided on his next step. He wrote to the State Department and resigned from the foreign service, then he drove to Indiana and rented an old house not far from his parents' farm. They were now advanced in their years and relied on Tom's brother to run the farm. When additional help was needed, Tom eagerly pitched in. He grew closer with his family and seemed to gain strength from the rich Midwest soil. He also started to write essays on foreign policy, international relations, and ethnic conflicts. At first he wrote only for himself, in an attempt to organize his thoughts and to gain a greater understanding of what he thought he had learned. As he grew more confident in his writing and reasoning, Tom began to send his essays to select journals and magazines. *Foreign Affairs*, the journal of the Council of Foreign Relations, one of the most prestigious journals of its kind, printed everything he sent them. As Suzie had counseled, Tom focused on the present, then followed where it led. Tom's writing led to a new career.

The first call came shortly after Tom's second essay was printed in *Foreign Affairs*. The article had pertained to hostage taking and possible responses by governments and NGOs. The call was from Georgetown University's School of Foreign Service. They were holding a seminar on Lebanon and wanted Tom to give a presentation and participate in a panel discussion on the role of the international community in ethnic conflicts. Tom's presentation was well received, and most of the questions during the panel discussion were directed at him. Word spread through the academic community, and soon Tom was flooded with requests to participate in similar seminars. Within six months he was so busy running around the country that it was no longer practical to live in Indiana, so he moved to Washington. Tom was also approached by Harvard to write a brief book on hostage taking for their Kennedy School of Government. The book was such a success at Harvard that it became a standard feature in universities and classes around the country, then overseas. A year after saying goodbye to Suzie, Tom found that his schedule was booked for the next six months. His bank account held a considerable amount from book sales and speaking fees.

Another advantage of moving to Washington was that Tom could live near Keith and Karen. He cohosted Keith's thirteenth birthday party with Barbara and even enjoyed being with Henry Bennett, his father-in-law. The old man was as conservative as ever, gloating over the Reagan presidency, yet the two men found common ground in their love of Keith and Karen. Bennett was also proud of how Tom had held up during his captivity in Beirut. They were able to discuss foreign policy, discussions that

Keith raptly listened to and often participated in. Keith was a bright lad who absorbed knowledge and debating skills from his father and grandfather. Regardless of his eventual political views, Keith was determined to be a diplomat like his father. Karen, now eleven, was a tender, thoughtful girl who loved reading and all forms of art. In an odd way, she reminded Tom of Suzie, a seeker of deeper, spiritual meaning. Karen often asked Tom questions about religion and philosophy, and she seemed drawn to the same qualities about Buddhism that had attracted Tom.

Five years after moving to Washington, Tom was offered a teaching position at his alma mater, Columbia. Although Tom didn't relish the thought of being away from Keith and Karen, he accepted the job. The five years had been fulfilling, yet also a bit overwhelming. He traveled four months of the year—domestically and internationally—attending conferences and giving presentations, and had become a consultant for the State Department, specializing in hostage situations and ethnic conflicts. At Columbia he taught foreign affairs and published the occasional book. During Tom's third year he bumped into Ira Blue.

Tom was walking home from class, and a light snow was falling from a dull gray sky. He turned a corner and saw a tall, lean man walking toward him. The man wore a bulky peacoat and a long muffler that was wrapped twice around his neck. His black cap was pulled down low and he had a long, scraggly reddish beard that obscured his face. Still, there was something familiar about him. When Tom was ten feet away, the man looked up, and they locked eyes.

"Hello, Ira."

"Oh. Hey." Ira nodded and began to walk past Tom.

"What's news?" Tom asked.

Ira turned and peered at Tom, his face blank. Tom tried again.

"What are you doing in New York?"

"Living." He started to walk away.

Tom was on the verge of doing the same, but then he thought of Ira and Suzie and their time together at Columbia, and he was struck by a wave of nostalgia.

"Can I buy you a cup of coffee?" Tom shouted at Ira's back.

Ira took a few more steps before stopping and slowly turning.

"Sure."

They walked in silence to a coffee shop where Tom often picked up coffee on his way to Columbia. They ordered, picked up their coffees, and found a table in a corner. Both took a few sips and sat looking at their cups. Finally, Tom broke the silence.

"So you're living in New York now. How long have you been back?"

"A few years."

"Still publishing *The Handless Monkey*?"

"The *Monkey* is now headless and heartless. It's dead."

"Sorry to hear that."

"Are you? Really?"

"Of course I am. It meant something to you, so it meant something to me. It was a newspaper with a conscience."

"It was fishwrap. It was a waste of time."

"You don't know that for sure. Maybe one person read it and decided to run for office and ended up passing some law that helped others."

The hint of a smirk turned up the corners of Ira's mouth. "All those years, all the shit you've seen, and you still have a bit of the Midwestern Boy Scout in you."

"I might have remained a Midwestern Boy Scout if I hadn't met you and Suzie."

"No, your life changed when you were accepted to Columbia and moved to New York. Suzie and I just happened to be there."

"We're all affected by the people we meet, sometimes in big ways, sometimes small ways. You were a major influence in my life. You deserve some share of the credit for whatever I achieved."

"That's not what you said last time we met up. You basically called me a bitter asshole and told me to fuck off."

"I was pretty upset at the time."

"As you should have been, what with Mary dead and me trying to keep the *Monkey* alive when it was already long dead and not giving two shits about your life." Ira shrugged. "Now the *Monkey* is dead and I'm stuck in New York. I came back to bury my dad a few years ago and decided to stay. I see my mom from time to time, do some editing and writing for a couple of radical papers, collect food stamps, just hanging on, waiting for…I don't know. I don't know if I was ahead of my time or too honest. I always thought people would get me some day, see the truth I'd been spouting, but most people just keep their noses clean, don't want to make waves. They just don't care." Ira looked up at Tom. "Except you. You always cared, about everyone and everything. You still do."

Tom's eyebrows rose in surprise.

"Yeah, I read about you. I know about your books and lectures, your teaching at Columbia. I even read that Bush asked you to meet and offer your views on the Middle East. You're practically a household name."

"Sure, all I had to do was get my ass captured and beaten for a year."

"You're being modest. You survived and escaped. You're also trying to offer hope to people who have lived in fear for years, telling governments how to help their people live in peace. You're doing good things, and you're not working at a multinational corporation or serving an evil government. You're working for the people. I respect that."

The look of surprise grew on Tom's face.

"Yeah, I know, praise from the guy who always gave you shit. I always saw that as my job. I suppose there was also a touch of jealousy. We both talked about doing good, but whereas I got stuck into thinking the *Monkey* was the only way, you followed your heart on a different path. I grew bitter, like you said. You remained a believer in the possibilities of mankind."

"You don't sound bitter as much as defeated."

"Maybe I am defeated," admitted Ira.

"There's a lot of life left."

"Sure, a lot of life." He didn't sound like he believed it.

"I'm working on another book, something about conflict resolution. I could use some help with research and editing."

"Throwing a bone to a hungry dog?"

"If you were ever a dog, you were a lean and aggressive one, only hungry for the truth."

"Thanks, I'll pass on your offer. I don't want any handouts."

Tom didn't press him. Ira drained his cup and stood up.

"I gotta run. Stuff to do. Take care of yourself. Keep telling it like it is."

"Yeah, you too. Give me a call if you ever want to meet for dinner. Here's my card."

Tom took out his wallet, pulled out a card, and gave it to Ira. Ira put it into his coat pocket without looking at it.

"Sure. See you around."

Ira walked out of the coffee shop. He didn't look back.

Tom blinked back some tears and stared into the darkness. He felt tired, more tired than he'd been in a long time. He realized that he missed spending time with friends. He'd lost touch with Sam Smith, hadn't heard from Omar in years, rarely talked with Stefan Boudreau. Maybe a trip to Vermont was in order. It would be good to see Suzie.

BIOGRAPHY: After teaching, traveling, and living on four continents, RJ Furth decided it was time to jump into something he'd been longing to do for many years: write. He started a novel twenty years earlier on the Thai island of Ko Samui and finally had a chance to complete it in Colorado, where he devoted himself to writing full-time. RJ has eaten dog in Sumatra, been threatened by a madman in Thailand, pulled leaches off his legs in India, and been frightened by daunting heights in Peru. It is his intention to write about some of these adventures while at the same time pursuing new ones. RJ is currently working on his seventh novel and a musical memoir. Many of his travel stories—fiction and nonfiction—as well as stories written by fellow world travelers can be found at rjfurth.com.

NOVELS BY R J FURTH

CHASING PALM TREES

Frank Rose had always dreamed of living overseas, and now that he and his new bride had been hired to teach in Malaysia that dream was coming true. Except his dreams had never included unfaithful colleagues, campus drug dealers, nude photos, run-ins with police in Malaysia and Nepal, or a climatic disaster that would bring his marriage to the brink. It was the year of El Niño, and the adventure of a lifetime would waver between dream and nightmare, leading Frank to realize that Iowa and Malaysia were separated by far more than a twenty hour flight.

CAPTIVE IN PARADISE

Young backpackers have been traveling through Southeast Asia for decades, blissfully unaware of the political and social turmoil that surrounds them. That ignorance abruptly ends when eight travelers are kidnapped by a revolutionary organization and held captive in the rainforest of southern Thailand. Maimed, beaten and facing death, each much decide: stay and hope for rescue or attempt an escape that stands little chance of succeeding. *Captive in Paradise* features Frank Rose, the protagonist of *Chasing Palm Trees.*

THE TAJ MALABAR MURDERS

Frank Rose is living in southern India, slowly recovering from the hostage ordeal he survived in Thailand, when he is framed for a brutal triple homicide committed at the Taj Malabar Hotel. Pursued by the police, Hindhu fanatics and a hired assassin, Frank must stay alive while he tries to solve the murders and clear his name.

Made in the USA
Charleston, SC
27 July 2013